ENTANGLED LOVE

"Natalie, we were destined to meet," Bryce murmured, lifting his hand to untie the bow that held the cape over her shoulders. And once that was done, he slowly laced his fingers beneath the hood and eased it from her head. He drew a deep nervous breath when her hair sprang free and began blowing away from her shoulders in dark, lustrous billows. Then in one quick movement, he swished the cape from around her shoulders and sent it falling in a flutter to her feet.

Natalie took a step backward, knowing what his next move had to be. She wanted his kiss, yet she was now a bit afraid. She wasn't so sure if having led him to such a secluded spot was wise.

"Bryce . . . I don't know . . ." she murmured as his long, lean body took a step toward her. She let her gaze rake over his face and saw that it was a mask of hungry desire for her. In his eyes, she saw victory.

"Natalie . . . ?" Bryce said in a husky whisper, testing her response. And when she stopped and held her arms out to him, he drew her gingerly to him—and lowered his mouth to hers. . . .

THE BEST IN HISTORICAL ROMANCES

TIME-KEPT PROMISES (2422, $3.95)
by Constance O'Day Flannery

Sean O'Mara froze when he saw his wife Christina standing before him. She had vanished and the news had been written about in all of the papers—he had even been charged with her murder! But now he had living proof of his innocence, and Sean was not about to let her get away. No matter that the woman was claiming to be someone named Kristine; she still caused his blood to boil.

PASSION'S PRISONER (2573, $3.95)
by Casey Stewart

When Cassandra Lansing put on men's clothing and entered the Rawlings saloon she didn't expect to lose anything—in fact she was sure that she would win back her prized horse Rapscallion that her grandfather lost in a card game. She almost got a smug satisfaction at the thought of fooling the gamblers into believing that she was a man. But once she caught a glimpse of the virile Josh Rawlings, Cassandra wanted to be the woman in his embrace!

ANGEL HEART (2426, $3.95)
by Victoria Thompson

Ever since Angelica's father died, Harlan Snyder had been angling to get his hands on her ranch, the Diamond R. And now, just when she had an important government contract to fulfill, she couldn't find a single cowhand to hire—all because of Snyder's threats. It was only a matter of time before the legendary gunfighter Kid Collins turned up on her doorstep, badly wounded. Angelica assessed his firmly muscled physique and stared into his startling blue eyes. Beneath all that blood and dirt he was the handsomest man she had ever seen, and the one person who could help beat Snyder at his own game.

PASSION'S WEB

BY CASSIE EDWARDS

ZEBRA BOOKS
KENSINGTON PUBLISHING CORP.

ZEBRA BOOKS

are published by

KENSINGTON PUBLISHING CORP.
475 Park Avenue South
New York, NY 10016

Second printing: July, 1990

Printed in the United States of America

With much love, I dedicate Passion's Web *to my uncle Chick Girot and his wife Elaine.*

A hundred years from now, dear heart,
The grief will all be o'er;
The sea of care will surge in vain
Upon a careless shore.
These glasses we turn down today
Here at the parting of the way . . .
We shall be wineless then as they,
And shall not mind it more.

—Bennett

KEY WEST, FLORIDA

1839

We met on roads of laughter—
Now wistful roads depart,
For I must hurry after
To overtake my heart.

—Divine

ONE

The black, stately carriage maneuvered its way down the narrow streets fronted by fenced-in yards bright with bougainvillaea, hibiscus, and poinciana. Natalie Palmer sat clutching her purse inside this carriage, quite unaware of eyes on her. She cast the handsome man sitting on the opposite seat a fast glance, feeling a sudden, strange wildness to her heartbeat. Her glance, meant to be brief, had somehow become lingering, capturing him in full detail, noting the smartness of his dress—the brown, snug-fitting breeches, matching afternoon coat, and lace-edged cravat at his throat.

His eyes were so startlingly blue that Natalie couldn't help but become lost in their magnetic stare which continued to look back at her from a sun-bronzed face with lean and smooth features. His face was framed by thick, blond hair that reached halfway to his shoulders.

When he removed a thin cigar from between his lips to direct a smile at her, Natalie quickly forced her gaze on past him, yet blushed at the knowing look she had seen in his eyes. She felt a nudge in her ribs and turned quickly

9

toward her best friend Myra Jones who sat at her right side.

"It is rumored that man is a pirate," Myra whispered, nodding toward their fellow passenger who was unnerving Natalie. "I've seen him on the waterfront before but always dressed much differently. He usually wears quite a charming outfit of gold silk."

"A pirate? Gold silk?" Natalie whispered back, her disappointment evident and her hope of ever being properly introduced to him crumbling. Her father would most surely hang this man if he, a pirate, even so much as spoke to her.

"Pirates are the worst lot of all men set loose on the face of the earth," her father had always warned.

He had refused even to allow her to go and experience the excitement of the public auctions on the waterfront, where salvaged materials from wrecked ships went for top dollar. "Too much riffraff mingling there for the likes of you, Natalie," he had further warned. "You're much too genteel . . . refined . . . to stand shoulder to shoulder with the class of people that frequents the waterfront."

"Yes. A pirate," Myra reaffirmed. "His name is Bryce Fowler. He's the captain of a magnificent ship called the *Golden Isis*."

Natalie lifted a carefully plucked eyebrow toward her friend. "You certainly know enough about this man," she whispered back, feeling sharp pangs of jealousy for the first time in her eighteen years of life. "How is it that you do?"

"Don't you see how truly male he is? Who could not ask questions about him?" Myra sighed, then giggled, causing the fleshiness of her round cheeks to loosely ripple. She touched her fingers to some loose strands of sandy hair that had fallen free from her bonnet. "Look at the way he's looking at you, Natalie. Oh, if it were only me."

Natalie cast Bryce another fast glance, scowling toward him, thinking him surely a scoundrel, yet sensuously moved when she saw that the velvet blue of his eyes was sweeping over her in a lingering, admiring fashion.

Tilting her chin haughtily, Natalie once more tore her gaze from him, although still filled with the wonder of his nearness. She was even becoming almost breathless with a strange desire for this man! But she knew that she could never become acquainted with him, much less let herself fall in love with him.

Yes . . . he . . . was most obviously drawn to her, not her friend Myra who ate too much Key Lime Pie and Conch Chowder. No. He was not attracted to Myra. It was apparent that he much preferred the slender woman Natalie could boast of being. With her long, midnight black, lustrous hair, her dark, luminous eyes, and oval, bright-cheeked face; she had even been called ravishing.

Straightening her back, Natalie was proud to show how the bodice of her peach satin dress clung so sensuously to her figure. She was especially glad this day that it emphasized the swell of her breasts by a plunging neckline and the smallness of her waist by being nipped in sharply before it fell into gathers past her ankles.

She realized that her eyes had to be twinkling as brilliantly as the diamond necklace at her throat. She quickly drew her fingers to the necklace, thinking now that maybe the diamonds were the full attraction here, not her after all. He was a thief! All pirates were low-down, murdering thieves!

11

When Myra once more sank her elbow into Natalie's right side, Natalie turned upon her with a dark frown. "What is it now?" she sighed languidly.

Myra leaned closer to Natalie and spoke into her ear. "I also have heard that he is quite a womanizer," she whispered. "He has such a reputation for loving, then leaving a woman. It's as though he's trying to prove something to the women of the world."

Natalie laughed sarcastically. "Or maybe to himself," she scoffed, casting him a shadowed, sideways glance of smugness. She cupped her left hand over her mouth and leaned even closer to Myra as she whispered further. "Maybe he's trying to prove to himself that he's a man. Maybe he lacks the skill to be a perfect lover."

Myra laughed softly. "I doubt that," she said, letting her gaze stop where his breeches fit so tightly at his crotch. She felt a flush rising to her cheeks as her pulse raced crazily. "Yes, I doubt that," she repeated throatily.

"I truly don't care to talk anymore about him," Natalie said stubbornly. "What he does or how he lives is truly no concern of mine." She placed her purse on her lap and reached to retie the bow of her straw bonnet beneath her chin. At that moment the carriage careened into and out of a hole in the street, and Natalie's purse slipped from her lap to land near the hem of her dress, next to her feet and her frothy petticoats.

"Oh . . ." she exclaimed irritably, and as she bent her back to reach for her purse, her bonnet flew from her head, also to settle softly at her feet. Heat rose from her neck upward onto her cheeks. She had never felt so awkward and clumsy as she did at this moment. When a male's hand reached down before her eyes as she was still bent to the flooring, her heart skipped a beat.

"Beautiful lady, may I be of service?" Bryce asked in a quite masculine voice.

With her hair cascading in dark, silken waves across her shoulders, Natalie looked into the face so dangerously close to hers and once more found herself lost in the deep blue pools of his eyes.

She slowly straightened her back, having the sudden need to look more ladylike. "That would be very kind of you, sir," she said softly. She wished her pulse would slow a bit. Could he see her uneasiness? Would he realize just how much his presence did disturb her?

As he handed the rescued bonnet and purse to her, lifting his beautifully shaped lips into a half smile, Natalie was reminded of Myra's earlier words. She could see in his eyes that he would like her to be his next conquest. And when his hand brushed against hers as she accepted her bonnet, then her purse, she realized that though she had never been with a man before in that way, she ached to be wanted by this man.

"Thank you, kind sir," she purred, casting him a veiled look from beneath her thick, feathery lashes.

"Bryce is the name," he said, settling back on the deep cushions of the carriage. He gave her a half-salute as he lowered his head a bit in a mock bow. "Bryce Fowler, to you, beautiful lady."

Natalie let a soft laugh escape from her throat. "Thank you, Bruce Fowler," she murmured. She replaced her bonnet on her head and tied its sleek, satin bow snugly beneath her chin.

"And your name . . . ?" Bryce asked, leaning a bit forward.

Natalie opened her mouth to speak her name but was

13

interrupted by the coachman suddenly opening the carriage door at her right side. She flushed a bit. She had been so enamored of this man Bryce, she hadn't even been aware that the coach had drawn to a halt.

The coachman, who had a pinched sort of face and was dressed in coarse, dark clothes, stuck his head inside the carriage. "We've arrived to Parrot Inn," he bellowed. "All out. I have more to do than stand here waitin'."

Bryce scooted across his seat but stopped directly in front of Natalie. He reached to capture one of her hands in his, eying her differently than before. Natalie swallowed hard. She could see in the depth of his blue eyes that he no longer seemed to be seeing her as *only* another conquest, but maybe as something . . . special. . . .

"Your name?" he said thickly.

"Natalie. Natalie Palmer," she whispered, almost melting inside from his steady, adoring gaze and from the steely grip of his hand.

The coachman intervened again. "Get along with ye now," he shouted, moving aside as Bryce released Natalie's hand and stepped slowly from the carriage.

"We will meet again," Bryce said, then turned on a heel and walked away from her and on into Parrot Inn.

Can you believe it?" Myra exclaimed to Natalie, beaming and taking the hand Bryce had so recently held. "He wants to see you, Natalie. What are you going to do?"

Still in a state of semishock, Natalie stared toward Parrot Inn. She had never been so stirred by any event in her life before. It was as though she had been struck by lightning and was glowing from the aftershock of it. "Do?" she murmured. "What can I do, Myra? You know my father. No father is as strict—as cautious—as

14

Saul Palmer."

"Ladies . . ." the coachman growled angrily from between clenched teeth.

"Natalie, come on in with me," Myra pleaded. "Your father need never find out. He didn't the other times. Come on."

Natalie ached to say yes, nevertheless she was aware that it wasn't only a question of obeying her father. She somehow knew that if she crossed the Inn's threshhold in pursuit of this Bryce Fowler, she would never be the same again. She was already aware of the different, disturbing feelings this man had aroused in her. She was still tingling from his brief touch. But she had to forget him. Her father would not allow such a relationship. She often wished to be as carefree as Myra whose parents let her do as she pleased. Even now Myra was going to be able to be with Hugh . . . the man she loved. . . .

She turned and hugged Myra affectionately. "Myra, you just go on and enjoy listening to Hugh sing his beautiful ballads," she encouraged. "Then when you're sharing wine by candlelight, all of your worries about me will be swept from your mind."

"Oh, Natalie . . ." Myra sighed. "Are you sure?"

Natalie gave Myra another final hug, glancing meanwhile at the red-faced coachman. "Yes. I'm sure," she said. "And best be on your way. The coachman is growing more angry by the minute."

"All right," Myra said. She gathered the skirt of her dress in her arms and stepped from the carriage and moved quickly toward the inn. The carriage then rolled away, toward the other end of town, where the rears of the neat and stately, three-storied houses faced the wide Southwest Channel that emptied into the At-

15

lantic.

These, the most beautiful homes of Key West, had been built many years ago by ship's carpenters who had become stranded on the island after their vessels had broken up on the treacherous Rebecca Shoals. The house to which Natalie directed the coachman stood tall and defiant against the brilliant backdrop of the ocean, its finely kept yard of green, protected by a six-foot high, black wrought-iron fence and gate.

Natalie had learned early in life of her father's wealth and understood the need for the protective fencing and his personal need to be surrounded by throngs of men at all times. When not away at his thriving cigar factory, he would be seated comfortably in his villa's library sharing, with his many followers, glasses of port and, more usually than not, the hand-rolled El Cuño cigars on which he prided himself.

Then on occasion, way late into the night after the men had gone their separate ways, Natalie had caught the scent of a strange perfume in the hallway and had glimpsed the fleeting, colorful flutter of skirts as one of her father's female companions had slipped in and out of the house.

"Since my mother's death, he has not let himself grow serious about another lady," Natalie said in a near whisper. She wondered why he had chosen not to wed again. Natalie could barely remember her mother. Had it truly been sixteen long years ago?

"I was only two," she whispered again. "I didn't know her long enough . . . to . . . even miss her. . . ."

Glancing from the carriage window, she could see that the gable-roofed houses were thinning at the side of the road; the ocean now was more visible. As the carriage pulled into a long, narrow lane, lined by beautiful orange-red, royal poincianas and purple bougainvillaea, Natalie knew that she was soon to be home. She had shared another day with Myra at the few shops of Key West where clothes and hats could be purchased or where one could place an order for dresses or frilly finery to be shipped from Paris. This time she had only watched as Myra had exhibited herself in dress after dress.

"Just a fun day away from the house," Natalie sighed. "Away from the stench of cigars and the fat, pompous men my father keeps introducing to me with the intention of finding one for me to wed."

She only hoped that no man would be waiting now. She had purposely stayed away longer than usual to avoid such a situation. Stars sparkled in her eyes when she let her thoughts wander back to Bryce Fowler. If she hadn't delayed her return home she would never have met him. Had it been fate guiding her movements this day? Had they been thrown together for a purpose?

Shifting her weight on the seat, she scoffed at herself. He was not the man for her, no matter how strangely he had made her feel. She had to remember that he was a pirate . . . someone no one could trust. Pirates would steal even from their own mothers!

Feeling the pounding of her heart when she allowed his likeness to form in her mind's eye, she knew that he had come close to stealing something from her all right. Her . . . *heart* . . . !

"But he would be an even worse choice than those pompous bores my father keeps forcing upon me," she whispered. "I musn't let his memory mesmerize me so. I musn't!"

As the afternoon sun filtered lazily through a window,

to settle in soft, hazy streamers on the cushioned seat opposite her, a sparkling of sorts being cast from something in the folds of the cushion attracted Natalie's attention.

"What is it?" she whispered, leaning forward. Her heart lurched when she saw that it was a key . . . a tarnished, brass key!

"A key," she said. "Whose? Someone has lost . . ."

Her fingers flew to her mouth as a slow sigh breezed softly through her lips. "It must be Bryce Fowler's," she murmured. "When he leaned over to assist me, it must have fallen from his rear pocket."

Circling her fingers about the key, lifting it from the seat, Natalie couldn't deny or escape the desire she had felt for the man, not with a part of him now with her, in her hand. She opened her fingers and looked downward at the key, feeling her pulse race. As long as she had his key, she would be assured of seeing him again. When he discovered it gone, surely he would come in search of it. How would he react when he learned that she had rescued it for him?

"I *must* see him again," she said softly. "Surely I can find a way."

She studied the key further. "What does this key unlock? Something of so much importance, he surely will miss it?" she whispered.

Feeling the carriage come to a sudden halt, Natalie composed herself. She swallowed hard and straightened her back. With eager fingers she opened the drawstrings of her bag and removed her smaller coin purse. She took a last, lingering look at the key. Somehow, she managed to see Bryce in its reflection; then she smiled coyly as she dropped it into the purse and withdrew a few coins with which to pay the coachman.

"I *will* see him again," she said determinedly. She then locked all further words and thoughts inside her heart as the coachman helped her from the carriage. Natalie dropped the few coins into the palm of his hand then swirled around and walked on through the gate, racing up the remainder of the drive in a light-hearted, skipping fashion. She lifted her eyes to the sky, never having felt so alive before . . . and a man had been the cause!

Colorful crotons and hibiscus bordered the veranda onto which she stepped, but she could already smell the cigar smoke curling from the open windows of the library and knew that her escape had probably not been long enough. She groaned inwardly, silently praying not to find another man awaiting her arrival—a man who would drool over her and her youthful, innocent beauty.

Sighing lethargically, she opened the heavy oak door and stepped directly into the parlor, consciously aware of the dullness it represented to her. Since there was no mistress of the household, there had been no female given free rein in this house's interior decorating. The furniture and floor coverings spoke only of a man's choosings. The room was spacious, filled with stiff-looking, high-backed leather chairs. A matching sofa sat opposite a magnificent stone fireplace, and beside this stood dark, mahogany tables at each end, a smoked kerosene lamp on each.

Candles dripped from black, wrought-iron wall sconces, and expensive paintings of all sizes and shapes hung obtrusively from walls that had been darkly paneled, making the room appear even darker and more unpleasant. Even the raw, white tropical sunlight streaming in through the windows cast a hard illumination all around Natalie as she began to inch her way on past the closed doors of the library. If she could only make it to the staircase . . .

The creaking of the door behind her and the sudden stronger stench of cigar smoke engulfing her made Natalie close her eyes and cringe. She clasped her purse to her bosom, waiting to hear her father's voice.

"Where have you been, Natalie?" he spoke forcefully from behind her. "There aren't enough shops in Key West to warrant such a lengthy stay from the house. Did you find some other way in which to pleasure yourself? Did you by chance go to an auction on the waterfront?"

Natalie sucked in a nervous breath then turned and faced him boldly; she was tired of having to be accountable to him for every move she made. But he was her father. He was all she had in the world. She had to continue to show her respect and gratefulness to him for being so devoted to her, for being both a mother and a father throughout the many years since her mother's death. Yet, she just couldn't hide her building displeasure!

"Father, when will you quit worrying so?" she sighed. "Do you forget my age? I'm no longer a child, with childish ways. I'm a woman. A grown woman."

"I'm even more aware of that than you are, Natalie," he grumbled, furrowing his brow. "I'll ask again. Were you at an auction. Your cheeks of pink reflect more excitement than you would have received while only trying on dresses."

Natalie took a step backward, remembering the few moments of eye contact with Bryce Fowler and the feel of his hand brushing against hers. Again she heard him ask her name, felt him hold her hand! Yes. She had reason to be a bit flushed but she wished that her father hadn't noticed. Oh, if the room could have been even darker at this

20

moment!

She glanced toward her purse, remembering the key and what it represented. To see *him* again! But her father could never know. Never.

Reaching to untie her bonnet, she forced a confident smile onto her face. "Father, I've never been to an auction. Not even with you," she purred. "Why would I today?"

He took a step toward her and took her hand in his. "You've appeared a bit restless of late, my dear," he said, bowing to kiss her hand. "When a daughter your age shows restlessness a father has reason to worry."

"I don't mean to worry you, Father," she said, relaxing her shoulders a bit as he returned her hand. "Truly I don't."

She smiled weakly toward him, as always feeling a deep hurt when she noticed that time had not been good to him. Though still an obese, robust man with the dark and penetrating eyes of his youth, he was fast losing his graying hair. Wrinkles seemed to swallow wrinkles on his face which displayed a wide scar on his left cheek; he had acquired it the same day he had lost three fingers on his left hand.

"A Cuban gone suddenly crazed one day in my cigar factory," her father had cautiously explained. "It was the sultry heat of the day. It seems he took it out on me because I was the handiest. . . ."

Saul Palmer. Her father. A pleasant enough man to her, yet Natalie had just begun to see something else about him. Was it . . . a ruthlessness . . . that she hadn't sensed when younger and even more innocent? She was just now realizing how hard he was on the servants. Also, at times, when she had passed the closed door of the library and paused to eavesdrop, she had heard him speak so coldly and angrily to those with him. . . .

Dressed all in black, as her older brother Adam always was, too, her father did present an almost sinister appearance.

"Natalie, remove your bonnet and leave it and your purse on the table," Saul said sternly. His gaze raked over her. "Yes. What you're wearing will do."

Natalie fought her feelings. She knew what he had in mind. She glanced toward the library then back to her father. "Father," she whispered, "please. I do not wish to see anyone today. You know how I feel about those men. I detest being near *all* of them."

"That will change, my dear, once you know this man better," Saul said quietly. He cast a backward glance over his shoulder toward the open library door.

"Know *who* better?" Natalie demanded icily.

"Albert Burns."

"Oh, no," Natalie groaned. She leaned into Saul's face and whispered harshly. "He's an ugly man, Father. How could you even *want* me to marry him!"

"He's a good man. He's respected," Saul replied tartly. "He's also very rich. He's a shipping tycoon with a sizeable fleet of ships. Your sons could inherit a fortune."

Heat rose upward onto Natalie's face, causing her eyes to burn. She jerked her bonnet from her head, feeling a thunderous, angry heartbeat pounding against her ribs. "Sons?" she hissed. "You not only have me married to the man in your thoughts, but you also have me bearing him sons? Oh, Father, sometimes I hardly feel I know you at all!"

Saul clenched his fists at his side, paling strangely. "I am your father," he whispered harshly. "Don't you ever forget that I am your father."

Seeing his paleness and the flashing of his eyes, Natalie dropped her purse and bonnet onto a table. She went and hugged him tightly. "I'm sorry, Father," she whispered. "Don't be upset with me. It's just that . . . well . . . yes . . . I guess I am a bit restless. But I shouldn't take it out on you."

He patted her back affectionately. "When a daughter grows restless, a father helps to find a husband for her," he said. He stepped back away from her and nodded toward the library. "Come on. Try to be pleasant. For your aging father. Eh? I won't always be around to protect you from rogues who travel the sea. . . ."

Natalie's eyes widened and once more she was thinking of Bryce. She shook her head to clear her thoughts; then she accepted her father's arm as she linked hers through his. "I shan't marry Albert Burns, father," she whispered. "But I shall be polite. I can at least promise you that."

"That's all I am asking, Natalie."

"How many more times do I have to go through this?" she questioned softly. "How many men have you now introduced me to? I've hated them all. You know that. I have."

"One day you will say yes," he persisted. "You will see the importance of saying yes to the right man. I can only hope that when the time comes, this man will be one of my choosing."

Natalie cast him a furtive glance, lifting her lips into a soft smile, again remembering Bryce. If her father knew that this man had sent her head into a crazy spin, then he

23

would know the kind of man with whom she wished to spend the rest of her life. He would know that no one of his choosing would ever do. She wanted to feel the arms of someone youthful and handsome around her. She wanted to look upward into the eyes that could look back into hers with the promise of enduring, passionate love. Yes, she wanted different things from a man than her father was offering her in the men to whom he had so eagerly introduced her. Somehow, she knew that her father understood this, yet he continued to bring only aging, ugly-smelling fools into their house! Maybe one day she would understand. Yes, maybe . . .

"Ah, my beautiful Natalie," Albert Burns said as Natalie was swept into the library beside her father.

Surrounded on all four sides by walls of books and more dark furniture, Natalie smiled stiffly toward Albert as he took one of her hands and bowed to kiss it wetly. He didn't remove his lips any too soon for Natalie, for she felt the same sick feeling inside that the presence of these older men always seemed to cause. She wiped the wetness from her hand onto the skirt of her fully gathered dress. "Good afternoon, Mr. Burns." She managed to respond coolly. Her gaze, raking over him once again, told her why she didn't care for this man. A little on the heavy side, he smiled broadly behind a pencil-thin mustache that fell past the corners of his mouth and gave him a look faintly Mexican. In his eyes, she could see the intensity of his interest in her as they shone with eager gray lights that matched the gray of his hair and attire. His shirt, having been left to gape at the throat; revealed a hairless chest.

Saul went to his liquor cabinet and removed from it three long-stemmed crystal goblets. He placed them on his desk and poured each half full with a vintage port. "Albert is sailing for Cuba tonight, Natalie," he said, lifting a heavy, gray eyebrow in her direction. "I'm traveling with him to check on my next supply of tobacco. Albert has requested that you also accompany us. His ship is well equipped for passengers as you know. It would do you good, Natalie. You need some variety in your life. I've already accepted the invitation for you."

"You've what?" Natalie gasped.

Saul's expression became harder than granite when he heard her dismay and realized that once again she was ready to oppose his wishes. Only recently had she begun to behave in such a way. But he had to believe it was her age. He would never forget how her mother had fought back at that age. Not only mentally, but physically, until the day one of Saul's rages against her defiance had been too heated. If Natalie ever found out how her mother had truly died, he would lose her forever. If Natalie ever found out *all* the truths about him, she might even wish to kill him!

"An ocean voyage could do you a world of good," Saul persisted, determined to remain firm; for to lose one inch of grip on her could mean to lose her for eternity. He strolled to her, extended a glass in her direction. "And drink this. Seems you need something now to calm you."

He leaned into her face. "Natalie, do not show your stubborn side to our friend Albert," he whispered angrily. "Smile, damn it, smile. And accept this glass of wine."

Natalie took a step backward, glaring toward Saul and then Albert. She grabbed at her stomach and feigned a sudden illness by forcing a painful-sounding groan to emerge from deep inside her throat. "Father," she cried weakly. "I suddenly . . . don't . . . feel so . . . well. . . ."

"Natalie!" Saul set the two glasses of wine down on a table then rushed to her side. Placing an arm about her waist, he let her lean into him. He lifted a hand to her forehead, feeling a clamminess. "Damn. You *do* feel as though you are ill. Let me help you upstairs to bed." He began leading her from the room, then took a fast glance back at Albert. "Maybe you'd better leave without us, ol' man," he said.

Natalie turned to Saul and clasped one of his hands in hers. "Father, you go on. I know how important it is for you to check the quality of the tobacco leaves for your cigars. Tami will take care of me. Please go on without me."

A tall and thin negro maid, colorfully attired in a long, fully gathered dress, came rushing down the staircase. Her wiry black hair was pulled into a chignon at the back of her head and her dark eyes were wide with fright. "Heavens, Massa Saul," she exclaimed shrilly. "Is our Natalie ill?"

Saul stepped back from Natalie and let Tami take his place at her side. "Seems like it," he said thickly. "Help her to her room, Tami, and see to her. Maybe I'd better send a message to Doc Raley."

Natalie's heart leaped. She turned and eyed Saul warily. "Father, it isn't necessary," she urged. "I just need some rest. That's all. I suddenly feel so hot . . . and . . . exhausted. It is quite a humid day."

"If you think—"

She interrupted. "Yes. I'll be all right," she whispered. "Now please. Go on to Cuba. Has anything ever happened to me while you've gone on such voyages before without me?''

Saul kneaded his chin. "Well . . . no. . . ."

"So it shall not this time," she further encouraged.

Saul paused, weighing his next words, then gave Tami a firm stare. "Now, Tami, you take care of her," he ordered. "I may be away for a lengthy spell. You know how I've grown to count on you."

"Sho' do," Tami replied, drawing Natalie closer to her. "Sho' can depend on Tami to do what's right fo' our Natalie."

Natalie hugged Tami back. "Yes, father," she sighed. "Tami's always been there when I've needed her. She's been like a mother to me. Please don't worry."

Saul glanced toward Albert who had moved to hover at the library door. "It's to Cuba then, Albert," he exclaimed. He looked back toward Natalie. "But this time without Natalie."

Albert didn't say anything, just looked sad and brooding as he watched Natalie being escorted up the stairs by Tami.

Natalie breathed a deep sigh of relief when she was safely inside her bedroom away from the watchful eyes of Albert and her father. Breaking free from Tami, she laughed throatily and whirled around in circles until Tami reached a hand to her shoulder and stopped her.

"Land sakes, child," she exclaimed. "Why, you're not sick at all."

Natalie grabbed Tami's hands and squeezed them affectionately. "I fooled them both," she giggled. "I truly did."

Tami's face screwed up in a doubtful frown. "Why, Miss Natalie?" she asked quietly. "You scared Massa Saul almost into his grave."

"Oh, Tami," Natalie said with a jerk of her head. "I did not." She dropped Tami's hands then reached up to unclasp her diamond necklace from around her neck. "And even if I did," she added nonchalantly. "It was quite necessary."

"I don't understand," Tami said. She went to Natalie and began unsnapping her dress at the back.

"I didn't want to travel to Cuba with father," Natalie sighed. "That's why. If I had to be on the same boat with Albert for any length of time I most surely would have become truly ill. Violently ill."

She stepped out of her dress and went to a mirror set into the door of her wardrobe. She lifted her hair from her shoulders and stood sideways, admiring the swell of her breasts beneath the lacy frills of her petticoat bodice.

"Yes, Tami, I did the wise thing," she quickly added. "Key West has suddenly become more interesting to me. I would feign illness over and over again if I had to, to be able to stay here. I have some ventures of my own that I am planning."

Tami rushed to Natalie and placed a thin dark hand on her brow. "Natalie, you must be ill," she said softly. "You've never spoken so strangely before."

"Tami, I'm not ill," Natalie laughed. "Truly I'm not." Remembering the purse that she had left downstairs, her smile faded. Inside it, she still held a part of him. She had to have it, to hold it to her heart. For she now knew what she must do!

She turned suddenly to beseech Tami with pleading eyes. "Tami, I left my purse and bonnet in the parlor. Would you please go and fetch them for me?"

"Yes'm. . . ."

Left alone with her musing, Natalie slipped her shoes

from her feet. She sank her toes into a plush, pink carpet, knowing that while her father was away, she would play. Never had she done this. But never had she met anyone like Bryce Fowler before. No matter that he had traits she didn't like . . . there was more to like than dislike!

While waiting for Tami's return, Natalie looked around the room, feeling quite comfortable in her own little niche in the world—her retreat . . . her hideaway. Though the rest of the house reflected her father's personal taste, he had let her choose fully for her own room.

Pink. She had always loved pink. Her favorite color was so feminine.

Natalie's passion for pink showed in the soft, pink satin of the drapes at her two windows and in the bedspread that lay gracefully across her magnificent, carved mahogany bed. The wallpaper she'd chosen was bedecked with tiny, pink rosebuds, and fresh long-stemmed roses rested in a crystal vase on a table at one side of her bed. At the other side, on another table, a kerosene lamp had already been lighted since the sun was quickly settling amid orange splashes, into the Atlantic.

Natalie pulled on a robe of full white eyelet lace and threw back the doors that led to a widow's watch platform. There she had a commanding view of the ocean, yet was shaded by giant sea-grape trees. As the sea breeze blew steadily against her face, lifting her hair sensuously from her shoulders, Natalie hugged herself tightly, wishing she were in Bryce's arms instead of her own. She closed her eyes at the rapture of the thought. She could so easily envision herself now as a wife keeping vigil, awaiting the return of Bryce's ship to the harbor. Soon Bryce would be there, to carry her to bed, to caress the whole of her with the blue of his eyes, then to worship her ceremoniously with his lips and tongue. . . .

"Natalie . . ." Tami spoke suddenly from behind her. "Miss Natalie. . ."

Flushed from her fantasy, Natalie swung around and smiled awkwardly toward Tami who stood with puzzlement etched onto her dark, sensitive face.

"You sho' nuff look feverish, Miss Natalie," Tami murmured, holding Natalie's purse and bonnet. "Maybe Doc Raley should come and take a look."

Flipping her windblown hair back from her eyes, Natalie rescued her purse and held it, strangely possessive. "Please place my bonnet in its proper box and quit worrying so about me," she said softly. "What I would like is a cup of café con leche."

"Yes'm, Miss Natalie." Tami sighed. "Coffee and hot sweetened milk might do you some good." She moved toward the wardrobe. "It might sweat the vapors from your pores."

"Whatever . . ." Natalie laughed silkily, then sighed with relief when Tami finally left the room.

With trembling fingers, Natalie released the drawstrings of her purse and, taking the key in the palm of her right hand, dropped the purse to the floor. A reckless passion for this man Bryce was sweeping through her; she remembered every detail about him, yet truly knew so little of his true worth.

She eyed the key once more. "What does this key unlock?" she whispered. "Can it even unlock the cold heart of this man . . . this pirate?"

The sound of carriage wheels moving away from the house grabbed Natalie's full attention. She rushed to her front window and stood on tiptoe to watch her father's carriage move from the protective walls of the gate and head on down the lane leaving only a spray of dust in the air.

"With father gone, I am free to do as I wish, am I not?" she whispered. She looked upward and saw a bit of day stubbornly lingering in the sky that was so serenely colored in streaked purples and crimsoms.

"Dare I?" she wondered, suddenly alive with excitement.

She glanced toward the lane and basked in its quietness. Even the Palmer's personal coachman wasn't on the grounds now to stop her from mounting her lovely, devoted horse Adora to take an evening ride.

"Wouldn't the wind feel delicious against my face?" she whispered further. Already she could almost feel it as she closed her eyes. But she laughed softly when she opened her eyes again and realized that indeed it was the wind caressing her cheeks, but only from her opened window.

"I shall do it," she said firmly, turning on a heel, and dashing toward a table beside her bed. "I will sneak down the stairs so quietly even Tami won't miss me."

Placing the brass key inside a drawer beneath some lacy finery, Natalie sighed pleasurably. "Tonight I shall ride with the wind," she said. "Tomorrow I shall seek him out. I *will* go to Key West. I *will* find him."

She paced the floor nervously until Tami came with her café con leche and then left again, leaving Natalie on her own for the entire evening and night.

Quickly Natalie chose a dark riding outfit and a black satin hooded cape, knowing that she would soon be a part of the night herself, her and her beautiful Adora. . . .

TWO

Refusing to let fear of discovery by her father enter her mind, Natalie urged her black mare Adora on past the wrought-iron gate. Sitting high in her saddle, she traveled down the narrow hibiscus-lined lane and onward, until she was on the road that led in one direction to the busier streets of Key West and in the other to the ocean.

Pulling her reins taut, she studied these two paths on which to travel, and Bryce entered her thoughts. She couldn't help but wonder what if . . . She clucked to Adora and determinedly headed her in a soft trot away from the ocean.

With her black cape fluttering in the wind around her ankles and its hood loose around her face, Natalie felt wickedly free and loved it. The amber-gray shadows of predusk clung to the ground almost sensuously, and the aroma of flowering trees hung like perfume in the air. On each side of the road coconut palms rustled their fingers peacefully in the breeze; yet Natalie felt her first stirrings of fright when she saw a tall figure astride a lively-stepping black stallion approaching her.

Stiffening her back, Natalie continued to travel at the same pace as before. She desperately hoped this passerby wouldn't be her brother Adam who might have decided to return home for a night. Rarely did he do this; he was so much a part of the sea now.

Natalie's heart began a furious pounding as soon as she was able to make out the true figure of the horseman. But no! It couldn't be! Why would he . . . ? She'd never thought she would be seeing him again so soon . . . if . . . ever . . .

Feeling a slow flush rising on her cheeks, Natalie smiled at Bryce as he drew rein next to her.

"Ah, can I be so lucky?" Bryce laughed, casting her a devilish grin as he raked his eyes over her. Even in the dimmed light of predusk and dressed in such a way, he could still see the loveliness of her and ached to pull her into his arms and make her his own. Damn, oh, damn! Why? Why was she any different from all the rest? But the nervous beat of his heart proved to him that she was.

"But . . . you . . . ?" she murmured. "How . . . ? Why . . . ?"

"You surely know the answer," Bryce said almost hoarsely.

So disturbed by this man's presence that she was all atremble inside, Natalie stroked Adora's sleek mane. She had wanted to see him again, but now that he was so suddenly near, she didn't quite know how to handle the situation. She was feeling even more awkward than she had in the carriage after having clumsily dropped both her purse and bonnet. And how did he just happen along?

Her gaze moved slowly to his, and she realized this was not just a chance meeting. He was seeking her out for a purpose, and between this man and this woman, there was only one definite purpose on this earth. They were attracted to one another. Yes, he was on this stretch of road for a reason. The reason just had to be her!

Her lids grew heavy with growing desire. She lifted her lips into a slow, sensual smile. "Are you saying that—"

He leaned forward and interrupted her by saying: "Yes. And you?"

With a tremor in her voice she said: "You've been on my mind since your eyes met mine in the carriage this afternoon."

"Then you were coming to—"

She interrupted him. "No," she laughed silkily. "I wasn't. I doubt if I could have been so brave as to go in search of a man at night. I was just getting a badly needed breath of fresh air." She lowered her thick veil of lashes. "But tomorrow? I most certainly would have if you were the man in question."

"And would I have been?"

With a racing pulse, she raised her lashes. She gazed rapturously toward him now, seeing his features clearly beneath the soft flow of the evening's new moon. "Oh, yes," she whispered. "I would have done that for none other. I have not done such a thing before for *any*one. You see, my father is quite guarded with me."

"And where is he now?"

"He should be boarding a ship bound for Cuba," she replied softly. "And you? Did you find Parrot Inn to your liking?"

Bryce looked quickly away from her and watched his horse paw nervously at the road. "I really couldn't say," he said thickly. He directed his attention back to her. "You see, I was only there for a moment when I decided that I must find you, or maybe never be able to again."

34

"How did you manage to find me?"

"I hunted until I found the coachman who had carried us together in the same carriage," he said. "I paid him quite well to tell me where he had taken you."

Natalie lowered her lashes. "Oh, I thought you had asked my friend."

"The friend who entered Parrot Inn after me?"

"Yes," she said, looking toward him again.

"She went immediately into the arms of . . . uh . . . a . . . uh . . . man," Bryce said quietly, appearing to be a bit uneasy about this declaration.

"Oh, that was Hugh," she said. "They are very much in love, those two."

"Eh?" Bryce said, as though shocked. Then he said: "The important thing is that I did finally find you."

Natalie swallowed hard. "And now that you have?" she murmured, lifting her delicate fingers to her face to brush back a wisp of windblown hair.

"I'd like to talk," he said thickly. He glanced around, studying the setting. Then his lean, smooth features were once more directed to her. "Would you like to go with me to my ship? We could talk in private there."

Once more his eyes were becoming magnets, drawing Natalie into their spell. Even with only the moon lighting their way, she could see the tantalizing blue of them. "I truly can't," she murmured, curving her lips down sullenly. "My father. Remember I told you he was boarding a ship for Cuba this very night. If by chance he might see me . . ."

"I take it you are afraid of your father?"

Natalie blew a silken strand of hair from her lips. "Yes, I guess I am," she said softly. "But not so much for fear of what he would do to me. It would be more for fear of what he might do to you."

"Oh . . . ?" Bryce said, leaning a bit forward, lifting an eyebrow.

"If he knew I was even talking with a . . . a . . ." Natalie said, but couldn't speak the word *pirate* for fear of angering him.

"A what?" Bryce mused, as soft flecks of a smile danced on his face.

"A . . . uh . . ." Natalie stammered, then blushed. "Nothing," she murmured, squirming uneasily in her saddle.

"If you fear discovery so much, maybe we'd best move from this road," Bryce said.

"Yes. You're right," Natalie replied softly. She looked in all directions and then steadily gazed more intensely at where the road curved to outline a bluff that overlooked the magnificence of the Atlantic.

With a slap of the reins, she urged Adora around, directing her horse in a gallop away from Bryce. She looked back over her shoulder. "Follow me," she shouted. "If you love the ocean, as you must, since you command such a masterful ship, then you will love the place I have chosen in which to have our private chat."

"Lead the way." Bryce laughed. He thrust his knees into the black stallion's sides and followed behind, watching her graceful outline, knowing that if she were dressed in white instead of black, in her cape she would look like an angel with lacy wings fluttering invitingly at him.

Bryce could not fully comprehend what had led him to her since no other woman had ever affected him in such a way before. But she seemed to understand and was even strongly encouraging him. The ache in his loins goaded him on even now; yet there was something else this time. He felt that maybe he had mercifully found a woman who could make him forget his painful past and this drive he always had to have constant power over women . . . even over many women. . . .

The wide breadth of the ocean was quickly reached. The surf was noisy and agitated, and the water appeared to be a giant chest of glittering diamonds, open for the taking. Adora neighed as Natalie guided her one careful stretch at a time down the sloping ledge where tangled thornbrush was scattered and gnarled mangrove trees grew crookedly from the rocky soil.

Glancing over her shoulder, Natalie saw that Bryce was following. She still couldn't believe that she was being so reckless . . . so utterly daring. In her dreams she had done such a thing many times. But now to be actually leading a man to a romantic interlude by the ocean? No. Not *her!* She had never thought herself capable of defying her father in this way. But lately, she had begun to feel a cold desperation rising inside her. If she didn't find a man to her liking on her own, then a wedding—one she would hate—would most surely be taking place in the near future.

"Well, I have found a man," she marveled to herself. "And not just *any* man. This man Bryce kindles my heart to flame!"

She turned her eyes from him now, frowning. "But oh, if he is a pirate," she worried, "what can I do about that?"

Tossing the thought aside she found herself traveling over smooth, white sand and felt tremors of joy sweep through her when Bryce pulled up next to her and cast her a slow, half smile.

Returning the smile, she let Adora carry her a bit farther to a protective cove where she had swum nude in the ocean in one of the other daring moments of her life. Her father hadn't been able to watch each and every move she had made, no matter how desperately he had tried.

"This is perfect," Bryce said, dismounting. He tied his reins to the root of a mangrove tree that jutted out awkwardly overhead.

"I thought you might like it," Natalie said, almost breathless now from the erratic pounding of her heart. As she reached to tie her reins next to his she found her hand encircled by his fingers. In wide-eyed wonder of him and his chiseled features outlined in the moonlight, she watched as he gathered her reins in his other hand and wrapped them securely in place.

With her hand still in his, he brushed his lips against her fingertips, eying her with lusty desire in the depths of his penetrating blue eyes.

"Natalie, you are so breathtakingly beautiful," he whispered.

She shivered with pleasure. "You remembered my name," she sighed.

"As I'm sure you did mine," he said huskily.

With her free hand, she touched his lips and felt a strange, soft pain between her thighs as she let him suck a finger and curl his tongue around it. "Bryce . . ." she whispered. "Yes. How could I not remember your name?"

She eased her finger from his mouth, not sure she was going to be able to keep control of her senses while alone with him. She was already crazily dizzy and her insides were melting.

"We were destined to meet," Bryce murmured, lifting

his hand to untie the bow that held her cape together. And once that was done he slowly laced his fingers beneath the hood and eased it from her head. He drew a deep, nervous breath when her hair sprang free and began blowing away from her shoulders in dark, lustrous billows. Then, in one quick movement, he swished the cape from around her shoulders and sent it falling in a flutter to her feet.

Natalie took a step backward, knowing what his next move had to be. She wanted his kiss, yet she was now a bit afraid. She wasn't so sure if having led him to such a secluded spot was wise. In her fantasies, it had been easy to let a man take possession of her body. But in reality? Bryce seemed to have taken possession of her mind!

"Bryce . . . I don't know . . ." she murmured as his long, lean body took a step toward her. She let her gaze rake over his face and saw that it was a mask of hungry desire for her. In his eyes, she saw victory. Was he a man who never experienced defeat? Did she wish to be the one to show him that he couldn't have every woman he hungered for? But the pounding of her heart and the aching pain deep inside her gave her the answer. She wished to never say no to this man! She needed him as she had needed nothing else in her life!

"Natalie . . . ?" Bryce said in a husky whisper, testing her response. And when she stopped and held her arms out to him, he drew her gingerly to him and lowered his mouth to hers.

Having never been in a man's arms before, Natalie felt awkward, not knowing where to place her own arms or how to fit her body into his. But his kiss . . . the sweet passion of it . . . the ecstasy it was stirring inside her . . . was her guide. She laced her arms silkily around his neck and wove her fingers through his hair. Then she slinked her body into the contours of his and moaned as she felt the steel frame of him moving erotically against her.

His lips set hers free momentarily as he whispered her name. "Natalie . . ."

He nibbled at her lips, setting sparks on fire inside her. "Sweet . . . sweet Natalie . . ." Bryce repeated huskily. His hot breath against her cheek seared her flesh and then her lips as he kissed her once more, this time with savage fury.

A low moan arose from somewhere deep inside Natalie as his hands reached between them and found the outline of her breast through her shirt. As his fingers worked the buttons free and touched the bare flesh of her skin, Natalie's breath caught in her throat. Had anything ever felt so delicious? His touch was creating the most exquisite sort of warmth between her thighs and that set off a tingling which reached her brain in fiery splashes.

While his hand caressed and learned the shape of her, his tongue worked her lips apart. And as his tongue began exploring inside her mouth, she felt as though she might explode from the ferocity of this rapture consuming her.

She let her fingers begin to move over him, feeling the wide, solid expanse of his shoulders and of the muscles straining beneath his clothes. Then she discovered the rapid beat of his heart when she pressed her hand against his chest, and she knew that he, too, was lost in this seduction, even as much as she. But something compelled her to wriggle free. She had always known that such feelings were only to be shared by husband and wife. Wasn't she no better than a waterfront whore if she gave herself so freely to him? Wouldn't he compare her to such? Hadn't Myra said that he loved, then left, his women? Why would she be any different to him?

"What's the matter?" Bryce murmured, reaching for her again.

"You appear to be quite skilled in the ways of women," Natalie said stiffly, pulling her blouse back together in front.

"Most men are," Bruce chuckled. He stooped to the sand and scooped some up into a hand. He began letting it sift slowly through his outspread fingers. "As most women want them to be," he added. He lifted an eyebrow in her direction. "As I'm sure even you want me to be."

Feeling frustrated, wanting him, yet fearing where her desire was leading, Natalie swung her riding skirt around and placed her back to him. "I'm not just any woman," she snapped angrily. "I will not be taken so easily." Her heart thundered inside her. She didn't want to discourage him so much that he might leave her to go to another. Yet, she did have pride. Thank God, she had remembered that she did before he had gone farther.

Fingers of force were suddenly on her waist, urging her back around to where Bryce stood, fire burning in his eyes, scorching her, igniting flames along her spine anew.

"You know there's something special between us," he growled. "We experienced it the first time our eyes met. You know that what I feel for you is more than what I usually feel for other women."

"But we don't truly know one another," Natalie pleaded. "We've barely just met. I was wrong to bring you here . . . to encourage you. I don't know what I was thinking."

Bryce lifted a hand to her face and traced her features,

41

running his fingers over the oval of her face, the sensuousness of her lips, and the straight line of her nose. Then he lowered his lips to her eyelids, kissing them closed, drawing a silken, tremulous sigh from inside her.

"But I don't want you to possess me, then . . . then forget me," she whispered, trembling as his lips found the soft curve of a breast.

"I would never forget you," Bryce whispered huskily. "It's taken me a lifetime to find you. How could I ever forget you?"

"You don't know me . . ." she argued faintly, giving in to him as he slowly began to free her of her blouse.

"After this night, we will know every pore of each of our skins," he said hoarsely. "Please just relax. We're alone. No one will ever know."

"I will." Natalie argued weakly. "I will . . . know. . . ."

"Hush," Bryce murmured as he lowered her skirt and feasted his eyes upon the magnificence of her breasts and the thin taper of her waist beneath the laciness of a petticoat.

As though in a trance, Natalie removed the rest of her things, even her boots, and let herself become lost in the magical moment of love's first awakening. There was no longer any fear or shame. Her need was the greatest drive now. Her need of him!

Bryce's heart pounded like a thousand drums inside him as he devoured her with his eyes. Beneath the moon's silvery flow, her fair skin glistened. The swell of her creamy breasts rose and fell in unison with the crashing of the waves onto the shore and their nipples were stiffening into two exquisite splashes of pink. As she self-consciously crossed her legs and covered her breasts with her arms, Bryce reached out to her, urging her gracefully to the sandy floor and letting his lips begin to taste the sweet flower fragrance of her flesh.

"Bryce . . ." Natalie moaned throatily when his teeth stopped to nibble a breast. And then when his lips moved upward and possessed hers, she knew that no matter what, she would give of herself freely to this man and would forever be his. She twined her arms about his neck and returned his kiss, caught now in a passion's web of her own making, getting more tangled by the minute.

She hated it when he withdrew his lips gently from hers. He eyed her feverishly.

"I must undress now," he murmured.

Natalie recoiled a bit, suddenly jolted back to reality by the realism of his words. "I'm not sure . . ." she said cautiously. "You've never seen a man nude before, have you?" Bryce asked, removing his coat, then his cravat.

"No," Natalie murmured, scooting back on the sand, once more very self-conscious of her own nudity as he stood over her, flooding her senses anew with the blue pools of his eyes.

"Which means you've never been with a man sexually," Bryce said huskily, stepping from his breeches and removing the rest of his clothes slowly, so as not to frighten her away.

"No . . ." she stammered. "I have not." Her breath lingered in her throat when she caught the full nudity of him in her gaze. The slim smoothness of his hips . . . the muscles of his legs . . . and the gold, curly fronds of his chest hair which traveled lower to where the part of him lay that waited to pleasure her. . . .

"I will be gentle," he whispered, easing down over her. His lips found a breast and sucked it hungrily while his hands searched over the silken flesh of her, gradually lowering to where she was soft and pulsating from renewed excitement. His fingers worked on her now, massaging, and her hips moved rhythmically with him.

"Bryce . . ." she cried out, almost incoherent from the pleasure/pain he was creating inside her. Seductively, she felt driven to begin nibbling at his flesh. She began at his shoulders, then at an earlobe. But this was halted when his lips sealed hers with another fiery kiss.

Clinging now, she wriggled her body into the shape of his. She relished this touch of flesh against flesh and let out a gasp when he lifted his hips and slowly eased his sex inside her.

"Easy does it," he whispered as he inched further inside her. He groaned out his pleasure the farther he drove. Then when she let out a sort of mewing sound of pain, she smiled and knew that the path of full pleasure had suddenly been opened to him.

His lips went to hers and kissed her pain away. He wrapped his arms around her and loved her tenderly when he tasted the salt of tears on her lips.

"Does it still hurt, my love?" he whispered, raining kisses along her brow.

Natalie trembled and looked rapturously into his eyes. "How can a hurt feel so delicious?" she whispered.

"Because, sweet Natalie, you are sharing with me the ultimate pleasure between man and woman," he said. He smoothed her hair back from her face, then sought her mouth again gently. While he kissed her he began to increase his movements inside her, almost to his peak now, loving the feel of her breasts meeting his with each body's movement. He combed his fingers through her hair and nuzzled her neck as their passion built.

Natalie clung to him, breathless now, opening herself to him so completely. She responded with abandonment, clinging with her wrapped legs around him. She lifted her hips to meet his every thrust, almost wild from the pleasure he was bestowing upon her. She bit her lower lip and closed her eyes as something even more painfully beautiful began. It was as though a warm ray of sunshine was inside her, splashing out farther and farther, getting hotter and hotter, until suddenly it exploded in magical torrents of ecstasy, making a clean sweep through her. Her body arched and trembled violently with pleasure as Bryce's body shuddered against hers.

Natalie clung to him, reeling from her moments of heightened passion, while Bryce burrowed his head against her shoulder, panting wildly.

"Natalie . . ." he finally whispered. "I don't know how it's happened that we have met, but I do know that I feel something for you that I've never felt for anyone else."

"There will never be anyone else but you," she whispered back.

"Then we can be together again?"

"Yes, oh, yes, yes. . . ."

Bryce rolled from atop her and reached for his breeches. "Tomorrow?" he asked, eying her still with hungry need.

Natalie reached for her clothes, blushing as his eyes never left her, though he was quite busy stepping into his breeches. "I'm not sure how," she murmured. "My father has me watched quite closely."

"You managed to elude him tonight," Bryce said, suddenly clasping her shoulders. "Surely you can tomorrow. In daylight it will be easier. It's only natural for a lady to go to the market or shopping for a fancy hat. Is it not?''

"Well . . . yes . . ." Natalie whispered.

Bryce moved his hands to her hair and laced his fingers through its thick, lustrous texture. Then he drew her lips to his and kissed her with tender ecstasy. "Then meet me at my ship," he said, breathing warmth onto her cheek. "Meet me at my *Golden Isis,* after the auction begins on the waterfront. Everyone will be too caught up in the excitement to see you."

"And how would I know your ship?" she whispered, drawing away from him to look devotedly up into his face.

"Its magnificent gold hull stands out from all the rest. You will have no trouble choosing which ship is mine."

"The name *Golden Isis.* It is beautiful," she murmured.

"Isis was the most important female goddess of the ancient Egyptians," he said, framing her face between his hands. "Her worship spread throughout all of Egypt. The worship of Isis even became popular among Romans during the period of the empire. She was the mother of all things, the lady of all the elements, the beginning of all time. This is why I chose her name. She is the symbol of life . . . of strength."

"That's beautiful," Natalie sighed.

"And you will come tomorrow?" he asked, lowering a soft kiss to the tip of her nose.

"Yes. I will. I will come on Adora," she said, trembling as his lips seared the flesh of her neck. "No one will guess that I will travel farther than the estate while on my horse."

His lips were too demanding on her breasts as he sucked one, then the other, causing the same wild desire

46

to grip her anew. "Please . . . Bryce," she sighed. "We'd best not."

Chuckling softly, he stepped back away from her. "I know," he said, stooping to rescue the rest of his clothes from the sand.

"It's not wise that I stay away from home too long," Natalie explained. She began to dress, now truly worrying about Tami. What if Tami checked on her? What if the coachman returned to the stable and found Adora gone?

"And I. I have some important business to attend to," Bryce said, tying his cravat.

"At Parrot Inn?" Natalie asked, pulling her riding boots on.

"Yes," Bryce grumbled, furrowing his brow. "At Parrot Inn."

"You do not act as though it is a pleasant thing you have to do," Natalie said softly, combing her fingers through her hair.

"I guess it's something I should have done ten years ago," Bryce said, now fully dressed. He went to Natalie, drew her gently into his arms and burrowed his nose into her hair, smelling the mixture of sea breeze and jasmine. "Yet, maybe I shouldn't even go at all. Not since I've found you."

Natalie clung to him. "I don't know what is troubling you," she whispered. "But whatever it was that pulled you to Parrot Inn today, I'm glad. For, you see, had you not had a purpose for going there, you wouldn't have been in that carriage and we would never have met."

Her eyes widened now, she remembered the key! His lost key! Not having thought to see him this night she had left it hidden in a drawer!

47

Pulling free from him, she said, "Bryce, I—" Then she stopped. She would surprise him tomorrow! She would give it to him when she arrived at his ship!

"Yes . . . ?" he said, lifting an eyebrow.

She laughed silkily, tossing her hair across her shoulders with a flip of her head. "Oh, nothing . . ." she said.

He took her hands in his. "I really must go," he said. "I hadn't planned to arrive at Parrot Inn so late. I hope you understand."

"Yes. I understand," she smiled. "Please do go on."

"Are you staying behind?"

"Until you are a bit ahead of me. It's too risky to be seen together on the road so close to my house."

He lifted her hands to his lips, kissed each fingertip reverently, and whispered: "Then I will say *au revoir*, for now, my love. Until tomorrow."

"Avec plaisir, monsieur," she giggled. "You see, I too can speak a little French."

"Is there anything you can't do?" he teased.

She sighed heavily. "Yes. Go with you now," she whispered.

"Darling . . ." Bryce murmured, drawing her close again. She trembled against him as his mouth rediscovered hers, kissing her ardently. But then he was away from her so quickly, on his horse, and only a shadow against the sand as he waved a final good-bye to her.

Aching for him, loving him so, she reached for her cape and placed it around her shoulders. She looked out to sea, noting the waves' restless sparkle, and wondered about the mysteries of the ocean—the way its tides rose and fell with the moon.

A slow panic began gripping Natalie. She'd just given

herself totally to a man about whom she knew nothing. He remained a mystery to her. Oh, God! Would she ever see him again? What if he boarded his ship and left this very night? What if he had used her for his own personal needs?

She smiled coyly. "But *I* have his key," she whispered. "Once he finds it's gone, won't he retrace the steps he took this day . . . *and night* . . . ?"

THREE

Taking long, masterful strides, Bryce entered Parrot Inn, purposely avoiding the dimly lighted tearoom to his left. To the accompaniment of a lone guitar the voice of Bryce's brother Hugh hushed all sounds except his own; his throaty ballad reached out, holding his audience captive.

"But my brother, that's the only strong point you have." Bryce whispered. "Only your voice has character."

He was reminded of what Natalie had said about her friend Myra. Hugh . . . in . . . love? How could any woman love *him*? He was less than a man. But maybe Myra hadn't tested him in that way yet. . . .

Clenching his hands into tight fists at his sides, Bryce began the ascent to the dark staircase to the second floor, where not only rooms could be let. There his father lay, possibly on his deathbed. Though Bryce made frequent trips to Key West, it had been ten years now since he had made any attempt to see his father, or his younger brother Hugh, whom Bryce hated with a passion.

Bryce had passed by the inn many times without even a glance toward it, never able to forget those long years of living there, feeling unwanted and unloved. It had been the Fowler's inn from its inception, yet Bryce had never felt kin to it and had blessed the day he had been given the opportunity to walk away from it and his family.

At the head of the stairs, Bryce was met by a long, narrow hallway which reached from right to left with closed doors along each side. The wooden floor squeaked noisily beneath his feet as Bryce made a turn to the right. Frowning, he began making his way to the far end of this hall to where the private quarters of the Fowler family had been established many years ago. Wall sconces with flickering gaslights were spaced evenly along the walls, and cast dancing shadows on the peeling, yellowed wallpaper.

The strong aroma of heated grease, rising from the first floor kitchen that served the many customers of the inn, caused his nose to curl with disgust and distaste. It seemed that nothing had changed in ten years . . . except . . . himself. He no longer begged for love he'd never received as a child. He took what he wanted and made sure never to give anything back.

"Except for tonight," he whispered. "Except for Natalie."

He was feeling a pressure in his loins, remembering her dark, luminous eyes . . . her voluptuous figure . . . and the magic they had found together. There was something different about her. Though she had given herself freely to him, he had found an innocent wholesomeness in her that he had yet to find in other women. Possibly . . . just possibly . . . he had met a woman from whom he could not only take, but to whom he could give in return!

"Natalie." Softly he repeated her name. "The name is even as lovely as she. . . ."

He wove his fingers through his hair in frustration. "This is a hell of a time to be thinking about a woman," he groaned aloud. "No matter how beautiful. I've got to concentrate on why my father sent me that damn key. He still knows me well enough. He knew the mystery behind the key would draw me back home since nothing else has succeeded in doing so."

The low, hacking cough that erupted from behind the closed door he'd approached caused Bryce to sense the pain of regret. He had at one time loved his father as most sons do, with a sort of silent, hero worship. But his father had been too wrapped up in his own silent wants and needs to return this devotion and kinship.

And now? Did his father want only pity on his death-bed . . . or . . . did he want love? Bryce set his jaw firmly. He wasn't ready to part with either feeling. He had only come to see what the brass key unlocked.

Lifting a hand, he rapped his knuckles against the door facing, causing a hollow echo to ripple up and down the full length of the hall. Bryce tensed, waiting for his father's voice to answer and when his father bade him to enter, Bryce felt tears burn at the corners of his eyes. Though he wanted to appear uncaring, his father's weakened voice tore at the inner core of his being. This was his father! And he most surely was dying!

Slowly turning the doorknob, Bryce stepped into semi-darkness then closed the door quietly behind him. Squinting his eyes he peered about him. Not much, even in this room that had been converted into a parlor, had changed. A smoking kerosene lamp reflected its shadowed light onto the faded overstuffed chairs and the one long sofa crowded into the center of the room. On the outer edges, odds and ends of tables were cluttered with books and papers. Only one window faced onto the street; yet it was so yellowed with grime no curtain was needed for privacy.

Each step taken on the bare, hardwood floor created a muffled sort of sound as Bryce moved toward what he remembered as his father's bedroom. When he stepped into that room, his attention was drawn quickly to the bed where his father sat with a pillow propped beneath his lower back, and his head resting on a mahogany headboard. From the light of another smoking kerosene lamp, Bryce could see the dark circles beneath his father's eyes; they blending strangely into the dark brown of his gaze. Where once he had sported thick, dark wavy locks, there shining almost obscenely toward Bryce was a head quite lacking hair. His loose, white nightsack gaped open at the front clearly showing the outline of his ribs under flesh stretched taut.

Bryce continued to stand there, quite speechless, staring at the ghost of the man who at one time had been so strong and vital, seeing his father's sunken cheeks and thin lips begin to quiver in unison. How could ten years have done this to a man! Would the next ten years do this to him? Damn! He most surely had to live life more fully!

"Bryce . . ." Tom Fowler said in a weak, gravelly tone. He reached a limp hand toward Bryce. "My son, you've come home."

Bryce stiffened his back and shifted his weight from one foot to the other. He didn't want to see the bones of his father's frail hand. He didn't want to hear the hurt in his father's voice. These things could tear his defenses down and make him less than a man if he showed the first

53

sign of emotion.

To occupy his own hands, Bryce removed some soiled clothes from a wooden chair and shoved the chair closer to his father's bed. Settling down onto it backward, he rested his arms on the chair's back and forced his attention back to his father. "I've come," he said icily. "But I wouldn't call this . . . this place my home. It hasn't been for many years now. I'm not even sure it ever was."

Tom's eyes wavered and tears shone from their corners. "Bryce, don't start on that again," he said shallowly. "I was hoping that time would erase all bitterness from your mind."

Bryce threw his head back in a sarcastic laugh. "Time heals all wounds? Is that what you're trying to tell me, Father?" he asked, narrowing his eyes. "Am I supposed to forget that my mother forgot she had another son—namely me—when Hugh was born?"

"You knew that she almost died while giving birth to your brother. . . ." Tom defended her.

"Yes and that Hugh almost didn't make it to his first birthday," Bryce drawled, kneading his deeply tanned brow. "Then why not continue with the family history of Margo and Hugh . . . mother and son . . . how they became so devoted to one another—so devoted I was never paid heed to. . . ."

Tom interrupted by leaning forward to cover one of Bryce's hands with the clamminess of his own. "Bryce . . . please . . ." he urged.

"Father," Bryce said, almost choking on the emotions he had forgotten dwelled inside him. "She didn't even ask for me on her deathbed. She only wanted Hugh. Even then . . . she forgot . . . me. . . ."

Tears splashed from Tom's eyes as he settled back

against the bed. "As you have managed to forget me, my son," he murmured, suddenly doubling over into a fitful, spasmic cough.

Being suddenly awash with love for his father, Bryce rose from the chair and kicked it aside as he fell on his knees at his father's bedside. When his father's coughing ceased and he sat there, pale and wheezing, Bryce circled his arms about his father's shoulders and drew him close. "I'm sorry, Father," he said thickly. "I'm so sorry."

Tom loved him back. "I'm the one to apologize, Bryce," he said shakily. "I saw your plight when you were a child. But I was too involved in my own problems. I failed to intervene in what was an embarrassing situation for me. You see, your mother also neglected her wifely duties to dote on her youngest son. Rarely did she share the pleasures of the night with me after Hugh was born. Thirteen years, Bryce. I put up with it for thirteen years; then suddenly she was gone. Dead."

Bryce pulled free from his father and clasped his frail shoulders. "Father, why didn't you talk with me then?" he asked quietly. "Instead you turned your back on me. That made it so easy to leave when I got the chance."

Tom's face became shadowed with deeper wrinkles as he frowned. "Rose. You mean Rose. She gave you that chance," he accused.

Bryce dropped his hands from his father's shoulders and moved from the bed, to pace the floor of the drab, crowded room. "I refuse to bring her into any conversation we have," he said flatly.

He turned on a heel and, boldly facing his father, stood there tall, lean and confident. "Before we do stray too much more into the past, maybe we'd best get down to business," he said, suddenly noticing the old sternness about his father's mouth and in the hard set of his jaw. Though desperately ill, he still could hold his own when talking about divided issues with his oldest son.

Rose. That was a subject Bryce had never discussed with his father. Though controversial she had been, be she dead or alive, Bryce still held her in high esteem. He would let no man speak disrespectfully of her.

"I assume the messenger boy delivered the key?" Tom said, leaning forward, his eyes suddenly asparkle. "You wouldn't be here if not for the key. Isn't that right, son?"

"Father, you know the answer to that."

"Yes, the answer is 'yes.' You do have the key."

"Secured in my rear pocket," Bryce said. He set the chair back in place beside the bed again and settled onto it. He leaned forward, eyebrows tilted. "Why did you send the key, Father? There was no message. Why the mystery?"

Tom coughed into a cupped hand. "I've been fighting this damned cough and fading away to skin and bones so I thought it best to tell one of my sons the best guarded secret of my life," he said, wheezing anew. "Never know what tomorrow'll bring. Thought it best to get my house in order."

Bryce refused to think about the true possibilities of his father dying. Instead he focused once more on the key. "Father, what about the key?" he urged.

"I purposely sent it by messenger boy without an explanation except for telling you the key was sent by me," Tom said weakly. "I know you well enough to be sure that would draw you back home since nothing else ever has. The mystery. The not knowing. And it worked, son. Here you are in the flesh."

Bryce pulled the chair even closer to the bed and, resting his elbows on his knees, leaned toward his father. "Yes. The mystery," he sighed heavily. "Will it remain just that? Do you plan to hold me in suspense forever?"

Glancing toward the door, Tom looked wary. "You did close the hallway door, didn't you, son?" he asked in a near whisper.

Lifting a golden eyebrow, Bryce shook his head in affirmation. "Yes," he said, seeing the guarded expression etched on his father's face. What was this all about? His father had never taken him aside to speak solely with him. Never! And now? What did it all mean?

"I've not kept a secret since my father's death to carelessly toss it away to a stranger who might be passing by my door," Tom growled, settling back more comfortably against the headboard of his bed.

"Secret?" Bryce said softly. "Father, what secret will you share with me? Is it something you've also shared with Hugh?"

Tom scowled. "No. Hugh isn't to know anything about this," he said flatly. "I've made my choice between my two sons and, Bryce, you've come up the winner."

Bryce shifted his weight on the chair, suddenly feeling awkward in his father's presence. Somehow he was being made to feel a young boy of fourteen instead of a man of thirty. Surely that was because at that age he had wished for such camaraderie with his father. But this was now. The present. He only wished to be done with these clumsy moments so that he could be on his way again. Surely no key could be worth all he was now putting himself through. He had managed to avoid this in all these years and was beginning to wish that he had done so again.

"Father . . ." He sighed. "Please get on with it. My ship and crew await my return. I have many duties needing my attention before returning to New Orleans."

A dreamy expression of sorts caused Tom's eyes to moisten a bit. He gazed toward the one window in the room on which a circle had been washed clean; through it could be seen the wide, blue stretches of the Atlantic. "I've often watched your magnificent ship move into the harbor," he said, choking a bit on his words. "Your *Golden Isis*. I've even stood in the shadows and watched you conduct your business at the auctions. I've seen how well you carry yourself, my son. I know many whisper that you are a pirate but I am aware that you are a legal pirate, a 'salvor,' one who looks for ships that have been wrecked, to rescue their crews and to be given a share of the salvaged goods to auction off for whatever price you can receive. Yes, there is a difference in pirates. You are among the respected set. You are someone I have secretly admired from a distance."

A fitful bout of coughing caused Tom's speech to be drawn to a sudden halt. Bryce rose from his chair, looking desperately about him for some sort of liquid to offer his father to possibly ease his coughing.

A half-emptied bottle of wine and a glass sat on a table on the far side of the room. Bryce went to it and, pouring his father a glass, quickly returned to the bedside, suddenly feeling protective of this old man—the father he had once more found.

Bryce leaned down over Tom and placed a hand behind his head; then he lifted the glass to his father's lips, relieved that the coughing had ceased.

"Here, Father," he encouraged. "Take a sip. At least

it will wet your lips and tongue.''

He tipped the glass and watched as his father swallowed a bit before brushing the glass away with a slow movement.

''That's enough,'' Tom said, taking a deep breath. He held his head back, closed his eyes for a brief moment before opening them in a flash, and smiled coyly toward Bryce. ''There is something else I'd like, Bryce,'' he said.

''Eh? What's that?'' Bryce asked. He set the glass down and stood over his father with his hands clasped together behind him.

''Your finely tailored coat smells of cigars,'' Tom said with wavering eyes. ''I'd like to share in the smoking of a fine cigar with you while revealing something I'm sure will be of interest to both you and your fine crew of the *Golden Isis*.''

This statement sparked renewed interest in Bryce. Anything to do with his ship and the sea had a way of causing his insides to blaze with burning excitement. His fingers searched eagerly inside his coat pocket until they found two perfectly round cigars. Smiling evenly he handed one to his father and placed one between his own lips. After both were lighted and the sour smell of the filthy room was replaced by the heady aroma of the cigars, Bryce once more sat beside his father's bed, leaning close, waiting. . . .

Tom took a long, lingering drag from the cigar and then sighed almost contentedly as he let the smoke roll lazily from his mouth.

''Father . . . will you please. . . .'' Bryce encouraged him to continue. He flicked ashes from his cigar into an ashtray. ''Father, if you've something to tell me, best

59

get on with it or we'll have to delay until another day. I told you I—"

"Bryce," Tom interrupted him quite abruptly. "The key. It unlocks a chest that my grandfather hid away in a vault. This chest has since lay buried, untouched, on Orchid Island."

"What chest?" Bryce said, feeling the wild pumping of his heart. "What vault? Where is this Orchid Island?"

"The chest?" Tom said in a whisper. "As my father revealed to me on his deathbed when he handed me the brass key . . . it is a chest filled with a king's ransom in gold. . . ." He coughed then added: "Even more than gold. There are many assorted jewels also inside the chest."

"What . . . ?" Bryce whispered. A key that would unlock such riches . . . and he had it in his possession!

"Father, I don't understand," he murmured. His face was flushing from this added excitement. He sat down on the bed and accepted his father's hand, encircling it with one of his own.

"Just listen, Bryce," Tom encouraged. "I'll tell it to you as it was told to me. . . ." He cleared his throat nervously then began the tale of the brass key.

"I was told that Orchid Island rises humpbacked and speckled brown above the horizon. The trade winds steadily blow across it, riffling the palm fronds and the gourds which hang from mahogany trees. Orchids grow in the savannas, and the creepers overhead are as bright as the iridescent butterflies among the shoulder-high ferns. My father said that the valleys lay lilac in the shadow. . . ."

Remembering having seen an island that resembled the one his father was describing in detail set Bryce's pulse to

60

racing erratically. How often had he pursued that black demon of a pirate ship, the *Sea Snake,* until it seemed to suddenly disappear into the horizon where an island stretched out almost crimson purple! Was this Orchid Island? Did this damnable pirate live on the island where the treasure chest lay secretly buried? He puffed eagerly on his cigar and listened even more intensely, leaning forward, stern and even more eager than before. . . .

"Many years ago, there was this Spanish treasure fleet that sailed from Havana," Tom continued, as though in a trance. "Each ship carried its own fabulous cargo. The twenty-eight homeward-bound vessels were laden with bales of tobacco, chests of indigo, tons of copper, silver from the mines at Potosí in Bolivia, and most precious of all, a king's ransom in gold and jewels.

"The next day a fierce storm ripped through the Straits of Florida, hurling eight of the ships, including three of the fortresslike galleons toward the Keys. When the hurricane subsided, one of the three, the *Santa Margarita* lay beached on Stock Island before going to the bottom with its cargo. . . ."

Tom took a deep breath and closed his eyes momentarily. Bryce leaned toward him and carefully shook a shoulder, fear grabbing him at the pit of his stomach. Was all of this too much for his father? What if he died before he finished his instructions about the chest . . . where on the island it could be found?

"Father," Bryce said, shaking his father's shoulder a little harder. "You must finish the story. I don't yet know enough to go to the island."

Tom's eyes eased slowly open. He licked his parched lips and lifted the cigar between them. After a shallow puff, he resumed his tale.

"My grandfather was a pirate."

Bryce's back straightened, his face paled. "He was . . . ?" he said. "You never told me."

Tom laughed quietly. "One doesn't go around bragging about a grandfather who plagued the seas with murdering and plundering, who was one of the fiercest pirates the Florida Straits ever came up against."

"God . . ." Bryce shuddered.

"Yes, he was one of the fiercest until he came up against someone stronger than he," Tom continued.

"Who?" Bryce questioned, mashing out his cigar in an ashtray.

Tom cast him a sideways glance. "I'll get to that," he said. "But I must take this step at a time or I'll forget some of it."

"All right, Father," Bruce said. "I'm all ears."

"As I said earlier," Tom said, wheezing a bit between words. "Before this ship, the *Santa Margarita,* went to the bottom of the sea, my grandfather and his lively crew slew her crew and rescued everything they could before the storm broke up the rest of the wreck."

"And this chest was among the items salvaged?"

"Yes," Tom answered. "My grandfather returned victorious to Orchid Island where his family waited in a mansion that had been built for them. But he wasn't victorious for long. Another pirate . . . one who traveled in a black ship called the *Sea Snake* came to the island and took it over."

Bryce bolted from his chair, a marked expression of surprise etched on his face. "The *Sea Snake?*" he said, almost breathless. "Surely you're wrong. There is a pirate who now navigates such a ship called the *Sea Snake.* I have chased her many times. . . ."

"I'm sure the great-grandson of the original," Tom grumbled.

Bryce clenched his hands into fists, anger and excitement intermingling inside him and almost causing his blood to boil. "Go on, father," he said. "Tell me the rest."

"Seems my grandfather had feared news of his prize would spread and expected looters on the island. He placed his best chest, the one from the *Santa Margarita*, in a vault in the family mausoleum beside the Fowler mansion there on the island," Tom continued. "Then shortly after that, this *Sea Snake* pirate and his crew came and tortured and killed all of the Fowler family and their ship's crew, except for one . . . my father . . . who escaped at age seven by way of a longboat and made his way here, where all Fowler's, except yourself, have since lived."

Bryce began to pace. "They were all tortured and killed?" he growled. "The island that once was our family's is, I am sure, still held by a pirate . . . my own personal enemy . . . the captain of the *Sea Snake!*"

Tom reached out a hand to Bryce. "I wasn't aware that a pirate still sailed these parts," he said quietly. "Piracy is all but dead. I thought it would be safe to tell you now. Bryce, you musn't tangle with pirates of that sort. Not for all the gold in the world. Perhaps I shouldn't have passed the key on to you. Perhaps I should have let the tale die with me."

Bryce fell to his knees at his father's bedside and reached a hand to his father's brow. "Father, do not worry about me," he said. "I will fight for the honor of the Fowler name. I will return to us what is rightly ours. If Orchid Island was once ours so shall it be again."

"But Bryce, the dangers—"

"My ship is powerful and so am I," Bryce scoffed. "But you must tell me. Does this Orchid Island lie halfway between Cuba and Key West? I've seen such a humpbacked island."

"Yes. That would be the one."

"Then, father, you must see to it that you survive a while longer," he said flatly. "For it is I who will bring you a piece of this gold to prove the success I will soon be seeking."

"I had no ship," Tom murmured. "My father before me had no ship. Only you, my son. Only you have gained the wealth to purchase such a ship."

Bryce's face flushed a bit at remembering just how he had managed to become wealthy at age twenty, but he wouldn't think about that now.

"Hugh, father?" he said quietly. "What about Hugh?"

"Aw, yes, and then there's Hugh," Tom sighed languidly. "There's *always* Hugh."

"Well? What shall we tell him?"

"Nothing," Tom said darkly. "He will continue to run Parrot Inn and sing his damn ballads. He has neither the strength nor the guts for much else. The murmur in his heart has almost made him an invalid." His voice dropped an octave. "As did your mother's constant pampering of him." He looked Bryce square in the eyes. "Son, Hugh will have the inn and you can have the treasure and the island if you can fight and win it."

Bryce rose quickly to his feet and towered over his father. "*If* you say to me," he stated flatly. "Father, I will succeed. The island will be ours. Soon. And also the treasure."

Tom's eyes closed lazily and his breathing became

64

shallow. "The vault . . ." he whispered. "Many . . . orchids . . ."

Bryce leaned into his father's face, anxious. "What did you say about orchids?" he said. "Father?" But words were futile now. Bryce straightened his back, realizing that his father had become fatigued from speaking at such length. Seeing the half-smoked cigar hanging limply between his father's fingers, Bryce reached down, rescued it, and mashed it out in an ashtray. He looked at his father for a moment longer; then he spun around and headed toward the door. Nothing had so stirred his insides except . . .

His eyes hazed over in a veil of blue; suddenly he was remembering her again! Natalie . . . the beautiful Natalie. In the excitement of speaking about treasure, he had let her escape from his thoughts.

He stepped out into the hall and stopped abruptly when he found himself face to face with his brother. He glowered toward Hugh, seeing his washed-out blue eyes, his hawklike face, and the sandy-colored hair that was pulled back into a pigtail that hung halfway down his back. Although he was dressed in a bright orange, full-sleeved shirt and full-cut trousers of sturdy black cotton, they didn't hide the fact that he was too thin and on the puny side. Being so close to Hugh was an ugly reminder of all the things he had hated about his past.

"Step out of my way, Hugh," Bryce growled.

Hugh stood his ground. "Why did father send for you, Bryce?" Hugh asked in a velvet-toned, vibrant voice that didn't match his looks.

Bryce leaned into Hugh's face. "It's none of your damned business," he snarled. "Now if you don't step aside I'm afraid I might have to make you."

65

"Why did father send for you?" Hugh argued back, ignoring the threat. "Surely he's not planning to leave *you* Parrot Inn when he dies."

"And why wouldn't he?" Bryce said between clenched teeth. "Because I had the backbone to leave this rathole ten years ago and you didn't? Didn't it ever occur to you that he admires backbone in a son? Eh?"

Hugh's face paled. "He just can't leave you the inn," he mumbled. "It wouldn't be right."

"Maybe you don't think so." Bryce purposely taunted him, having fun. "But maybe father does."

Hugh took a step backward, teetering a bit. "No," he said in a near whisper. "I won't let you. . . ."

Tired of the game, Bryce tossed his head a bit. "Damn it, Hugh," he growled. "Just move. I've things to do."

"No. I won't let you have Parrot Inn," Hugh shouted.

"Hugh, I don't even want—" Bryce began but was crudely interrupted.

"You're not even legally father's son," Hugh bellowed. "You can not legally take possession of Parrot Inn."

Bryce's heart skipped a beat. His eyes wavered as he said: "What's that you just said?"

"Mother told me before she died," Hugh bragged. "She wanted me to know, just in case you tried something crazy like this."

A sick anger raged inside Bryce. He grabbed Hugh by the shoulders and glared sharply into his face. "What the hell are you talking about?" he snarled.

"Bryce, you're hurting me," Hugh whimpered. "Please remember my heart."

"I might even kill you, Hugh," Bryce threatened. "Now tell me. What the hell is this all about? What lies have you invented? What's this that you say mother told you?''

"Even father doesn't realize you're not his,'' Hugh stammered, quite ashen in color.

Bryce shook his head and blinked his eyes, hardly able to grasp what was being said to him. "Father . . .'' He choked, dropping his hands to his side.

"Mother told me the full truth,'' Hugh bragged. "She made no pretense about how it happened. She told me quite mournfully that she had played a dangerous game with a dark, handsome man and, in a way, lost. You see, she became pregnant. Wanting a more respected person as a husband, she tricked father into marrying her.''

Bryce shook inwardly. "What . . . ?'' he gasped.

"Yes,'' Hugh said quite smugly. "When father married mother, she was already with child . . . another man's child. That child was *you* Bryce.'' Hugh lifted his lips into a mocking smile. "And she hated your true father,'' he sneered. "That's why she hated *you*.''

A bitterness began rising in Bryce's throat. The past was making more sense to him now. It hadn't only been after Hugh's birth that his mother hadn't wanted or loved Bryce, but from his own conception. She had blamed Bryce for the inconvenience in her life, for having gotten pregnant by a man she never truly loved. The only reason Bryce hadn't realized she hadn't loved him earlier was because he had been too young to notice. . . . Yet he still didn't want to believe any of this.

"Hugh,'' he whispered harshly. "You have to be making this up. This can't be true.''

"It's too bad I don't have further proof,'' Hugh laughed. "But, you see, even your true father Saul Palmer doesn't know the truth. Mother never told him about the child.''

Bryce's insides froze. His mouth dropped awkwardly open. He grabbed one of Hugh's arms and yanked Hugh next to him. ''Who did you say?'' he gasped.

''Saul Palmer.''

''Any . . . relation . . . to Natalie Palmer?'' Bryce asked thickly.

''She is his daughter.''

''God!'' Bryce said, choking on his feelings. He stepped away from Hugh and saw the triumph in his brother's eyes, the cold hate. Bryce just couldn't help himself. In a fit of fury, he doubled a fist and drove it angrily into Hugh's face. With a pounding heart he watched Hugh bounce back, slam against the wall, then crumple to the floor. Then feeling nauseous and sick at heart, Bryce fled down the stairs and out onto the street. Crying for the first time ever since his mother had turned away from him on her deathbed, Bryce ran blindly toward the waterfront.

''Natalie,'' he cried. ''Oh, Natalie, what have we done?''

He looked into the star-speckled sky. ''Is that why she was so different? So special?'' he cried. ''Because she in truth is my sister?''

Then he buried his face in his hands. ''God. I thought it was because I'd found a woman I could finally give my heart to. . . .''

FOUR

"Tami, quit fussing so," Natalie scolded as she pulled her riding boots on. "You knew that I was feigning illness last night. Why should you fret so over me wanting to take a simple ride on Adora this morning? You must know I need the exercise."

She cast Tami a sideways glance. Tami did not know that Adora had been ridden the night before! How easy it had been to slip back into the house unnoticed! And today? Natalie even had a planned rendezvous with Bryce. The thrill of it all had caused Natalie quite a sleepless night. But who needed sleep, when in love?

Tami busied herself picking up and folding Natalie's nightgown. "Miss Natalie, your father depends on me to keep a watch on you while he's gone," she worried. "Land sakes, if anything'd ever happen to you while he was gone, he'd take a bullwhip to me fo' sho' . . . probably until I'd neva' walk again."

With her boots now securely on, Natalie swung the long tail of her dark riding skirt around. She reached for a colorful, silk neck scarf to use as a decoration and thereby

69

to brighten the drabness of her longsleeved, white shirt-waist blouse. She hated the thought of meeting Bryce in the same plain attire, but to dress differently would draw too much attention to herself and to her true purpose for taking an outing on Adora.

"I'm old enough to fend for myself, Tami," she said. "Now will you please go tell Matthew to saddle Adora and bring her around to the front?"

Tami went to Natalie and touched a cheek with the velvet brown of her hand. "You'll stay on the estate grounds, won't you?" she asked softly. "I don't like the look in your eyes. They be adancin', Miss Natalie. Since your return from your outing yesterday you've been a different young lady. Did you by chance make the acquaintance of a man? Is a man why you are behavin' so strangely . . . so defiantly?"

Natalie turned her face from Tami to hide her blush from Tami's dark, knowing eyes. She reached deep into her front skirt pocket and circled the key with her fingers. To be sure she wouldn't lose it she had tied a bow to it and had pinned the bow to the inner lining of the pocket. This morning, as it had last night when she held it during the wee hours, the key made her heart pound with excitement. The blue of Bryce's eyes swam before her, drawing her magnetically into thinking of him, but Tami stepped before her, drawing her quickly back to the present. Tami surveyed her face even more intensely.

"There is a man," Tami murmured. "Miss Natalie, your eyes speak the truth. The flush of your face confirms it."

"So there is a man," Natalie said stubbornly, stomping away from Tami. "Why shouldn't there be? Am I so ugly that I cannot attract a man on my own? Must I be at the mercy of my father and those he so unjustly chooses for me?''

She picked up a brush and stroked her hair until it shone as a blackbird's wings glistened beneath the brilliance of an afternoon sun. Then replacing the brush with the dexterity of her fingers, she laced their delicate tips through her hair, to lay it above and over each ear.

"Natalie!" Tami said, her breath short and raspy.

"Please, Tami," Natalie said, suddenly afraid that she had let her belligerent self reveal too much to her personal maid. Was Tami actually more loyal to Saul Palmer than to his daughter? Such a thought sent bubbles of fear bouncing through Natalie's insides. She went to Tami and clasped both her hands tightly. "You musn't tell father. You musn't."

The whites of Tami's dark eyes brimmed slowly with tears. She worked a hand free and reached it to Natalie's cheek. "Old Tami ain't gonna do nothin' to stir up trouble for Miss Natalie," she murmured. "The years have made you my own."

Also feeling teary-eyed, Natalie threw her arms about Tami's frail shoulders and hugged her tightly. "Then Tami, you do understand?" she whispered.

"More than you know, Miss Natalie," Tami sighed, patting Natalie's back affectionately. "Yes'm, more than you'll ever know."

Natalie pulled away from Tami and eyed her speculatively. "No more questions?" she asked softly. "Trust me to do what's right for myself?"

"Yes'm."

"Then please go and ask Matthew to ready Adora for me?"

"Yes'm. . . ."

71

Sighing with relief, Natalie watched Tami lift the fullness of her skirt into her arms and glide away from the room. With the sweep of her own skirt she took a last look in her mirror, amazed at how different she appeared this day. She reached a hand to her cheek, seeing what Tami had seen. "It's as though I'm glowing," she whispered. She laughed softly to herself. "If one time with him can do these things to me what might I be like after today?"

The sound of a carriage approaching the house was cause for Natalie to move quickly to a window. She stood on tiptoe and watched as the conveyance drew to a halt next to the front veranda. She frowned, wondering who might be ready to spoil her outing. She had lain awake all night awaiting the moment to mount Adora, to go to Bryce. It no longer mattered that he was a pirate! It no longer mattered that he was a womanizer! She would make him forget both passions! Hadn't he made love to her with true feeling? Hadn't he even asked to see her again? Well, she would go to him and be damned to her father and his aging, ugly cohorts!

She strained her neck some more, oh, so afraid the morning visitor might be one of those foolish, doting men! But then another thought sprang forth, causing her heart to skip a beat. With a hand to her throat, she whispered, "Oh, but what if it is my brother Adam returned from one of his lengthy voyages? He most surely would see to it that I don't stray from the estate on Adora. Hasn't he so often said that it is unladylike to go unescorted to town in any fashion other than by carriage?"

But even when she had gone by carriage she had always been under the close scrutiny of an escort. Charles. The Palmer's personal coachman. He had been instructed not only to deliver her to her destination but also to stay close by her and to protect her at all costs from Key West's waterfront riffraff. Only yesterday had she succeeded in eluding him, by slipping out the back door of a shop with Myra to get a taste of freedom as they went laughing, quite alone, from shop to shop.

Surprisingly, her father hadn't reprimanded her for this little escapade. But with Albert Burns having been waiting for her already too long, Saul had most surely thought better than to detain him longer to take time to scold his naughty daughter.

Not able to contain her curiosity any longer, Natalie flew from her room and down the staircase, then she burst into a smile when she found Myra waiting.

"Myra," she exclaimed quite silkily. "It's only you." She embraced her best friend and gave her an affectionate hug before stepping back to look Myra over. "But why are you dressed so formally so early in the day, Myra? Gloves? Fancy hat? All these just to visit me? We didn't make plans to go shopping this morning." She eyed Myra even more intensely. "And, Myra, velvet? When the sun rises to midday you will smother!"

"This is the dress I ordered from New York a short while back," Myra said quietly. "It is quite beautiful, don't you think?" Her petticoats rustled voluptuously beneath the fully skirted, pink velvet dress. Her breasts filled out the low-cut bodice in an almost breathtaking fashion, yet the thickness of her waist made one quite aware of her pleasure in eating. A wide-brimmed straw hat hid the sandy color of her hair, and the shadows the hat made on Myra's face mercifully hid her filled-out jowls.

Natalie smiled an answer back to Myra. "Yes. It is

quite beautiful,'' she said. ''But you still haven't told me why you're so dressed?''

Myra went to a table where a silver bowl displayed a variety of fruit. She chose a cluster of grapes and began devouring them, one plump grape at a time; then she plopped down onto a leather chair, scowling. ''I will need the warmer fabric against my skin for the cooler temperatures I will be coming up against,'' she sighed heavily. ''You see, I must take a trip to New York with my mother.''

Natalie sat down on a chair opposite Myra. She leaned forward, wide-eyed and puzzled. ''But you didn't say anything about this yesterday,'' she said. ''Why not?''

''Natalie, it took all I had in me to come and tell you this morning,'' Myra whimpered. ''The ship sails quite soon. I only had time to tell you . . . and also . . . Hugh.''

''Hugh?''

''Yes,'' Myra said, lowering her eyes. ''I had to tell him good-bye. I was going to last night but didn't. He was too upset about something else. But I couldn't have broken the terrible news to him anyway.''

Natalie interrupted. ''What terrible news, Myra?'' she said exasperatedly. ''What on earth are you talking about?''

Myra's eyes scanned the parlor, then looked toward the closed library door. ''Is your father in there?'' she asked, nodding toward the door. Her face paled a bit, then she added, ''Or even . . . your brother . . . Adam?''

''No.'' Natalie replied. ''Neither are here at the moment.''

''We are free to talk?''

''Yes, Myra,'' Natalie sighed. ''Quite free. Father left

for Cuba late last night. And Adam? Who ever knows where he might crop up?''

Myra thrust several more grapes inside her mouth, spit some seeds into her gloved, right hand, then beseeched Natalie with miserable, watering eyes. "Natalie, you've been my best friend for years," she said. "And through those years we've shared secrets as though we were sisters. But there's been one secret I've kept from everyone, even you, until recently, when my mother had to be told.''

Natalie threw her head back with exasperation. "Myra . . . *please*. . . !" she said between clenched teeth. Then she went to Myra and took her hands and urged her up from the chair to stand before her. She squeezed Myra's hands affectionately. "Myra, you know that you can tell me anything. What is it?" She searched Myra's face. "You are so pale this morning and you've dark circles beneath your eyes. Are you ill? Is that what you're trying to tell me? Are you going to New York to see a doctor?''

Myra swallowed hard. "Yes," she said softly. "A doctor. But a much different kind of doctor than you've ever had the need to make the acquaintance of.''

"Myra, what do you mean?"

Myra worked her hands free and turned slowly away from Natalie, now avoiding eye contact with her. Her shoulders began to shake as soft sobs filled the room. "I'm pregnant," she whispered.

Natalie took a clumsy step backward, suddenly numb. She placed a hand to her mouth and whispered through her fingers: "Pregnant?"

Myra's face was awash with grief as she sucked in her lower lip. She couldn't speak. She just slowly shook her head up and down.

"Myra, I can't believe you can be pregnant," Natalie said in a strained whisper.

"Natalie, it's true," Myra blurted. "And please quit looking at me as though I am a criminal. Please—"

"I'm not, Myra," Natalie whispered. "It's just that . . . Oh, Myra."

Then as friends do, Natalie felt the hurt and humiliation Myra was feeling. She rushed to her and turned Myra to face her. Seeing the torment in Myra's green eyes tore at Natalie's own heart. "This trip to New York . . . ?"

"Yes. I cannot . . . I *will* not carry this child," Myra cried softly. "My parents told me last night that they had finally managed to make arrangements in New York."

"God!" Natalie gasped. Then she asked the inevitable. "Is Hugh . . . the one . . . responsible?"

Myra turned her eyes away from Natalie with a crimson blush coloring her cheeks. "No," she whispered shallowly. "It's not Hugh's."

Natalie's mouth went agape. She had known that Myra was a free spirit, but was she even more than that? Did she so freely give of her body that she could love one man and go to bed with another? "Then . . . who?" Natalie whispered.

Myra swung around and went to stand at a window, staring from it. She was wringing her hands as she answered. "I cannot say," she murmured. "But I can tell you that it is a man I detest."

Natalie stepped cautiously to Myra's side and took a hand. "You were . . . raped?" she murmured. "Is this what you're trying to tell me?"

"Yes." Myra sobbed. "So you see why I cannot have this child? It was *not* conceived of love."

76

Natalie drew Myra into her arms and hugged her tightly, drawing Myra's grief into her own heart. "I'm so sorry, Myra," she whispered. "But the innocent baby. Are you sure?"

Myra jerked angrily away from Natalie. "I will not have his child," she hissed.

"Who's . . . ?" Natalie asked quietly.

Myra ducked her head. "I cannot say."

"How were you able to keep all this from me?" Natalie asked. "You didn't once act as though plagued by such a nightmare. And, poor Hugh. Whatever did you tell him?"

"I've been walking a tightrope of taut nerves," Myra said, relaxing her shoulders. "But I had to hide my feelings from you. You have enough trouble of your own with such a strict father watching your every move." She lowered her eyes and chewed her lower lip. "Maybe if my parents had been more strict . . ."

"Don't say that," Natalie said flatly, clasping Myra's shoulders. "Don't blame anyone now but the man responsible. Don't make it any harder on yourself than it already is."

"Of course Hugh doesn't know the true reason I am leaving," Myra said softly. "How does a woman tell the man she's in love with that she's carrying another man's child?"

"What did you tell him?"

"That I was going to New York on a shopping spree with mother."

"And when you're gone for so long, what shall he think?"

"It doesn't take long to rid one's body of a child," Myra said, engulfed with tears again.

77

"Good lord," Natalie whispered, aghast at the thought. "If ever I become with child, oh, I pray that it will be conceived by the man I love."

Myra wiped the tears from her eyes with the back of one of her gloved hands. "I must go, Natalie," she said, forcing a stiff upper lip and tilted chin. "My mother waits at the ship."

Natalie walked Myra to the door then clutched an arm. "Myra, while at Parrot Inn yesterday afternoon, did you—" she said, then stopped, thinking better of speaking of Bryce and how he had chosen to leave Parrot Inn to go in search of her. No. This was her own kind of secret to be kept hidden inside her heart.

"What about Parrot Inn?"

"Oh, nothing."

"Are you sure?"

"Yes."

"You know the man we saw in the carriage?" Myra asked. "You know . . . the man Bryce Fowler?"

Natalie's heart lurched at the mere mention of his name. "Yes, I remember," she said thickly. "What about him?"

"Well, it was the strangest thing," Myra sighed. "He left for quite a spell then came back. And when he did, you should have seen him dash up the stairs to the second floor." Myra giggled a bit. "Of course you have to know what there was of interest up there."

Paling, Natalie made a quick turn and hid her displeasure from Myra. She placed a knuckle to her lips and bit down onto it. She knew what the upstairs of the inn held. Many rooms and some whispered to be used for only an hour at a time by skirt-lifting whores! Bryce surely must have planned a rendezvous there with such a lady! He

78

certainly didn't make his residence in such a dowdy place. But . . . maybe he did! Maybe his interest in her was because of the wealth she'd displayed in her diamonds!

The thought ate away at her heart, surely she had fooled herself into believing his interest in her was genuine. But no matter. She still was driven to go to him . . . be with him again. . . .

She swung around and let her gaze move slowly downward to settle on Myra's abdomen. Oh, God, she thought desperately to herself. What if that happens to me?

Feeling a blush warm her face, she moved her gaze upward and saw that Myra had noticed her bold stare, but no words were exchanged between them about the embarrassment of the moment. Instead, Myra hugged Natalie once more; then she flew from the house and on into the carriage, leaving Natalie to stand staring from the door until the carriage became as only a small speck upon the horizon.

A sudden shudder raced through Natalie, the aftereffects of Myra's revealing visit. But she forced all fear from her thoughts when she stepped out on the veranda and saw Matthew strolling casually from the stables, directing Adora toward the house.

"Nothing will change my mind," she murmured. "No man has ever stirred me so. I must see the reason why. What *is* the mystery about this man Bryce who in one breath is called a pirate and in the next . . . the man I have hopefully fallen in love with."

Then her thoughts once more went to Myra and the secret she had so skillfully kept. Best friends shared secrets of the heart! Why hadn't Myra? But now wasn't the time to wonder further about that. Bryce was surely waiting!

She flashed Matthew a smile of welcome as he handed her Adora's reins.

"Ride her slow and easy, Miss Natalie," Matthew drawled in his thick Southern accent, looking humble as his dark eyes turned guardedly toward her. She felt that his past had not been pleasant . . . that someone had not been kind to this dark-skinned man. Gray, kinky curls framed his black face on which the skin was drawn taut across his high cheekbones, and his shoulders never straightened as though he was always ready to bow if so ordered.

"The sun comes up hot and darin' this day," Matthew quickly added.

Holding Adora's reins, Natalie stepped from the veranda and began stroking her horse's sleek, black mane. She smiled as Adora shimmied and snapped her tail at a fly on her rear. "I always ride her gently, Matthew," she said, speaking more loudly, since he was half deaf. "I'll bring her back to you safe and sound. You'll see."

"You just be sho' to bring yourself back home safe and sound," Tami said suddenly from behind Natalie as she stepped out onto the veranda. "Massa Saul. Remember Massa Saul."

"Oh, Tami," Natalie sighed disgustedly. "I told you. I can take care of myself." A sort of shiver trailed up and down her spine when she saw Tami and Matthew exchange quick, brooding glances. Then without any further thought, she placed a foot in a stirrup and swung herself up into the saddle. She dared Matthew and Tami to respond, defiance in her set stare. "I can," she stated flatly. "I am a Palmer, or do you forget?"

With her chin tilted haughtily, she clucked to Adora and ignored the two pair of eyes still watching her and almost projecting a threat to her planned morning of freedom. Following her bidding, Adora trotted across the straight stretch of yard, away from the drive, until the back gate was reached. Swinging herself from the saddle, Natalie opened the gate, then once more mounted Adora and traveled along a rose-tangled bluff that overlooked the wide expanse of the Atlantic.

She lifted her eyes to the sky and inhaled deeply the fresh, clean smell of the sea. Ah, how she loved the soft caress of the damp breeze against her face, tasting only the faintness of sea-water salt on her lips. She was once more free! She laughed into the wind and enjoyed the rise and fall of her hair on her shoulders as the sea breeze played through it. It was as though the dark, glistening threads of her hair were the strings of some magnificent harp, and the wind was many, many fingers, touching . . . lifting . . . teasing.

"Yes, I am free," she shouted. "And it is because of you, my pirate friend. Your eyes. I cannot forget your eyes. . . ." Nor his kiss . . . nor his touch . . .

Looking out across the Atlantic she caught sight of a tall-masted ship. Something compelled her to pull Adora to a quick halt to study the ship more closely. "With its body of black, it looks so sinister," she whispered.

She had heard whispers of a pirate who navigated such a black ship. The *Sea Snake*. She had heard that this pirate was a seagoing robber who recognized no government and obeyed no law other than his own—a man who was an enemy to all and friend to none.

"I wonder who . . . ?" she said in a hushed whisper.

Natalie veiled her eyes with her left hand and leaned a bit forward, now seeing another tall-masted vessel on the horizon, traveling along behind the black ship. Barely breathing she watched as the black ship held back and the smaller vessel passed it and headed on toward Key West.

"Does this *Sea Snake* pirate own a sister ship?" she murmured, dropping her hands from her eyes.

Then her mouth grew a bit dry. "No. It cannot be," she said. "That looks like Adam's ship. Why would he . . . my brother . . . ?"

She forced a nervous laugh. "No. I'm sure it's not," she tried to reassure herself. "So many ships look alike. That just can't be Adam. Why would he be traveling with that black, ugly ship?"

Shrugging, she snapped her reins and once more urged Adora to travel in a soft trot. "Enough of my dallying. I've got to hurry on," she whispered. "I've already lost precious time that could have been spent with Bryce."

The fullness of her skirt lifted daringly above her knees as the wind caught its gathered folds, and she shook her hair free as it curled and whipped around her eyes. How she enjoyed the tropical setting, the somber greens of the palmettos and the weirdly tangled mangroves that dotted the shoreline. In the woods, aromatic trees offered spices, and wild pigeons flitted about by the dozens.

But as the houses at the side of the road multiplied, a tingling of sorts raced through Natalie, and she hoped that she could indeed, fend for herself. She did understand the dangers of the waterfront. Though there were many women of the night who offered their services—even at all hours of the day—there was always a man who would enjoy taking the virginity from an unsuspecting, innocent girl.

"As one did with Myra," she hissed.

She touched a bulge at her thigh. She was smart enough not to travel to the waterfront without some means of defense. She had sneaked a knife and its protective leather sheath from her father's desk earlier in the morning and now had it tied securely to her leg. If any man besides Bryce would try to touch her wrongly, she would show him the spirit of the Palmer's in the flash of her knife!

Now deep into the heart of the city, Natalie slowed Adora's pace. She kept a close watch on all sides of her as she worked her way toward the waterfront. Cuban and American women mingled in the streets in their brightly colored cotton skirts. They were busy shopping at the outdoor booths which displayed tropical fruits such as coconuts, papaya, and Spanish and Key limes. Also, assorted fresh seafood such as lobsters, stone crabs, crayfish, and conch meat were offered by vendors. Others sold hot *bellos,* ground black-eyed peas seasoned with Cuban spices and then deep fried.

From the many saloons which lined the busy streets, she could hear Spanish, Bahamian Calypso and junkanos songs. These hideaways drew many from the streets, but Natalie had only one destination in mind—the waterfront where Bryce's gold-trimmed hull was said to stand out from the rest of the ships.

Now, approaching the crowd where the daily auctions were held, Natalie brought Adora to a halt. She slipped gently from the saddle and held tightly to the reins as she stepped more deeply into the crowd. The unruly group of men and women who had come to seek a bargain proved that one man's loss was another's gain; for the goods being auctioned off were the remains of the misfortune of others at sea.

Natalie could see the many ships moored at the Quay, their high masts towering above the heads of the crowd.

Her heart pounded with eagerness. Which mast belonged to Bryce's *Golden Isis?* With so many people clamoring around her, she couldn't see the hulls of the ships!

Frustration caused her to push her way on through the crowd. Though she had always begged her father to let her attend the auctions, she did not care to be there today. Not with Bryce so near. She could hardly wait to feel the magical warmth of his hands against her flesh. . . .

A fight suddenly broke out beside Natalie and cutlasses shone wickedly beneath the rays of the sun. She moved closer to Adora. With all her might, she clung to her horse, watching in disbelief when blood was suddenly spilled before her eyes as a man's finger fell to the ground.

Feeling spasms in her throat, knowing that she was about to retch, Natalie held her stomach with one hand and guided Adora away with the other. She now realized why her father had refused to let her be a part of such a violent scene! She tried to close her ears to the cries and goadings behind her, now knowing that the half-crazed crowd hungered for even more of the violence they had just witnessed.

With trembling, weak knees, Natalie once more mounted Adora. Now instead of working her way through the crowd she moved to its outer edge and was finally able to get a full view scan, she looked for Bryce's. Her heart plummeted. It wasn't there!

"Surely, I've overlooked it," she whispered, halting Adora. She leaned a bit forward and read the name painted on the side of each vessel, but saw none called the *Golden Isis*. Nor did she see a hull trimmed in gold!

What Myra had said about Bryce slowly began to haunt Natalie. "He has such a reputation for loving, then leaving, a woman. . . ."

Biting her lower lip nervously, Natalie directed Adora around and away from the ships. Tears blurred her vision as she now realized she had been played for a fool. Oh, how had she let it happen?

She sank her knees into Adora's side and slapped her with the reins, having the need to put a quick distance between her and the mockery of the tall-masted ships.

"Why did he do this to me?" she cried to herself, feeling an agonizing pain around her heart. "He seemed so genuinely sincere while with me."

Wiping tears from her cheeks, Natalie had another thought. "Maybe he had a reason for leaving," she whispered. "Or maybe someone else is using his ship today. Perhaps he could even be at . . . the Parrot Inn."

But if he was . . . would he be . . . alone?

"I must find out," she said stubbornly. *"I must!"*

Flipping her hair back across her shoulders, Natalie focused her eyes forward. Determinedly she left the ugliness of the harbor area behind her and directed Adora to a more pleasant section of town where Spanish and Bahamian architecture intermingled and where one of the buildings had been turned into an inn . . . Parrot Inn.

Full of anticipation mixed with fear, for she had never entered such an establishment alone, Natalie dismounted from Adora and tied her reins to a hitching post. Then, gathering courage, she made her way toward the door and, slowly opening it, stepped inside.

The soft strumming of a guitar drew her attention to a dimly lighted room to her left. There candles flickered romantically on dark mahogany tables, reflecting in the clean shine of the tops. A few customers sat sipping hot tea and a caged parrot, breaking open sunflower seeds it intended to eat, sat on a perch at the far end of the room.

Natalie turned slowly on a heel and let her gaze travel up the dark staircase at her right side. From somewhere above her she could hear someone lost in body-wracking coughs. When footsteps approached behind her, Natalie swung around and sighed heavily with relief. "Oh, Hugh," she laughed. "You gave me a fright."

Hugh Fowler, his face hawklike moved on toward her with his awkward gait. He was dressed in his usual attire, a bright orange, full-sleeved shirt and full-cut breeches. His sandy-colored hair was pulled back into his usual pigtail and hung halfway down his back. But there was something quite different about him this day. He sported a black eye! Yes! His right eye was swollen half-shut and the circle of black beneath it shone smoothly and menacingly back at Natalie. She wondered who could have done this? Hugh was too gentle to fight another man! But she couldn't embarrass him by asking!

"Natalie Palmer," he said in his vibrant tone of voice. He looked around her, then eyed her quizzically. "And alone?" he added, lifting a furry, sandy eyebrow. "You've never come to Parrot Inn without Myra."

"Yes, alone," she murmured, almost ready to challenge anyone who might question her right to go where she pleased, yet feeling uneasy at his mention of Myra. She would avoid answering this question.

But then she had to smile, having been touched almost sensuously by his voice and its resonant quality. That had been Myra's attraction to Hugh. When he sang, it seemed he could reach into a person's soul. But that was his only asset. If it were not for his voice, he would have nothing with which to draw attention to himself. "What would your father say if—" Hugh began but was interrupted by her sudden bluntness. He took a step backward, not having yet learned the skills to protect himself even from a woman.

"Hugh," she exclaimed sharply. "If you were to question everyone who entered your inn you'd soon be out of business."

"I didn't mean to imply—"

Natalie scowled toward him. "Yes. You did," she said. She recognized his uneasiness, his cowering as though he were a scolded puppy, and was drawn to take one of his limp, thin hands in hers. "Hugh, it's all right," she reassured him. "Truly it is. Of late I have a way of speaking my mind too brusquely. Forgiven?"

He laughed reassuredly. "Only if you'll have a cup of tea with me," he offered, nodding toward the tea room.

"You're not going to be singing any of your beautiful ballads? You have time for tea?"

"I don't usually sing until afternoon," he said. He took her by the elbow and guided her into the tea room where he chose a table at the back.

Lifting the tail of her skirt, Natalie let him assist her into a chair, feeling strangely wicked to be sitting in the dark corner of this controversial establishment with a man. She smoothed her hair back behind her ears and smiled to herself, studying Hugh as he carried a silver tea service toward the table. With his feminine stride, she had to wonder how much of a man he was. What did Myra see in him besides the velvet texture of his voice? But then she had to remember that Myra had had trouble attracting a man and most surely had swooned at Hugh's feet when he'd said his first word to her.

"But I must remember where Myra is going now," she thought to herself. "Did the man responsible find her at-

87

tractive? Or did he rape her because she was handy when his warped mind decided he wanted to take a lady by force?''

''And now,'' Hugh said, settling down opposite her, ''tell me what brings you here?''

Natalie blinked her thick lashes quickly, realizing that she had been lost in thought; for already the tea was poured in a tiny china cup and steam was spiraling upward from its brown liquid.

She moved her fingers to the cup but, instead of lifting it to her lips, turned the cup in circles on its saucer. She suddenly felt embarrassed. She couldn't tell Hugh her true purpose for being there. One fast sweep of her eyes had told her that Bryce was not in the room, but her gaze had stopped and held at the staircase which was visible out in the foyer. If she happened to venture up those stairs, would she find him? Would he perhaps be making love to a beautiful Spanish señorita?

Such a thought tore at her heart. Surely she had been banished from his mind the moment he had turned his back on her to walk away.

''Natalie?'' Hugh persisted. ''Is something troubling you? Myra's told me the reasons you've never been free to come here. Do you now wish you hadn't? Are you afraid your father might find you here?''

Natalie felt a blush splash her face crimson. She lifted the tea to her lips and took a soft sip from it; then she replaced the cup in the saucer. Suddenly she was awash with courage. ''Hugh, I met a man yesterday,'' she said softly, leaning over the table, closer to him. ''I'm wondering if you may have seen him today.''

Hugh's eyebrows lifted into two sandy arcs. ''A man?'' he said. He met her halfway across the table as he, too, leaned toward her. "Natalie, what man are you speaking of? Why would you even want to know about him?"

Glancing quickly around her, Natalie replied softly, "Why does any woman ask about a man?" She squirmed a bit under his ensuing, steady stare, suddenly feeling quite uncomfortable as his blue eyes studied her almost reverently. His eyes disturbed her, but not in the same sensuous manner as the blue of Bryce's had.

"Hugh!" she whispered harshly. "Why are you looking at me in such a way?"

He smiled a bit bemusedly. "You're different than I have always thought," he said. "The untouchable, beautiful Natalie? I would never have thought you would go in search of a man. Most surely you have gentleman callers by the dozen. Why would you need to come to an inn to seek a man?"

Natalie's liquid, brown eyes blazed in a sudden fury. "That's none of your affair, Hugh Fowler," she snapped angrily. Then her face paled a bit as she whispered his last name again. "Fowler . . . ?"

She gave Hugh a lingering look and let her gaze settle on his eyes and the blue of them. Her pulse racing, she wondered why she hadn't made the connection earlier. The name Fowler . . . Bryce Fowler . . . Parrot Inn, owned by a family of Fowlers . . .

But could this weak-appearing, dowdy man—Hugh —be related to the virile, handsome Bryce? Surely Natalie was wrong!

Toying with her teacup, Natalie lowered her eyes to it, wondering how to approach him with the question. . . .

Hugh cleared his throat nervously and rose suddenly from the chair. "Seems I've offended you, Natalie," he said moving to stand beside her. With gentlemanly grace he bowed toward her, lifted one of her hands to the narrow line of his lips, and kissed it wetly. "For that I wish to apologize."

Slowly withdrawing her hand, Natalie watched him as he turned to leave. Feeling panic rise, driven by the need to find out if Hugh's name, Fowler, could be connected with Bryce's name, Natalie pushed her chair back and blocked Hugh's way. She was a bit embarrassed when she saw the look of dismay etched across his face and somehow felt she had overstepped the boundary of a proper lady.

But all thoughts of Hugh and Bryce were cast from her mind when she heard a deep, growling voice speak her name from across the room.

With fear grabbing her heart, Natalie spun around and boldly faced her brother Adam. "Adam . . ." she said in a near whisper, knowing that she had just been caught and by one whom she dreaded even more than her father. There had always been a strange tension between her and Adam. But she had always thought it due to their age gap, that being fifteen years, he being the oldest.

As she glared back at him, trying to look brave and defiant, she saw that even though he was her brother, she couldn't help but always notice how darkly handsome he was with his rugged features. Yet there was a ruthless quality about him. Yes, it was the cold hardness of his eyes. They were even darker than Natalie's and blended in with his dark hair and his everyday attire of black. Even now, dressed in his billowing, full-sleeved, black shirt, open halfway to his waist, and his snug, fitted breeches, he looked the role of a sinister pirate. But Natalie knew better than that. Adam traveled the seas in one of his own fine ships, delivering the family's cigar shipments to such faraway ports as New York and sometimes even China.

Her hands went to her throat as she remembered having seen the ship that so resembled Adam's sailing away from the black pirate ship the *Sea Snake*. But, no. That couldn't be! It was foolish to even dwell on it.

Adam moved toward her, and his scowl caused his thick, dark brows to almost shield his eyes. His black leather boots caught the shine of the candles as he took heavy, determined steps around the tables, till he stood with his right hand on a pistol strapped at his waist. "Natalie, what the hell are you doing here?" he stormed angrily.

"How did you know?" she asked, glancing toward Hugh who now stood watching her with not a trace of color on his face.

"I saw Adora," Adam growled. "Only you ride Adora. But I couldn't believe you would be visiting such a place as this without a proper escort."

Spoiling for a fight, he cast Hugh a scornful look. "Are you responsible for Natalie's being here?" he said, threatening Hugh with a heavy-booted step toward him. His lips then lifted in a sardonic smile. "But, no. Natalie wouldn't risk being locked in her room for the likes of you," he derided. "At least she would be in the company of a man, which you surely do not profess to be."

"Adam . . ." Natalie gasped. "Please don't—"

Adam grabbed Natalie's right wrist and roughly began to urge her from the room.

Feeling angry and humiliated, Natalie fought against his hold. "Let me go, Adam," she hissed, cringing when the firmer grip of his hand caused sharp pains to shoot

91

from her wrist up to her elbow. She breathed harder, too stubborn to confess that he was hurting her. And when the dark foyer was reached, Adam swung her around and immobilized her against the wall as he held both her wrists above her head.

"I will not allow you to become a waterfront slut," he said from between clenched teeth.

"You will not allow me," Natalie argued, flashing her dark eyes back at him. "Who are you to tell me what I can or cannot do? Adam, you're my brother. Not my keeper. Now release me. Do you hear?"

"Only after you tell me why you've lowered yourself to come here," Adam argued. He nodded toward the dark staircase. "Whoring goes on up there. Is that why you're here? To become as those women who sell their souls for money?"

Shame engulfed Natalie with fierce icy stabs. At this moment she felt no better than a whore. With Bryce, she had forgotten how a true lady was supposed to act. But even now, she knew that again she would willingly throw caution and pride to the wind just to be with him!

But she still would not let Adam realize he had caused her to think twice about what she had done. She would not give him the satisfaction or the pleasure of having won a battle with her.

"I was ready to leave, Adam," she said coolly. "Just release my wrists and I shall leave."

"Not until you tell me why you are here," he said hotly into her face.

Realizing that she was indeed cornered, Natalie knew that she had to tell him something, to be set free, to leave this humiliation behind her. She couldn't tell him the truth . . . but she could tell him a half-truth. Thank God she had the key. It could be her excuse this time and perhaps provide the means for a meeting with Bryce. Yes! The key could protect her from possible threats from Adam and her father if ever the need arose again! She knew just how to use this key. It would open all doors that led to Bryce!

"I found a key," she said blandly, testing him, watching his reaction, seeing a dark eyebrow arch upward.

"So you found a key," he argued. "What does that prove?"

"I've come in search of the man who lost it, to give it back to him," she said, lifting her chin defiantly. "So now, Adam, you know. You can release my wrists."

His mouth tightened and his eyes narrowed. "What man? What key?" he grumbled.

She sighed heavily. "Isn't it enough that I told you the truth? Must you persist with this hateful questioning?"

She worked against his grip of steel, almost hating him. "And, Adam, you've had your fun. Unhand me this instant. Do your hear me? This instant!"

He laughed scornfully. "When I get the answers I seek, only then will I release you."

Natalie glanced toward the tea room, angry that she hadn't received the answers she had been seeking before her brother had entered the inn. Though she now realized that she'd behaved in a shameful manner it didn't lessen her need to see Bryce Fowler and to be with him. Was he related to Hugh? Oh, now would she ever know the truth? Only Myra could help her . . . and Myra was on a ship, bound for New York. It could be weeks—maybe months —before her return!

"All right," she said. "I'll tell you but only if you'll release me first."

"That's more like it," Adam said, laughing sardonically. He released his hold on her and took a step backward, so dark he blended into the setting as if he were a part of it.

Natalie rubbed her wrists, scowling toward him. "Yesterday I was in a carriage with Myra and this man sitting opposite us lost a key from his breeches pocket," she said quickly. "I have the key and I plan to return it to him."

Adam grabbed her by the wrist again. "You were in a carriage with a man?" he snarled. "God, Natalie, today isn't the first day you've behaved so loosely?"

"I was with Myra," she said stubbornly. "We had been shopping."

"I've warned you about being with that tramp," he hissed vehemently. "She's going to get you in trouble. You must stay away from her."

"Well you don't have to worry about Myra for a while," she hissed right back.

"Eh? And why not?"

"She left for New York," she snapped. "Some terrible man raped her and she's going to New York to rid herself of the child."

Natalie's heart skipped a beat when she realized what she had just disclosed. She should never—But seeing Adam's reaction caused Natalie's full attention to focus only on him.

Dropping her hand, Adam took a step back from her. His face was strangely shadowed and his eyes were even darker than usual—even more threatening. "What's that you said?" he said quietly. "What about Myra?"

Natalie eyed him questioningly, then denied him an answer. "Nothing," she whispered. "I said nothing about Myra.''

''By damn, I heard you well and clear,'' Adam said, kneading his brow. He turned on a heel and rushed toward the door, swinging around only long enough to say, ''You get the hell home, Natalie. Now! Do you hear? And don't let me ever hear tell of you coming in this place again!''

Red-faced with anger, Natalie clenched her fists at her sides. She placed her hands on her hips and, with her chin tilted, defied him anew. But this time he ignored her and was soon lost from sight, leaving her to wonder about his reaction to what she had said about Myra! He had become so upset he had failed to pull the name Bryce Fowler from her lips.

Hugh's velvet voice floated from the tea room, luring Natalie back inside for a brief moment. He was sitting on a stool next to a man strumming a guitar. The song he was singing sounded so hauntingly touching . . . Natalie was about to speak to him again.

But thinking better of it and remembering her status in the world, she swung the gathers of her skirt around and raced outside to where Adora peacefully waited. Grabbing the reins, Natalie stepped up into the stirrup and eased herself onto the saddle. She glanced toward Parrot Inn and let her gaze linger there awhile.

''Bryce Fowler . . .'' she whispered. ''Where did you disappear to? Shouldn't I hate you?''

The pounding of her heart at the sound of his name was her answer.

FIVE

The dipping sun, red in the hot and coppery sky, reflected its shimmering haze through the master cabin's skylight. The refracted beams of light became ruddy when they fell against the great scrolls of mahogany on the door frame opposite where Bryce lay sprawled on his bed. In a half drunken stupor, he reached his hand out to touch the golden-haired beauty next to him, tracing the soft whites of her breasts. "Hello there, wench," he said thickly.

"Are you sorry I sneaked aboard your ship while in Key West?" Cara Thomas asked, twisting her body into a sensuous curve, making herself even more accessible to him and his needs.

"You came close to being pitched overboard," he snapped. "I was in an ugly mood, one I'm sure you were aware of."

"Yes, I noticed, Bryce," she laughed. "But you didn't order me from the ship, did you?"

"Ah, hell," he snarled. "I needed someone. You were there."

"As I always would be, if you'd just ask."

"Cara, how many times do I have to tell you—"

She brushed a kiss against his lips. "I know where I stand with you," she said. "As you know *I* don't reserve all my time for you. It's probably best that way, Bryce."

"How the hell are you going to get back to New Orleans?"

"I've many friends with ships," she purred.

"So I've noticed," Bryce commented dryly. He lowered his lips to the swell of a nipple and sucked hungrily from it, but he was thinking of the eyes of the ravishing Natalie. Ah, Natalie with the dark, innocent, luminous eyes and body he would never forget. Oh, if only it were *her* breasts he was now teasing with his lips. The thought of not being able to draw her into his arms ever again sent splashes of anguished torment through him. Subconsciously his teeth sank into a nipple, causing Cara to wince with pain and to draw away from him.

Rubbing her raw breast, she eyed him vehemently. "Bryce, cut out the rough treatment," she hissed. "Don't take your anger out on me in that way."

Bryce laughed scornfully and drew her against him. "So how do you want me?" he asked huskily, trying his damnedest to erase Natalie from his mind.

"Do you even have to ask?"

She then gave herself fully to him as his lips traveled over her abdomen, then lower. When he saw her writhe and open more to him, he mounted her and filled her fully with his hardness. In only a few brief strokes he had received all the pleasure from her that he sought for release at the moment—a release that he hoped would drown his torturous thoughts of Natalie and of who in truth, she was . . . and who, in truth, he was.

Sighing lethargically, he rose from the bed, thick-tongued and heavy-hearted. It seemed nothing could ease this pain of discovery. Not Cara . . . not any woman. He had been foolish to think she could. Every time with her had always been the same. She had never stirred anything special inside him and now aroused him even less. Since Natalie, no other woman would do. Yet, Natalie was not his for the asking. He now knew that he was no better than a bastard. His father was Saul Palmer! God, how the knowing hurt!

Angry and trembling, he pulled his breeches on.

"Bryce, where are you going?" Cara pouted. She rose from the bed and tried to fit her body into his, to taunt him into returning to the bed.

"I need a breath of fresh air," he said brusquely, avoiding the pleading of her devilish green eyes. He nodded toward the cabin's interior, gesturing with a hand. "But you stay here. Away from the eyes of my men. I offer you the best of luxury aboard my *Golden Isis*. Where else would you find the master cabin of a ship such a commodious place of gold, plush settees and over-stuffed leather chairs? Enjoy it, beautiful lady, because at sunup it will be only a memory to you." He gave her a glowering, dark look. "And, Cara, don't *ever* sneak aboard my ship again," he growled. "In fact, I never even want to see you again."

Grabbing a shirt, he left her standing there, gasping, not caring that he had once more humiliated her. It seemed that with each women he had bedded, he had repeatedly been trying to repay the sorrowful debt of his past.

"The whole cause of my misery is my mother," he thought angrily to himself, stepping out onto the main deck. He had realized long ago that when he degraded a woman, in a sense he had been doing it to his mother. At times he hadn't been proud of this but had continued to be driven to conquer as many women as were introduced to him. And his reputation had followed him. Yes, he knew this and wasn't proud of it.

With his shirt left open, revealing a chest of golden hair, he walked barefoot along his ship's desk, a deck that was as white as the ship's snowy sails bosomed out before the favoring wind. His *Golden Isis* was a tall, stout vessel, a three-masted schooner of full-rigged design, which carried eleven brass guns in each broadside. With these showing prominently through a white strip on her gold-painted hull, no pirate had ever bothered her.

There was a great deal of copper and brass on deck, even brass belaying pins; and the toprails, stanchions, skylights, and coamings were made of mahogany. At this hour of dusk in the last of the sunlight, she glistened in a russet, gold radiance.

Stepping to the ship's railing, Bryce bent and leaned his full weight against it. The topsails creaked overhead as his crew noisily performed their duties on all sides of him. But he was oblivious of these sounds. He was watching the sparkling foam below him, becoming lost in deep thought. His past had been painfully revived upon entering Parrot Inn, and more than that, many questions had been answered, though crudely, by brother Hugh.

As the sea breeze lifted his golden hair from his shoulders and whipped inside his opened shirt, Bryce let himself be transported back in time when he was a boy of fifteen. . . .

The room smelled of death as Bryce lurked in a dark corner, watching his father place cool, damp cloths on

Bryce's mother's beaded brow. She was now only a shadow of what she once was, her skin drawn taut over her bones and her eyes hollow in their sockets. Each breath was now a challenge for her and death rattles rose threateningly from somewhere deep inside her.

When Bryce's father gestured to his two sons, Bryce crept to one side of the bed while his brother Hugh crept to the other. Each child was dressed in coarse, dark breeches and white, open-throated shirts, and both boys were weepy-eyed.

Bryce took one of his mother's hands in his and said her name. "Mother? It's me . . . Bryce. I love you, mother. Please open your eyes. Please let me know that you can hear me. Please tell me you love me."

When he received no response and her hand continued to lay limply in his, Bryce braced himself against the bed as thirteen-year-old Hugh, frail-boned and thin-faced, made his own try at drawing her from her deep sleep.

"Mother?" he said in a voice that had matured way before his body. "It's Hugh. You'll awaken for me, won't you? I'll just simply die if you don't."

With a slow tearing at his heart, Bryce watched his mother's other hand, seeing her fingers slowly curve around Hugh's and her eyes open to stare lovingly up at her younger son. Ignoring Bryce's presence, his mother moved her hand from his and, trembling, reached to stroke Hugh's cheek affectionately.

"Hugh . . . my darling Hugh . . ." she murmured shallowly. "I shouldn't . . . shouldn't leave you. What's . . . what's to happen to my . . . my . . . baby . . . ?"

Hugh fell to his knees, sobbing, and circled his mother's neck with his arms while Bryce stood looking on, growing more numb by the minute. A desperation was seizing his insides, and he felt himself an outsider, one who didn't belong. But hadn't he felt that way since age two when Hugh had been born? Hadn't he seen . . . ? Hadn't he felt the rejection? The fact that Hugh had been born in poor health and seemed to need the added attention hadn't eased the pain of rejection in Bryce's heart. And now? With death so near for his mother? It was twofold!

"Mother . . ." he said, tugging at Hugh, trying to make room for himself in her arms. But when his mother cast him an angry, impatient look, refusing to let him share in these last moments with her, it was all that Bryce could bear. He turned and ran. Blinded with tears, he fled down the steep, dark steps and out onto the street.

Lifting his long, lean legs high and wiping scalding tears from his eyes, he brushed through the crowded waterfront. He ran on and on until he finally reached an isolated spot on the beach where only the slap-slappings of the surf and the cries of the sea gulls were there to comfort him.

But being more distraught than ever before in his life, Bryce couldn't stop crying. He threw himself down onto his belly on the white, warm sand and pounded his fists and cursed the air about him. He would never forget this humiliation—the ultimate of all rejections—that of his mother denying him love, even on her death bed. He tossed his thoughts angrily around inside him, trying to understand why he would be treated so unjustly. Didn't he deserve better? Hadn't he always given her his undying love and devotion? And now, though his mother was dying, he couldn't help but hate her.

A smell, similar to that of jasmine, slowly drew Bryce

to his senses and caused his eyes to open. When he saw the soft silk flutter of skirts swaying so close to his eyes, he jumped to his feet, alarmed. His mouth went agape when he saw what he thought had to be the loveliest lady he had ever set eyes upon.

Wiping wetness from his eyes and sand from his clothes, Bryce felt the first stirrings of manly lust for a woman when he let his gaze slowly rake over this intruder on his private moment of grief and humiliation.

Her hair, circled fancily high on her head, with tiny ringlets cascading over her brow and ears, matched the color of a gorgeous, crimson, tropical sunset. And as she was so carefully shielding herself from the sun with a fancy parasol, he could see that her skin was as fair as that of a procelain doll he had once seen on display in a Key West store window.

Her green-flecked eyes danced amusedly as his eyes moved from the sensuous pout of her lips to the magnificent swells of her breasts that blossomed out from her low-cut red silken dress . . . and then on down to the curve of her hips as the wind caused the flimsy material of her gown to cling and reveal even the shape of her thighs.

"My name's Rose," she said, suddenly thrusting the long, tapered fingers of her free hand toward him.

Bryce wiped the palms of his hands on his breeches then awkwardly accepted her hand in his, surprised to find her grip firm and strangely satisfying. "Bryce is my name," he said quietly, shifting from one foot to the other. "Bryce Fowler."

Something compelled him to cling to her hand. Somehow it took the place of what had just been denied him at his mother's bedside.

Rose looked out across the Atlantic and let her parasol

rest on her shoulder as she lifted her chin, to inhale deeply of the sea smells. "I like to come here," she said contemplatively. "Clears my head." Then she cast him a troubled glance. "And you?" she added. "Young man, what causes you red eyes and a long face on such a beautiful day as this? Can anything be as bad as what I see in your beautiful blue eyes?"

Bryce released her hand and took a few steps away from her, looking out across the ocean, seeing the waves white with peaks. The clouds on the horizon appeared to be a part of the ocean—to break and move with the water.

"Young man, let Rosie help you," Rose said, moving toward him. Dropping her parasol to the sand, she drew him into her arms and let him place a cheek on the heaving rhythm of her bosom. "There, there," she crooned into his ear, patting his back affectionately. "Now isn't that better?"

As though driven by a force previously unknown to him, Bryce slowly wrapped his arms around her and drew from her what his mother had denied him for so long. Yet . . . this . . . was different! Though he was being comforted, there was something quite different in her approach. It was not a mother's embrace. It was the embrace of woman . . . to . . . man. . . .

"Rosie has a way of making a man forget," she whispered. "Even young men. Will you let me show you my skills?"

Bryce, red-faced and with a pounding heart, slipped out of her arms and eyed her warily. "Why would you do this?" he murmured. He knew that she was older. Much, much older than he. Maybe forty? Yet she couldn't be much older than that and still be so beautiful!

But he placed all questions behind him when she bent

her juicy red lips to his and kissed him gently, then more passionately as she pulled him down on the sand beside her. He let her fingers work with his shirt, then his breeches, until he lay quite nude beneath her feasting eyes.

With a hunger gnawing at his groin, he didn't question . . . just enjoyed. He was finding that there were means of escape from the woes of the earth. He was quickly forgetting what had prompted him to seek this isolated corner of a beach as he let himself get lost in the smell and touch of her.

"You've never been with a woman before, have you?" Rose whispered as her fingers moved silkily over his youthful body.

"Am I even now? Surely I am dreaming," Bryce said throatily, enflamed with arousal and desire for a woman, for the first time even in his life. "Are you truly real?" he added. He panted wildly and closed his eyes as her fingers played with the nipples of his breasts.

"Look at me," Rose laughed softly. "Open your eyes and see just how real I am."

Bryce did so and felt the pounding of his heart grow stronger when he saw that she was undressing before his eyes. When her breasts were fully exposed to him, he was quite aware of strange stirrings in his groin. And when he felt the blood fill his manhood, he became ashamed and covered it with a hand.

"No," she urged, reaching for his hand. "Do not cover yourself. You're becoming a man today. Be proud."

"But why are you . . . ?"

She placed a forefinger to his lips. "Hush," she whispered. "You have many needs. I will teach you how to fulfill the ultimate of all needs."

"But where do you come from?"

"The same as you. Key West."

"I've never seen you."

"Young man, from this day forth I won't let you out of my sight."

Leaning up on an elbow, he watched her step from her lacy underthings and remove her shoes and stockings. And when she released the pins from her hair, letting it cascade dramatically across her shoulders to settle in lustrous, red waves across her breasts, Bryce couldn't hold back his need of her and what she offered him.

With trembling fingers he reached out and touched the large peak of a breast. Involuntarily he drew a sudden, deep breath. Had he ever felt anything as soft? His fingers crept to the nipple and he watched wide-eyed as the pink tip grew under his lingering touch.

"Ah, yes," Rose sighed heavily, bending down over him. "Touch me. Discover all parts of my body. Memorize them with your fingers."

Both his hands molded a breast, and as she leaned down closer to him, he understood her and replaced his fingers with his mouth. Nibbling first, he felt a bit awkward, but when she lifted a hand and guided her breasts more firmly against his lips he opened his mouth and inhaled as much of her flesh as was humanly possible. As though he had done this many times before, he let his tongue do the exploring. With quick flicks he discovered a taste of milk and honey and let his hands now begin to move demandingly over her.

"My love," Rose whispered, easing her breasts from his mouth. Her lips captured his and became hot and sensuous, causing a strange quivering to begin inside him.

His fingers entwined in her hair. He pulled her lips even harder against his and eased her body around on the sand so that he was now above her, ready to guide his throbbing manhood where she so gracefully opened to him.

"Ah, yes . . ." Rose said huskily, lifting her hips to his thrusts. "I don't have to teach you. You already know."

Feeling the sweet pain of desire mounting inside him, Bryce once more cupped a breast and squeezed it; then he let his lips press against the hollow of her throat. "You're beautiful," he whispered.

With a moan of ecstasy, she looked up at him, seeing his face a mask of reckless desire. She reached her hands around behind him and held him even more strongly against her, crying out her own pleasure as he filled her with his youthful juices of fulfilled passion.

Still dizzy from the overwhelming feelings he had just experienced, Bryce refused to move from atop Rose. As though drugged, he clung to her, raining kisses on her lips, eyelids, and brow.

"Rose made you forget?" she whispered, tracing the muscles of his shoulders, knowing that when he developed fully, he would be as no other man she had ever known. Fate had drawn her to the beach today and somehow she knew they had been destined to meet.

Bryce rolled gently from her, crimson-faced and tingling with aliveness. His eyes devoured her nudity, she lay so seductively spread with her hair a halo of roses around her head.

"You are all right now?" Rose persisted, reaching to touch him gently on a ehcck.

Blushing, Bryce filled a hand with sand and let it

trickle through his outspread fingers. "Yes," he murmured. "But I don't understand any of this. Why would you do this with me?"

Rose leaned on an elbow and eyed him carefully. "Like I said. You were in need," she whispered. "It is my job to make a man forget. And I pride myself in doing my job well."

With a lifted brow, Bryce studied her back intensely. "It is your job . . . ?" he said in a shallow whisper.

"I own the Pleasure Palace on Wharf Street," she laughed silkily. "You *have* heard of my establishment, have you not?"

Bryce blushed anew. "You are *that* Rose?" he gasped.

"Don't look so alarmed," she said, rising to pull her clothes on.

Bryce reached for his breeches. "I'm not," he chuckled. "It's just that I didn't ever believe that *I* would meet the beautiful Rose who can steal a man's heart as well as his purse."

Rose laughed throatily. "So you have heard," she said, replacing the pins in her hair. "Do you now think less of me?"

Straightening his back, looking rapturously toward her, Bryce murmured: Never. I could never think anything but good of you. You see, I know you did this today for something besides money."

"And, that is . . . ?" she purred.

"You saw a young man who could have stepped into the ocean and let the waves grab him beneath to the dark pit of death," he said thickly. "Rose, you saved me. I now know there are reasons to go on."

Circling her arms around his neck, she eased his body

107

next to hers. "Tell me all about it," she murmured. "Then let me tell you what my plans for you are. . . ."

The wind was fair and soft, the sun now only a ghost on the graying horizon. Bryce trembled in the damp chill of the air and drew his shirt together, still thinking of Rose. She had taken him under her wing once he had confessed his problems to her. Then from age fifteen to twenty he had spent more time with Rose in her "establishment of girls" than he had at home. Rose had taught him all the ways to make love while he in turn made her feel young again.

But that had not been enough for Bryce. Rose's type of love and attention had not been enough to make him forget his bitterness toward his mother. And at age forty-five, five short years after having met Bryce, Rose died suddenly from consumption. Bryce was once more alone in the world, no less bitter, but a lot smarter, and a damned sight richer!

To his amazement, Rose had willed him all her possessions and personal wealth. After selling her bawdy house and gathering together all her assets to turn into cold cash, Bryce had found that he was, indeed, quite a wealthy man.

Having always secretly longed to be a part of the sea, Bryce had purchased his grand ship. He then sailed to New Orleans where he established himself as the proud owner of his own private bank, and had since led a dual life.

"And now?" he sighed, kneading his brow. "What in my life will change because I've met and lost a woman whose eyes have melted my soul? And what about the key father gave me? When do I go in search of that island?''

Leisurely reaching a hand behind him and into a rear pocket of his breeches, he felt for the key. He grew numb when he realized that it wasn't there. Frantic, he half-turned to search even deeper; then he felt his heart turn to icy stone.

"God . . ." he gasped. "It's gone. The key . . . is . . . gone . . . !''

With fear lacing his heart, he turned and ran back to his cabin, throwing its door open with a bang. He thundered inside, oblivious of Cara's nude body on the bed as he began lifting and tossing furniture around, searching and growling crazily with each added movement.

"Bryce . . ." Cara whispered, shrinking away from him as he loomed over her with hands on hips. "What's . . . the . . . matter . . . ?''

"Get off the bed," he ordered, doubting now if he would ever find the key. And if not, what was he to do? It most surely had no duplicate!

"Have I done something . . . ?" Cara whimpered, reaching for a robe and gathering it around her as she eased from the bed.

"No," he grumbled. "But seems *I* have.''

With a racing pulse he threw the blankets from the bed and shook each of them carefully. Then heavy-shouldered, he slumped down on the bed, thinking how careless he was. The key had been kept safe all those years, until he happened along.

Hanging his head in his hands, he wondered how he could tell his father. His father had trusted him! When his father had chosen between sons, his choice had been Bryce because Bryce was the stronger and more dependable of the two.

109

Bolting from the bed, Bryce began to pace. "I can't tell him," he whispered. "I just cannot. I'll have to find a way to open the chest without a key."

"Bryce . . ." Cara said, going to him, pacing along beside him. "What is the matter?"

Bryce turned and gave her an icy glare. "Nothing," he grumbled.

"Then what . . . ?"

"Be ready to leave the ship at dawn's awakening," he said. "My carriage will deliver you to an inn."

"So you meant it when you said that you didn't wish to see me again," she hissed.

"I usually do mean what I say, don't I?"

"Then that is the way it shall be," she said stiffly. "I've grown tired of your moods anyway. I can find a man who will treat me much better. I am sure of that!"

"Then do it," Bryce said coolly.

He left his cabin and stepped out where a night fog was beginning to settle in all around him and his masterful ship. A light spray of water settled on his lips and his mood was a heavy one.

Then his heart beat went suddenly wild. "What if Hugh tells father the truth about me?" he worried to himself. "He's angry enough at me to do such a damnable thing. If he does, I will have to forfeit my rights to the chest even if I do find it and its treasure of gold. . . ."

NEW ORLEANS

Your mouth that I remember
With rush of sudden pain
As one remembers starlight
Or roses after rain . . .

—Russell

SIX

Royal Street was quiet, except for a few passing carriages and lone horsemen. On each street corner, large oil lamps swung with the breeze and flared dimly in the fog. Bryce stepped next to a lamppost, flicking ashes from his cigar and pondering his next move. He looked toward his two-storied bank building with its stucco front, then at the name painted in bold black print between the iron bars at the front window.

"Fowler's Bank of New Orleans," he mumbled. Then he laughed a bit amusedly, yet not amused. "Damn name, that Fowler. Just happens it's truly not my own after all."

He tested another name on the tip of his tongue. "Bryce Palmer," he said, lifting an eyebrow. He thrust the cigar between his lips and clamped his teeth onto it. He hated the name. He hated the knowing! And what must he do to erase Natalie from his mind? What had she done when she had discovered his ship gone?

He kneaded his brow frustratingly. "How can I ever tell her she's . . . my . . . sister . . . ?" he worried.

113

"To be near her would be a torment of all torments."

Seeing that his partner Abe Clawson had lighted kerosene lamps in the bank, Bryce was drawn inside. Business for the day had waned with the onset of darkness and Abe was now busy going over his ledgers.

"How goes it, Abe?" Bryce asked, his inner struggle obvious in the lethargic way in which he spoke. He sat down behind a heavy oak desk next to Abe's and placed his cigar on the edge of an ashtray.

Lifting his gold-framed spectacles from a wide nose, Abe squinted toward Bryce. "Things are farin' well enough here," he said. "But looks as though you've had a few rough nights. Your Pa pass away? Eh?"

Not wanting to discuss his father, Bryce ducked his head a bit. Damn it, how could he explain to anyone that the father he had always known wasn't *his* father?

To busy his fingers he began sorting through a stack of letters piled high on his desk. "No," he grumbled. "My . . . uh . . . father is still hanging on. Won't be long now, though. He's nothing but skin and bones."

Abe leaned over, screwed the wick higher on his desk lamp, and studied Bryce more studiously. "That ain't all that's troublin' you, is it, son?" he asked, clicking his false teeth nervously as he awaited a response.

Knowing Abe's good intentions, Bryce lifted his eyes and smiled shallowly toward him. "You've guessed right, Abe," he said softly. "Seems many things have suddenly gone awry in my life."

"What can I do to help?" Abe asked, placing his glasses back on.

"I'm afraid I have to work it out by myself," Bryce said, easing back in his chair, sighing. He smiled more warmly toward Abe. "Just you keep things going here at

114

the bank. I may have to be gone for a spell.''

With a wife of thirty years, Abe was a dependable and hard working sort. He never fretted over his balding head nor the fact that his eyesight was slowly leaving him. And he just accepted his rounded shoulders and bulging waistline, saying even those were gifts from God. A religious man, yet crafty when it came to business and making money for the bank.

Abe adjusted his silk, maroon cravat, then the sleeves of his black frock coat. ''Business has been good,'' he said. ''The ledgers prove it.''

Bryce placed his fingertips together before him and let his gaze move slowly around the room. The richness in its décor proved the success of his venture. Bryce had invested his money and Abe his knowledge of numbers. Together they had drawn accounts from as far away as St. Louis, with the Mississippi River being the handy link between the two river-front cities.

All business was transacted at the desks, behind which stood a five-foot-square wall safe. Marble walls and expensive oak flooring met in matching grace. High-backed chairs covered with black leather sat opposite the two desks in the room. Various other chairs sat amid pots of flowering oleanders, and ferns hung in baskets from the ceiling.

At the far end of the room, a staircase led to the second floor where the private offices of Bryce and Abe were situated.

''I guess I should be a happy man,'' Bryce finally said. ''A man can't ask for more than what I have at such a young age. I have my bank and my *Golden Isis*. Two different worlds, with two different sorts of excitements.''

Abe leaned toward Bryce. ''Seen that *Sea Snake* as of

late?'' he asked with a twinkle in his eyes. "Gone achasin' it much?''

"Been a while,'' Bryce stated flatly. "That damn pirate seems to have been away from these waters for a spell. Must be up to something big somewhere else. There's a lot of traffic up New York way. Probably after some fancier prize to take back to his island.''

His face drew shadows into it. The island. Was the pirate's island truly that of the Fowler's? Was Orchid Island and the pirate's island one and the same? Would he ever find out? Maybe it wasn't his right. He wasn't a true descendant of the Fowler's.

His insides tingled suddenly. Whether or not he was a Fowler by name, he still had been given the right to the treasure. And, by damn, he would take it, one way or the other. But how could he . . . without the key . . . ? The only way to settle this was to return to Key West and retrace his steps—steps that might bring him face to face with Natalie.

"Are you ever going to follow this pirate on into his island?'' Abe quietly queried. "You know this could be doin' Key West and all surrounding islands a favor.''

Bryce made a low growling noise from somewhere deep inside his chest. His eyes were stormy blue. "Up to this point the chase has been more exciting than the thought of killing the devil pirate,'' he snarled. "I have always thought the fun of the chase would be missed. But now? Nothing would please me more than to show the power of my guns to that sea robber.''

Abe's face screwed up in wonder. "Bryce, what's happened to change your mind?'' he asked with caution.

Bryce cast him a sardonic grin. "One day I'll tell you,'' he said. "But not now. It's best left unspoken at

116

this time.''

The squeaking of the front door attracted Bryce's attention. He cleared his throat nervously and forced a warm smile toward the gentleman entering as he rose to meet him. "Good evening, sir," he said politely, extending his hand in friendship. "What might we be able to do for you?''

"Are you Bryce Fowler?" the man asked, accepting the handshake.

Bryce's stomach rolled a bit. It was the first time that he had been addressed by the name *Fowler* since having found out the truth. But he knew that was foolish. His name *was* Fowler. It had always been and would always remain so in the future. Nothing that his mother had done in the past would change that. It was her sin. Not his.

"Yes. I'm Bryce Fowler," he said with determination. "May I ask what might be the nature of your business?"

"The sea," the man said. "The . . . sea . . .''

Bryce winked toward Abe and smiled broadly. It was a code they had worked out. Each knew that when the word *sea* was spoken it had nothing to do with banking. Bryce's duties were to the sea. Abe's were to the banking. It had become a perfect relationship—a marriage consummated, with dreams of added wealth the goal, instead of children.

Bryce's insides were churning with excitement. Maybe this was what he needed to get his mind off his troubles. Yes, the sea—the adventure—was a catharsis, purging him of all doubts and fears. When on the sea there was nothing else. . . .

"The sea it is," Bryce said, squaring his shoulders. He nodded toward the staircase. "Please follow me to my private office upstairs. I don't think I caught your name,

117

sir."

"Clarence. Clarence Seymour," the man replied, half-bowing.

"Well, Clarence, let's go to my office and see what I can do to be of assistance to you," Bryce said, gesturing once more toward the staircase.

Bryce watched the tall, lanky fellow move on ahead of him, knowing that he was already aware that the banking business was only a cover. Yes, Bryce was a respected business man, yet to many he was a skilled seaman. He chuckled amusedly when called a pirate. For to those who knew him this statement was far from the truth.

Lifting a lighted kerosene lamp, Bryce left Clarence move on ahead of him. He eyed him speculatively. He was attired in a beige evening coat and matching breeches. The cravat at this throat was dark brown and seemed to accentuate the thinness of his neck and his long chin. Bryce had noticed how faded his brown eyes seemed and, reminded of his ailing father, realized that this man with the thick head of gray hair was probably about his father's age.

Lighting the staircase, Bryce moved up past Clarence to the second-floor landing. He then stepped aside and motioned for Clarence to enter the room at the right side of the hall. Clarence smiled warmly and nodded his thanks. Bryce then followed closely behind him and went to a desk positioned beneath a window hidden behind expensive ivory-colored, brocade draperies.

Placing the lamp on the desk, Bryce gestured toward a high-backed, leather chair. "Please be seated," he said; then he settled himself into a chair behind his desk. He lifted the lid on a small, gold-encased box and pulled two cigars from inside it. "Cigar?" he asked, offering one to

Clarence.

Clarence spoke softly, showing that he was of a gentle nature. "No thank you," he said. "Hard on my lungs. I chose to give them up some time ago when I discovered smoking caused me to have a dull, raspy cough. Feel much better now that I've given up the nasty habit."

Lifting an eyebrow, Bryce glanced from Clarence to the cigars. His need for a cigar was no longer as strong, so he shrugged and replaced the two he'd taken. He settled back against his chair and smiled broadly toward Clarence. "Now tell me. What brings you here?" he asked, already tasting the thrill of adventure on his tongue. "What sort of problem might I solve for you? You are here for my services as the captain of the *Golden Isis*, are you not?"

"I was given your name by an associate of mine," Clarence said, leaning forward to rest an arm on the edge of Bryce's desk. "I know that you mainly travel the sea as a 'salvor' but I've also been told that your ship can give a merry chase when the need arises."

Bryce's eyes twinkled and his lips curved upward in a smug, half smile. "Yes," he said smoothly. "You've heard right."

"Bryce, I own an import/export business here in New Orleans," Clarence said dryly. "Seymour's. I'm sure you've heard of it. I've got one of the finest buildings on the river front."

"Yes, I'm quite familiar with your dealings," Bryce said. "You're an honest dealing man. That's what's spoken of you about town."

"Yes. I try to deal fair and square," Clarence responded, settling back in his chair. His narrow shoulders slumped a bit. "But seems some people have never made

119

an honest move in their lives.''

"Eh?" Bryce said blandly. "Who might you be referring to?''

Dark shadows of hate fell across Clarence's usually
gentle features. "That damn pirate who travels on the *Sea
Snake*,'' he growled. "Bryce, someone has to rid the seas
of that devil. Surely you can. You have the ship. You
have the prowess. I've come to offer you a commission. I
hope you are free to accept.''

His own hate and the need of vengeance caused
Bryce's blood begin a slow boiling. He rose from the
chair, stepped to the window, pulled the drapes back a
bit, and pretended to be looking down onto the street.
Momentarily he had to hide his true feelings from this
stranger to prevent him from realizing that he had struck a
raw nerve when he'd mentioned the *Sea Snake*. Strange
how things happened. Bryce, who now had his own reasons to earnestly pursue that devil pirate, was also being
asked to do this for another!

He waited for the racing of his heart to slow a bit; then
he turned and directed his full attention back to Clarence.
"What's this pirate been up to?" he asked, clutching
onto the back of his chair.

"Bryce, are you a man to be trusted? You'll give your
word not to speak of what I tell you, except to the crew
under your command?''

The air of mystery behind Clarence's words sparked
Bryce's interest even more. He leaned forward a bit. "I
am,'' he commented dryly. "And, yes, you can trust that
what you disclose to me will be kept in confidence.''

Clarence smiled crookedly and looked self-consciously toward Bryce. "Honesty has been my guideline.
I do treat everyone fairly and squarely,'' he said. "But I

only recently became involved in something quite under-handed.''

"Eh?'' Bryce said, lifting a heavy, sandy eyebrow. "What's that you say?'' He chuckled a bit into a hand held over his mouth, finding it hard to believe that this genteel man could ever do anything dishonest. But most of us are tempted at least once in our lifetimes. Bryce knew that there had to be an awful lot of money involved to lure Clarence Seymour into a scheme beneath his usual dignity.

"Have you heard of the East India Enterprises who work from Malwa on the Indian coast?'' Clarence suddenly blurted.

Bryce kneaded his brow, barely breathing. He was beginning to understand. He also understood the dangers. "Yes,'' he murmured. "Who in business hasn't heard of the East India Enterprises? They control the opium trade.''

Clarence's face grew red. "Exactly,'' he said softly.

"Then . . . you . . . ?'' Bryce said in a near whisper.

"Yes,'' Clarence said dryly. "I've just recently tried my luck in smuggling opium. I've been working with East India Enterprises.''

Bryce hit his brow with the palm of his left hand. "Well, I'll be damned,'' he whispered. Then he raised his voice. "Opium. I'll be damned.''

"Yes, opium,'' Clarence said, lowering his eyes. "Now you see why we have to keep this only between us and your ship's crew.''

Bryce sat down on the corner of his desk. He crossed his arms and studied Clarence for a moment, then said: "How does the pirate and his *Sea Snake* fit into this?'' he asked cautiously.

"They confiscated my opium shipment," Clarence growled. He rose from his chair and began pacing the floor. "He and his men boarded my ship and took it all. Damn. I thought my ship captain and mate were tough, and the crew up on their gunnery. Any opium clipper requires it. But I guess nobody is more skilled than that damn pirate." He ceased his pacing and went to bend his face into Bryce's. "Except for you, young fellow," he said. "I know you could beat him. I know it."

"Not only beat him but get your opium back," Bryce said smoothly. "That's what you're asking of me, isn't it?"

"Exactly. . . ."

"Clarence, you knew before getting into this that the opium trade was filled with danger," Bryce said. "Outside of war, no trade could be more so."

"Three-hundred-thousand dollars is cause for daring, wouldn't you say?" Clarence said, pacing again.

Bryce rose from the desk, feeling the erratic beat of his heart. "What's that you say?" he murmured.

Clarence settled back in his chair. "There's always an enormous profit to be made from the opium traffic," he murmured. "My ship traveled to Malwa and purchased the opium from the East India Enterprises. The ship was en route to Havana when that damn pirate showed up. Somehow they knew we were hauling more than tea and spices."

"How did you carry it?"

"The opium had been made up into balls about the size of thirty-two-pounder shot and wrapped and packed in dry leaves; it has been mixed into our shipment of nankeens, chinaware, and tea. There's no smell so no one could have noticed opium was aboard," Clarence said

122

wearily. "But my ship's first mate, thank God he survived the theft, said this pirate dressed in full black knew right where to look."

"So you want me to get your opium shipment back," Bryce said, slouching down onto his chair. He narrowed his eyes, deep in thought. He needed time to return to Key West to try to find the key. For if he was to seek out Orchid Island to recover the opium shipment, while there he could see to his family's fortune. He wouldn't only see to the fortune, he would rid the island of all its pirate scum and retain the island as his. He would do that not for himself but for his ailing father who as well as Bryce, had been betrayed by the same woman—Tom Fowler's wife . . . Bryce's mother!

"I'll pay you quite well," Clarence said. "Forty percent of what you're able to return to me."

"Forty percent of the worth of the opium you mean," Bryce said. Then he laughed softly. "Damned if I want to be paid in opium."

Clarence rose from his chair and extended his hand toward Bryce. "In hard cash, Bryce," he laughed. Then he grew serious. "Let's shake on it."

Bryce shoved his chair back and stood, accepting the handshake. "It's a deal," he said thickly. "There's only one problem."

Clarence straightened his back and clasped his hands together behind his back. "And what's that?" he murmured.

"I've got something to do before searching out the pirate," he said. "Something of vital importance to me and my future."

"How long will it delay you?"

"I can't say."

"I guess that won't matter." Clarence looked worried. "The pirate would be a fool to try to unload the opium at any port at this time. He'll have to lay low for a while, I'm sure."

"Then you'll trust my judgment to move when I see fit?"

"Bryce, if I didn't trust you implicitly, I wouldn't be here," Clarence said flatly.

"Then we understand one another," Bryce said, throwing an arm about Clarence's shoulder. He lifted the kerosene lamp from the desk and guided Clarence toward the door. Once the lower floor was reached and Bryce saw the full figure of a woman standing with her back to him, staring from the window, Bryce's heart began to thunder inside him. It was the midnight black of her hair and the way it hung sensuously across her shoulders. In a soft-colored dress of blue silk, nipped in at the waist, revealing her petiteness, Bryce knew this had to be Natalie! Had she . . . followed him . . . ?

Then Clarence spoke, breaking the spell Bryce had become caught up in. "Ah, Brenda. You grew tired of waiting in the carriage," he said, taking long strides across the room toward the woman.

"Brenda . . . ?" Bryce whispered, eyes wide. "Who is . . . ?" Then when she swung the fullness of her skirt around to face Clarence, Bryce took a step backward, in a near state of shock. It wasn't Natalie but she so resembled her that it was uncanny. He watched, awe-struck, as she and Clarence embraced. Bryce stood as though frozen, feeling a tremor surface, as she cast him a half smile across Clarence's shoulder. Though she did so strongly resemble Natalie, there was something else in her dark eyes.

Whatever it was, she appeared to be wicked and untrusting. Even her smile was devilish. Yet she also possessed all of Natalie's fine qualities in the delicate features of her face . . . and the provocative swells of her breasts which Bryce was now able to see as Brenda swung out of her father's arms.

"Bryce Fowler, this is my cherished possession, my daughter Brenda," Clarence said proudly, beaming from Bryce to Brenda.

Bryce swallowed hard, still speechless. He still couldn't believe his eyes. How could any two girls resemble each other so and not be related?

Noticing Bryce and how strangely he was acting, Abe rose from behind his desk. He went to him and eased the kerosene lamp from his hand. "Bryce, what the hell's the matter?" he whispered. He followed Bryce's steady stare to Brenda Seymour. He had never seen Bryce so affected by a woman before, yet Abe knew that Bryce had quite a reputation with women. Had one suddenly appeared who could change his ways . . . ?

Bryce reached his hands to his hair and nervously combed his fingers through it. He finally looked away from Brenda and into Abe's searching eyes. "It's the damnest thing," he whispered. "I could swear she's someone else."

"Ah," Abe shrugged. "That happens all the time. Lots of people favor each other."

Clarence approached Bryce. "What seems to be the matter?" he asked, lifting a gray eyebrow. He cast Brenda a quick look, then focused back on Bryce. "Something to do with my daughter?"

Bryce placed his hands awkwardly into his front breeches pockets and gave Brenda another sideways glance. When she smiled back at him again, he did not experience the same stirring he'd felt when smiled at by Natalie. Instead, shivers ran up and down his spine.

"Yes. It's your daughter," Bryce finally said in a near whisper.

"What about my daughter?" Clarence insisted, his face reddening. "I don't like this one damn bit, Bryce. What the hell's causing you to behave so oddly?"

Bryce felt foolish, yet he had to pursue this. "She resembles someone I just recently met in Key West," he said softly. "So much about her is the same. In fact, at first, I thought it was her." He furrowed his brow as he watched Clarence's color blanch.

"You say you met this . . . this woman in Key West?" Clarence murmured. "How old would you say she might be?"

"She is eighteen. . . ."

"God," Clarence said, teetering a bit. "If my Kathryn would've given birth to a daughter, my daughter would have been eighteen. . . ."

Bryce saw the state Clarence was in and grabbed him by the elbow. Brenda rushed to his other side, anxious. "Papa?" she whispered. "What is it? I've never seen you like this before."

Clarence forced a smile and patted her reassuringly on the hand. "Honey, I'm all right," he said. His eyes grew hopeful as he looked up into Bryce's face. "Maybe even more than that if what I'm thinking could be a reality."

"Come and sit down," Bryce encouraged. He helped Clarence down onto a chair opposite Bryce's desk, then went and sat down also, behind his desk.

Brenda settled on the floor at her father's feet, beseeching him with her dark, luminous eyes. "Papa, what

126

did you mean? Was Mama pregnant when the pirate stole her away from you?'' she asked softly. ''Are you saying that the woman this man is speaking of could in truth by my sister?''

Clarence smoothed a lock of hair from Brenda's fair brow. ''My pet,'' he murmured. ''It is very likely. The minute Bryce made the comparison, I knew. There was only one other woman on this earth who could compare to you and that was your mother. So if there is now another, she could be your sister.''

Bryce watched the stirring scene, then felt pinpricks of fear pressing into his heart. He had to wonder if Clarence was seeing what he was seeing? In Brenda's eyes, there was no joy at hearing this news of family. Instead, there was a quiet, brooding anger that could only be jealousy.

''Papa, I'm sure you are wrong,'' Brenda said with the quick toss of her head. ''Mama surely lost the child. The pirates surely even tortured Mama until she died.''

Clarence's face took on an ashen color as his eyes wavered toward Brenda. ''My God, Brenda . . .'' he gasped. ''Such a horrible thing to say.''

Brenda rose from the floor, straightening the folds of her dress. She shrugged nonchalantly. ''I'm sure it's true,'' she stated flatly. She strolled away from Clarence with her chin tilted haughtily. There was suddenly a strained silence in the room. All that could be heard was the voluptuous stirring of Brenda's petticoats beneath the silk of her dress. All eyes followed her as Brenda opened the door and stepped out into the darkness of night.

''She is a moody one,'' Clarence finally laughed. ''I never seem to know from one minute to the next what to expect of her. I guess I can blame it on raising her alone. Maybe I should have married again. But I never found a woman Brenda approved or got along with.''

"I'm sure," Bryce said stiffly. He leaned both elbows on his desk, ready to get on with the subject at hand. "So. You do believe I may have seen your daughter. Well, Clarence, I hate to break the sad news to you that it really cannot be.''

"And why not?''

"Because Natalie—the woman I was referring to—is the daughter of Saul Palmer, of Key West.''

"And who is this Saul Palmer?''

Bryce cringed inside. He hated knowing Saul Palmer existed! Saul Palmer. His father. He hated to discuss him but he had no other choice. He now felt foolish for having upset Clarence Seymour. Natalie most surely was not Brenda's sister. "Saul Palmer is a wealthy businessman in Key West," he said somberly. "He's a dealer in tobacco.''

"And how well do you know this Saul Palmer?'' Clarence asked, leaning forward. "Was he a successful businessman, let's say, eighteen years ago? Or could he in truth have been a marauding pirate? How do you know that he isn't a retired pirate?''

Bryce felt the first stirrings of doubt. Then another thought came to him, causing his heart to thunder inside him. If what Clarence was saying could be true . . . then Natalie and he weren't blood related! The thought of being free to go to her and draw her into his arms again made a delicious spasm of delight flood his insides.

He kneaded his brow, frowning. He was again feeling foolish. Yes. He was full of foolish hopes and dreams. Clarence was also filled with the same.

"Do you happen to know Saul Palmer's wife's name?'' Clarence interjected candidly.

Bryce rose suddenly from his chair and began pacing. "I know none of these things," he grumbled. "I only saw Natalie twice." And on one of those two occasions, they had engaged in mutual seduction! How was it that he hadn't shown enough respect for her to inquire about her personal life? As usual, he had taken what he wanted and gone on his way. But it had been different with her. It *had*.

Oh, God. If only he could prove she wasn't his sister . . . !

He swung around and boldly faced Clarence. He settled back onto his chair. "I want to know everything," he said flatly. "Where you were and how it was the pirate managed to get your wife from you."

"I'd like a glass of port if you have some on hand," Clarence murmured, staring blankly ahead. "I might need some added courage to relive that day."

Bryce flashed Abe a look. "Abe . . ."

Abe nodded and hurried up the stairs, returning a moment later with a tray that carried a crystal decanter of port and three long-stemmed wine glasses. After the glasses were poured and shared, Bryce encouraged Clarence to tell his story. . . .

"We were traveling from England to New Orleans," Clarence began. "My beautiful wife Kathryn and our year-old daughter Brenda. Kathryn was with child and ailing the whole sea voyage. She was only three months pregnant and we so feared she'd lose the child. But as it was, I don't know what happened to Kathryn or the child."

"The pirates . . . ?" Bryce interjected.

"The ship that approached ours was black, like a sea demon risen from the pits of hell," Clarence growled. "It all happened so quickly. Before anyone could do anything about it this ship's crew had boarded our ship and, without even a battle, had taken their booty and . . . and . . . only one woman of all the passengers. . . ."

"Kathryn? Your wife . . . ?"

"Yes. My beautiful wife," Clarence said, hanging his head in his hands. "I'll never forget the pirate who jerked her from my arms. He was huge. He wore all black. And he had a wide scar on his left cheek and three fingers missing on his left hand."

"How did you manage to stay alive?" Bryce asked solemnly. "Didn't the pirates take the ship as their prize?"

Clarence took a quick shallow of wine, afterward wiping his lips free of it with the back of his hand. "All but my wife were set out in a longboat to drift at sea," he said. "After a full day in the scorching sun, we were rescued and taken on to New Orleans."

"Seems some luck was with you, Clarence," Bryce said. "Most wouldn't have survived the pirate attack, let alone a full day's drifting in a flimsy longboat."

Clarence laughed a bit as his hands went to his hair. "Yes," he said. "My gray hair? Acquired it through that bad time in my life."

Bryce rose from his chair and began pacing, kneading his chin contemplatively. "So you said your wife was with child," he said softly. "And the pirate was obviously unaware of this since she wasn't showing yet. When he took your Kathryn as a prize, he got, instead, two prizes in one. He got himself a baby six months later."

"Though we knew the ship was black, we never could find her again," Clarence complained. "Damnedest thing. Seems pirates are always taking from me. First my wife and unborn child and now my opium shipment.''

"And both black ships," Bryce whispered. "Could it be the son of the pirate who took your wife who is now the owner and captain of the *Sea Snake?*"

"No," Clarence scoffed. "Surely not."

Bryce's pulse raced. Though it was a bit unbelievable, it could be true! Maybe his earlier perception wasn't so foolish! Maybe . . . even . . . Natalie was . . .

Swinging around, Bryce went and urged Clarence from his chair. He clasped Clarence's shoulders solidly. "Clarence, I think we may have something here," he said. "It is very possible I may have been in contact with your daughter. So much of what you have said leads me to believe that this woman who so resembles Brenda could be the daughter you've never seen."

Clarence lifted a hand to Bryce's arm and clutched him, eyes wide and hopeful. "And Kathryn?" he said thickly. "Maybe Kathryn? Do you think that maybe after all these years, I may even see, her again . . . ?"

Bryce furrowed his brow. "I don't know," he worried. "We may have false hopes here. But, damn it, you'd better believe I'm going to find out. And soon."

Clarence studied the intensity of Bryce's expression. "Bryce, there's more here than you're revealing to me," he said softly. "What is it? Why are you so eager to get to the truth?"

Bryce moved away from Clarence, red-faced. "It is something quite personal," he murmured. "In fact, my whole future depends on what I find. My happiness depends on it."

"I don't see why . . . or . . . how."

"I can see why you wouldn't understand. But it is true.

131

Yes, what I say is quite true.''

Bryce's insides were bubbling with excitement, hope, anticipation. If Natalie was not Saul Palmer's daughter . . . His heart turned icy cold. If Saul Palmer was once a pirate, his grandfather and his father before him may have been also! Then did Saul have a son who now rode the seas in the *Sea Snake*. . . ?

Circling his hands into two tight fists at his side, Bryce swung around on a heel to face Clarence. ''I will leave on tomorrow's tide,'' he snarled.

''If it is Kathryn and my daughter that you find, bring them back to me,'' Clarence said flatly. ''I will pay you extremely well.''

''And the opium shipment?''

''My wife . . . my daughter . . . are worth much more to me. We will deal with the opium shipment later.''

''And if I find it is your wife and daughter and they are attached to their ways of life in Key West and do not want to leave?''

Clarence's face shadowed. He turned and placed his back to Bryce, lowering his head. The fists at his sides revealed the hate seething inside him. ''Bring them to me,'' he growled. ''At all costs, bring them to me.''

''Even if I have to abduct them?''

Clarence faced Bryce, glowering. ''Yes. Do whatever you must,'' he snapped. ''In the beginning they were mine. So shall they be again.''

Bryce clasped Clarence's shoulders once again. ''Clarence, don't get your hopes up,'' he encouraged. ''If none of this is true, you could be shattered, just as you were the day you lost your Kathryn. It might be the same as experiencing it all over again.''

"I've lived the loss, over and over again in my mind," Clarence said sorrowfully. "The hurt has never lessened. It couldn't be more painful now if the truth is not in my favor."

"All right. I have warned you."

"You will sail tomorrow?"

"Yes. When the sun rises copper in the sky, my sail's will be filled. . . ."

KEY WEST

Miss you, miss you, miss you;
Everything I do
Echoes with the laughter
And the voice of you.

—Cory

SEVEN

Feeling alone and dejected, Natalie tried one hat on and then another. Standing in Grace's Millinery, she gazed into a mirror, tilting her head first one way and then another. She tied the satin bow and untied it, too heavy-hearted to make a decision. It had been a full week since she had shared those magical moments with Bryce. She had thought he would have returned by now with a simple explanation as to why he had disappeared from her life so quickly. She hadn't wanted to believe that he had used her, as any man might, thinking her a waterfront whore.

That tore at her heart now, making her cheap and degraded. She might even hate him if she didn't love him so. Hate! Oh, it was such an ugly word! And once it took possession of one's heart, it could fester like an open wound. No! She didn't want to hate him! She wanted to leave her heart free, to love him!

She jerked the hat from her head, near to tears. "Oh, but I should hate him," she whispered. "How could he have done this to me? How?"

Stubbornly, she chose another hat. As she placed it on

her head she smiled at her reflection in the mirror. "Ah. I do like this one," she whispered. It was of green satin, trimmed with folds of matching velvet. It went quite well with her green chiffon dress, on which the velvet trimming was pressed to look like ribbing. She reached for the hat's velvet ribbons that hung loosely, waiting to be tied. Then she became breathless when another reflection appeared suddenly in the mirror and hands reached to tie the ribbons beneath her chin.

"Bryce . . ." she gasped, feeling a weakness enter her knees. Still looking at him in the mirror, her gaze swept over the full height of him and she noticed how differently he was dressed this day. A belt of sorts crisscrossed his chest upon which could be seen a pistol at each side. This was worn over a gold, full-sleeved silk shirt, opened halfway to the waist.

His full-cut breeches of heavy cotton were also of a gold coloring and he sported soft-looking, black, wide-topped leather boots.

Her gaze moved back to his eyes, seeing the passion in their silken, blue depths.

"Beautiful lady, I would choose this hat if I were you," he said thickly, now resting his hands on her shoulders and staring lovingly back at her.

Natalie became quite aware of the heaving of her bosom, and with such a revealing neckline, she knew that he had to notice it. Well, she didn't want him to! She didn't want him to realize how much his presence disturbed her. But there was no stopping these wild feelings surging through her as there was no stopping the urge she felt to turn and become once more a prisoner of his arms. She forced a stiff upper lip and stepped away from the burning imprint of his fingers on her flesh.

Seething, she untied the hat and placed it back on display with the others. "Who are you, Bryce Fowler, to have a say in anything I wear or do?" she snapped moodily. She gathered the skirt of her dress into her arms and swung around and boldly faced him. "Some nerve you have even daring to approach me after what you did to me."

Bryce glanced toward the female sales clerk who stood watching, then back to Natalie. "I'd like to talk with you in private," he whispered. He reached for her elbow. "I don't know how I can explain but I will try."

With anger flashing in her dark eyes, she jerked away from him. "I don't think so," she said haughtily. "It would probably be all lies. I'm sure you've already practiced a pretty speech . . . probably one you use on all the women you play games with."

"Natalie . . ." Bryce growled. "You've got to listen to me. We have to talk. It's very important to both of us."

Slinging her hair back from across her shoulders, to hang in black, lustrous rivulets down her back, she grabbed her purse and headed toward the door. "You've waited too long for this talk you say is so important to us," she said with a backward glance across her shoulder. "I really must run now, Bryce. Good-bye."

With a throbbing heart, Natalie stepped outside into the humidity of the day. The splash of the sun against her skin was almost as hot as the heat of desire Bryce's presence once more had aroused in her. How could she walk away from him? Hadn't she dreamed of the moment they would be together again? But she couldn't appear to be so wanton as to do everything to his bidding. He would have to come after her and prove that he was indeed sorry that

139

he had treated her so poorly. But how could he prove this? Would she ever be able to truly trust him?

One glance toward her private carriage revealed that the lazy heat of the day had taken its toll on Charles. He was fast asleep, head bobbing and arms crossed over his chest. To her pleasure, this gave Natalie the opportunity to exercise her free will. She began to stroll casually along the narrow, crowded walkway, barely breathing, for want of being able to hear Bryce's footsteps behind her.

Bryce stood speechless, staring at the void left by her exit from the shop. It had been hard being near her again . . . touching her. Harder yet to realize that until he got some answers from her, he couldn't truly get his life in perspective. But hardest of all was not being able to draw her into his arms, to shower her with kisses and to confess his undying love.

Watching her now through the shop window—the way she so teasingly began to stroll down the walkway—he set his jaw firmly and rushed after her. He would not take no for an answer. She was even more important to him than finding the key! She was more valuable than any treasure that had been locked away to collect mold.

Ignoring the passersby, Bryce captured Natalie by a wrist and forced her to meet his gaze as he stepped in front of her. "Damn it, Natalie," he snarled. "You will listen to what I have to say."

Not quite ready to give in yet, Natalie glared back at him, anger flashing in her eyes. "Unhand me, you . . . you . . ." she hissed. She struggled until the tender flesh of her wrist began to burn. "Bryce Fowler, you do not have to be so rough. Let me go. Do you hear?"

"I will not. Not until you agree to go to my ship with

me. We can talk in private there.''

Stepping up on tiptoe, she spoke angrily, yet softly, into his face. "So you can seduce me, you mean," she said. "That's all you truly want of me, isn't it?"

Bryce couldn't help but feel amused at how enticing she was when she was angry. Somehow it lightened his mood, enough to make him want to tease her, to possibly cause her to give up this pretense of hating him. He knew how she felt about him. He had been the first with her. She did not make a habit of lifting her skirts for just any man.

Yes, he had to believe that once she played this game to its full gamut, then they could get down to some serious talking. And if he received the answers that he was after, then they could share much more than talk!

Yes, he would just tease her a mite, before he laughed and told her that it was all in jest.

He leaned into her face and spoke softly, so no one else could hear. "I forgot to pay you for the one night with you," he said, chuckling beneath his breath. He released his hold on her and reached inside his front breeches pocket and jangled some loose coins noisily together.

"Let's see. How much do you want? And how much can I pay you for today's services? You are just playing hard to get, are you not? You will lift your skirts if paid well enough, won't you?" he added, wondering if she could see the twinkling in his eyes.

Natalie blanched. She forced back the tears that were building because of this sudden humiliation. Then her embarrassment turned to venom-filled anger. "You are an ass," she hissed and, raising a hand, slapped his face sharply. When she saw his expression cloud up and his eyes grow dusky blue with his own anger, she took a step

141

backward and covered her mouth with a hand.

Bryce refused to stroke his face where her finger's imprints most surely showed red. He would not give her that satisfaction. Neither her nor her temper were amusing any longer. She had overplayed her hand. Though he loved her with passion, he would not get caught up in its web. For no woman had ever had the opportunity to slap him twice.

He placed a hand on one of his pistols. "I will get the answers I was seeking from someone else," he stated flatly. "And I am not speaking of the questions I asked about whoring. Natalie, I was only jesting. I truly needed you today, but for much more than what a few coins would buy me."

Natalie felt the plummeting of her heart when he turned and strolled briskly away from her. She wanted to call out to him—run to him—but she felt that nothing she could say now could right this wrong. With hot tears wetting her cheeks, she rushed to her carriage and commanded Charles to take her home.

In wide, angry strides, Bryce hurried on to Parrot Inn. He would pull answers from his father. Surely his father knew of the Palmer's . . . whether or not Natalie's mother's name was Kathryn. Maybe his father even knew if Saul Palmer had at one time been a pirate! He only hoped that his father wasn't too weak to share in a bit more conversation.

"But how can I tell him I lost that damned brass key?" he grumbled. "Suddenly so much is taking me away from my pleasures of the sea. . ."

At the inn, Hugh met Bryce's entry with a weak smile on his hawklike face. His orange, silk shirt, with its flowing sleeves and open throat seemed to be a mockery of Hugh's true personality. He wasn't gay and carefree. He was usually withdrawn inside himself except for when he was singing. Then he became a different person, a part of many worlds, not just his own.

"I wouldn't advise going upstairs to talk to father," Hugh said boldly, shying away from Bryce as Bryce stepped farther into the dark shadows of the foyer.

"I can guess why you'd say that," Bryce said, glancing up the stairs. "You told him, didn't you? Damn it, you told him."

Hugh stroked his chin. "After you hit me, did you think I would not tell him?" he whined. "And you should know. Father has promised to leave Parrot Inn to me. Not to you."

Bryce leaned into Hugh's face, almost growling. "I think I told you before. I wouldn't want this rat-infested bird cage," he laughed scornfully. "You think you've got yourself a treasure here? Well, just try to spend your nights counting the gold pieces. Ha! You'll find them in your head . . . not in your pocket!"

"It's more than you'll get from father," Hugh argued back. "He won't give you a pot to p—"

"Shut up, Hugh," Bryce growled into his face. "If I'm provoked into hitting you again, believe me, I won't be as kind as I was the last time." He placed his hand on one of his pistols. "In fact, I might even show you how well my pistol discharges."

Hugh recoiled from Bryce, ashen in color. "You wouldn't . . ." he gasped.

"I wouldn't dare me if I were you," Bryce said. He laughed across his shoulder as he moved quickly on up the stairs. Then once the upstairs landing was reached, his laughter died to a soft sigh. At least his father was still alive. Even if his father demanded the key back the last laugh would be on Hugh, for the key now belonged to no Fowler! Maybe it was a blessing that he had lost it. At least he wouldn't be forced to hand it over to Hugh!

With caution, he opened the door that led to his father's quarters. When he came to stand over his bed, a slow agonizing pity for this ailing man seeped into his heart. With his mouth wide open and eyes so doggedly closed, his father looked already dead.

Bryce turned his head away to swallow. But when he felt eyes on him, he turned slowly around and saw that his father's expression did not reflect hate, as Bryce would have expected.

"Bryce . . ." Tom said, lifting a bony hand toward him. "You've come back. Is it because you've . . . returned . . . with good news?"

"Good news?" Bryce asked, seeing the disarray of his father's bedding and smelling his body odor.

"The key, Bryce . . ." Tom murmured. His fingers trembled violently as he let his hand settle back down onto the bed. "Did you go . . . ?"

Bryce pulled a high-backed wooden chair next to the bed and settled onto it. "No." he said softly. "Father . . . I—"

"You haven't had a chance yet," Tom said, coughing spasmodically. "I understand." His dark cavernous eyes explored Bryce. "You're in your salvor costume, eh?" he said, chuckling a bit. "Kind'a flashy, son. Kind'a flashy."

Bryce was confused. Hugh had said that he had told his father the truth. Yet his father wasn't acting any differently toward him. In fact, he was even more lighthearted than usual.

"Father," Hugh said.

Tom scooted up on an elbow. "Place a pillow behind my back, son," he said shakily. "Then I want to explain something to you."

Bryce leaned over and fluffed a pillow, cringing at touching the yellowed case. He placed it behind his father's back, then sighed heavily as he once more tried to relax against the chair. "I've much to ask you, too, father," Bryce said huskily, remembering Natalie. Now he regretted that he had treated her so coldly. Maybe he had deserved that slap.

"I'm glad you're still calling me father, Bryce," Tom said wearily. "I was afraid I would never see you again."

"Hugh shouldn't have told you," Bryce said darkly. He shifted his weight on the chair and rested his hand on a pistol. "Not in your weakened condition, he shouldn't."

"He didn't tell me what I didn't already know."

"You knew . . . ?"

"All those years I knew."

"Then it didn't matter?"

"I guess this is why I kept busy," Tom said dryly. "This is why I never had time for you."

Bryce leaned forward. "But you gave *me* the key, father. Not Hugh."

"I explained earlier . . ."

"You said I was the strongest of your two sons."

"You still are," Tom said flatly. "Now, Bryce, I'm weakening. If you have something else on your mind, you'd best get on with it. I'm not sure I can stay awake much longer. I have to take talking in small doses."

Bryce now knew that he definitely wasn't going to worry his father with the loss of the key at this time. He

145

would, but later. Right now, he had to find out about Natalie! He only hoped that when he left this room, he would be able to search her out again for the best reason possible. For himself! Now that his anger toward her had left him, he did not want much time to pass between now and their next meeting. To be without her would leave more sting in his heart than any blow to the face inflicted by the delicate fingers of her hand. He had been foolish to react so forcefully. Hadn't she shown spunk by defending her reputation in such a hot-tempered fashion? He admired that in a woman! A woman of that temperament was a woman who loved fiercely! Ah, and yes, she had. . . .

"Father, I've recently become acquainted with a man —Clarence Seymour, from New Orleans—who lost a wife and unborn child at the hands of a pirate eighteen years ago," Bryce said. He cleared his throat nervously, then continued. "Father, I hate to bring Saul Palmer's name into the conversation for any reason, but, by chance, do you happen to know his wife's name?"

Scowl wrinkles shadowed Tom's face. He coughed into a hand. "He hasn't got a wife," he said.

Bryce's eyebrows lifted. "He hasn't?" he blurted.

"He never did have a true wife," Tom said throatily.

Bryce's color paled. "But he has . . . a . . . daughter." he said shallowly.

"As well as two sons," Tom said falteringly. "You and Adam."

"He . . . has . . . another son?" Bryce said quietly.

"Yes . . . your half brother. Adam is your half brother."

Bryce lowered his face into his hands. "God . . ." he said. Then he met his father's soft gaze in a challenge.

146

"Father, what does it all mean?"

"Bryce, it means that Saul Palmer is not at all what he appears," Tom stated flatly. "Who and what he is is only known by a few of us old-timers."

"What are you talking about?"

"Before Saul Palmer decided to look respectable, he was one of the fiercest pirates traveling the Caribbean."

Bryce rose so abruptly, his chair fell backward and crashed noisily against the floor. "My God," he gasped. "He *was* a pirate."

He dropped to one knee beside his father's bed. "Father," he said quietly. "Do you by chance know the name of Natalie's mother? It doesn't matter that she isn't Saul Palmer's wife. The name is all that's important."

Tom reached a hand to Bryce's shoulder and limply clasped onto it. "Bryce, why do you ask?" he queried. "Why am I reading so much into your voice and seeing so much in your eyes?"

Bryce set his jaw firmly. "Father, I have been commissioned to find Clarence Seymour's wife and daughter," he said thickly. "His daughter would be eighteen. He has another daughter, Brenda, who lives with him who so resembles Natalie Palmer, she could be Natalie Palmer. He thinks that his wife Kathryn could have given birth to this daughter after her abduction by this pirate."

Tom's lower lip began to quiver. He leaned away from his pillow. "Did you . . . say . . . Kathryn?" he gasped. "This man's wife was named . . . Kathryn . . . ?"

Bryce felt the hair raise at the nape of his neck, realizing that from his father's reaction to the name Kathryn, surely, she must be Natalie's mother. "Father, do you know?" he persisted. "Is Natalie's mother's name Kathryn?''

Tom studied Bryce in a moment of silence, then said: ''Natalie Palmer's mother's name was Kathryn,'' he said stiffly.

''Was . . . ?'' Bryce said in a near whisper.

''She died when Natalie was two.''

''God . . .'' Bryce mumured. But the news of this Kathryn's death was not as alarming as the discovery of Natalie's true identity. Bryce felt warm pleasure as this knowledge crashed through him in waves. It was as though he was standing on the beach and the effervescence of the water's foam was tickling his insides, making him almost giddy with delight.

''Bryce, you are smiling almost drunkenly,'' Tom said, reaching a hand to Bryce. ''Will you tell me why?''

''Before Hugh broke the news about . . . uh . . . Saul Palmer and what he was to me, I had found myself quite taken by Natalie,'' he confessed. ''Then after Hugh told me who Saul Palmer was, I immediately became aware of the fact that she must be my sister. Now I have just found that she is not and that I am free to go to her. Yes, I am quite ecstatic.''

''But I thought you said you were seeking information about Natalie for some man? You said you were commissioned.''

Bryce cleared his throat nervously. He sat the chair upright and settled onto it again. He was anxious to go to Natalie but he had been paid quite well to get all the answers to her past. So that he must do before trying to approach her again.

''Yes, I am,'' he said thickly. ''I must not lose sight of that. Now, father, just a few more questions before I take my leave. Could you tell me about Natalie's mother?

Was she forced to stay with Saul Palmer? Why didn't he marry her? And why has Natalie stayed with him?"

"Like I said before," Tom grumbled. "Only a few of us old-timers know about Saul Palmer's past. It was at the time of Kathryn's abduction that he laid down his cutlass. He didn't marry her, of course, because she was already married. But she stayed with him willingly. And after she died, Saul kept Natalie on and raised her as his own."

"Then you're saying Natalie has never known?"

"No. She doesn't know. And Saul has spread word to us who know the truth that if anyone tells her, he'll show that he hasn't lost his skills with his cutlass even if fingers are missing on one hand," Tom grumbled. "But not much left he can do to me. I'm already at death's door."

Bryce's pulse raced. "Fingers . . . missing . . . ?"

"Three on his left hand . . ."

Bryce kneaded his brow. "That confirms it," he growled.

"Clarence said that the pirate who stole his wife from him had the same fingers missing. He also said the pirate vessel was black." His words caught in his throat. "His son Adam," he whispered. "Could . . . he . . . be . . . ?"

He rose suddenly from the chair, filled with nervous excitement. He had much to do. But first Natalie . . . Ah, Natalie!

"Bryce, when are you going to travel to Orchid Island?" Tom asked wearily. "I'm just not sure how much longer . . . I . . . can hang on. I'd like to see . . . to see at least one gold coin rescued from that chest."

The euphoric madness sweeping through Bryce was momentarily halted. His eyes wavered, yet he stood straight-backed as he said: "Father, don't you fret," he murmured. "You will share in the treasure. I will promise you that."

"When, son?"

"Soon, father. Soon . . ."

He couldn't tell his father about the key. He just couldn't! That seemed to be the only thread of life to which his father was clinging—the hope of seeing the Fowler's get revenge. Bryce had to wonder. Hadn't his father ever wondered if Saul Palmer's family of pirates might have been responsible for the Fowler family slaughter all those many years ago?

And Saul Palmer's son Adam. Yes, his son Adam . . .

"My brother Adam . . ." he thought angrily to himself. "And the . . . *Sea Snake?*"

Hoping that Bryce's anger would cool and that he'd remember the hidden cove, Natalie paced, anxious. She had been so foolish to let him walk away from her. She held her right hand before her, still seeing the stunned expression on his face after she'd slapped him. She could feel goose pimples rise on her flesh as she remembered thinking that she had so expected him to hit her back. Why, she had never done such a thing before! And she most certainly would never do it again.

"But I have probably driven him so far away from me, he will never want to be near me again," she said aloud. "Oh, what shall I do? Should I have gone to the ship instead of this cove?"

But, no. She knew that she couldn't have. She had risked trying that once. But no suspicion was raised by her riding Adora. It had been simple enought to flee once more atop her horse from the back gate. And now, as the water lapped lazily at her bare feet, she still waited, full of hope, not letting despair enter her heart.

With her boots pulled from her feet and tossed aside, she stepped farther into the water. Lifting her dark riding skirt into her arms, she enjoyed the caress of the warm water against her flesh. The tropical sun was ablaze above her, sultry, hazy red, and puffy clouds of white were being wind whipped along the horizon. The neighing of a horse, then another, as two horses communicated, drew Natalie around with a start. When she saw Bryce approaching on horseback, she forgot the knee-high water and let her skirt fall free of her arms. As it soaked up water, so did Natalie soak up the growing nearness of him.

"Bryce . . ." she whispered, moving toward the beach. She was consumed by her heartbeats. He had remembered! The cove had become a special place to him also! And surely he wasn't angry with her any longer. He wouldn't have come to her if still angry.

The wind, catching the full sleeves of his gold shirt and his hair, emphasized his handsomeness. All the contours of his body rose and fell gracefully with the horse's further approach. His familiar, lean and smooth features . . . his sun-bronzed face . . . the muscles flexing in his legs and shoulders. All these things made her pulse race even more. She wanted him. She needed him.

Bryce drew Hugh's horse up next to Natalie's and quickly dismounted. As he secured the reins, he was breathless. Hadn't she looked seductive with her skirt above her knees, revealing the silk of her skin to his hungry eyes? Then when she had discovered his approach, hadn't she looked as anxious, as delighted, as he was to see her?

One day they would share laughter when he revealed

that he had for a short while thought they were brother and sister. But for now, she would not learn his true identity or that this Saul Palmer wasn't her true father . . . but his.

His insides softly quivering, he wondered how he was going to tell her about Clarence Seymour. Seymour's words kept eating away at him—that Bryce was to bring his wife and daughter back, no matter what! Well, his wife Kathryn was dead. There was only a daughter. What if Natalie refused to leave Key West? All she had ever known was Saul Palmer's way of life. But once she knew the truth wouldn't it be simple? Surely she would be willing to leave such a man as Saul Palmer to go to her true father.

"But if not, I must take her any way," he thought. "I've been paid quite well and I always deliver."

He knew that he had to practice caution with this commission. He had to be tactful. It would be quite a shock for her to hear the truth. At least the blow would be softened because he would be the bearer of these tidings.

He could feel her nearness. He could smell the jasmine scent of her hair. He turned and she was there, her dark, luminous eyes gazing rapturously into his.

"I'm sorry," she whispered. "I shouldn't have—"

Not able to hold back any longer, Bryce gathered her gently into his arms and tested her with a slow, lingering kiss. "You have nothing to be sorry for," he murmured, raining kisses on the delicate features of her face. "Just be glad that we've found each other again."

She trembled beneath his kisses and twined her arms about his neck. Fingering his hair, she sighed. "Bryce, I do love you so," she whispered. "The days . . . the nights . . . have been so long. I couldn't understand why you left or why you didn't come back. I thought that you loved me just as much as I loved you."

Tilting her chin with a forefinger, Bryce directed her eyes to meet his. "One day I will explain," he said huskily. "But now? Must we waste time talking? Beautiful lady, my heart is about to race from inside me."

She curved her lower lip into a half pout as she cast him a brooding look through her veil of thick, black lashes. "I want you," she whispered. "But I would simply die if you are playacting and not truly in love with me. I don't wish to be used, Bryce. I am not a . . . a . . . tramp."

Bryce drew her quickly into his arms and burrowed his nose into the thickness of her hair. He laughed throatily. "No. You certainly are not a tramp," he said. "You now understand that I was jesting before, don't you?"

He felt her silent nod of assent against his cheek then moved his lips to the silken hollow of her throat and kissed her softly there. "No," he murmured between kisses. "You are no tramp. You're *mine*. I won't allow another man to ever touch you."

"But will you leave again?"

He pulled slowly away from her and held her at arm's length. "You know that I must," he said thickly. Then his heart pounded harder and his eyes lit up. "But, darling, you can go with me. Travel to New Orleans with me. I will show you the magnificence of my Creole home. You can be my guest . . . even more than that. . . ."

Natalie's face flushed warm. "Are you asking me to . . . ?"

Bryce shook his head. "Yes," he whispered. "Travel to New Orleans. Become my wife . . ." He felt suddenly smug. Getting her to New Orleans was going to be

153

easier than he thought. And, yes, by God, he would marry her! He had never thought it possible to love and respect a woman. Not after he had lost all respect for women because of his mother. Then there had been the women at Rose's bawdy house. He had wondered if any woman could be treated with respect . . . until he had met Natalie. Yes, he would marry her!

"Bryce, I just can't leave," she whispered. "My father. I have to think of him. Except for Adam, I'm all he's got." She didn't want to question him about his reputation of a pirate. Wasn't he even dressed this day as a pirate might dress? Or was this what he wore while in command of his great *Golden Isis?*

Bryce drew quickly away from her and directed his attention elsewhere. He kneaded his brow, feeling many things inside. He had never proposed to a woman before. And now that he had humbled himself in such a way, she had actually turned him down! And for what? Because of damned Saul Palmer? Suddenly Saul Palmer was a thorn in his side. Not only one thorn . . . possibly even dozens!

Natalie took a step forward and placed a hand on Bryce's cheek. Just the feel of him sent a burning ache through her. She forced his face around and let her fingers discover his chiseled features again. His gold eyebrows were thick and bristly and his brow showed traces of lines that deepened when he frowned toward her.

"Are you saying that you won't travel with me to New Orleans?" he argued.

"Bryce, my father has done so much for me, I can't just up and leave him."

"Yes. Your father . . ." he grumbled.

"Shh," Natalie whispered, blocking his words with a

154

finger sealing his lips. "I will tell him I've found the man of my dreams. I will tell him I want to marry you. You could then court me."

Bryce brushed her finger away. "Natalie, I've got something to tell—" he began, but was stopped again, this time by the sensuous softness of her lips pressing invitingly against his. When her fingers reached inside his open-throated shirt and began moving slowly over his body, he was lost to the burning ache in his loins that only she could release.

He reveled in this touch of her fingers. With slow, circular motions, she rubbed her thumbs over and around his nipples, drawing a nervous groan from deep inside him. Then when she lowered a hand from his chest to touch his swelling need of her, he couldn't hold back any longer.

Drawing her into the cool shadows of the bluff and the jutting rocks, Bryce eased her downward, onto the sand. With mounting desire for her, he released her from her clothes, then paid homage to her nudity by worshiping her creamy skin with the fire of his lips.

"What if someone should see us?" she whispered, reaching a hand to his brow, to push a gold lock of hair back in place. She devoured him with her eyes, seeing the serious love mask of his face and the intensity of his blue pool-like eyes.

"Do you really care?" he asked huskily.

"No," she said, releasing a heavy sigh.

"I love you, Natalie," he whispered back. "What we're doing together is perfectly normal and healthy. Don't feel guilty."

Natalie smiled. "Bryce, you don't have to explain all these things to me," she said. "I'm an adult. I do what I do because I love you. And, no. I don't feel guilty. How

155

could I?''

"You've seemed to have your reservations.''

"When you speak of marriage—''

"And why should it be so unbelievable to think of us as married?''

Natalie tensed. Then she began running her fingers over the silk of his shirt. "Bryce, it is whispered that . . . that you are a . . . a . . . pirate," she said softly. "Bryce, surely pirates don't wed.''

"What . . . ?'' Bryce exclaimed, drawing away from her. He tore into a sudden fit of laughter, then eyed her amusedly when the laughter faded.

Natalie pushed herself up on an elbow. "What's so funny?'' she snapped, furrowing her brow. "Are you or aren't you a pirate?'' Her eyes swept over him. "You are dressed as a pirate. A fancy pirate.''

In slow, yet deliberate motions, Bryce began to undress. When he stood over her, proudly displaying his risen passion, he laughed huskily. "Now I don't wear a pirate costume," he said. "Do you like me better this way?''

Giggling, Natalie reached her arms out to him. "Bryce, how can you joke at a time like this?'' Her blood was running hot. Seeing him ready to send her senses reeling into another world that she had only known once made her not care that he might be a pirate. She was in love with the man.

Following her bidding, Bryce lowered himself over her. With a reckless passion, he gathered her into his arms and kissed her demandingly. Natalie closed her eyes and let euphoria begin to possess her, becoming almost mindless as his lips pressed even harder against hers. She gave of her body willingly when Bryce's fingers sought and captured a breast. As his hand played and caressed there, she began tracing the sinewy muscles of his shoulders, then on downward, past his waistline, where his skin was smooth and hairless.

As his knee parted her legs, his tongue parted her lips and plunged inside her mouth, a sweet torture to her that stimulated her passionate need for him. His hands played along her throbbing flesh, downward, until one found the soft spot between her legs and cupped the vee of it. The physical contact—the warmth of his hand—sent spasms of delight to Natalie's brain.

"I could never love another," Bryce said, pulling his lips away from hers. "God, I didn't know I could ever totally—truly—love at all."

"Bryce . . ." Natalie whispered, flushed with desire and mounting pleasure as his mouth eased over the nipple of a breast. His hand began a slow caress between her thighs sending Natalie into an almost mindless frenzy. She nibbled at the flesh of his shoulder, tasting the manliness of him. She laced her fingers through his hair and drew his mouth more firmly to her breast. Then she drew in her breath as she felt him enter her from below. Sighing, she lifted her legs around him and clamped her ankles together.

Bryce lifted his lips to hers; they seemed magically soft as he kissed her sweetly and gently. Twining his fingers through her hair, he whispered her name against her throat. "Natalie," he sighed. "My sweet, sweet Natalie . . ."

Consumed with fiery rapture, Natalie met his eager thrusts; filled with such intense joy, she hated to think this moment could ever end. She clung to him. She reveled in his long, sweet strokes. They were igniting flames inside her that would forever burn for him.

She twisted her head from side to side when the exquisite sensations began. She trembled when Bryce lowered his head and caught a nipple between his teeth. Then she felt the glow inside her spread and she cried out her pleasure.

Breathing hard, she opened her eyes to see him still laboring inside her. He looked at her with burning eyes, then burrowed his face between her breasts when his body began a frantic spasm.

Natalie smiled, knowing that he had now also reached that pinnacle of love and was proud that he had shared it with her. She ran her fingers through his hair, feeling the beat of his heart against her flesh.

"Bryce . . ." she whispered. "It was so beautiful."

With tenderness, he held her close and kissed her parted lips. "Beautiful lady, it's because we are as one, you and I. *Êtes-vous heureuse?*"

"Mais oui," she murmured.

"And how is it that you can speak in French?"

"My father," she replied softly. "He taught me. As he has so much of life."

Bryce cringed inside, once more reminded of his assignment to lure Natalie from the clutches of Saul Palmer. "No love could be as perfect as ours," he whispered into her ear. "We belong together. Please say you'll travel to New Orleans with me."

Natalie squirmed from beneath him. She moved to a sitting position, wrapping her arms around her bent knees. She stared out across the ocean, seeing the whitecaps rise and fall, torn between her wants and needs. "Bryce, I explained earlier," she said. "You will have to properly court me."

"Because of Saul Palmer?" Bryce said hotly, rising from the sand. He grabbed his breeches and stepped angrily into them.

Hearing the disrespect for her father thick in his words, Natalie rose to her feet, glaring. "Because of my father," she snapped. "I will not repay his years of kindness and dedication to me by deserting him now."

Bryce took one bold step toward her and clasped her shoulders. His face was tight with anger. "Not even for me?" he whispered.

Natalie's lips quivered. "Bryce, don't force me to make a choice," she whispered. "It would be much simpler to agree to courting me. Father would adore you as *I* do. He would forget forcing those old, pompous friends of his on me. Even tonight I have to attend a masquerade ball at Albert Burns's house. Don't you know that I'd much rather be with you?" She reached a hand to his face and touched it softly.

Bryce drew roughly away from her and proceeded to dress. Natalie, feeling his added rejection, also began to dress, once more wondering if she had been wrong to give herself so willingly to him. He was a man who obviously didn't live by any set rules! If he didn't think enough of her to properly court her, then she had been a fool again! Was his brooding silence his way of answering? Refusing?

Fully clothed now, except for her riding boots, she yanked first one on, then the other. Angry and hurt she placed her hands on her hips and glowered toward him. "I will now take my leave, sir," she said haughtily. "Maybe Albert Burns isn't such a bad choice after all. My father may have chosen the man I will wed."

Feeling tears near, Natalie spun on a heel and rushed

toward Adora. When she reached to untie her horse's reins, Bryce's hand was there to stop her. With resentment flashing in her eyes, Natalie swung around and boldly faced him. "What do you think you're doing?" she snapped.

"I've something more to say to you, Natalie, and damn it, you're going to listen," Bryce said flatly. He took her by a wrist and led her back to the cool, shadowy cove. He nodded toward the sand. "Sit," he commanded. "You sit down and listen to what I have to say."

"I won't listen to further talk about marriage," she said stubbornly. She flinched when his grip on her wrist tightened as he forced her downward.

"I said sit," he growled. "And, no, I do not plan to talk of marriage. But I do plan to talk about Saul Palmer."

Irritated, Natalie eased down onto the sand. She sat on the folds of her skirt and watched him as he settled down beside her. Aware of the worry in his eyes and the set of his jaw, she lost some of her anger and began to be filled with wonder. What was he finding so hard to say? And what could he have to say about her father? She was finding out just how complex Bryce Fowler was.

Bryce began sifting sand between his fingers, averting his eyes from Natalie. He could feel her gaze on him and could even feel its questions, almost like arrows piercing his flesh. Damn! How could he tell her? She was a devoted daughter who obviously loved . . . maybe even worshiped the man who she thought was her father. Her bubble was about to burst. Her whole life was soon to be changed. If only she had first agreed to marriage. At least that would have been something for her to cling to as her life shattered about her.

"Bryce . . ." she murmured. "What is it?"

Heavy-lidded, Bryce looked her way. "Natalie, what I have to tell you will be hard for you to take at first," he said thickly. "But, God, Natalie you have to know."

Natalie swallowed hard. She didn't like this. There was something different about Bryce. There was a threatening quality in the way he spoke. "Bryce, whatever is it?" she demanded.

Bryce hung his head in his hands. "Damn," he mumbled. "I've never run into a problem like this before."

Natalie eyed him questioningly. "What problem?" she whispered. "Bryce, don't leave me wondering. Tell me what you have on your mind."

Bryce slowly lifted his gaze to meet hers. He reached a hand to her hair and caressed its full length tenderly. "Your mother's name was Kathryn?" he said in a strain.

Natalie recoiled, watching his hand tremble a bit as it eased from her hair. "How did you know?" she gasped. "And why have you made it your business to know?"

"Natalie, I recently saw a woman in New Orleans who so resembled you, I thought she was you."

"What?"

"Yes," he said flatly. "Her name is Brenda Seymour. She's nineteen. Her father is Clarence Seymour."

Natalie rose quickly to her feet, hands on hips. "And what does this have to do with me?" she snapped angrily. "I know of no Brenda or Clarence Seymour. Should the fact that she resembles me mean something to me? Should her father?"

Bryce rose to meet her height. He clasped her shoulders and held her at arm's length. "Yes," he murmured. "They both should and will mean something to you. If

161

you will only listen.''

Natalie's face flamed red. "Bryce," she whined. "I don't like this game you're playing with me. Why are you doing it?''

"This is no game, Natalie," he said flatly. "This is life. This is a part of your life that I recently discovered. It is your right to know. It is your right to know that Saul Palmer is not your true father.''

The color drained from Natalie's face. She tried to step back from Bryce, but he held firmly to her shoulders. He knew to release her would be to lose her. He could see flight etched across her face.

"How could you say such a thing?" she said in a strained whisper. "Why would you? I've loved you and now you play such a cruel trick on me? Bryce, I . . . I hate you. I will never let you touch me again.'' She squirmed, flailing her hands toward him. "Let me go. I hate you. Do you hear? Hate you.''

"Would you feel better if you could slap my face again?" he stated flatly. "Natalie, that will not erase the truth that you must hear. Now, calm down. Just listen to me. Then do what you want. Slap me, or let me pull you into my arms to comfort you.''

"Never. I never want your arms around me again,'' she hissed, tears wetting her lashes.

"You might as well quit struggling," he said. "I do plan to continue holding you until you hear everything.''

"Bryce . . . please . . .'' she pleaded, curving her lips into a soft pout. "I just want to go home. Please . . .''

"Natalie, eighteen years ago, Clarence Seymour, his one-year-old daughter Brenda and his pregnant wife Kathryn were traveling from England to New Orleans,'' he boldly stated. "A pirate ship intervened. Kathryn was taken hostage. The rest of the ship's passengers were set out in longboats to drift at sea. But Kathryn was taken by this pirate . . . and this pirate's name . . . was . . . Saul Palmer."

Natalie felt her heart plunge. She looked at Bryce, not seeing him, for her vision was going into a crazy kind of swirl. She blinked her eyes frantically, wanting to keep control of her senses. A sinking feeling in the pit of her stomach was grabbing hold of her insides, as though she was far away from shore, in the ocean, drowning, slowly drowning. . . .

"No!" she suddenly screamed, closing her eyes. She shook her head back and forth until she became even dizzier. Then she felt the warmth of his arms around her shoulders and momentarily gave in to that comfort. But she jerked herself free, eyes flashing. With her composure regained, she took a step backward.

"It can't be true," she hissed. "It just cannot be true. My father speaks of piracy with venom. He would—he could—not have been a pirate."

"I have reason to believe that Adam, your . . . well . . . what you thought to be your brother, is the pirate that roams the seas in the *Sea Snake*," he said softly. "Everything points in that direction. I could almost swear to this, Natalie."

Feeling a bitterness of sorts rising in her throat, Natalie placed her hands to her mouth. "Adam . . ." she whispered, remembering her own doubts about him. She recalled the sinister, black ship . . . then Adam's personal ship moving from the black ship's shadow. . . .

Once more she closed her eyes, trying to squeeze the truth away. "Adam . . . father . . ." she whispered.

Then she eyed Bryce again. "Bryce, who told you these things?" she said icily. "I still cannot believe them. I love my father so much. He's such a good man."

Even while saying that he was good, she was remembering the times when she had wondered about his rudeness, his brusqueness to the servants and to some of the men he would lock into the library with him. She was remembering Matthew, the stable hand, and how he cowered at the mere mention of Saul Palmer.

Oh, please let none of this be true, she prayed to herself.

"I cannot reveal the source of information for the full truth about Saul Palmer," he said thickly. "You see, he has threatened to kill anyone who breathes a word of his past. Don't you see now why he keeps such a close eye on you? He doesn't want anyone near you who might tell you."

"No . . ." she whispered, shaking her head. "It just can't be. It just . . . can't . . . be . . ."

"It is true. Clarence Seymour—he had come to me with a commission, to go in search of an opium shipment that the pirate who rides the *Sea Snake* had so wrongly taken from him," Bryce said. "It was then that I met Brenda. I told Clarence of you, of the resemblance, and he told me the story about his wife Kathryn and the child she was carrying when the pirate abducted her. This child was you, Natalie. Kathryn was your mother. I found this out from someone else after Clarence paid me a commission to find Kathryn and bring both of you back to him. You are rightfully his, you know. Of course, he will be shattered by the death of your mother. . . ."

Natalie's insides turned cold. His words were penetrating her brain. He had been paid to seek her out! All along he had planned to trick her into returning to New Orleans with him. He hadn't planned to marry her! He had planned to deliver her to this Clarence Seymour for the gold he was being paid! Her heart turned to stone when she eyed him coldly.

"Bryce Fowler, do you do everything for money?" she hissed. "Even . . . love . . . ?"

Blinded with tears, she turned and rushed to her horse. So many tumultuous thoughts inside her brain were causing her to feel disoriented. Surely Bryce was wrong. Surely he had made this up. Yet, why would her?

Money. Gold. Yes. When money was involved, surely he would stoop to anything. He was a pirate, was he not? Yes, he was the pirate! Not her father! Not her brother Adam!

Hearing him yelling for her, Natalie quickly mounted Adora and sunk her knees desperately into her horse's sides. Flicking the reins angrily, she found Adora quite responsive to her needs and was quickly on the road that led to the protective fence that separated her from all the hurts in the world.

Hearing the horse behind her growing closer, Natalie leaned lower over Adora and shouted into her ear. "Hahh," she screamed. "Hurry, Adora. My life depends on it. I never—never again—want to let him near me." But her thunderous heartbeat told her differently. Though she hated him, she loved him.

"Natalie," Bryce yelled. "Please wait. You mustn't go. Not until you've resolved yourself to the truth. Natalie . . . !"

Thankful the gate had been left open, Natalie rushed Adora through it; then she jumped down and ran to secure its lock in place. Not waiting to see Bryce's desperation at finding himself eternally separated from her, she once more mounted Adora and fled onward, toward the safe cocoon of her house. Now would she ever be able to flee from it again? There was no one she could trust?

"Surely father," she cried to herself. "Surely I can trust my own father. I must stay near him now at all times. I cannot let Bryce interfere in my life again. For if he gets the chance, he might even abduct me. . . ."

Her thoughts went to her mother. Kathryn. Oh, if only her mother had lived to tell her the truth . . .

She shivered, realizing that she had just acknowledged the doubt simmering inside her brain.

Pulling Adora to a halt, Natalie looked toward the house, confused.

EIGHT

There was no doubt about it. Natalie had to admit that Albert Burns's house was charming. On the walls were cheerful hand-painted murals, and crystal chandeliers and wall sconces caught and consolidated the light overhead and all about.

With her trim, black mask only hiding a portion of her face, Natalie began to work her way around the edge of the room, feeling the need to escape the crowd. After her trying afternoon with Bryce, she had wanted to hide away in her room, to think. But now that her father and Albert Burns had returned from Cuba, her father had insisted she accompany him to this masquerade ball and she had been compelled to obey.

All the while he had been speaking to her, she had studied his features, trying to find a trace of her likeness in him. But nothing! She didn't even resemble Adam . . . her brother! Only their dark eyes and hair—nothing else. Her features were soft. Theirs were hard.

Later, when her father had stepped from his bedroom, her heart had skipped a beat. Attired in a pirate's black costume, even sporting gold loops of earrings on each ear lobe, he had taken on a complete different identity! He, indeed, had looked the role of a pirate! His dark wig had been heavily pigtailed and behind his black mask, his eyes seemed to reveal an evil glint that the costume appeared to have drawn from inside him. Natalie had even let her thoughts wander farther . . . wondering if this was the way her mother had seen him those many years ago? But no! She had to brush such thoughts from her mind. He was her father. He *was*.

A four-piece, string orchestra ensemble was keeping Albert's guests entertained. All those in attendance were masked and many were costumed. Some were dancing and swaying in time with the music, while others stood idly by, chatting.

In her flared, elegant dress of blue silk, Natalie moved on into the dining room. And there, too, eyes followed her. She had pulled her hair up over her ears and at her brow. The many petticoats beneath her dress rustled enticingly with each step she took. Her low-cut bodice displayed the splendid white swells of her breasts and the sparkle of diamonds at her throat. Matching diamonds had been set into the folds of her hair as well as on the lobes of her ears. Though she wore a mask, it seemed everyone knew her; so many had whispered about "Natalie . . . beautiful, beautiful Natalie."

Hearing these remarks made her blush and feel the need to escape from the stares and whispers, but mainly from Albert Burns who had already claimed her for three dances.

Not hungry, but with the need to busy her fingers, Natalie stepped up to a long and dark mahogany table that shimmered with rows of wine glasses and massive, crested silver. There was champagne, claret, and port to choose from. For the hungry, there were heaping platters of classic Cuban food prepared by master Latin cooks. She picked up a delicate piece of chinaware and tried to choose something to nibble on. Her gaze moved from item to item, seeing what was offered. Among the choices were *arroz con pollo*, rice with chicken, and *picadillo*, ground meat with black beans and yellow rice. The desserts offered were *flan*, a custard, and *arroz con leche*, rice with milk.

Truly not wanting anything, she placed the plate back on the table and started to walk away when a voice—oh, so familiar—spoke from beside her.

"Something has taken your appetite away, *sí?*" Bryce said amusedly, pretending a Spanish accent.

When she slowly turned and saw him standing there, dressed so ridiculously, she momentarily forgot her anger toward him and covered her mouth with a hand to suppress her giggles. "Bryce . . ." she whispered. "What . . . are . . . you . . . ?"

"I am here to pleasure the beautiful *señorita,*" he said, bowing ludicrously.

Natalie's gaze swept over him when he once more straightened his back to stand before her. Attired in a flashy, flowered shirt and extremely baggy, red breeches, and with a red bandanna tied snugly to hold a wiry, black hairpiece in place, he looked the role of a Mexican musician. But even the bushy, black mustache glued beneath his nose couldn't hide his true identity. The piercing blue of his eyes, revealed behind his thin strip of a black mask, danced back at her, almost mockingly.

She was once more remembering. . . . "Bryce Fowler," she whispered, glancing nervously on all sides of her. "What are you doing here? This is a private party. Surely you don't know Albert Burns."

"No," he laughed. "But I do know you. And that should be enough."

"I told you that I didn't ever want to see you again," she hissed, leaning into his face. She felt her pulse race when he reached for her hand and began kissing each fingertip, one at a time. The bristles of the mustache tickled the palm of her hand and once more she wanted to giggle. But she had to stand firm. He had to get out of her life. Since having met him, she hadn't had one restful thought.

"Tell me again, *señorita*," he slurred, now sucking a finger between his lips, flicking his tongue over it. "Tell me you want me to go."

Feeling a dangerous, sweet pain pleasuring her insides, she jerked her hand away and placed it, along with her other one, behind her back. "Have you been drinking?" she whispered. "Surely you have. You're behaving very recklessly. What if my father . . . ?"

Bryce placed a forefinger to her lips, sealing her words. "Correction, beautiful lady," he said softly. "Your father isn't even here. He's in New Orleans, awaiting your arrival. He wants to know this daughter he's never had a chance to meet."

Anger flashed in Natalie's dark eyes as she shook his finger away. She set her lips in a straight line, then whispered shallowly: "I will not let you subject me to this again."

She tilted her chin and walked from the dining room into the parlor. When a strong arm circled her waist, her breath caught in her throat. And once in Bryce's arms, dancing, moving with the crowd, in time with the music, she had no choice but to cling to him. To cause a scene, could mean disaster for him.

"You are despicable," she whispered into his ear. "Why do you persist at this game? This man who has paid you to find a woman that is his daughter will only be disappointed to find you did not succeed."

"Ah, no, my sweet *señorita*," he whispered back. "I never disappoint those who pay me well."

She struggled against his hold, only causing his arm to strengthen against her, to pinion her more in place. "I will soon scream if you do not release me," she hissed into his ear; but she was unable to quell the fire of passion burning her insides. She loved his warm breath against her cheek . . . his smell of cigars and sea water. She melted into his embrace when his lips kissed her ear. . . .

They swirled in unison, becoming lost in the enchantment of the music, and the mystery behind the masks. The aroma of wine and champagne was heavy in the air, but that wasn't the cause of Natalie's building intoxication. . . .

"So you want to scream?" Bryce teased. "Go ahead. I'm sure Albert Burns would come to your rescue. Then he would expect a reward. Now wouldn't you enjoy kissing that pompous ass?"

Natalie stiffened. Her euphoric state had just been invaded by Bryce's persistent teasings. She drew away from him, feigning dizziness. "I must get a breath of fresh air," she murmured. "I will go out on the terrace. Bryce, you stay here and find yourself another pretty thing who might enjoy your amusing sort of charm."

He took her by an elbow and began guiding her toward a side door. "Oh, no you don't," he said. "You won't

171

get away from me that easily this time.''

Casting him a sideways glance, she followed along beside him. If her father caught sight of him then what would he do? She looked slowly around the room, wondering where her father was. Then she spied the library door closed and knew that her father and his cohorts were smoking and drinking, talking over whatever business matter may have arisen through the day.

''And, sir, what are your next plans?'' she snapped angrily. ''You can't stay here for long. You most surely will be discovered.''

Bryce opened the terrace door and gestured with an arm. ''Beautiful lady, step out into this splash of moonlight,'' he said hoarsely. ''Many women's minds have been changed beneath the mystical glow of the moon.''

Natalie groaned inwardly. He didn't give up so easily! Sighing heavily, she glided out onto the terrace and felt the sudden damp chill of night wrap itself around her. Looking toward the wide sweep of the Atlantic, she watched a distant, tall-masted ship follow the path of the moon's beams shimmering in the water. It caused a shiver to ride her spine. She couldn't help but envision a sinister pirate abducting a pregnant woman. How horrible it must have been for her. Could this Kathryn truly have been the only Kathryn Natalie had ever known? Could it have been her . . . mother?

Bryce drew Natalie around to face him. ''What are you thinking at this very moment?'' he asked, studying her face, seeing the far away look in her eyes.

''That's none of your concern,'' she snapped, jerking away from him. ''Bryce, you have done nothing but bring confusion into my life. Why don't you just leave me alone? Please?''

With one bold sweep, Bryce had her in his arms and was raining kisses on her face. "Beautiful lady, you know the impossibilities of that," he said thickly. "And you also know that you do not want me to forget you. You could not live without me now, as I could not without you."

His lips searched and found hers, eager . . . waiting . . . soft . . . warm. His hand traveled to the front of her until he found a breast. Slowly caressing it through the sheerness of her dress, he felt her response weakening and knew that the time had come to make his move.

"Darling, let's go to the privacy of my waiting carriage," he whispered. "I need to be with you. Alone. Anyone could step out here at any given moment. Maybe even your father."

Natalie's head was doing a slow spin. He always had this effect on her and she hated him for it. But there was no denying the need of her body; she hungered to be alone with him. She wanted to melt into his arms and to let his lips fully possess her. She wanted even more. . . .

"Yes, Bryce," she murmured. "But for only a little while. Albert may miss me and go to my father."

"Only a little while," Bryce said. "I promise."

Natalie cast a fast glance into the parlor. "I do feel so wicked when I'm with you," she laughed. "Bryce, I hardly know myself any longer."

Assisting her from the terrace, down onto the ground, Bryce then guided her toward the front of the mansion, where he had paid a coachman to wait. When they reached the stately carriage, one which displayed flickering lamps on each side, the coachman leaped down to open the door.

Lifting the skirt of her dress, Natalie stepped inside the carriage and settled herself on the plump cushioned seat. Almost breathless with desire, she waited for Bryce to close the door so she could once more be in his arms. Something deep inside warned her of the danger of being so reckless, but her heart told her differently. And at this moment, her heart would be her guide.

"Like it?" Bryce asked, settling next to her, gesturing with his hand. "The fanciest carriage for hire in all of Key West."

An inside lamp was flickering lazily, casting dancing shadows on the pale green velvet interior of the carriage. The fringed swags at the two windows were pulled to provide privacy.

Natalie was suddenly reminded of the other time she'd been in a carriage with Bryce. She had later found his key. She kept forgetting to tell him. Maybe it was of importance to him. Turning her gaze to meet his, she said: "Bryce, I found . . ."

Then, feeling the carriage beginning to move, she paused. Her eyes widened and her heart began to thunder inside her. "Bryce, the carriage . . ." she whispered. "It's . . . moving. . . ."

"Just relax," he said quietly. "I instructed the coachman to take us to a more romantic setting once we were inside the carriage."

"You did what?" she gasped. "Bryce. I told you I could only be away from the ball for a short while." She crossed her arms angrily across her chest. "You order the driver to stop. Right this minute."

Bryce chuckled amusedly. He slowly peeled the mustache from beneath his nose, lifted the mask away from his face, and brushed the wig off his head. "Beautiful lady, now wouldn't you rather make love aboard my magnificent ship while traveling the seas? There's no more romantic setting in which to share intimate embraces."

A coldness was circling Natalie's heart. Surely he wouldn't! "Bryce, you're not saying what I think you're saying, are you?" she snapped angrily. "Are . . . you . . . actually abducting me?"

"You might say that," he said, laughing softly again. When he reached for her, she slapped his hands away.

"You're a madman to try this," she hissed. "My father will track you down. You'll be sorry you ever laid eyes or hands on me."

"No. Never," Bryce said. "I'll never be sorry to have found you."

Natalie reached for the door. "Oh, yes. I forgot," she spat. "You've been paid quite well to find me. But, Bryce, the gold coins you've received can't warm your heart like my love for you could have."

She struggled with the door handle, growing numb with fear. The door had been locked from the outside. There was a conspiracy between Bryce and the coachman.

"You may as well settle back in my arms and decide to enjoy the sea voyage ahead," he said, once more reaching for her.

"You've tricked me," she cried, stiffening when his fingers brushed against her heaving bosom. She jerked her mask from her face and threw it at him. "How could I have been so dumb? I should have known you couldn't be trusted. You're no better than that pirate who abducted that woman named Kathryn so many years ago."

"Your mother, Natalie," Bryce corrected. "That

Kathryn was your mother. When will you ever let yourself believe the truth?''

''The truth?'' she cried. ''The truth is I am a Palmer. And a Palmer will kill you for what you're doing to me. Just be warned, Bryce Fowler.''

''Temper, temper,'' Bryce teased. He took Natalie by a wrist and forced her to his side. With fierceness he swept her into his arms and kissed her on the lips. When he felt her pushing at his chest, he held her even closer, hoping the passion they shared would weaken her defenses into complete surrender.

But this time he wasn't the victor. Though she was petite, she exerted much force behind her kicks and blows. He knew that his next move must be to get her onto his ship unnoticed. To hold her anger in check, he reached for the red bandanna that had been wrapped around his wig and began tying her wrists together.

''Bryce, what are you doing?'' she cried, continuing to struggle. ''Untie me this instant.''

Testing the knot, seeing that it was secure, he let her hands rest in her lap. He lifted his lips into a half smile. ''And I will also have to gag your mouth shut if you continue to refuse to cooperate with me,'' he said. He raised a hand to her hair and began setting it free of its pins and diamonds.

''My jewels also?'' she hissed. ''Are you going to take everything of value from me? You've already stolen my self-respect.''

''The diamonds?'' he scoffed. ''Natalie, I have access to a chest that has a treasure of gold locked inside it, just for the taking. Diamonds have a tendency to lose their glitter when in the shadow of gold.'' He slouched his shoulders a bit and kneaded his brow. ''But, damn it,'' he grumbled. "I do have a problem."

"You?" she laughed. "Hah! You do not know what a problem is until you come face to face with my father after he comes to my rescue."

"That's nothing," he scoffed. Then he spoke in a softer tone, almost meditatingly. "The key I lost is of much more significance to me. Without it, I do not know how I can unlock that damn chest. I guess I'll have to shoot the lock open. But then, there's the chance of damaging the chest's contents."

"A . . . key . . . ?" she whispered, feeling her pulse race.

"I seem to have lost it from my rear pocket that very first day I met you," he grumbled. "Once I get you safely to Clarence Seymour, I will have to return to Key West, to go in search of it. Surely retracing my steps will uncover it."

Natalie smiled smugly. She was glad that she had never given him the key. If it meant so much to him, then wouldn't he continue to suffer by not having it? Though it was a silent revenge, it satisfied her. It gave her a delicious sense of power, knowing that she had something of value that she could keep from him.

Bryce peered around the edge of a fringed swag at the window, checking to see if the moon-splashed sails of his ship were in sight. He had given strict instructions to his first mate Dominic to be ready to set sail the minute he stepped on board with his prize. He had dropped anchor away from the busiest wharves. Though dark, a tied and gagged passenger being forced aboard his ship could cause serious repercussions. Bryce was trying, at all cost, to keep the truth of Natalie's abduction from reaching Saul Palmer. Bryce had too much to do to risk a battle with that old man of the sea . . . his own father.

"We're just about there," he said, gazing intensely toward Natalie. He hated taking her by force. By doing so, he was lessening his chances of her ever trusting him again. But this was a risk he had to take. By delivering Natalie to Clarence Seymour, he was not only making her more accessible to himself but at the same time getting even with Saul Palmer who had blackened Bryce's name by being his father.

Ah, the web of life . . . he thought to himself. Saul Palmer hadn't just lost a daughter, but he had in her place gained a son.

Natalie struggled with her bonds, fuming inside. Once on the ocean, there would be no chance to escape. She had to make her move soon, or all would be lost to her. Her eyes wavered as she found Bryce staring at her. She just couldn't understand this man. He had seemed to love her, yet now she only appeared to be an inanimate object to be bought and paid for—a prize, taken by a pirate.

"You are a pirate, aren't you?" she said, jaws set. "What is whispered about you is true."

"I'm sure there have been many things whispered about everyone," he said thickly. "I am no exception."

"Bryce, you've always managed to evade the question," she snapped. "By not answering you are in a sense admitting the ugly truth."

Bryce laughed softly. "Beautiful lady, the truth is I am a most respected banker in New Orleans," he said, glancing from behind a swag again. "I own my own bank. One I'm damn proud of."

Natalie leaned forward, flipping her fallen hair back from her eyes. "But, Bryce," she murmured. "Your ship. What you're doing with me . . ." Her gaze traveled over him, remembering the golden attire that she had last seen him in. "Your clothes. Why . . . ?"

His face was directed to hers again. "I am also a salvor," he said flatly. "One who rescues the crews and the goods of ships that have been wrecked at sea."

"A salvor?" Natalie whispered. "Yes, I am familiar with the reputation of a salvor. My father has explained their connection with the Key West waterfront auctions. Most are a respected lot. But, Bryce, a salvor does not take a woman captive. Why are you doing this?"

"Because it is in your best interest," he argued. "You should be with your true blood relation. You should even detest Saul Palmer now that you know the truth. And if you really think about it, I'll bet he is somehow responsible for your mother dying at such a young age."

Tears streamed from Natalie's eyes, anger and remorse intermingling inside her. "I just can't believe any of this," she murmured. Then she forced a stiff upper lip. "I won't believe it," she snapped.

Her heart stilled when she felt the carriage come to a halt. She tensed her back, listening. It was quite evident where the carriage had taken her. The slap-slap of the waves against the shoreline and the creaking of the moored ships sounded to the one side of her. The aroma of sea water and fish drifted lethargically through the carriage door as the coachman opened it.

"I don't want to gag you, Natalie," Bryce said, pulling a silk neckerchief from a front trousers' pocket. "But I will if I have to. What must it be? Will you go quietly to my ship?"

"Yes," she said quietly. "I'll not utter a sound." No. She wouldn't scream but she would run. As soon as she stepped foot onto the wooden flooring of the pier. He had been foolish to tie only her hands.

"Why have you decided suddenly to be cooperative?" Bryce asked, lifting an eyebrow. "I can't believe the fight has gone out of you. What are you up to, Natalie?"

"Can't you guess?" she purred, teasing him with the soft flutter of her lashes.

"Eh . . . ?"

"You, Bryce," she murmured, tilting her head. She ran her tongue seductively across her upper lip, wetting it. "I want to be with you. At least the sea voyage will allow us to be together as never before."

Bryce chuckled amusedly. He took her by the elbow and propelled her toward the door. "Natalie, if you think I believe that, then you must think I'm daft," he said. "You're so angry with me at this moment the last thing on your mind is making love. Come on. Step down from the carriage. My ship waits."

Feeling her anxious heart pounding against her ribs, she did as he bid. But what she hadn't counted on was the force with which he held her to him as he began to lead her toward a beautiful, three-masted ship. Beneath the full moon, the ship's sails shone as if they were giant ghosts fluttering in the night. And though the breeze was light, she could almost feel the ship strain to be free of its moorings as she heard the wind catch against canvas in a sound almost a groan and a sigh.

Looking back over her shoulder, Natalie saw how quiet the waterfront was. Had all deserted their duties to go and partake in Albert's masquerade ball? How was it that no one was about to give her a helping hand?

But a wider span of vision was handed her when she was guided up the gangplank and she found that Bryce had moored his ship at a wharf unknown to her. There were no other ships about, nor waterfront buildings. Yes, he had planned this escape quite well. She had no other direction to go now but straight ahead, on to his ship. Her next chance to escape would have to be after her arrival in New Orleans. Surely there would be a ship's captain whom she could promise to pay if he returned her to Saul Palmer. Saul Palmer was known for his riches.

Stepping down onto a pure, white deck, Natalie found herself almost glad Bryce's arm was holding her securely against him. The ship was a hubbub of activity carried on by many strange-looking men, and once Bryce was noticed, Natalie could tell that the crew was quickly making ready for departure from the quay. Suddenly one man stepped forward. He was a burly sort, even taller than Bryce, and was attired in a loose white shirt with flowing sleeves and glossy black, snug breeches. His carrot-colored hair reached beyond his shoulders and his face was hard and determined.

"Heave anchor and set sail," Bryce ordered, saluting the man. "Dominic, let's get the sails filling and set our course for New Orleans."

Dominic's voice was almost a growl as he glared toward Natalie. "This one'll be trouble, eh, Cap'n?" he said. "You've never brought one on board by force before."

Bryce set a hand heavily on Dominic's shoulder. "Dominic, don't forget who is captain here and who is first mate," he said flatly. "Natalie is my concern. Getting the ship safely to New Orleans is yours."

Dominic's dark eyes flashed. "Aye, aye, air," he growled. "But I still don't like it. I've never liked women aboard our ship. Especially one who's hands are bound. Bad luck. I know she'll be bad luck."

181

"Be on with you, Dominic," Bryce sighed. "Save your growlings for the crew. It's them who can bring you a piece of bad luck if not handled well."

"Aye," Dominic yelled across his shoulder, moving away from them.

Natalie had absorbed each of Dominic's words. She had most definitely heard the reference made to other women. She begrudgingly followed alongside Bryce as they moved on down a short flight of steps and into a dark passageway which showed only a few closed doors on each side. Their way was lit by dim flickerings from whale-oil lamps on one side wall. "So you've done this before," Natalie snapped, tripping a bit on the skirt of her dress as Bryce swung her around to lead her into a cabin.

"What?" he asked, urging her down onto a plush, gold leather settee.

"Women," she hissed. "You've apparently shared this very cabin with many women."

As her gaze moved about her, she was unable not to be impressed. A whale-oil lamp revealed several matching chairs and a nice-sized bed which sat beneath a beautiful stained-glass skylight. Mahogany panels glistened on all four walls and a large oak desk showed an exuberant amount of paperwork strewn across it.

Bryce slipped off his flashy flowered shirt and stretched his sinewy arms over his head, yawning. "There have been women," he drawled. "Many women before you." His blue eyes twinkled as his lips curved in a small smile. "And believe me, Natalie, none have had to be forced as you have."

Jealousy sent pinpricks of pain into her heart. Yet she would never let him know this. Suddenly he had become her enemy. "I will always fight for my rights," she said haughtily. She did not want to see how his muscles flexed so invitingly as he stepped from his bright, red breeches. She didn't want to feel that weakness in her knees occasioned by his half nudity. The warmth rising to her cheeks caused her embarrassment when Bryce stepped before her and tilted her chin upward so that their eyes could meet.

"Even for the right to share my bed this night?" he said thickly.

Natalie gasped. "You have my wrists tied . . . you force me aboard your ship . . . yet you think I would want to . . ."

Bryce fell to his knees before her and busied himself at untying her wrists. Then he took both her hands in his and tenderly kissed each palm. Being once more drawn into his magnetic spell, Natalie felt the slow warmth taking over inside her. It was a delicious sort of feeling, as though she were standing in a slow tropical rain, absorbing it and its sweet freshness one single pore at a time.

But the clanking of the rising anchor and the jerk of the ship as it moved from the quay drew her back to her present dilemma.

In one fast movement she was at the cabin door and had it open, but was met with a wild spray of water on her face and Bryce's forceful hands around her waist.

"Come back in here, Natalie," he growled. "Damn it, do I have to tie you to a chair for the entire voyage?"

Natalie fell clumsily back against the bed as Bryce slammed the cabin door shut and slid the heavy bolt lock across it. Feeling completely beat now, Natalie threw herself down onto the bunk and began sobbing. "We're already out to sea," she cried. "How could you, Bryce? How could you?"

Bryce settled on the bed beside her. He reached a hand to her face and wiped her wet hair back from her eyes. "Darling, one day you'll thank me," he murmured. "This has to be right for you. I only wish I could have returned you to your rightful father many years ago. The adjustment will be hard."

He swallowed uneasily. "I know," he said. "I have my own cross to bear. I've just been recently made aware of secrets kept from me for even more years than you."

Leaning up on an elbow, she sniffled. "But you have no one forcing you to accept what you don't want to accept," she hissed. "If I were a man, I'd show you—"

Bryce silenced her words by the sudden onslaught of his lips against hers. A hand moved over her, settling on a breast, cupping it. The burning ache was troubling his loins and he could feel the heat rising higher and higher.

Natalie didn't want to respond, but his kiss was causing her to be awash with desire that could not be quelled. And his hand on her breast was making her heart race out of control.

Bryce nibbled at her lips. "Thank God you are not a man," he said huskily.

"If . . . I . . . were—" she argued, moaning hungrily when his lips drew the breath from her as he once more kissed her with a hungry, reckless passion. Her mind and body fused with her need as she slowly laced her arms around his neck. She was aware of the hard strength of him as he pressed his thighs into hers. She responded to the virile male magnetism of him. She twined her fingers into his hair and, closing off her earlier frustration and hurt, let his hands take control.

While his tongue searched inside her mouth, sending spasms of delight crashing like thundering waves throughout her, his hands were deftly removing her dress. When her breasts were fully exposed she guided his head down and threw her own head back in a rapturous ecstasy when his mouth searched and found the stiff, throbbing peak of a nipple that was waiting to be washed with the love of his lips.

Writhing, Natalie leaned into him and waited patiently as he completed his task of unclothing her, even down to her shoes. Her eyes became hazy with desire when he stepped from the last of his clothes and once more revealed his male strength to her. Then her senses slowly reeled when his lips began to slowly nibble at her toes, and traveled up the calf of her leg to the responsive spot that ached for him. When his tongue speared her there, Natalie opened more. The devotion of his mouth caused a sweet pain which urged her to reach out to him, to become lost in him—heart, body and soul. All she wanted was him. The force inside her had become almost a torture.

"Bryce . . . please . . ." she whispered. "I can hardly hold off any longer."

"Natalie . . ." he sighed and rose farther up on her. A shudder of drugged passion breathed through him as he locked his arms about her. Feeling the upward arch of her body, he slowly fit his hardness inside her and began to draw magic into himself as she began to work with him.

Natalie was transformed by the thrill of their union. The voyage had suddenly taken on a different light. How could she not have remembered how he could send her into another world, one full of joyous swirling sensual colors? She strained herself upward, breathless with the sudden need of release. Her hands traveled over his back. She clasped his hips ever closer to hers. She was drifting, blazing, then shuddering as her passion crested in one bright flash of glory and his body also shook with violent tremors against hers.

Once she had descended from her silky cloud of pleasure, Natalie rose quickly from the bed, red-faced and disappointed in herself and the uncontrollable needs of her flesh. Stooping, she swept her petticoat up into her arms and held it in front of her, quite aware of Bryce's eyes following her every movement.

"Seems you don't only hold me captive," she said coolly with the toss of her head. "I can't seem to help it that my heart is also your victim."

She pulled her petticoat angrily over her head and straightened it over the sensual curves of her body. With hands on her hips, she defied him. "This one time will be the last, though," she said haughtily. "I won't let you near me again."

Bryce watched her in silent amusement, stretched leisurely on his back. He lifted his lips in a smile and gave her a slow wink.

NEW ORLEANS

Look from thy window, and see
My passion and my pain.

—Taylor

NINE

Along Orleans Street, houses stood shoulder to shoulder, each with balconies of ornate ironwork. The street was not paved but had narrow, brick walks which clung close to the facade of the brick and plaster houses.

Brenda Seymour stepped in and out of the shadows of the balconies, the darkness of the late evening hours giving her a cover under which to go to Adam Palmer, her partner in crime and her ardent lover.

Attired in a hooded, black velveteen cape, she rushed breathlessly on; she had thought her father would never retire to bed for the evening. Since Bryce Fowler had entered their lives with his tale, Brenda's father hadn't been the same. A love he had thought he had lost all those years ago was now haunting his every breathing moment.

"And he even thinks he has another daughter," she scoffed aloud. "Doesn't he know that one daughter is all he can handle? I've tried his patience more than not."

She circled her fingers around a key in her cape pocket. "And if he ever suspected I was letting Adam search through his ledgers, he would most surely disown me. . . ."

Not having wanted to worry Brenda with the full details he had gathered after she had taken her leave from the bank, Clarence hadn't told her any further news of the past that Bryce Fowler had brought suddenly back to the present. Brenda was glad. The less she knew, the easier it was to scoff at the tale. She was glad that names hadn't been mentioned except Natalie's . . . the sister she was supposed to have. No last name had been spoken. But, yes, it did not matter to Brenda. She didn't ever want to hear the name Natalie again!

Not wishing to think about the possibility of having a sister and the disruption her entry into Brenda's life would cause, Brenda made a quick turn and headed toward the buildings that lined the river front. Lamps flared dimly in the fog. Through this misty haze, Brenda could make out tall-masted ships and paddle wheelers moored side by side on the Mississippi River. Green bunches of fruit gave a vivid touch of color to the wharves where a throng of men were being kept busy unloading bananas from a ship.

"Brenda . . ."

Brenda stopped short and peered into the darkness; then she smiled her wicked smile when she saw Adam step from the shadows. She rushed toward him and threw her arms about his neck. "Adam," she whispered. "I'm so glad you've come."

"You've brought your father's key?" Adam asked in his deep growl of a voice.

"Yes . . ." she murmured, clinging. His dark eyes showed their usual cold hardness and his attire of black made her heart race. She liked sharing everything with him. The realization that he was a pirate made her drive for danger and excitement even greater.

"Then let's be on our way," Adam said, brusquely brushing her aside. "I don't like all the activity on the wharves. I hadn't counted on a banana shipment to cause such a stir in New Orleans' population."

Brenda sulked a minute as she moved along close beside him, never understanding his moods. But knowing this was his way, she linked an arm through his and just accepted him for what he was. She didn't have enough time with him as it was. She wasn't about to waste precious moments arguing about why he didn't even kiss her this time.

"There's no need to worry about these men helping unload the bananas," she encouraged. "Most are not residents of New Orleans. Most are sailors from tramp schooners putting in an idle night's work. No one will pay any attention to a light shining from my father's office windows."

"And your father is at home, fast asleep?"

"He appeared to be asleep."

"The key, Brenda," Adam said, stepping up to a solid, oak door. He opened a palm to her, waiting.

Feeling only a slight stirring of guilt, Brenda gazed upward at the six stories of this brick building which housed Seymour's Import/Export facilities. The many windows, though they were dark, resembled eyes staring accusingly back at her. But having done this one other time without being discovered, she drew the key from inside her pocket and determinedly placed it in Adam's outstretched hand.

The door creaked ominously as Brenda stepped inside with Adam. "Where's a lamp?" he whispered.

Feeling around, Brenda found one on a desk. "Here,"

she whispered back. She lifted the chimney from the kerosene lamp and watched as Adam set his burning match to the wick.

"Don't screw the wick up much," he said, shaking his match out. "We can't chance much light. Just enough to see our way up the stairs, to your father's private office."

Brenda replaced the chimney onto the lamp and let the soft flicker of light guide her and Adam across the room toward the darker shadows of the staircase. Lifting it, she nodded for Adam to go on ahead of her. Then after glancing back across her shoulder and thinking the many chairs and desks appeared to be animals crouching in the dark, she shivered and followed along behind him.

"Adam, I sometimes feel that you care nothing for me at all," she said softly, watching his majestic stride as he stepped up on the second-floor landing and moved on up to the next flight of stairs. "You only take . . . never give."

"You knew me for what I was from the beginning," he grumbled.

"Yes, I know," Brenda sighed. "But surely you can manage to spend more time with me. Your love affair with the *Sea Snake* keeps you traveling the seas much too much."

Adam turned and glowered toward her. "In my business I am taken anywhere, anytime," he said. "You know that. Now keep your voice down. When we reach the safety of your father's office, then say what comes to your mind."

Brenda didn't want anger to possess her. Yet she didn't like being scolded by anyone. Not even Adam! She brushed on past him, chin tilted haughtily. Turning, she leaned her face into his. "Adam, if it wasn't for me, you wouldn't have even known about my father's shipment of opium,'' she hissed. ''Now treat me respectfully, or I shall never tell you a thing again.''

Adam grabbed her by a wrist. His eyes darkened menacingly. ''I don't like to be threatened,'' he snarled. ''If you don't help me, I'll manage quite well, Brenda.''

''But you wouldn't have access to my father's records,'' she snapped back, wincing when he tightened his hold on her wrist.

''Do you truly think a locked door would keep me out?'' he laughed scornfully. ''Brenda, don't be so naïve.''

Her eyes narrowed angrily. ''Then why do you even bother with me, Adam?'' she hissed.

''As long as I do have you to aid in these adventures, why take chances I don't have to take?'' he said flatly. ''Now. Are you going to shut up or am I going to have to lock you in a room until I'm finished with what I have to do?''

Brushing the hood from her head, Brenda turned around and stomped on up the stairs until the door that led into her father's private office was reached. She watched with a pounding heart as Adam worked the doorknob and then slowly pushed the door open.

''Bring the lamp,'' he ordered. ''I don't want to take all night.''

Almost hating him at this moment, Brenda moved begrudgingly into the room. Then, seeing her father's spacious oak desk, she withdrew a bit. She was remembering the many times as a child when he had sat at this desk with her on his lap. With one arm he had held her in a tender embrace while with his free hand he had diligently placed figures in his ledger. He had tried to be both mother and father, yet that hadn't been enough. From birth, there had been an untamed wildness in Brenda just waiting to be unleashed. With Adam, she had found a way to release some of these tensions; yet she still hadn't experienced enough. She now hungered for the time he would take her with him on his *Sea Snake*. . . .

"Place the lamp on the desk," Adam said, already searching through papers in cupboards that lined one whole side wall.

"Adam, you must be careful," Brenda said, seeing the disorder he was creating. "You mustn't cause suspicion by leaving my father's office any way but how you found it."

"Just you let me worry about that," he growled. "I don't want to leave any stone unturned. If there's any reference made to future shipments that I can get my hands on, I want to find it."

Brenda set the lamp down on her father's desk; then she unbuttoned her cape at the neck and let it hang loosely from around her shoulders. Frowning, she went along behind Adam and placed everything back in order as he moved from cupboard to cupboard. If things weren't put exactly in place, then her father would have reason to suspect her. Only one man held a key to this building and that was the owner . . . Clarence Seymour. It wouldn't take long for him to figure out who else had easy access to it.

"I can't find a damn thing," Adam growled. He went to the desk and began scattering papers and throwing them onto the floor.

"Adam . . ." Brenda said, covering her mouth with a hand.

He moved around behind the desk and tried to open

one drawer and then another. "Locked," he snarled. He hit at the drawers. "They weren't locked before."

"Adam, maybe we'd better leave," Brenda said, hurriedly picking up the papers from the floor. "Something isn't right here. Maybe father suspects."

Adam ran his fingers through his hair. "The ledgers," he said. "They're surely locked inside these drawers."

Brenda went to Adam and framed his face between her hands. "Adam, you must listen to me," she whispered. "We must leave here. Things aren't right. Father has never locked his ledgers away inside a drawer. Since I was a child they've always been displayed on the top of his desk. This could . . . be . . . a trap."

"But . . . why . . . ?"

"The opium shipment, Adam," Brenda said softly. "No one but the crew knew of the opium shipment. Father has to have guessed how an outsider found out."

"The ledger—"

"Yes. The ledger. *I* showed you the ledger."

Adam brushed her hands aside and clasped her shoulders. "As I will once again see the ledger," he said flatly. "It is now up to you to find the key to his desk."

"Oh, Adam," Brenda sighed. "Must I?"

"Yes," he growled. "The opium showed me the worth of your father's shipments. I now want all access to his future dealings. I want to know what and when. It makes my ventures much easier. Do you understand?"

"But, Adam, the opium alone will make you rich," she argued. "Why must you take more from my father?"

"I can't make a trade for the opium yet," he said. "Too many ports are watching for it. So I'd like to take a prize that I can trade right off without arousing suspicion."

"All right . . ." Brenda sighed. "But you will have to wait. I refuse to take the chance of getting that key for you tonight."

"It's too late to do anything else about it tonight," Adam said, swinging away from her. He lifted the lamp and headed toward the door. "Let's go to my ship. I've other things on my mind now."

"And what might that be, Adam?" she whispered, slinking up next to him. She clung to his arm as they began a slow descent of the stairs.

His free arm circled her waist. "You, my wicked wench," he growled. "Besides my adventures on the *Sea Snake*, you also have ways of warming my blood. I've yet to find anyone who quite compares to you."

Brenda's heart skipped a beat. What would he do if he were to meet this woman who so resembled her? Would she even take Brenda's place in Adam's heart? It puzzled Brenda that Adam could be from Key West and not have met this woman with whom Bryce Fowler had become so enamored. Surely Adam didn't keep that low a profile. Yet, he had told her he did everything possible not to draw attention to himself. It would be too easy to make comparisons between him and the man dressed in black who commanded the *Sea Snake*.

Brenda was relieved when the first-floor landing was finally reached. She couldn't help but worry about being caught. She had to wonder what her father would do if he ever found out.

"Let's hurry on," Adam whispered. "And blow that damned light out."

"All right," Brenda whispered back. Then her words caught in her throat when she heard a rattling at the front door. She looked quietly toward the doorknob and saw

196

that it was being tried.

"My God . . ." she whispered, placing her free hand to her throat. "Maybe it's father."

Adam jerked the lamp away from her and blew the flames out. Then, with quiet, catlike steps, he went to the door and pulled a corner of its dark, green shade aside. His shoulders slumped with relief.

Brenda stood frozen on the spot, eyes wide. "Who is it, Adam?" she whispered.

Adam laughed hoarsely. "Some waterfront scum," he scoffed. "Come on," he urged, motioning with a hand.

"But, Adam—"

"Come on," he growled. He set the lamp down on a desk. "We'll leave by the back door. We'll follow the water line to my ship."

Once more clinging to Adam's arm, Brenda followed him in the dark. Their route, punctuated by fumbling and bumping into things, finally led them to the door that led to a private wharf. Standing in the damp chill of the sea breeze, Brenda slipped the hood back on her head, then went, like a ghost in the night, with Adam to his ship.

Breathless, she watched as Adam closed his cabin door. She swung the cape from her shoulders and eased down onto a chair, panting. Her hair was clinging to the perspiration on her brow and her low-swept dress revealed the heaving of her chest. She closed her eyes and held her head back against the chair. She always felt safe on Adam's fancy ship. Though it wasn't the *Sea Snake*, it was one of the most impressive ships that traveled the sea. It smelled strongly of tobacco, since that was the only cargo ever to be placed in this ship's hold. And its dark, mahogany paneled walls and plush, red leather furnishings smelled of fresh wax and cleaning products.

Lips being applied on the exposed flesh of her breast drew Brenda's eyes slowly open. With one sweep of her eyes, she saw that Adam had already discarded his clothes. The door was bolt-locked and a whale-oil lamp flickered in soft tones upon a waiting bed.

Without further adieu, Brenda kicked her shoes from her feet and rose to undress slowly before his feasting eyes.

"And shall I pour us a glass of port?" Adam chuckled, strolling casually toward a wine cabinet.

Brenda's eyes traveled over his masculine frame, seeing the broadness of his shoulders, his slim trunk and the dark tendrils of hair that scattered across his chest and down to where he showed that he was ready to share the most ultimate of adventures with her. . . .

"Yes," she purred, reaching to toss her long, lustrous hair back across her shoulders. Laughing wickedly, she approached him and ran her fingers over his body, feeling smug when she saw the rippling of his flesh. It was at times like this that she felt the power she held over him. When unclothed, he became vulnerable, no longer a fierce pirate, but a man . . . a humble, eager to please man.

Bending, to place a brief kiss on his risen sex, she watched his face become distorted, as though he were in agony. She then went to the bed and slithered onto it, laughing throatily as he handed her a long-stemmed glass filled with sparkling red wine.

He settled down next to her. "And what shall we drink to?" he said thickly, eying her greedily.

"To us," Brenda murmured. "To us and all that we shall conquer together."

Adam raised a dark, thick eyebrow. "Eh?" he questioned.

Brenda moved to her knees and leaned into his face. "Adam, I want to go with you on the *Sea Snake*'s next voyage," she said huskily. "I want to experience what you experience. Just hearing about your adventures is no longer enough. I want to feel what you feel when you approach a ship to take it as your own. Adam, you must let me. You must."

"My ship's crew would not approve," he grumbled. "They all feel that a woman aboard would give the ship bad luck. No. It wouldn't work."

"Oh, Adam," she scoffed, settling down on crossed legs. "That's so foolish. It's even childish to be so superstitious." She turned the glass between her fingers, seeing her reflection in the liquid. An evil glint appeared in her eyes. "I will tell you a secret, if you promise to take me with you, Adam," she teased, now lifting her thick veil of lashes in his direction. She hadn't planned to tell Adam about Bryce Fowler and the possibility that he might be a threat to Adam's future sea ventures. She hadn't known much about why her father had contacted Bryce, but she had guessed that it had to do with the missing opium shipment because her father did his banking elsewhere, not at Fowler's Bank of New Orleans.

At first Brenda hadn't thought this important enough to tell Adam, but now she could use the information for a better purpose. In a sense, she could use it to blackmail Adam into giving her her way.

"No matter what approach you try to get me to take you with me, I will refuse," he said flatly. He tapped his glass against hers. "To tonight," he said hoarsely. "Only tonight."

Brenda's eyes narrowed as her lips lifted into a sly

grin. She would show him how she got what she wanted from a man. In the end, she would be the victor. "To us," she mused.

She lifted the glass to her lips and tipped it, feeling the warmth of the wine move slowly down her throat. And once it was all consumed, she tossed the glass aside as he also did, both lost in laughter as the tinkle of breaking glass reverberated throughout the cabin.

"Come here, you witch," Adam growled. He lowered himself over her and crushed her lips beneath his. His fingers cupped a breast and squeezed it while she fit her legs up and around his waist.

In one stroke, he was inside her, already feverishly working his body with hers.

Hearing his low moan, she tightened her legs about his hips, causing him to lose freedom of movement.

"Brenda . . . what the . . . ?" he growled. His eyes were dark pools of passion, ebbed with an unfulfilled need.

"Promise me I can go on your ship with you, Adam," she hissed, holding herself firm. Her hands circled behind him and locked into his hair. Slowly pulling, she watched his eyes close to the pain.

"Promise me, Adam. . . ."

"Yes . . ." he panted. "Soon . . ."

Brenda released both her hands and legs and sighed heavily. "Oh, Adam, I *do* love you so," she whispered. When his lips parted hers and found the cavern of her mouth eager for his tongue, Brenda gave in to the pleasure he was so skillfully arousing inside her.

As his palms moved seductively over her, she was even more awakened to the wild excitement building in her. Then much too quickly, the magical fire burning rampant inside her spread out for an instant, glowing bright, only to be snuffed out by the cool breeze of evening as he shuddered momentarily and quickly withdrew from her.

Grabbing one of her wrists, Adam almost growled out his words. "Don't you ever try anything like that again, Brenda," he said darkly.

She felt the pain at her wrist and tried to jerk free. But no amount of struggling helped. He held her, as though in a vise. "I don't know what you're talking about, Adam," she said silkily, yet feeling fear in her heart when she saw his eyes darken even more.

"I should have slapped you silly," he spat angrily. "But you know the depth of my needs. You knew that I was powerless at that point."

"Adam . . . I . . ." she said, swallowing hard. His hand across her face made her neck snap with the jolt.

"That little secret you were toying with," he said, dropping her wrist as though she were a limp, rag doll. He rose from the bed and stepped into his breeches. "If you want to see daylight again, I'd suggest you enlighten me on this subject of secrets."

Feeling dejected and with a slow throbbing headache engulfing her, she shied away from him. She rubbed her aching jaw, glowering toward him. "I was only jesting," she said flatly. "There is no secret." She would never tell him. *Never.* He had never been this cold-hearted before. Yet, she had to remember . . . she hadn't either! Had she been a man, she would be ready to kill for having been as humiliated as he had been by her insensitive use of her power.

Stepping to a wardrobe, Adam withdrew a polished cutlass. Testing its edge with a thumb, he went and stood over her. "Seems you forget who you are in the presence of," he said icily. He leaned the cutlass down close to her throat. "Now, do you want to tell me the truth?"

With a feverish heartbeat, Brenda inched back against the wall. "You . . . wouldn't," she whispered shakily.

"Test me further," he snarled.

"But, Adam . . ."

The sharp edge of the cutlass made contact with her flesh. Afraid to move, she whispered: "Adam, I will tell you. Just . . . please . . . remove that thing."

Adam placed the cutlass on a chair and doubled over with laughter. "I never thought I'd see the day Brenda Seymour would fear anything," he shouted. "But your life is of some importance, eh?"

Seething, Brenda rose quickly from the bed. She reached for her clothes and began dressing. "It is *I* who should use a cutlass against your throat," she hissed. "That is not a funny game you just played on me."

Adam took two steps and had her helpless beneath his grip of steel. "It was no game," he growled. "Just because I was amused at your reaction didn't mean that *I* was playing a game. No. I want the truth, witch. And now."

"Adam, I never know what to expect from you one minute to the next," she sighed, squirming against his hold.

"My next move? Maybe it's to let you walk the plank, to send you into a school of swarming sharks."

Blanching, Brenda held her chin taut. Then she said: "Do you know a man by the name of Bryce Fowler?"

A slow, soft laugh rumbled through Adam. "Ah, yes," he said. "The man who persists in chasing me in his *Golden Isis*. What about him?"

"I think my father may have hired him to cause you some problems."

Adam stepped back away from her, kneading his chin. "What sort of problems?"

Brenda finished dressing, then began slipping into her shoes. "I think it has to do with the missing opium shipment," she murmured. "I'm sure he's been hired to go in search of it."

Amused, Adam tossed his head absently. "Let him give me chase," he said icily. "Maybe this time I'll let him catch me. It could be fun taking his ship as my next prize."

"And there's something else about that man," Brenda said, combing her midnight black hair with her fingers.

"And what is that?" Adam asked, pouring himself a glass of wine.

"Bryce Fowler told my father something that I found quite strange."

Adam tipped the wine to his lips, watching her. "Well? What is it?" he demanded, circling the glass between his fingers.

Brenda bent to rescue her cape from the floor, shaking particles of the broken wineglass from its folds. "He, this Bryce Fowler, said that he had seen a woman in Key West who so resembles me, she could be me," she said quietly. She took a step backward when she saw the rush of alarm enter Adam's eyes. Then she gasped noisily when he smashed the glass between his fingers.

"I've feared this day would come," he snarled. His face had become red cast and he began to pace the floor. Then he turned on a heel and boldly faced her. "And what did your father say?" he said guardedly.

"He said that she might be my sister . . . that . . .

203

that my mother Kathryn had been taken by a pirate.''

Adam started flailing his arms. ''Enough . . . enough,'' he shouted. He went to Brenda and clasped her shoulders forcefully. ''And then what? What's to be done about this?''

Brenda's heart raced. ''Adam, you're scaring me,'' she cried. ''It's as though . . . as though—''

''As though I already knew?'' he finished.

''Well . . . yes.''

''Well, I do,'' he stated flatly. ''This woman Bryce Fowler has seen is my stepsister Natalie.''

Brenda's heart plummeted. She suddenly felt deathly ill. But what did it all mean? ''Adam, how can she be . . . ?'' she whispered.

''Didn't Bryce Fowler reveal the name of Natalie's family to your father?''

''I left the room before—''

''Then you failed to hear that Natalie is the daughter—in truth the stepdaughter—of Saul Palmer . . . not even that since he never did marry her mother Kathryn.''

''Her . . . mother's name is Kathryn?'' she questioned, paling even more. ''God, Adam, I don't understand.''

''Brenda, she is your sister,'' he said hoarsely. ''My father was the pirate who abducted your mother all those years ago.''

Brenda teetered a bit. ''Oh, my God . . .'' she murmured.

''But you still haven't told me what else was said between Fowler and your father,'' Adam said, strengthening his grip.

''Adam, my father has also hired Bryce Fowler . . . to . . . go and rescue my sister and mother,'' she whis-

pered, finding it hard to actually speak those words: *sister
. . . mother*.

Adam's eyes went wild. He dropped his arms to his
side, stunned. "He . . . what?" he gasped.

"Yes, he has," Brenda said. Then she placed a hand
on Adam's arm. "Is my mother—"

Adam shook his head. "No. She's now been dead for
sixteen years," he said solemnly.

Biting her lower lip, Brenda turned her back to him.
"She's dead," she whispered. "My mother's dead."

Adam went to Brenda and rushed her toward the door.
"You must go now," he said. "I've things to attend to."

Swinging around, anger flashing in her eyes, Brenda
narrowed her lips into a straight line. "You can reveal
such truths to me then so coldly send me on my way?"
she cried. "Adam, you have no heart."

"I was poured from your same mold, witch," he
growled. "We are the same, you and I. You'll get over
the shock of the moment and be ready to ride the sea with
me as you have been longing to do."

Brenda's pulse raced. "Adam, can I . . . really?" she
sighed.

"You've earned many voyages on my *Sea Snake* this
night," he said flatly.

Brenda threw her arms about his neck and hugged him
tightly. "Oh, Adam, I'm sorry for talking in such an ugly
way to you," she cried. "I only want to make you
happy." Then she withdrew slowly from him, suddenly
silent, her color paling.

"Adam . . ." she said shallowly. "If my . . . my sister looks so much like me, how is it you can come to me
and—"

"Because until now, I've always had to pretend she

205

was my true sister," he said huskily. "When holding you, I—"

Something tore at Brenda's heart. "My God . . ." she whispered. "What have I done by telling you the truth?"

Adam laughed amusedly and drew her back into his arms. He tilted her chin with a forefinger. "Witch, I was only jesting," he said. "There's a world of difference between you two sisters. And I prefer the one with fire in her veins."

Brenda's eyes wavered. She wondered if she could ever be sure of him again.

TEN

"Though it's a late hour, I've sent a messenger ahead to tell Clarence Seymour of our arrival," Bryce said, leaning against the swaying of the carriage as it moved over the uneven cobblestones of the streets of New Orleans. He placed his cigar between his lips and eyed Natalie out of the corner of his eyes. He felt as though she were a tigress, ready to pounce at the first opportunity. There was even a wildness in her eyes.

Shivering from the tension and the cool of the night, Natalie hugged her arms about her chest. Still in the same dress she had been wearing when abducted, she felt less than presentable. Bryce had forgotten one thing about a woman. Her pride in herself and her appearance. If she was going to have to meet this Clarence Seymour, she most certainly would have rather done it in a dignified way.

She cast Bryce a sideways glance and saw that he was watching her. Not wanting to give him the satisfaction of knowing that she was the least bit unsettled, she sighed and relaxed her arms onto her lap. There was no getting out of this. She must get by in any way she could for the moment. Then, later, when alone, she would make her move. He would not hold her against her will. Not with ships moored at the river front—ships that traveled day and night to Key West. She might even run into Adam! She knew that he had delivered shipments of cigars to New Orleans. Yes, she would search him out at the first opportunity!

"Cold?" Bryce asked, slipping an arm about her shoulders. "I wish I could have had a shawl to offer you. But I don't make a habit of traveling with women's apparel on my ship."

"Hah!" she scoffed. "I don't know why not. You most certainly must have had your pick of women. I'm surprised you don't have a complete wardrobe to offer your 'prizes,' as you must surely think of me now that you have succeeded at bringing me to this city to hand me over to Clarence Seymour."

Bryce chuckled and ran his fingers down over the swell of one of her breasts. "Yes, I've had many," he said thickly. "But none to compare to you."

"Oh, yes, I am sure," she sighed casually.

"I've never asked a woman to be my wife, until you, Natalie," he said, now smoothing his fingertips across the hollow of her throat and upward to the soft curve of her chin.

Feeling the racing of her pulse, Natalie pulled free of him. "Bryce, just leave me alone," she said softly. "I believed you at first. Now I shall never again trust anything you do or say."

Bryce flipped ashes from his cigar. "I was afraid of that," he growled. "But I had no choice. I had to do what was right. You shouldn't have had to live one more moment with Saul Palmer. You will soon be with the true family you've been kept from since your birth.''

His insides rippled. How ironic that he should be telling her what he only recently had found to be true of himself. In a sense, they were two people lost together between two worlds.

"Bryce, please . . ." Natalie sighed lethargically. "I shall never believe this tale. All you're interested in is money. You've just found it to your convenience to capture me since I so foolishly fell into your web of passion. Seems I got even more tangled than I had at first thought possible. If it hadn't been me, it would have been somebody else. Anything to collect some gold."

Bryce furrowed his brow. "Do you forget the resemblance between you and this Brenda Seymour?" he said, tossing his cigar from the carriage window.

"I will only believe that when I see it," she snapped. "And even if I do resemble this woman, that could just be a fluke of nature. It does happen, you know."

"Too many things fall into place," he growled. "Remember the name Kathryn. . . ."

Natalie looked quickly away from him. "I do not wish to hear anymore," she whispered. She placed a finger to her temple, feeling a soft throbbing. Too many things did point to the truth . . . a truth she did not want to accept. She would not let herself believe any of this. She wanted to return home . . . to her father. Surely he was beside himself with worry. He probably had a ship at sea, in search of her. . . .

"I won't say anything else," Bryce said. "I'll just wait and let you see the truth with your own eyes."

Natalie glanced at him, realizing how handsome he was in the flickering light of the lantern. His attire, a navy blue frock coat and matching breeches, was set off by white ruffles at his throat and cuffs. He smelled of men's cologne and cigars, an aroma that made her want to melt into his embrace, though she did hate him at this moment.

Love. Hate. They so often blended into one moving force inside her. It was becoming hard to distinguish between the two.

Inching away from him, Natalie peered from the side window of the carriage, now focusing on her new surroundings. From what she could see beneath the soft flares of the street lanterns, the houses were quite different from those in Key West. These houses were built flush with the sidewalks and had fancy balconies overhanging the streets. At this time of the night, she noticed that most houses were close-shuttered against prying eyes.

There was an intoxication of sorts in the scent of the city; it was heavy with the sweet smell of magnolias and other lush, tropical vegetation. Thick-growing vines of wisteria, with their great, graceful clusters of bluish-lavender blossoms and heavy, green foliage, drooped from along the front of many buildings. Through masonry arches, palm trees could be seen in which were large courtyards lighted by their own private lanterns swaying gently in the breeze.

The soft twanging of a guitar floated almost mysteriously through the air from a cabaret and a man's voice could be heard singing a song of the *toros*. This appeared to be a gentle city, filled with gentle people. In Key West, there was always trouble brewing, both day and night. But that had been attributed to the pirates who had made Key West their home long before the genteel people had arrived.

The carriage coming to a halt drew Natalie from her

thoughts. She tensed when Bryce placed a hand on her arm. Then her heart thundered inside her when the carriage door was thrown open to reveal a large, two-storied house. It was grand, bedecked with black, wrought-iron trim, and its shutters were opened wide at each window, a soft glow of lamplight being emitted from each.

"Natalie, try to relax," Bryce encouraged, squeezing her arm affectionately. "I know this must be hard. In truth, it could be like becoming a new person . . . with a brand new identity. I am aware of the inner turmoil you must be feeling."

"You could never begin to understand what I am feeling at this moment," she murmured. "Bryce, I shall never forgive you for this."

"Be civil, will you, Natalie?" Bryce asked, leaning into her face. "Please do not show Clarence Seymour that his daughter has a spiteful tongue. Let him see you as I know you. As sweet. As loving."

"Oh, hush, Bryce," Natalie fumed. "I do know my manners. You will see that I am quite a lady when meeting strangers. Though I have been abducted, I will still represent the good breeding my father Saul Palmer has taught me from childhood."

"Saul Palmer," Bryce groaned. "Natalie, when will you quit fooling yourself?" He took her by the elbow and guided her across the carriage cushion. "There is only one way to settle this. We must go on inside. You must meet Clarence and his daughter Brenda. Then all arguments will be placed behind you. You will know that you are in your rightful place. You will be home."

Bryce stepped from the carriage and lifted a hand to help Natalie down. Stubbornly, she brushed his hand aside and, lifting the tail of her dress into her arms, stepped on out beside him. When the front door opened just a few feet from where she stood, Natalie quickly drew in her breath at seeing what appeared to be her own shadow standing in the doorway. She grabbed Bryce's arm and looked beseechingly into his eyes, but found that they were saying more than words. They were saying, "I told you so."

"So. You are this Natalie Palmer," Brenda said icily, stepping out from the shadows and letting a lantern's light play across her face. She felt a cold stirring of hate splash through her insides—jealousy—for both her father and Adam were now free to love this woman who professed to being her sister as she saw the resemblance. It was as though she were looking into a mirror.

Natalie covered her mouth with her hands, thinking, too, that she was looking at her own reflection. The sensation was uncanny. It gave her a keen sense of dread. What Bryce had said . . . was it possibly true? Was this a . . . sister . . . she had never known existed.

Oh, yes, surely. How could any two people look so alike?

Her gut began to slowly twist as she thought about her father, Saul Palmer. Had he been a pirate? Had he taken her mother and used—defiled—her? Had he kept her held prisoner? Why had he treated her daughter any better? Natalie had never felt herself a true prisoner. The only times she had felt stifled she had assumed he had loved her so much he hadn't wanted harm to come to her.

Her head began a slow spinning; she was hardly able to accept all these realizations being presented to her so crudely. Surely there could have been a gentler way! Why hadn't Bryce known of a gentler way?

Reeling a bit, Natalie once more grabbed for Bryce's

arm and held securely to it. "Bryce, please take me back to the ship," she pleaded. "I'm not sure I am ready for this. Please . . ."

"Natalie . . ."

A deep voice, gentle and smooth, broke through the silence of the night. "Natalie . . ." Clarence repeated. "My daughter . . . Natalie . . . ?"

Clarence stepped out of the shadows, next to Brenda, tall and lithe, his thick head of gray hair accentuated by the dark brown of his clothes.

Bryce took a step forward, urging Natalie on. He held a hand out to Clarence. "Clarence, it's good to see you again," he said, feeling his damp handshake being returned. Damn. He was glad that he had wired ahead about Clarence's wife Kathryn. The shock of discovering his wife's death and seeing his other daughter for the first time simultaneously could have been too much for his aging heart. Yes, he had been right to wire ahead. Even now, he feared for this man whose eyes were heavy with emotion.

Bryce turned his eyes toward Natalie. "Clarence, this is Natalie," he said softly. "Natalie, this is Clarence Seymour, your true father." He nodded toward Brenda. "And this is your older sister Brenda."

Natalie took a step backward, wary. She glanced first at Bryce, then Clarence, then Brenda. It wasn't real. None of this was real. Surely she was living a dream. No. Not a dream. A nightmare! Only a few weeks back she had been content with her life. A bit restless, but happy with her life-style and with her father . . . the father she had always known. And now? Everything had suddenly changed.

Clarence moved toward Natalie with an outstretched

213

hand. "Natalie, won't you please come into my house?" he said softly. "Let's become acquainted. I know how hard this must be for you."

Natalie swallowed a lump in her throat and nodded a yes toward him. "Yes," she murmured. "It is hard. Quite hard."

"Natalie, it's best if we go inside out of the dampness," Bryce encouraged quietly. "Without a proper wrap, you might catch a chill."

Natalie cast him a hurt-filled glance. "All right," she whispered. He placed a supporting arm around her waist and ushered her slowly forward. As Natalie stepped past Brenda, she smelled a strong aroma of expensive perfume and felt Brenda's cold, steady stare. It was quite apparent that Brenda was more angry than uncomfortable with this situation. That was understandable. Brenda had not shared her father or her life with anyone else, ever. Bryce had explained that Clarence Seymour had never married again, always hoping that his Kathryn might possibly be alive . . . somewhere. . . .

The light from at least fifty tapered, white candles displayed in a cut-glass chandelier lighted Natalie's entrance into a magnificent parlor. Instead of focusing her attention on the people in the room, knowing that she would have to be doing that soon enough, Natalie let her gaze move slowly around.

The softness, the feminine grace of this room, almost took her breath away. It was like nothing she had been accustomed to. In the Palmer's parlor, darkness and hardness had characterized the furnishings and wall décor. In this room, soft-colored, silk-covered sofas took precedence and were heaped with multi-colored, velvet pillows. Seventeeth-century French tables and white dam-

214

ask-covered chairs accented the sofas, and numerous paintings graced the wallpapered walls.

Clarence went to a liquor cabinet where a showcase of crystal beakers and glasses sparkled beneath the light. "Maybe we all need a glass of wine," he said softly.

"Yes," Brenda said, hurrying to his side. "I'm sure *I* need something to help me through the rest of the evening."

Natalie had become suddenly deaf to all words being spoken. Feeling the nervous beating of her heart while standing in a trance like state, she studied a huge portrait hanging, well lighted, above the fireplace mantle.

Flashes of the past began to ignite inside her brain. . . . She was running along the beach, loving the feel of the warm sand sifting between her toes. The hand that was holding hers was so soft . . . so frail. The voice, too, was soft; it was magical. Then Natalie's mother was laughing as she reached down and captured a sand dollar from the surf and handed it to Natalie. Thrilled, Natalie had cupped her mother's face between her hands as her mother knelt down before her.

Natalie had told her mother how much she loved her. Her face, the adorable face of a serene angel, had looked devotedly back at her. . . .

Tears splashed from Natalie's eyes. She was now looking into that face. In the portrait, her mother sat, poised and sweet, her dark eyes radiant with happiness, her cheeks pink from an inner glow.

Hanging her head in her hands, Natalie moaned lightly. "Oh, mother," she whispered. "It took the portrait to truly remember."

She felt a slow spinning in her head and blackness begin to swim before her eyes. Natalie let Bryce rescue her by guiding her to a sofa.

"It can't be, Bryce," she whispered, shaking her head back and forth. "Oh, God. It just can't be."

"But you've seen."

"I don't want to. . . ."

"Natalie . . ." Clarence said, extending a long-stemmed glass of wine down toward her. "Drink this. Maybe it will help."

Natalie turned her eyes slowly upward. She let her gaze take in the faded brown eyes, the long chin and neck, his total thinness. She once more focused on his eyes, seeing almost into his soul, seeing his gentleness. Had he ever spoken a harsh word in his life? In comparing him to Saul Palmer, there was no comparison. Clarence Seymour had surely never known any enemy, but one, the pirate who had taken half his life from him.

"Thank you," Natalie whispered, taking the glass.

Clarence took a step away from her, a heaviness in his movements. "The voyage," he murmured. "Was it pleasant enough?"

"I imagine any voyage on the *Golden Isis* is pleasurable enough," Natalie volunteered. "It was . . . the . . . uh . . . circumstances of my voyage that was not to my personal liking."

Bryce settled down beside Natalie and took her free hand in his. "Natalie, would you rather get into this to-morrow?" he asked quietly. "I'm sure you are tired. Too much at once, I'm sure."

"Maybe a full night's rest would be best," she whispered back, glancing toward Brenda who stood tight-lipped, arms crossed, glaring back at her. Natalie knew there would never be anything but a coldness between the two of them. The look in Brenda's eyes told her—the evil

216

glint that showed her true personality for what it was. It even caused an icy shiver to travel up and down Natalie's spine. She couldn't get out of this house fast enough. Even the portrait of her dear, departed mother wouldn't hold her there. No matter what her true identity was, she only knew one home . . . one father. No matter how Saul Palmer had managed to have her to raise as his own, he had done so, and in the most loving sort of manner. She would not let ill feelings for him enter her heart. If he had been a pirate, that had been long ago. Now? He was a respected gentleman . . . with a respectable business. And she was his daughter. If not by proper birthright, by claim.

Surely her mother had loved him. Why else would she have looked so happy on the beach with her? The same sort of radiance was obvious in the portrait—a portrait that had been painted while she lived with her true husband. One love . . . then another. Yes, it could be possible. Yet, Natalie knew deep down inside her that she could never love anyone as deeply as Bryce.

"If you would prefer to talk tomorrow, that can be arranged," Clarence said, setting his empty glass on a table. He gave Brenda a brief glance. "Take Natalie . . . no . . . take your sister to the room we have prepared for her, Brenda."

Brenda's hands circled into tight fists at her sides. She hated that reference to sister. To her, no one had a rightful claim to that title, and no one had a rightful claim to her father! And, then there was Adam . . . what would he do now?

"Brenda," Clarence repeated. "Please take Natalie to her room."

"Yes, father," Brenda said quietly. She nodded to-

217

ward Natalie and headed up a steep staircase at the far side of the room, opposite the large, stone fireplace. "Come on. Your room is ready. Father even made sure there were roses placed beside your bed."

Natalie flashed Clarence a soft smile. "That was nice of you," she said, handing him her empty glass.

Bryce helped her from the chair. He drew her into his arms and comforted her with a soft embrace. "Things will be all right," he murmured. "You'll see. You'll be glad that I've done this for you."

"Never," she murmured. "Bryce, I feel as if I were a foreigner setting foot on a distant shore. I want to be home. I want to be in my own house."

"You will get used to things in due time," he whispered, caressing her thick mane of midnight black hair. "I'll be back tomorrow. To check on things. I want to do everything I can to make you happy."

Natalie drew back a bit and gazed into his eyes of blue. "There was only one way to make me completely happy," she sighed. "That was to properly court me in Key West. It is quite impossible now. You have proven that it is not myself that you want at all. Why would you have brought me to someone else, when you could have had me all to yourself?"

She eased out of his full embrace and moved on toward the staircase, giving him one more quick glance from across her shoulder. Then, feeling defeated, she lifted the skirt of her dress into her arms and followed Brenda until the landing of the second floor was reached. Family portraits lined the walls of this long and narrow hall. She could feel them watching her as she moved behind Brenda. When a room was opened to her, she found herself in a delicate setting of pale orchid and green carpeting and drapes, and scrolled, expensive furniture made of mahogany.

"I hope you don't plan to stay long," Brenda said icily. "I, for one, will make your stay quite unbearable."

Natalie turned on a heel and faced Brenda. "I'm sure there is no love lost," she said softly. "I, for one, don't plan to stay long. In fact, I may be even gone at the rising of the morning sun."

"I will aid in your escape, if you wish," Brenda said softly. She closed the door behind her and moved on toward Natalie. "I can understand why you wouldn't want to leave the home you have always known." Then she grew clammy cold inside. If she helped to send Natalie back to Key West, wasn't she, in fact, sending her back to Adam? What if Adam's intentions toward her were improper? What if . . . ?

"Why do you hate me so?" Natalie asked, eying Brenda closely. She felt a strange vibration at the pit of her stomach at the sudden realization that this was, indeed, her sister. Now there was no doubt about it in her mind. Yet there was nothing but coldness between them.

"Hate?" Brenda scoffed. "You just think about it. How would you like some strange woman to suddenly enter your life, saying she was your sister?"

"It has just happened to me," Natalie said icily, turning on a heel, moving toward the window. She stared down at the carriage and at Bryce who was just climbing inside it. A part of her ached for him, yet a part of her never wanted to see him again.

"So? What are your plans?" Brenda asked, stepping to Natalie's side.

"I'm not sure," Natalie sighed. She held the skirt of her dress out away from her, seeing the soiled wrinkles of it, even remembering when and where they had been made. Bryce had eased the dress from her shoulders prior to making love to her. The dress had been left to lie on the floor of the ship through most of the voyage while she had so shamefully reveled in his love.

But that was all behind her now. She had to make plans for her future. Her near future!

"I can't do much dressed in this thing," she sighed annoyingly. "Bryce Fowler did not have a change of clothes aboard his ship. I even lack a proper bath."

Brenda began pacing, tossing the long, sleek hair that hung down her back. She was torn between her needs. She didn't want Natalie to stay and share her father . . . yet she didn't want Natalie to return to share Adam! Oh, what was she to do? She swung around and headed toward the wardrobe. She slung the door open and gestured with a hand. "My father asked me to supply you with these dresses," she said quietly. "You can choose whichever you wish, and if you want, I will make sure you will be delivered to the waterfront before sunup. We can surely find passage for you aboard another ship. Most travel quite frequently to Key West."

"What's in this for you, Brenda?" Natalie asked icily, going to the wardrobe to inspect the many delicate fineries. "Surely I am not that much of a threat. Fathers are only fathers. Or, is he your life?"

Brenda swung her skirt around, went toward the door, and opened it. "My father has been my life since mother's death," she hissed. "But, no, he is not all my life. I also share a part of it with Adam Palmer!"

Natalie's breath caught. She felt the color leave her cheeks as she turned and looked at Brenda studiously. "Adam?" she whispered. "Did you say . . . Adam?"

"None other," Brenda said, tilting her chin haughtily.

"You and . . . Adam?" Natalie repeated softly. "All along he has . . . known about me and you and he never revealed the truth to me?"

Brenda laughed scornfully. "And why would he?" she said. "His father Saul also knew and didn't tell you. What would you expect? For them to reveal their heritage of piracy? That our mother lived with Saul Palmer willingly? That she didn't even return to our father when she had the chance?"

Natalie set her jaw firmly. "I can understand that," she said flatly. "Saul Palmer is quite a wonderful man."

Brenda took a step forward, glaring. "And you are saying my father is not?" she hissed.

Natalie let a small smile lift her lips, glad to see that she had annoyed Brenda even more. "Our father, Brenda," she taunted. "Our father." She felt her inner tensions lessening. If she could tease and torment in such a situation, surely she would be all right. She ignored Brenda's further presence and began sorting through the many dresses, already planning her escape. Yes, she would let Brenda aid in this escape. All that mattered was that she return to Key West in any way possible. She had many questions that needed answers.

ELEVEN

"Brenda, you seem quite skilled at slipping in and out of the shadows," Natalie said, clutching a valise to her chest. She watched all sides through the darkness, waiting for any sudden movement that might be a threat to her safety. Both she and Brenda were attired in dark, hooded capes, and they resembled sinister criminals fleeing the clutches of the law as they rushed on toward the river front.

"I'm quite skilled at many things," Brenda said coolly. "As I'm sure even you are. Being raised as Adam Palmer's sister was surely quite an education." She laughed sarcastically. "Did you ever learn the ways of piracy? Or didn't Adam ever take you on a voyage aboard his *Sea Snake?*"

Natalie stopped short, suddenly numb. In the confusion of the past several days, she had ceased to think about the possibility of Adam commanding the *Sea Snake*. And now to have the truth blurted out so . . . so nonchalantly . . . as though it was something so natural, so right . . .

"Adam?" she murmured, "He is the pirate everyone dreads?"

"Like father like son," Brenda laughed wickedly.

Natalie leaned into Brenda's face, glowering. "You're enjoying all of this, aren't you?" she hissed. "You like knowing that my world has suddenly been turned upside down. Do you pull strength from the misfortune of others?"

"It makes me no weaker," Brenda laughed scornfully. "Nor does it make me stronger. Truthfully, it matters not to me at all how you've been affected by this. You've never been anything to me nor will you ever be. Just because we've found that we're sisters doesn't automatically force us to love or respect one another."

"You have a heart made of stone," Natalie whispered. "You are evil. Clarence Seymour seems so gentle. How could you be so wicked?"

"Like mother like daughter," Brenda mocked. "Seems I inherited mother's love of wickedness and pirates."

Natalie's vivid memory of her mother and her gentle, loving ways was so fresh in her mind that she couldn't hold back her rage. She raised a hand and slapped Brenda across the face; then she smiled and proceeded onward. The tall masts of the ships were quickly taking shape before her eyes and hope sprang forth when she recognized the hull of one of them. It was Albert Burns's *Sea Gull*, moored and rocking gently on the waves. She despised the man, but for now, she would only look to him as her means of escape. . . .

Feeling hands on her arm, stopping her, pulling at her, Natalie swung around just in time to receive a blow on her chin. Her head snapped back and she saw momentary stars flashing on and off inside her head, yet she soon se-

223

cured her balance and found herself once more face to face with her hateful sister.

"You witch," Natalie said between clenched teeth. She dropped her valise to the ground and reached for Brenda's cape. With force, she pulled the hood from Brenda's head and quickly secured her fingers in the thickness of Brenda's hair and began pulling.

Brenda grimaced. "Ouch," she cried. She began kicking and clawing at Natalie until both were on the ground in quite a pitched battle.

Natalie grunted and groaned as she rolled across the cobblestone street with Brenda, refusing to set Brenda's hair free. With one hand she pulled and yanked at her hair while with the other she slapped Brenda across her nose.

"You'll be sorry," Brenda panted, ripping the bodice of Natalie's dress as her fingers clawed and scratched.

A deep, scornful laugh floated suddenly downward, causing Natalie and Brenda to stop and become breathless.

"Don't let my presence put a halt to your fun," Bryce chuckled amusedly. He placed his cigar between his lips and took a deep drag from it. Standing with his hands on his hips and legs widespread, he let his gaze move from woman to woman. He had never witnessed women in battle before and, damn it, somehow it was stimulating!

Natalie's pulse raced. "Bryce . . ." she gasped. She released her hold on Brenda and began inching away, eying her borrowed valise out of the corner of her eyes. A fast glance across her shoulder showed her the waiting *Sea Gull,* but she knew that her chances of escape this night were now gone. She glared back toward Brenda. If not for her, everything could have gone smoothly! Natalie knew that Albert already would have had her safely hidden in a cabin on his ship!

Bryce moved to Natalie and offered her a hand. "Seems I was right to think you might try to take leave from the Seymour house this night," he said. "I'm glad I stood watch." He looked toward Brenda. "But I sure as hell didn't expect you to aid in your sister's escape," he growled. "I'm sure your father will find that fact quite interesting."

Brenda straightened her cape about her shoulders. Her hair was wild, as were her eyes. "If you tell my father that it was I who helped Natalie, he would not believe you," she spat angrily.

Natalie ignored Bryce's offered hand and pushed herself up from the street. "As I am sure he wouldn't believe that you are having an affair with Adam Palmer," she said scornfully. She inspected her ripped bodice and blushed at seeing one fully exposed breast.

Bryce jerked his cigar free from his lips, brows lifted. "Adam Palmer?" he said in a shocked whisper, staring unbelievingly toward Brenda. "You . . . ?"

"Tell him," Natalie laughed. "Tell him that Adam is not only your lover but also the commander of the *Sea Snake*." She pulled her cape closed and tied it at the neck. Then she secured her valise in the crook of her left arm.

"So Adam Palmer is the damn pirate I've chased so often," Bryce growled, tossing his half-smoked cigar away, across his right shoulder. Then his gut twisted a bit. He couldn't help but wonder if knowing this could make it harder to send the *Sea Snake* and its crew to the bottom of the Atlantic. He and Adam were blood related. Could he in truth kill his own flesh and blood? His half brother?

225

But as for Natalie, no love had been exchanged between kin. And remembering the deviltry of Adam and the heartache, even bloodshed, he had scattered from coast to coast, it still would be a pleasure to see him defeated, even dead. The fun was no longer just in the chase. The full pleasure would come in the kill!

Brenda slunk back a bit, cowering. She hadn't intended that Bryce Fowler learn Adam's true identity. No one else was supposed to know. Why had she been compelled to tell Natalie? Why had she bragged of the truth? Now Adam will probably hate me, she thought to herself. I may even be the cause of his death!

She knew that as long as no one knew the identity of the *Sea Snake*'s commander, the chances of his being captured were not great.

But now? She swirled the tail of her cape around and fled into the darkness of the night.

Bryce soon forgot Brenda. He went to Natalie, his only true concern. "Natalie, what the hell do you think you're trying to prove by running away tonight?" he asked, clasping her shoulders. "Do you think that by turning your back on the truth, it will not be so?"

"The truths are all twisted together into a jumble of knots inside my head," she murmured. "I just wanted to return home . . . to where I belong."

"You belong here, Natalie."

"Bryce, what's the matter?" she said icily. "You have earned your gold coins once. Must you do so again?"

He jerked his hands free of her and combed his fingers through his hair. "Damn it, Natalie," he growled. "You know that money . . . that payment for what I do is not the issue here."

"Then you have been misguided in your judgments,"

226

she said stubbornly.

Bryce took her by the elbow and began leading her away from the sight of the ships. "I won't force you to return to Clarence Seymour's house tonight," he grumbled.

Natalie squirmed beneath his grip of steel. "Where are you taking me?" she argued.

"I'm for sure not returning you to where Brenda can get her clutches on you again so soon," he said flatly. He then chuckled amusedly. "But I do believe you are quite capable of defending yourself. You do pack a powerful blow, beautiful lady."

Natalie felt a blush rising and remembered the one time she had slapped him. After tonight, he must think her quite a hellion! "I've told you before," she murmured. "I will defend myself in whichever way is needed at the moment."

"Well, right now, you don't have to worry about such a thing. We're going to get you settled in bed," he said flatly. "Tomorrow we shall start all over again. I will send a messenger to Clarence first thing in the morning before he's even had a chance to miss you."

"Ha! What do you mean I don't have to worry about defending myself? Don't I have you to worry about? I take it you plan to take me to your own quarters, where you also will try to seduce me one more time," Natalie said sourly. "And when you do succeed, that treat will do until payment by gold is handed you tomorrow. Ha! I'm sure Clarence Seymour will once more pay you quite well."

Bryce threw aside a wide expanse of wrought-iron gate then guided Natalie down the full length of a corridor that led into a courtyard. Moon beams played in shining tremors on water cascading from a fountain. Shadowed palms swayed gently in the breeze and many trillium plants, with their erect stems and solitary white flowers, lined the wide expanse of stucco-covered wall that encompassed the three sides of the courtyard.

The aroma of magnolia blossoms flowed toward Natalie, its sweetness enveloping her like a rush of a rich perfume. She faltered a bit on the blue flagstone walk, letting her gaze move upward, toward a balcony that reached outward from the rooms on the second floor of this magnificent Creole house of cream-colored stucco.

"This could be all yours, Natalie," Bryce said softly, leading her up an outside winding staircase. "Your father would not hesitate one moment if I sought his permission to ask your hand in marriage."

"By speaking of father, you mean to say Clarence Seymour, do you not?" she said haughtily.

"There is no other," he growled.

"I still would argue that," she said. "A father means different things to different people."

"God. What does it take, Natalie?"

"My feelings are my judge as to who is what."

"I saw you reaction to your mother's portrait."

"That meant nothing to me," she lied. "Nothing."

"So you still insist on fooling yourself?"

"You are the true fool."

"And what makes you say that?"

"Because you refuse to listen to what my heart aches for."

"Oh, God." Bryce groaned. "You will still choose a family of pirates over someone as gentle as Clarence Seymour. It is hard to understand."

"You truly have no reason to bother yourself any longer about me or what I want," she said icily. "In the end it is *I* who will get what *I* want."

"And, that is . . . ?"

As they stepped upon the balcony flooring, Natalie swung around and faced him. "I most certainly no longer want you," she hissed. "You can be assured of that."

Bryce's back stiffened. He set his jaw firmly and tipped her chin with a forefinger and studied the dark pools of her eyes. Then in a flash he had her in his arms, crushing her lips beneath his. Holding her pinioned next to him, he ignored her struggles. Instead, he shaped his body to hers and let her feel the male hardness of him grinding into her as he began slowly to gyrate his body against hers.

Forcing her lips apart with his tongue he began searching inside her mouth, smiling inwardly when he could feel her defenses slowly melting into soft moans of pleasure.

Though she didn't want it, desire once more had Natalie in its grip. She didn't even fight him when he swept her up into his arms and carried her to a dimly lighted room. With her arms laced around his neck and her cheek against his chest, she even forgot her reason for having been on the river front. He and the pleasures he could offer her had become her immediate purpose in life. All else could wait until later.

"I love you so," Bryce said in a husky whisper, sending butterfly kisses across her face as she lifted it adoringly to his. "I need you, Natalie."

She kissed the taut line of his jaw, loving the male taste of him. "As I do you, my love," she whispered. "Oh, how I do love you, Bryce."

His blue eyes twinkled. "I thought you hated me," he

chuckled.

She curved her lips into a pout. "I do," she murmured.

His eyebrows forked. "Which is it? Love or hate?"

"Both," she whispered. "First I hate you, then I love you. Right now all I can think about is how my body aches for you."

"I thought you said I could never touch you again," he growled.

"That was when I hated you," she smiled.

"Damn." he said thickly. He carried her to a wide expanse of bed and placed her gently on it. Sitting down next to her he untied her cape and brushed it slowly from her shoulders before tossing it to the floor.

Natalie's whole body responded when Bryce's fingers found her exposed breast and caressed it tenderly.

"It is as soft as the petal of a rose," he whispered then bent and let his tongue replace his hand. "Your body even smells and tastes of rose petals," he murmured.

Feeling the sweet pain between her thighs, Natalie reached her hands to his head and guided his lips to hers. She sighed pleasurably when his mouth covered hers with its magical warmth. She kissed him back with a wildness, twining her arms about his neck and urging his body down next to hers. Her hands went desperately over him, pushing his coat from his shoulders and opening his shirt to her hungry, searching fingers. She twisted and sighed as his lips once more lowered to her breast.

"Bryce, love me," she whispered. "Love me now."

"You feared my seduction earlier," he teased, flicking a tongue across the beige tip of the taut nipple.

"My words do not always match my thoughts," she laughed silkily.

"And now?"

"You are my thoughts. My words are not important. Only you are, my love."

Smiling softly, Bryce began methodically disrobing her, kissing each newly exposed piece of flesh with the flames of his lips. And when she lay exquisitely pale in her complete nudity, he once more rained her with kisses.

As he undressed, she devoured him with her eyes, seeing the male strength of him swollen and ready to pleasure her. Reaching her arms out to him, she watched as he lowered himself down over her and spread her legs even more for his entrance inside her.

Feverish now from her building excitement and anticipation, she drew him closer. Each thrust sent her into an almost frenzied passion. She lifted her hips to him, clung to him, and her lips parted seductively as he once more kissed her with a fiery passion.

Their bodies rose and fell, waves on an ocean, their blended lips and flesh bathed in the effervescence of their love's glow. They were rising higher now on their pinnacle of love, reaching for that moment of united pleasure, when both bodies shuddered together and both minds were lost to everything but release and joy.

Bryce kissed the hollow of her throat and ran the palm of a hand over her silken face. "My beautiful lady," he sighed. "My beautiful Natalie . . ."

Now down from her cloud of pleasure, Natalie looked slowly around her, quite aware of what she had so wantonly participated in again. She didn't even know herself anymore. First she was fighting on the river front like some gutter tramp, and then she once more willingly let herself be seduced by the man she ought to detest! Shame engulfed her in cold splashes, causing her to rise from the bed.

Her toes curled into a soft carpet of a pale green coloring. The room was dark paneled, matching the dark, heavy-looking mahogany bedstead and the other various furnishings. The windows bore no drapes, only shutters that had been closed against the damp spray of night. She turned with a start when she felt Bryce turn her to meet his gaze.

"It's late," he said. "Let's turn in for the night. Once I've delivered you to Clarence Seymour in the morning, I must return to Key West. I've important business to tend to there."

Natalie suddenly remembered the key she had found. She knew what it meant to him. But what could she do about it now? It wasn't even in her possession to give to him. It was still in her bedroom at Key West, deftly hidden beneath her finery.

Once there, she would send it to him by messenger. She no longer had use for it. Though her heart would bleed for Bryce, she knew that, once having returned to Key West, she would have to forget him. To be involved with him further held many elements of danger for both her and him.

Looking toward her soiled dress and cape and then toward the valise Brenda had so generously given her for the trip and thinking of the fresh clothes within, Natalie felt somewhat better. As soon as Bryce was fast asleep she would once more make her move. Surely Albert's ship had been moored for the night. . . .

Feigning a lazy yawn, Natalie crept to the bed and tossed its mussed spread aside. "I am tired," she sighed. "It's been a long day."

She crawled beneath a layer of blankets, spreading her hair out beneath her head in glossy, midnight black tresses.

Seeing her look so seductive, Bryce felt renewed heat in his loins. "I'm not so sure if either of us will get any sleep if I get in that bed beside you," he chuckled. He glanced toward the door, then back to her. "But I sure as hell can't leave you alone for you would surely slip from my clutches."

Natalie yawned again, lacing it with a quivering sigh. "Bryce, I'm too tired to share in further lovemaking or to escape," she whispered. "So much has happened to tire me both physically and mentally. I'm sure you understand."

"In that case, I'd best blow out the flames of the lamp and help you drift off to dreamland."

"But, Bryce . . . I said I was tired. . . ."

"Honey, I am too," Bryce chuckled. "All I want from you now is the softness of your body to cling to through the night. Then maybe, after you see how nice a full night with a man can be, you'll reconsider my proposal of marriage."

Natalie closed her eyes to her heartache. Leaving him for good would be the hardest thing she had ever had to face. She could never love again as completely. Without him, a part of her would be dead.

"Natalie . . . ?" Bryce murmured as he crawled beneath the blankets beside her. "Did you hear what I said?"

Feigning sleep, she found it hard not to respond to his warm breath on her cheek or the pleasure of his hands stroking her arms with desire.

Tears glistened on the tips of her lashes. She was glad that the room was dark and he could not see the sadness that these tears represented. She hadn't even left him yet and she already missed him!

Oh, how could she do this? How?

But the only world she had ever known silently beckoned. She had no choice but to answer its call. She was a stranger in New Orleans. Key West, like gold, glittered . . . yes, luring her back.

Natalie continued to lie beside Bryce, tense and breathing shallowly. She only hoped he wouldn't take long to fall asleep. Now that she'd made her plans, she wanted to carry them out quickly. The later the hour, the riskier her escape. What if some waterfront riffraff grabbed her and dragged her away to use . . . to degrade?

Swallowing hard, Natalie shook such thoughts from her mind. Instead, she focused on what she would say to Albert when taken to his personal cabin upon her arrival at his magnificent ship. How could she explain this all away? Oh, what if he would not believe her? What if he thought she had come willingly? What if he told her father of his doubts and called her a tramp?

Natalie tensed even more as she heard the steady rumble of snores surfacing from somewhere deep inside Bryce. Though she was tense, hearing him made her smile. The snoring was comical. It made Bryce so human. She loved him even more. She wanted to lean over and kiss his snores away but knew that the time had finally arrived to ease herself from the bed and into her clothes. What if Bryce's loud snores awakened him?

With a racing pulse, Natalie crept slowly from the bed. Fumbling in the dark, she finally found the valise. She could not wear the ripped dress, so she had to pull something different from inside the bag. Though wrinkled, at least it would be respectable in appearance.

Hurrying, doing the best she could in the dark of the

room, Natalie finally succeeded in readying herself for the escape. Once more she was mostly hidden beneath the dark confines of her cape.

With one last, lingering look toward the shadowed heap on the bed, Natalie fled from the room and through the courtyard to the street.

One thing was in her favor. Bryce's creole house was in walking distance from the river front. But she wasn't walking. She was running. Every shadowy movement on the walk and street gave her a fright. Even the swaying of a tree's branch represented a hand reaching out to her.

Fog swirled in ghostly whites as Natalie drew closer to the river. But this gave her a soft cover of sorts as she moved on toward the ship named the *Sea Gull*. When finally at its gangplank, she threw the hood of her cape back and peered ahead, seeing no activity whatsoever on the topdeck. But having traveled on the *Sea Gull* before, accompanied by her father, Natalie knew which direction to take to Albert's cabin door.

"Just the thought of being near the pompous old goat sets my stomach to turning," she whispered, shivering. "If I could succeed at traveling unnoticed, even as a stowaway, I would do it so I would not have to be near him."

But she knew that was not a wise thought. The crew of any ship would be a threat to her if she was found hidden away. No. Such a thought was not wise. She would have to travel in the open—even in the accompaniment of such a man as Albert Burns—knowing that was the only way this time.

Lifting the tail of her cape and dress into her arms, Natalie stepped lightly onto the ship's deck and moved stealthily down a small staircase. The corridor she had reached was dark, barely lit by a single whale-oil lamp at the far end. The ship rocked smoothly in the gentle waters of the Mississippi and a faint odor of tea and spices drifted up from the hold of the ship.

A door creaking open along the corridor drew Natalie's courage from inside her in one quick gasp for breath. With her hands at her throat, she waited, then sighed heavily when she saw that it was Albert. If it had been one of his crew, anything could have been expected. Possibly even rape!

Surely Albert could be trusted, especially if he valued his life. Saul Palmer's daughter was untouchable, a virgin, so he thought!

Attired in a long, red nightsack, Albert came toward her, yawning and rubbing his eyes. It was obvious that he had not yet seen her. Her black cape blended in too well with the darkness.

Trembling, Natalie stepped out of the shadows. "Mr. Burns . . . uh . . . Albert?" she said in a low whisper.

Albert stopped jerkily. He reached a hand to the side wall to steady himself. "Natalie Palmer?" he gasped. "How? Why?"

With caution in her step, Natalie moved on toward him. "Albert, I have come to seek your help," she said. "Will you please see to my return to Key West?"

Securing the belt tied at his waist, he met her approach. "Natalie, why would you need my assistance?" he said hoarsely. "Are you not this far from home in the company of your father?"

Natalie stopped within inches of him, now clearly able to make out his pencil-thin mustache and thick head of gray hair. His obeseness showed in his loose-hanging jowls and the pudginess of his fingers.

"Albert, it's quite a long story," she murmured, casting her eyes downward. "Is there someplace we can talk? I do feel a bit exhausted from my travels and traumatic experience."

Albert reached for her elbow and guided her into his personal cabin. "I shall pour you a drink of wine, my dear," he said softly. "Then you can talk to me the entire night, if you wish. You know how much I have wanted to have some time alone with you. Damn if I can believe you are here even how."

Once inside his cabin, Natalie stiffened a bit, hoping he wouldn't try to take advantage of her. If he did, she would not have bettered herself by having enlisted his services. To be in the same room with him was unbearable enough, let alone to have him touch and fondle her.

"Here," Albert said, reaching his hands to her cape. "Let me take your wrap."

"Thank you," she murmured, swinging it back from her shoulders. Her eyes took in the magnificence of the cabin. As in most ship's master cabins, the walls were finely paneled and the furnishings were of plush leather and heavy oak. The bed that sat beneath the skylight showed disarray in its blankets. Natalie knew that sleep had been eluding him this night. Was it because he had been feeling the need of a woman at his side?

She shivered at the thought of possibly having handed him the answer to this need by having so boldly boarded his ship.

Out of the corner of her eye she watched as Albert poured wine into two tall-stemmed crystal glasses. She could see the trembling of his fingers. She could see the nervous twitch of a cheek. Oh, what was she to do to prevent him from touching her? Wasn't she now at his

237

mercy? Would he expect that kind payment for her return to Key West?

He turned to her and handed her a glass. "Now you drink this and tell me all about it," he said thickly.

The gray of his eyes was lost in the black of his dilated pupils. Natalie was quite aware of his building excitement. In fact, what was the strange odor in his room?

Oh, God! No! It surely wasn't opium! She had been given a sniff once by her brother Adam. He had said that he had taken it from one of his ship's crew.

With a racing pulse, Natalie accepted the glass of wine and slowly settled into a chair. She was quite aware of her heaving bosom and just how much of herself was exposed. The plunging neckline of her silk dress afforded no comfort to her in this situation.

She sighed heavily when Albert finally sat down on a chair opposite her. His nightsack gaped open in the front and his hairless chest shone beneath the soft rays of the whale-oil lamp's flickerings. His lower anatomy was slowly also peeking through.

Clearing her throat nervously, Natalie averted her gaze. She took a sip of wine then began telling how it was that she was in New Orleans. At the end of her tale, she glanced toward him and saw a look of mockery in the slow curve of his lips. Her insides froze. He most surely had known all the untidy details of her past. He had known Saul Palmer since they both were youths. They had settled in Key West at almost the same time.

Natalie inched farther back in her chair, eyes wide. "You knew," she gasped.

"Yes," he said, laughing amusedly. "I remember your mother quite well. I was aboard the ship when your mother was taken captive. I have watched you grow up to

238

be just as beautiful.''

"You . . . were also a . . . ?'' she whispered shallowly.

"Yes. A pirate,'' he sighed. "Until I felt it was for the younger gents. Yes, gents like your Adam. Those days were fun. Full of danger and excitement. But I don't have the scars to show it as your . . . eh . . . father does. I'll never forget the day he lost his fingers.''

Natalie's insides suddenly trembled. "You mean the day the Cuban attacked my father at the factory?'' she asked cautiously.

"Is that what he told you?'' Albert asked, lifting an eyebrow.

"That's not the way it happened, is it?'' Natalie said dryly. "My father lied to me.''

She hung her head and shook it slowly back and forth. "In fact, my whole life has been one big lie,'' she whispered.

Suddenly it was as though someone had hit her in the stomach—the truths and the lies merging into a seething, hurtful anger. Bryce had been right to try to make her face up to reality. This man who had posed as her father all these years did not deserve her love! Though he had treated her well, it had always been under the cover of a malicious deceit. He had known all along that her true father was out there, somewhere, full of anguish and sadness over his loss.

Oh, how had Saul Palmer had the nerve to play at God by keeping true kin apart? Oh, she had been so wrong to deny herself the truth once it had been placed so neatly before her eyes.

"I was wrong to come here,'' she murmured, slowly rising from the chair. She felt a strong need to return to

239

Bryce . . . to find comfort in his arms. He had offered her even more than that. He had offered her security . . . as his wife. That could be the answer. Being married meant that she didn't have to answer to either man who professed to be her father!

Albert rose from his chair and met her at the door, blocking it with the wide expanse of his body. "And where do you think you're going?" he growled.

"I have decided not to return to Key West," she said flatly. She placed her glass on a table and took a step toward him. "Step aside, Mr. Burns," she said, lifting her chin haughtily. "I plan to take leave of your ship."

"I think not," Albert argued. "I'm going to return you to Saul. Then he can decide what to do with Bryce Fowler for his unwise abduction of you."

Natalie swallowed back her mounting fear. "You cannot do this," she whispered. "I demand that you set me free."

Albert placed his glass on a table and opened the door, watching her closely all the while. "I will see to it that you are comfortable while on my ship," he said. "You can have my cabin. Please try to make yourself at home. None of my men will abuse you. And since Saul is my closest friend, I won't take advantage of you either. The pleasures I want from you will come later after I have made you my wife."

"What?" she gasped, paling in color.

"Saul will reward me well for your safe return," Albert laughed. "When I am asked what would make me happiest, I will say you. And under the circumstances, he will be more than willing to have you wed to a man of his choosing, away from the clutches of such a man as Bryce Fowler."

Unable to control her anger any longer, Natalie slapped Albert in the face. "I will never wed you," she hissed. "Never."

Albert reached a hand to his flaming cheek, glowering. "If you weren't Natalie Palmer, I would make you pay for that," he snarled. "But once you are Natalie Burns, you will pay . . . yes . . . you will pay. . . ."

The hair at the nape of Natalie's neck rose; she heard so much in his voice that frightened her. She watched in stunned silence as the door slammed closed in her face. The sound of a bolt lock being slipped into place made her realize that she had once more become a victim of circumstances . . . and of her own careless doing.

Swinging around she threw her hands up into the air. "Oh, how do I get myself into these messes?" she cried. "Now what am I to do?"

She tensed and grew silent when she heard a sudden rush of feet on the outer deck. Yes, Albert had alerted his crew. They wouldn't take the chance that Bryce Fowler might find her missing and come in frantic search of her.

The creaking of the anchor being raised from the river floor caused goose pimples to scatter across Natalie's flesh. She went to the door and leaned her ear against it, already hearing the sails whipping in the wind.

KEY WEST

You may stretch your hands out toward me,
Ah! You will . . . I know not when. . . .
I shall nurse my love and keep it
Faithfully, for you, till then.

—Procter

TWELVE

The house smelled of roses. Huge vases of many varieties had been placed around the rooms to create a garden like atmosphere and a feeling of celebration. There was to be a wedding . . . the first ever in the Palmer villa.

Attired in her sleek, white satin wedding gown, with her hair piled luxuriously atop her head and pearls braided into it, Natalie paced her bedroom floor. The veil that had been chosen for her hung heavy with lace and netting, from the back of a chair, an ugly reminder of what the next hour would hold for her.

The steady sound of horsedrawn carriages arriving for the ceremony drove Natalie into an almost nervous frenzy. She wrung her hands; she continued to pace.

Her low-cut dress showed the white, classic swells of her breasts. Its nipped-in waist revealed her exquisite thin waist. The full gathers of the gown were held out from her by yards and yards of petticoats trimmed in Valenciennes lace and they rustled enticingly with each step taken.

Moving out onto her private balcony, Natalie gazed intensely across the wide breadth of the yard and out to the Atlantic darkened by the impending gray shades of night. A high-masted ship, its white sails weaving in the breeze, drew her most devoted attention. Her heart began to beat wildly. Though darkness was quickly approaching, the hull of the ship showed through the gloom in shimmering golds.

"Bryce . . ." Natalie gasped.

With one hand, she leaned her full weight on the balcony railing and with the other reached toward the ship. "Oh, Bryce," she cried. "It is your ship."

She watched the direction in which it sailed and became breathless. The ship was drawing closer to shore. Had the message reached Bryce? Had he come to save her from a life that she dreaded more than death? Had he figured out a way to truly . . . rescue her? Would he know how to reach her without being discovered by Saul Palmer and the guards who surrounded him?

Natalie had been made a virtual prisoner since her return home from New Orleans. But Tami had managed to get that one message out for her. Natalie didn't know how it had reached New Orleans, but she was now convinced that it had; for surely Bryce had come to take her away with him on his *Golden Isis*. If he did succeed in reaching her, she wouldn't fight him this time. She would go willingly.

"But can he get here fast enough?" She fretted aloud. "Within the hour . . . within the hour. . . ."

A light tapping on her bedroom door drew her quickly around. "Tami?" she whispered.

Hope sprang forth. Surely Tami could help her again. The wedding must be delayed!

Running to the door, Natalie jerked it open. She smiled

with relief when Tami stepped hurriedly into the room.

"We've got things to do, Miss Natalie," Tami said, rushing out onto the balcony. She stretched ner neck and looked toward the ocean.

"Tami, I don't want to finish getting ready for the wedding," Natalie fussed. "It must be delayed. It must."

Tami moved quickly back into the room. "Shhh," she said, placing a forefinger to Natalie's lips. "I'm not talkin' 'bout no weddin'. I'm talkin' 'bout him. Massa Bryce. His ship is in sight. He got the message. Now we've got to proceed with the plan."

Natalie grabbed Tami's thin arm. "Tami, what plan?" she whispered. "What are you talking about?"

"It was all in the message," she said, going to the bed to pull the spread back. "He knows what to do."

"Did you alter my message, Tami?"

Tami's dark eyes glistened. "Yes'm," she said softly.

Natalie leaned into Tami's face. "How?"

Tami moved away from her and began to muss up the bed; then she folded the spread and placed it at the foot. "You'll see," she giggled. "You'll see. . . ."

Natalie raised an eyebrow. "Why are you mussing the bed, Tami?" she queried softly. "What are you up to?"

"We must see to it that you look quite ill," Tami murmured. "You must appear to be in need of a doctor."

Natalie sighed heavily. She swung her arms up into the air. "What are you talking about?" she cried. "Why must I pretend illness?"

Tami grabbed Natalie's hands. "Shhh," she insisted. "No one must know what we're up to. But, Miss Natalie, it's the only way to get you out of here unwed to Massa Burns."

"But . . . how . . . ?"

"Massa Bryce will arrive soon, posing as a Doctor Jamieson. There is a new doctor in town with the name of Jamieson, one Massa Saul hasn't yet met. Massa Bryce will disable the true Doctor Jamieson momentarily until Massa Bryce will have time to get you on his ship."

Natalie placed her fingers to her temple, shaking her head back and forth. "Wait . . . wait . . ." she cried softly. "This is all spinning around inside my head. I just don't understand."

"Massa Bryce will be sent for as soon as I tell Massa Saul that you're ill," Tami continued. "Massa Bryce will be waitin' in the shadows. I'll send Matthew for him. Matthew wants to see right done by you the same as I do."

Natalie felt heat rise in her cheeks. She worked her hands free from Tami's and began pacing the floor again. She shook her head frantically. "It won't work. Bryce will get caught."

She swung around and faced Tami, her eyes wide with fear. "Surely someone in the parlor will recognize Bryce," she whispered. "Surely someone will have met the real Doctor Jamieson."

"Nobody'll see him," Tami reassured her. "Matthew will bring Massa Fowler up the back way. It would only look right not to bring the doctor in where the guests could see him. Knowin' Massa Saul, he wouldn't want to cause alarm. He wouldn't want his guests wonderin' 'bout what's happenin' to the bride to be."

"But I still don't see how . . ." Natalie worried further.

"After Massa Bryce arrives, you will escape with him out the back way," Tami said with a jerk of her head, showing confidence in the strength of her words.

Natalie clasped Tami's frail shoulders. "All right, Tami, let's say this does work," she said. "What about you? What you're doing will bring danger to yourself. Once I am gone with Bryce, father will know that you and Matthew are responsible. He might even—"

Once more Tami silenced Natalie's words with a pressed forefinger against Natalie's lips. "Shhh, Miss Natalie," she whispered. "Ol' Tami here and Matthew are too valuable to Massa Saul. He may take a whip to us but he won't harm us in any other way."

Natalie circled her hands into two tight fists at her side. She once more began pacing. "He won't even take a whip to you," she said.

She swung the skirt of her dress around and met Tami's dutiful stare with flashing eyes. "No," she said firmly. "He won't have that chance. You and Matthew are going with me."

Tami's lips began to quiver and her eyes became filled with tears. "Miss Natalie, how kind," she murmured. She wiped the tears from her eyes. "But we can't. Our escape could slow things."

"You will get a head start," Natalie said, nodding her head, liking the excitement of the upcoming adventure. The element of danger gave her a strange sense of euphoria. Or was this warmth swimming inside her head because she knew she'd soon be with Bryce again?

She went to the balcony, but no longer saw the ship. She could envision Bryce, now on foot, racing along the bluffs toward the estate grounds.

Moving back inside her room she went to the bed and slipped her shoes off. "Yes," she said softly. "As soon as Bryce enters my room in the guise of Doctor Jamieson, you leave by the back way with Matthew, Tami, and hightail it as fast as you can to Bryce's ship. When the coast is clear, Bryce and I will follow. By the time father, or should I say Saul Palmer, misses activity in this room, we shall all be gone!'' Natalie sighed heavily. ''Yes, Tami, I like your plan,'' she said.

Tami laughed nervously. ''My plan has taken a different turn than expected,'' she said. She went and leaned her dark face down into Natalie's. ''He'll be fit to be tied, Massa Saul will. He'll come afta' us fo' sho'!''

''But we will then be aboard the magnificent *Golden Isis*,'' Natalie said proudly.

She threw herself back on the bed and placed a hand to her brow. ''Oh, Tami, I am so sick,'' she said, giggling. ''You must go tell father and send Matthew for a doctor. I think I feel too faint even to walk as far as the parlor.''

''Oh, Miss Natalie,'' Tami said, laughing softly. ''Y'all do tickle my funny bone at times.''

Natalie cast Tami a serious look. ''We must both be very convincing,'' she murmured. ''So much depends on how my father reacts to my condition. He may not even believe me. He knows I dread this marriage. So let's do the best we can, Tami.''

Tami squared her shoulders. ''Don't you fret none,'' she said firmly. '' 'Fore long, ya'll be aboard the *Golden Isis* with the man you love. You deserve that, Miss Natalie. Y'all sho'nuff do.''

Natalie leaned up on an elbow. ''We will be aboard that ship, Tami,'' she said. ''Don't forget. You and Matthew must leave when I do.''

Tami's eyes wavered and her voice weakened. ''Yes'm,'' she said; then, amid a flurry of skirts, she left the room.

Her heart pounded so Natalie found it hard to breathe as she listened for her father's approaching footsteps. She wondered if he would be furious? He did have a house full of waiting guests. Was Albert even now watching for her to descend the stairs? The sound of violins had just begun; it floated up the stairs and into Natalie's bedroom creating a sensation of almost magical enchantment.

Tears burned at the corners of her eyes. Oh, if only the planned wedding ceremony could have been for her and Bryce. If only she hadn't found out those awful truths about Saul Palmer. But this was no time to dwell on these things. She must concentrate on appearing ill.

As the door suddenly burst open Natalie's heart leaped. But she kept her eyes closed, already sensing Saul Palmer's presence at her bedside.

"Natalie," he growled. "What's this all about? Tami said you're feeling so poorly that she encouraged me to send Matthew for that new Doctor Jamieson. Are you truly ill? Or is this just a bit of fright caused by the wedding?"

Feigning a soft groan, Natalie slowly opened her eyes. "It's my stomach," she whispered. "I'm having terrible pains. I do need the services of a doctor. I do."

His eyes dark pits of mistrust, Saul leaned over Natalie and touched her brow with the back of his right hand.

Out of the corner of her eyes, Natalie saw his left hand and the void left there by his missing three fingers. All those years she had thought he had been wounded while making an honest living, yet all the while . . .

"You don't seem feverish," he growled. He straightened his back and clasped his hands together behind him.

Studying her still, he raised an eyebrow, and then said, "I will go downstairs and see to our guests. I will come

251

and get you as soon as the doctor has given me the word that you can proceed with the wedding. Albert anxiously awaits. He even has his ship readied for a voyage to New York, where he plans to take you and to let you buy all the dresses and hats your little heart desires.''

The mention of New York caused Natalie's thoughts to wander to Myra. ''Father, has Myra arrived for the ceremony?'' she asked softly.

''Natalie, I didn't want to break the news of Myra until after the wedding,'' Saul said guardedly. ''But now that you've asked, perhaps it's best I tell you.''

Natalie blanched. She didn't like the caution in her father's words. She had tried over and over again to get a message to Myra, but with no success. It seemed Myra still hadn't returned from her unfortunate voyage to New York.

''What is it?'' she murmured. ''What about Myra?''

''I received word today that Myra didn't reach New York nor did she return to Key West.''

''What . . . ?'' Natalie gasped, now really feeling ill, but with worry. ''Where is she?''

''Seems she was abducted while traveling to New York,'' Saul murmured, lowering his eyes. ''A ship came broadside the one on which she was traveling and the only prize taken by the pirate was Myra.''

''No . . .'' Natalie exclaimed, rising to a sitting position. She hung her head in her hands and shook her head back and forth agonizingly. Then she dared to stare boldly at her father.

''Seems pirates make a habit of abducting women from ships,'' she snapped angrily. ''And what pirate, father? I thought there was only one pirate left roaming the sea and I know Adam wouldn't abduct Myra. He hates her.''

"Don't speak disrespectfully of your brother," Saul growled.

"He is not my brother," Natalie hissed. "As you are not my father. I only keep calling you that because I tend to forget. It is only by habit that I ever will call you father again. Believe me when I say that!"

A sly smile lifted Saul's lips upward. He smoothed his fingers over his black evening coat. "Hmmm," he snarled. "Seems you've quickly recovered."

He glanced toward the door, then back to Natalie. "But I'll let the doctor examine you anyway. I don't want Albert complaining later on that I married him off to you while you were ailing."

Natalie reclined on the bed, pulse racing. She had momentarily forgotten! She'd almost ruined the whole thing!

Natalie did not watch him take leave of the room, but she listened to his footsteps grow fainter as he descended the staircase. Then she rose quickly from the bed, loosened her braided hair, and threw the pearls aside.

Hurrying to her wardrobe, she chose appropriate attire in which to make her escape. A heavy riding skirt and white shirtwaist blouse. And just as she slipped into her last boot, she looked up and saw Bryce standing there in the costume he had worn at Albert Burns's masquerade ball.

Though they both were in danger of discovery, his bold, black mustache and wig drew a quiet chuckle from deep inside Natalie. Then she rose from her chair and rushed into his waiting arms.

"Bryce . . ." she whispered.

His lips kissed the hollow of her throat, then he held her away from him, feasting his eyes upon her.

"Beautiful lady, we've got to get out of here," he said

thickly.

His blue eyes touched her heart. She reached a hand to his cheek and touched the smooth, sun-bronzed softness of it.

"Thank you for coming," she whispered.

Bryce nodded toward the door. "Shall we?" he asked.

"Yes. Just follow me, darling," Natalie said, grabbing one of his hands.

She stepped to the door and slowly opened it. Looking from side to side, she saw that the way was clear for them to move to the back staircase. By now, Tami and Matthew should already be on their way to the ship. Before long, they would all be free. . . .

"It's okay," she whispered, glancing toward Bryce. Then her heart skipped a beat. How could she have forgotten his key? She hadn't had a chance to send it to him. She had to get it now . . . or never.

She turned her eyes to him. "I've got to get something before we leave," she whispered.

"Surely it's not so important," he argued. "I'll buy you whatever it is when we arrive in New Orleans."

"This is something that no one can buy anywhere," she murmured softly. She didn't want to take the time to explain how she had the key. That would cause too much delay. "Just keep watch while I get it."

"Get what?" he persisted.

"Bryce . . . please . . ." Natalie sighed.

"Oh, all right." he said. "I'll keep watch. Go ahead. Get your damn whatever."

Smiling her thanks, Natalie rushed to her night stand and, opening the drawer, searched until her hands came in contact with the coldness of the key. Circling her fingers around it, she pulled it from beneath her lacy underclothes. Then, speedily, she pinned it securely in the depths of her skirt pocket and once more went to Bryce's side. Wouldn't he be surprised!

"Well?" he said, forking his eyebrows. He glanced down at her hands, seeing nothing. "What was it you were so eager to take with you? I see nothing."

She tapped her pocket. "It's safely hidden away," she said. "I'm now ready to go, Bryce."

Bryce rolled his eyes upward. "Women!" he sighed. "Who can understand them?"

"In time I hope you will understand everything about me," Natalie said, once more checking the hallway. She couldn't help but worry about the men who constantly surrounded her father. But, hopefully, they would be mingling with the crowd, enjoying the wine and Palmer's fine cigars.

"But for now," she quickly added. "Let's get this place and the waiting people behind us."

With Bryce at her side, Natalie moved down the hall to the back stairs and when they reached the lower floor, she led Bryce on through another narrow, dark hallway to the back door.

Natalie tensed at the noisy squeak of the opening door. Then she sighed heavily, aware that the noise of conversation and music in the parlor predominated over the slight disturbance caused by the door.

"Natalie, we must hurry," Bryce encouraged her softly, taking the initiative to pull her out onto the back veranda.

With a pounding heart, Natalie ran down the steps beside Bryce and then lifted her skirt and began running beneath the protective shadows of the trees. The sea breeze was fresh and cool and smelled faintly of fish. The whispering of the palm fronds was left behind as they neared the jutting bluffs edging the Atlantic.

Natalie reached a hand to Bryce, stopping him. She was panting. "Bryce, I . . . must . . . rest," she whispered hoarsely.

She looked back across her shoulder, relieved that they had left the Palmer estate way behind them. "I do believe we're safe," she sighed. "I see no one following."

Bryce drew Natalie into his arms and burrowed his nose into the depths of her hair. "We will not be safe until we are far out to sea," he whispered huskily. "Only then will I know that I have once more succeeded in rescuing you from the clutches of that evil man, Saul Palmer."

Natalie leaned back from Bryce and studied his face. There seemed to be more to what he felt than what he was saying. Were there even more mysteries to unveil about Saul Palmer? What could they be?

But wanting to think of nothing now except Bryce and the reality that she was with him again, she reached her fingers to the false mustache and slowly peeled it away from his skin. She giggled at his loud "Ouch."

She dropped the mustache to the ground then slowly brushed his black hairpiece from his head. Running her fingers through his thick head of golden hair, she felt the familiar pain of love for him causing a dull, sweet ache between her thighs.

Bryce reached a hand to her hair and, lifting it from her shoulders, watched as the wind blew it in sensuous rivulets free from his fingers. Then he lowered his lips to hers and kissed her hard and demandingly.

Natalie laced her arms about his neck but found their intimate moment was too short-lived. Bryce abruptly drew away, once more taking her hand in his.

"Come on, Natalie," he urged. "It's a dangerous game we're playing. Let's get the *Golden Isis* sails filling with the wind; then we can make love for the rest of our lives."

An involuntary shiver raced through Natalie when the giant shape of the *Golden Isis* towered above her. She felt a strange pride seize her as she stepped on the gangplank. She felt that she was just as much a part of the ship as Bryce. His pride was her pride. When together, they were as one.

Bryce's crew became active as soon as he stepped aboard his ship. Dominic, his long, carrot-colored hair blowing wildly in the wind, saluted Bryce as he stepped before him.

"Get the ship out to sea and fast, Dominic," Bryce shouted. "We don't have much time."

"You didn't have to tie 'er this time, eh?" Dominic sneered, eying Natalie with a hardness in his deep-set eyes. The flowing sleeves of his white shirt rustled noisily as the wind whipped them around.

"No. She came willingly," Bryce said flatly. "But you knew that, Dominic. You knew my purpose in coming to Key West. This is no time to cause problems. Just get to your duties."

"Aye, aye, sir," Dominic growled, turning on a heel, already shouting orders to the rest of the crew.

Natalie looked from side to side, growing a bit numb. "Bryce," she said tensely. "I don't see Tami or Matthew on board."

"Who?" Bryce said, scratching his head questioningly.

"Tami. My personal maid . . . the one who sent you

257

the message," Natalie said, now hurrying along the deck searching all the dark corners.

The sound of chains clanking made her quite aware of the anchor being lifted from its water grave. "And Matthew, the stable hand," she said even more anxiously. "They were supposed to come ahead of us and board the ship."

"I wasn't told," Bryce said, loosening his collar and letting the sea breeze move down the front of his shirt.

"Tami and Matthew were supposed to leave with us," Natalie said, wild-eyed.

She put a knuckle between her lips and bit down on it. Then she hurried to the side rail when she felt the jerk of the ship as the sails filled and whipped the vessel farther out to sea.

"They apparently didn't make it, Natalie," Bryce said, moving to her side.

He placed an arm about her waist. "I'm sure they just changed their minds," he tried to reassure. "They'll be all right."

"No, they won't," Natalie cried. "My father—I mean Saul Palmer—will know they aided in my escape. I'm not sure what to expect of him. Bryce, we must go back. We should wait. . . ."

The landscape was only a blur on the horizon now, and the waves were causing the ship to lift and fall steadily on a set course now for New Orleans.

Bryce clasped Natalie's shoulders. "We can't," he said thickly. "We must think only of your safety at this moment. I came close to losing you. I won't let that happen again."

"But, Bryce . . ."

Bryce kissed her lips closed, then whispered, "Hush,

my darling. Hush.''

"Please?" she pleaded softly.

"I'm sorry to have to say no to your pleadings, Natalie" Bryce said thickly. "Come. We will go to my cabin. Maybe I can make you forget."

"Oh, Bryce . . ." Natalie argued weakly; yet she accepted his arm about her waist and let him usher her to his cabin.

He locked the door behind them and drew her into his arms, weaving his fingers through her hair. "You're safe now," he murmured. "You can place all ugliness behind you."

"Can I? Surely you understand how hard this has been for me. It's as though I am someone else, Bryce, living another life. I did love him for so long. I loved him as any daughter would love a father. How does one learn not to love? I want to hate him. I do."

"Just remember his deceit. Saul Palmer deprived you, Natalie. He forcibly deprived you. Just remember that."

"A part of me will always love him, no matter what he was or is."

"That's understandable."

Natalie gazed rapturously into his eyes. "Had it not been for this planned marriage to Albert Burns, I most surely would have stayed in Key West," she murmured. "You see, Bryce, when I love, I love completely."

Bryce framed her face between his hands. "I'm counting on that," he chuckled. He lowered his lips to hers, combing her hair back from her face with his fingers.

"Love me, darling," she whispered, moving her hands desperately over his body. "Make my mind leave me as only you can. Help me forget my sadness over Tami, Matthew, and Myra. . . ."

Her breath caught in her throat and her eyes opened wide. She reached a hand to Bryce's cheek. "Bryce, I forgot about Myra," she gasped. "My father—Saul Palmer—told me that she had been abducted by a pirate on her way to New York. How could this be? Piracy is all but dead. Who would take Myra from a ship, but no one and nothing else?"

Bryce took her hand in his and held it to his chest. "You say she was abducted by a pirate?" he said, furrowing his brow.

"Yes."

"Was it . . . Adam? Was the ship recognized?"

"I do not know. My father told me very few details."

Angrily, Bryce drew away from her and smacked a fist into the palm of one hand. "Why would he?" Bryce worried. "With all the prizes to choose from why would he choose one lady? Unless. . ."

"Unless?"

"Surely he loves her. Maybe she refused his hand in marriage. Pirates do not like to be refused anything as you, yourself, have so rudely been made aware."

"But Myra . . . ? Adam . . . ?" Natalie whispered. She shook her head back and forth. "No. No, I'm sure it couldn't have been Adam. You see, Myra . . . well . . . she was with child."

Her words faded away as she remembered Adam's reaction when she had told him why Myra was going to travel to New York. Then she laughed nervously and said, "No, it couldn't be. It just couldn't be. . . ."

"What?"

"Never mind," Natalie murmured, going to him and shaping her body to his. She sighed, feeling his hardness and smelling his familiar aroma. She had always hated the cigar smell of the pompous, old fools of Key West, but on Bryce, it was intoxicating, aphrodisiacal. His scent caused her senses to reel. Yes, while with him, she could forget. . . .

"Did you hate me when you found me gone from your house in New Orleans?" she whispered, running her fingers through the hair at the nape of his neck. It was becoming easier by the minute to forget. . . .

"I should have expected it," he said huskily. "When you want to do something, nothing stops you, does it?"

"I've only recently become so daring," she whispered.

"And what changed you?"

"You, Bryce," she said silkily. "You . . ."

Bryce's eyes hazed over with passion as he unfastened her blouse and slipped the lace of her undergarment down from her breasts.

Natalie felt the nerves in her body tighten. She exhaled a nervous sigh as Bryce kissed the deep valley between her breasts while he continued to undress her. Then as though in a trance, Natalie let him lead her to his bed and eased her down onto it, while his lips paid homage to the white satin of her flesh.

She eased his coat off, then his shirt and caressed the corded muscles of his shoulders lightly, with her fingertips. When his lips moved across the sensitive area of her abdomen with soft, feathery kisses, Natalie felt a tingling at her spine and became breathless as he went lower and lower, then stood before her and quickly removed his breeches and shoes.

Seeing the part of him that would once more fill her with his pleasure seed, she smiled invitingly and held her arms out to him.

When Bryce lowered himself over her, Natalie's head began slowly spinning as she reveled in the touch of flesh against flesh. And as he entered her she tossed her head from side to side, filled not only with him, but with a wild ecstasy that threatened to explode inside her.

"I love you so," she whispered, now raining kisses on his face as she framed it between her hands.

"And I you," he said huskily. He began making slow movements inside her, while watching her with a drugged passion in his hypnotic blue eyes.

Hearing a slow moan ease from between his lips, Natalie locked her legs around him to draw him even closer. They moved together, body to body, soul to soul. Bryce kissed her with intensity, his hands searching from breast to breast. Natalie clung to him, molded herself against him in her mounting desire. She let herself be lost to the warm glow of pleasure that built inside her until the ultimate plane was reached and together they shook and quaked as though a volcano were sending out magnificent rivulets of molten lava to spread . . . and spread. . . .

Within moments, however, Natalie drew away from Bryce, her eyes downcast. Though she was still feeling aftershocks of spent passion for him, she also was suddenly filled with guilt. How could she have let herself be carried away to such heights of pleasure when there were those whom she loved whose lives could be in danger? Where could Myra be? Was Tami all right?

Bryce threw an arm lazily across her stomach, letting his hand rest possessively against the velvet of her flesh.

"Now that I've rescued you from that scum, I have other matters to take care of," he said softly. "I must go to Orchid Island. I'm sure I will find the treasure chest there and also Clarence Seymour's opium shipment. And if I can succeed in ridding Orchid Island of all its pirates, then I will feel free to take you there, where we may even be able to build an empire of our own.''

He sighed even more lethargically. ''Just imagine, Natalie. An island all to ourselves.''

Natalie didn't respond; she just turned her face into his chest and tried to think of the moment . . . of him. . . .

''But there's only one problem,'' Bryce murmured. ''That damn key. I lost the damn key.''

Natalie's ears perked up as her heart skipped a beat. She leaned up on an elbow and smiled coyly at Bryce. ''Bryce, I have a surprise for you,'' she said. ''Just you wait right here while I get it.''

Feeling awkward in her nudity, she slipped her petticoat over her head.

Bryce rose from the bed and put on his breeches. ''What sort of surprise?'' he said, lifting an eyebrow.

Fumbling with her skirt, Natalie was finally able to get the key unpinned from its inside pocket. Curling her fingers around it, she moved steathily toward Bryce, smiling mischievously. Then, as though playing a game, she thrust both fists toward him, crossing her wrists at an angle.

''Choose a fist.'' She giggled. ''Inside one is a prize of all prizes, just for you, Bryce Fowler.''

Bryce placed his hands on his hips. ''Games, my love?'' he chuckled amusedly. ''What of such importance could you have hidden inside such delicate fingers?''

Natalie straightened her back and set her jaw tightly. ''Bryce . . .'' She sighed. ''Choose. Choose a hand!''

Bryce absently scratched his head, then lowered his hand and tapped one of her clenched fists with a forefinger.

Smiling brightly, feeling her heart hammering against her ribs, Natalie slowly opened her hand and watched his mouth drop open in silent amazement.

Bryce's face flushed crimson when he saw the brass key shimmering back at him beneath the flickering light of the cabin's lone whale-oil lamp. He eyed the key . . . then Natalie.

"Is that . . . ?" he murmured, his throat suddenly dry, his pulse keenly racing.

"It is your key, Bryce," she said, fitting it into the palm of his hand. "I'm sorry that I didn't give it to you earlier. But circumstances just wouldn't allow it."

Bryce went closer to the lamp's glow and studied the key, turning it from front to back, over and over again. "By God, it is the key my father gave me," he drawled.

He clasped his fingers tightly around it and held it to his heart. He closed his eyes and, though he was not a religious person, mouthed a silent prayer of thanks toward the cabin's ceiling.

Then he swirled around on a heel and eyed Natalie wonderingly. "How did you happen to have the key?" he asked softly.

"Bryce, I've had it since the day we met in the carriage."

"You . . . what?"

Smiling Natalie placed a cheek against his chest. With her arms twined about him, she said, "Darling, it must have fallen from your pocket when you so gallantly rescued my purse and bonnet from the carriage floor. I discovered it later, after you were gone."

"Well, I'll be damned," Bryce murmured. He placed a forefinger beneath her chin and lifted her face to meet his gaze. "All along you have had it. Why didn't you tell me earlier? I've been sick with worry."

Natalie felt a blush rising. She lowered her lashes as she spoke. "I know," she whispered. Then she met his gaze with a soft, glowing smile. "It's truly not important why I didn't give it to you sooner, is it? You have it now. That's what matters, isn't it?"

Bryce placed the key safely inside the drawer of his desk, lifting his lips in a slow smile. Then with one fast movement, he placed his hands at Natalie's waist and lifted her into the air.

Laughing merrily, he began swinging her around. "Yes, darling," he shouted. "All that matters now is what this key will unlock for us. You, my sweet, will never want for anything the rest of your life!"

Feeling dizzy, yet deliriously so, Natalie joined him in laughter. After he took a last turn, he eased her slowly to the floor, devouring her with his eyes, then drawing her passionately into his arms. With a fierceness, an almost uncontrollable fury, he kissed her.

Their lips parted, tongues met, and once more they became entangled in their passion's web.

"I must have you again," he said huskily. He swept her up into his arms and carried her to the bed.

"With this key in our possession, the world is ours, Natalie," he whispered. "All ours. . . ."

NEW ORLEANS

It binds my being with wreath of rue . . .
This want of you.

—Wright

THIRTEEN

The kerosene lamp belched black spirals of smoke from
its chimney while Brenda stood watch at a window. From
her father's office, she could see only faint movements
below her on the street which was enveloped in a low
hanging, ghostlike fog. She glanced toward Adam as he
turned the key in the drawer of her father's desk. It hadn't
been hard to steal the key from her father's key chain.
Since he had a full circle of keys, the loss of only one
wouldn't be noticed. And, anyway, she would replace it
before he needed it on the coming day.

"Hurry, Adam," she whispered. "Someone might see
the light."

Adam drew the kerosene lamp closer as he placed the
ledger on the desk. "The fog's so heavy," he muttered,
"no one will see the light. Quit worrying about it."

Brenda brushed the hood of her cape from her head and
shook her hair until it cascaded in midnight black tresses
across her shoulders. She strolled to the desk and leaned
against it.

"Father's been quite moody since Natalie left," she

murmured. "It's as though I don't even exist. I don't understand. He's had me all of his life and now . . . it's as though she's the only one that matters."

She clenched her hands into tight fists. "I hate her, Adam," she hissed. "I hate her. Her entrance into my life has caused me nothing but heartache."

Adam continued flipping the pages of the ledger, scanning their contents, searching. "You don't have to worry about her any longer," he laughed. "Like I said earlier. She's surely wed to Albert Burns by now. The house was like a damned garden the day I left. Roses everywhere. That's why I left. I couldn't stand the sight or smell of it."

Brenda curved her lips into a pout and slinked around the desk to drape an arm about his neck. "Or was it because you couldn't stand to witness her marrying another man," she whispered harshly. "Is it because your father gave her to Albert Burns and not to you?"

Adam knocked her arm away and glowered at her. "Don't ever say that again," he snarled. "If I had wanted her, I would've taken her. I take everything I want. You know that, Brenda. I have killed many times to get what I want."

Ripples of pleasure coursed through Brenda's veins. She liked his strength. She liked his greed . . . his evil ways. Excitement was her main goal in life. With Adam, she had found it. He never seemed to be lacking ways to set her heart racing.

"All right," she said, moving back to the window to stare from it. "I understand. I should have known that, Adam."

Adam's fingers now were running slowly along a page. "Since I seized the opium shipment, seems your father's business has drawn to a sudden halt," he said. "There are no more entries."

Then he folded the ledger pages back even more, seeing a ragged edge. "Hmmmm" he murmured. "Seems someone has torn a page loose. . . ."

The sudden shuffling of feet drew Brenda's and Adam's eyes toward the door.

Brenda's color faded from her cheeks when she saw her father standing there.

"Could you be looking for this?" Clarence growled. He held up a lined sheet of ledger paper with one hand while leaving the other hidden in his right coat pocket.

Clarence's gaze met Brenda's, hurt and anger fusing. "I suspected you had something to do with the missing opium shipment," he declared. "I didn't want to. Not my own daughter. But a hired detective found the answers I was seeking."

Brenda's hands went to her throat. "A . . . detective?" she gasped.

Adam rose slowly from behind the desk, his right hand now resting on a pistol at his waist. Brenda rushed to his side. "No, Adam," she whispered. "Please. Just let's leave."

Adam cast her a fast glance. "And you think he plans to let us?" he snarled. In one quick movement he was pointing the pistol toward Clarence and edging away from the desk. "Now, ol' man, just step aside and you won't get hurt," he said smoothly, motioning with the pistol and a nod of his head.

"I wouldn't if I were you," Clarence said flatly. "I have my fingers on a trigger in my right pocket. One more move and I'll be forced to shoot you."

"Father . . ." Brenda pleaded. "Please just step

271

aside. Let Adam leave.''

''And you?'' Clarence said softly. ''What are your plans, Brenda?''

''I will stay here with you, father,'' she said, swallowing hard. ''I'm sorry. . . .''

''I don't want any part of you, Brenda,'' Clarence said icily. ''You not only stole from my business but also aided in Natalie's escape. You are a she-devil, someone I no longer know, nor want to know.''

''But, father, I didn't think—''

''No. I guess you didn't,'' he grumbled. ''Why, Brenda? Why? I've given you everything. You never wanted for anything.''

Brenda clenched her hands into tight fists. ''You gave me everything but excitement,'' she hissed. ''You doted over me, father. I became bored. I needed more. Adam has given it to me.''

Her voice grew softer and her hands relaxed. ''But I still love you, father. Please tell me that you don't hate me.''

''I don't hate you, I pity you,'' Clarence stated flatly. His icy gaze moved to Adam. ''Now very slowly place your pistol on the desk,'' he ordered. ''I then will take you to the authorities. They'll be pleased to know that I, single-handedly, have captured the *Sea Snake's* captain.''

Clarence emitted a short, raspy laugh. ''Seems your career as a ravaging, thieving pirate has just come to a sudden halt,'' he bragged.

''Adam . . .'' Brenda pleaded.

''Shut up,'' Adam growled.

Brenda saw Adam's finger slowly squeezing the trigger and felt panic rising inside her. She couldn't let him

272

kill her father! She just couldn't!

Plunging her body sideways, she grabbed for Adam's gun, and while doing so, caused it to discharge in a loud explosion.

Brenda's knees grew weak as she watched her father crumple slowly to the floor, clutching at his chest. "Father!" she screamed. She lifted the trail of her cape and dress into her arms and hurried to him.

"Damn it, Brenda," Adam snarled, rushing along behind her. "What the hell did you think you were doing?"

He bent and grabbed the ledger page from Clarence; then he went and held it beneath the lamp's soft glow, studying the entries.

Brenda fell to her knees at her father's side, full of torment and grief. She had never dreamed her thrilling escapades could lead to this. "Father . . ." she whispered, touching his brow.

Her eyes searched his face and then traveled downward to where the blood had splashed outward in ruby reds onto his white shirt and black coat. With trembling fingers she removed a maroon cravat from his throat and loosened his shirt until it was open to the waist, exposing the full extent of his wound. Since blood covered his chest, she couldn't see the full extent of the damage inflicted on his upper right chest. But she could see that although he was unconscious he was not mortally wounded.

"Can't make head or tail of this damn scribbling," Adam growled. "Seems like some sort of damned code."

He folded the page and thrust it inside his front breeches pocket. Turning, he saw Brenda kneeling over her father. He kneaded his brow. He couldn't leave her here. Her life would be in danger and she was too valuable to him to let anything happen to her. He had never met anyone quite like her before and doubted if he ever would again.

He loved her daring, reckless nature. She would make a perfect companion. She would never be one to settle down with children. He would ride the seas with her at his side.

With determination in his stride, he went to her and yanked on her arm. "Come on, Brenda," he said. "We've got to get out of here."

"But, father . . . ?" she said, beseeching him with her wide, dark eyes.

"Forget him," Adam said, placing his hands on his hips.

"But he's unconscious."

"You had better hope he doesn't regain consciousness," Adam argued. "He knew me, Natalie. It is now out that I am the pirate of the *Sea Snake*. I must keep a low profile for a while."

"But, Adam—"

Adam drew her roughly up before him. "Are you, or aren't you going with me?" he snarled.

"Oh, Adam. I can't stay. You know that," she said. "You heard my father. He no longer wants me. If you'll have me, I want to go with you."

"I'll take you to Orchid Island with me," Adam said. "I have a mansion there that is so huge one can get lost just going from room to room."

Brenda took a last lingering look at her father then ran from the room with Adam and down the steep staircase. Stepping out into the darkness of night, she clung to him. Then she yanked at his arm, to stop him, almost numb because she saw Natalie looking directly at her from a carriage window. In the light of the street lantern, she easily recognized her. But why was Natalie back in New Orleans? And who was she with?

Brenda glanced toward Adam, relieved that he hadn't also seen her.

"Brenda, we must get out of here," he growled. "Why are you stopping?"

Brenda pulled the hood of her cape up over her head and loved closer to him. "I needed to place my hood on my head," she said softly.

She watched the carriage move away from them, in the direction of her house. She now believed that Bryce Fowler had stopped the wedding and was once more returning Natalie to her rightful father.

Tears burned at the corners of Brenda's eyes, jealous tears. Natalie was taking the place of the daughter who had just been cast from the fold.

Then she couldn't help herself. Something compelled her to smile, knowing that maybe . . . just maybe . . . Natalie wouldn't have the opportunity to be loved by Clarence Seymour. Surely he would die!

"I'd rather he be dead than loving her," she thought angrily to herself.

When they were aboard Adam's ship, locked safely in his cabin, Brenda tossed her cape aside and threw herself down on the bunk, exhausted. She watched Adam as he unfolded the ledger page and sat down at his desk to study it. He was all she had now. Loving him as she did, she felt that he was worth all she had just lost.

But what if he found another woman he loved more than her? What would become of her then? Why was she feeling so empty at the pit of her stomach?

Slowly, methodically, she began to disrobe. She

needed to prove to herself and him that what they had together was enough for both of them.

At last, lying quite nude, Brenda whispered seductively, "Adam . . ."

Adam kneaded his brow, eying the jumble of words and figures on the page. He turned the page from side to side, then upside down, grumbling obscenities beneath his breath.

"Adam, come here," Brenda said silkily.

"Brenda, shut up," Adam snarled. "Can't you see I'm busy? There's got to be a way to figure this out."

The swaying of the ship and the splash of the waves against her hull made Brenda quite aware that they were now easing away from New Orleans and would soon be in the waters of the Atlantic. Then on to Orchid Island!

She had heard Adam speak so dramatically of Orchid Island. He had said that at one time pirates his father shielded from the hands of the law ran amok on it.

But now only Adam and his crew were occasional inhabitants. The island had become a storage place for the prizes taken from ships at sea. Brenda could hardly wait to become the mistress of such an island and the riches it most surely held!

"Adam, will you stop what you're doing for just one moment?" she said, a tone of impatience in her voice.

Adam slammed a hand against his desk top and swung his head angrily around. But his eyes wavered when he saw her there, her arms stretched out to him, inviting him to join her on the bed. As though in a trance, feeling the heat rising in his loins, he shoved his chair back, stood, and began undressing.

"You temptress . . . you witch," he said huskily, stepping from his final piece of clothing. He chuckled as he moved toward her. "You must have a heart of stone. Your father may be dying of a gunshot wound and you're only thinking of the hungers of the flesh."

Brenda's eyes misted over a bit. "Make me forget, Adam," she whispered. "Make . . . me . . . forget. . . ."

His dark eyes were pits of passion as he lowered himself down over her. "We're safely at sea now," he said. "And if your father is able to reveal our identities, the search will be for my *Sea Snake*. We're safe aboard her sister ship; no one will recognize it as mine."

"I know . . . I know," Brenda said, already feeling the headiness that his presence caused. Her heart pulsed wildly, her insides trembled. She reached a hand to his hair and weaved her fingers through it as she guided his lips downward.

"Love me, Adam," she whispered.

His lips crushed hers and his hands molded each of her breasts. His thumbs circled and teased their nipples until they peaked to tightness. When he entered her, Brenda moaned with rapture and moved with him as their bodies blended into one.

"Always love me, Adam," Brenda sighed. "Always love me. . . ."

The carriage wheels clattered noisily over the cobblestones of the street. Natalie placed a hand on Bryce's arms. "Bryce, did you see?" she said anxiously.

Bryce covered her hand with his, deliciously content to have her so near again. And soon they would be man and wife. With Natalie, it was easy to forget his childhood torments. Without her, he probably would have spent his life searching. . . .

277

"Did I see what, darling?" he said, brushing a kiss against her cheek.

"It was Brenda and Adam!" she exclaimed. "I know it was. They were rushing from one of those buildings on the river front. It looked as though they were up to no good."

"God," Bryce said, tapping on the front carriage wall, alerting the coachman to stop.

"What is it, Bryce?" Natalie asked, seeing the worry in his eyes and the hard set of his jaw.

"It may have been your father's warehouse and office building," he said hoarsely. "Point out which building you saw them leave."

As Natalie pointed, Bryce tensed. He looked the building over carefully, then his gaze stopped and held on the sixth-story window, from which a light dimly shone.

"Clarence Seymour said he never works at night," he said quietly. "He says no one is even allowed in the building late at night."

Bryce opened the carriage door and leaned his head farther out. "Then . . . who . . . ?" he mumbled. "I wonder . . ."

Natalie moved closer to him. "Bryce, what is it?" she whispered. "Is something wrong?"

"Could be," he murmured. "Could be."

He climbed from the carriage and held his hand toward her. "Come on. We've got to find out."

Natalie took his hand and stepped out onto the street. "Find out what?" she asked, staring upward through the fog as Bryce still studied the lit window. "Bryce, what is it?"

Bryce nodded toward the building. "That's your father's import/export building," he said flatly. "There's a light in his office window. I've been there recently to visit him. I know that's his private office. No one should be even in the building much less his office. I don't like it, Natalie. I think Adam and Brenda might have been up to their usual tricks.''

Natalie clung to his arm as they moved stealthily toward the building. Like dancing ghosts, the fog swirled around them as they stepped up to the entrance and Natalie shivered involuntarily. When Bryce tried the door and it crept slowly open at only a slight shove of a finger, she clung even more solidly to his arm of steel.

''The door is unlocked and was left ajar,'' Bryce whispered. He covered Natalie's clinging hand with one of his own, glancing down at her in the total darkness.

''Maybe you should wait in the carriage,'' he said, furrowing his brow. ''I'm not sure what we might find.''

''No,'' Natalie said stubbornly. ''I want to go with you.'' Then her eyes wavered. ''What do you expect to find, Bryce?'' she murmured. ''Do you think Clarence . . . my father . . . might be here?''

''I'm not sure,'' Bryce said.

He let his left hand go to the pistol he wore hidden beneath his coat. Then he left Natalie's side long enough to search through the dark until he felt around and found a kerosene lamp on a desk. He lit it and then held it up to look slowly around him. Everything was quiet. The only sound that could be heard was the lapping of water against the wharves outside the windows. The room was filled with the shadows of desks and chairs, and cubbyholes lined the walls, filled with what appeared to be scrolls of maps. The aroma was musty and damp, and the sudden appearance of a racing rat drew a scream from Natalie.

Bryce chuckled and drew her next to his side. "It's only a rat," he said. "Most buildings by the water have them. And let's hope a rat is all we find."

Natalie swept the folds of her skirt up into her arms as she began a slow ascent of the stairs at Bryce's side. Her eyes continuously darted around her, watching for any signs of life. From landing to landing, her heart beat out her apprehension and fear. Then when the sixth-floor landing was finally reached, Bryce and Natalie began to move quietly toward the opened door that showed faint light from it.

"Bryce, I'm scared," Natalie whispered. She flipped her hair back from her eyes and stared boldly toward the door that was now within reach. When they stepped inside, her pulse began to race at seeing Clarence Seymour leaning on one elbow, blood streaks across his clothes and across his exposed chest.

"Good Lord," Bryce exclaimed. He went to Clarence and placed the kerosene lamp on the floor beside him. Then he placed one hand behind Clarence's head to support it, while with the other he checked the seeping wound.

"Good Lord, man, what happened here?" Bryce asked, arching an eyebrow.

Natalie fell to her knees beside Clarence, all eyes. She reached a hand to his brow and eased some locks of thick, gray hair back from his eyes. "Who . . . could have . . . done this?" she asked thickly. Her heart was pounding against her ribs, and she felt something for this man for the first time. She swallowed hard when his soft, brown eyes met hers in a wondering manner.

"You've come . . ." he said, lifting a hand to cover one of hers. "Natalie . . . you've decided to come home.''

"Yes," she murmured.

"Clarence, what happened here?" Bryce persisted, reaching for a handkerchief from his inside coat pocket. He placed it over the wound and held it solidly in place.

Clarence's eyes misted over with a veil of tears. His gaze went back to Bryce. "I hadn't wanted to believe it," he murmured, almost choking with emotion. "But I found my suspicions to be quite valid."

"You're talking about Brenda?" Bryce asked, now dabbing at the wound.

"How did . . . you . . . know?" Clarence said, coughing a bit. His hand left Natalie's to move to his wound as he emitted a soft groan.

"Natalie saw Brenda and that damned Adam rush from this building," Bryce growled.

He rose and began searching around the room. When he found a bottle of wine in a liquor cabinet, he took it to Clarence. Leaning down on one knee, he removed the cork and offered Clarence a drink. "Might ease the pain a bit," he encouraged.

"Thanks . . ." Clarence said, groaning as he tried to rise a bit more on his elbow.

Bryce tipped the bottle to Clarence's lips. "Take it easy," he said. "Maybe not too much at a time. . . ."

Natalie reached for the handkerchief and folded it so the clean side could now be placed on the wound. "Mr. Seymour . . . uh . . . Clarence," she murmured, "did . . . Adam . . . shoot you?"

"I wasn't fast enough." Clarence laughed absently, wiping the wetness from his lips. "I trusted that he wouldn't shoot, not with Brenda there. But . . . when she tried to stop him . . . well . . . I'm not sure if she made the gun go off by accident or if he got the shot fired before she reached him.''

Natalie rose quickly to her feet and turned her back to the watchful eyes. She stifled a sob, hating to know that Adam was capable of shooting a man and leaving him to die. All those years of thinking he was her brother would surely haunt her for the rest of her life.

''Darling . . .'' Bryce said, drawing her around into his arms. ''Please don't be upset. But I think I do understand.''

He certainly did for he was experiencing the same feelings but for different reasons. It was his brother who was so heartless and cold. They had the same blood in their veins; they shared the same father. . . .

''I guess I will be able to accept all of this one day,'' Natalie murmured, wiping a tear away. She glanced down at Clarence. Would she ever feel comfortable calling him Father? Then she noticed his labored breathing and realized how selfish she was being. Here Clarence lay—her father—wounded . . . and she was requiring comforting by Bryce! Clarence Seymour needed and deserved devoted attention from her and Bryce at this time.

She pulled free of Bryce and once more dropped to her knees beside Clarence. ''We've got to get a doctor,'' she stated, caressing his brow.

''No,'' Clarence argued. ''Since you've cleaned up the blood a bit, I can tell it's only a flesh wound. Thank God. You'd probably even be able to find the bullet lodged somewhere in that wall back there.''

He took a deep, shaky breath. ''What I want is to get home. My bed is all I need.'' He eyed Natalie intensely. ''Maybe you'd even play nurse?'' he chuckled, reaching to pat her hand.

Natalie blinked back tears. "Yes, I'll do that for you," she said. "Gladly."

Clarence's eyes misted with tears again and he sniffled. "Brenda . . ." he whispered. "I can't believe she'd . . . But I've always realized she was different. Just didn't know how much. . . ."

"Don't think about it now," Natalie crooned, squeezing one of his hands.

Clarence gazed upward at Bryce. "He took a page from my ledger," he said hoarsely. Then he laughed. "Damned idiot," he said. "He's going to have a hell of a time figuring out what I placed on that page."

"Why's that?" Bryce asked, busying himself drawing Clarence's shirt and coat back in place, to hide the wound.

"You see, I knew they'd be back," Clarence chuckled. "I planned it."

"So what's recorded on the ledger sheet?" Bryce asked, placing the cork back on the wine bottle and setting it aside.

"I made it look like some sort of code," Clarence said. "But it doesn't mean one damned thing. I made up this page just for Adam Palmer."

"Well, I'll be damned," Bryce chuckled.

"Enough about Adam and the ledger sheet," Natalie said firmly, casting Bryce a fast, angry look. "What's important is getting Clarence home so I can properly dress his wound."

"You're right, Natalie," Bryce said. He picked up the kerosene lamp and handed it to her. "You take the lamp and I'll help Clarence to the carriage."

He looked toward Clarence. "Think you can make it down the stairs and to the carriage with my aid?"

283

"Sure as hell can," Clarence said, groaning as he pushed himself a bit farther from the floor.

Barely breathing, Natalie took the lamp, as Bryce lifted Clarence slowly upward. Once on his feet, Bryce let Clarence rest his full weight against him.

"God, I think I can do it." Clarence laughed nervously. He placed his right arm about Bryce's shoulder and let a dizziness rush into his head and away again.

"You probably lost more blood than you realize," Natalie said, lighting the way out to the staircase as Bryce half-dragged and half-carried Clarence toward it.

"Easy does it now," Bryce said as each step was taken with care.

Natalie sighed with relief when the lower floor was reached. She turned her steady gaze toward Clarence and saw how pale he had become. She was suddenly aware of how close she had come to losing him just after having found him! She felt awash with a strange devotion, even love for him, so much so that it frightened her. Was it a built-in instinct because they were actually daughter and father?

Whatever the reason she felt the need to go to him and ease herself into his arms . . . to ask about her mother . . . about their lives together . . . about the night she was conceived.

She had these needs—to see if she had even been wanted! So far, all of her life had been a lie. Had he wanted it to be different for her? But she had to keep telling herself that when his wife had been taken from him, she had only been a fetus, contentedly growing inside a womb. . . .

"Just a little farther," Bryce urged.

When they reached the carriage, Bryce was glad that

the coachman jumped down and helped to place Clarence inside. They rested Clarence's head on Natalie's lap; then Bryce instructed the coachman to proceed carefully to Clarence Seymour's house.

"Once I get you safely settled in bed, I'll go after that son of a bitch," Bryce growled. "It's time I showed him my *Golden Isis* can outrun any ship in the Atlantic. Even his damned *Sea Snake.*"

Clarence reached for Bryce. "I don't think you'll be wanting to do that just at this time," he said. "God. How'd I forget to tell you? Earlier this evening I received a message for you."

"From who?"

"Abe, your partner, came to my house, hoping you had returned from Key West with Natalie," Clarence said, coughing a bit.

"Well? What did he want?"

Clarence covered his eyes with the back of a hand. "I really don't know how I forgot to tell you the minute I saw you," he grumbled. "Such a terrible thing. . . ."

Bryce scooted to the edge of his seat. "What is it? What was the message?"

Clarence sent Bryce a wavering glance. "It's your father," he murmured.

Fear grabbed at Bryce's heart. His pulse raced. "What about my . . . father?"

"Seems he passed away two days ago."

"What?" Bryce gasped. Then his whole body seemed to melt into a depressed state. "My father is . . . dead?"

"Yes. Sorry, Bryce," Clarence mumbled.

Natalie reached a hand to Bryce, then drew it back, seeing his quiet, remorseful mood.

"Damn . . . damn . . . !" Bryce then snarled. "I let

285

him down. He won't ever see what is rightfully his."

He withdrew the key from his inner coat pocket. "He won't ever see what this key unlocks."

"The message said nothing will be done with his remains until you return to Key West," Clarence continued. "Something about your brother Hugh not knowing anything about making appropriate arrangements . . ."

"Yeah. I can understand that," Bryce growled. He reached for Natalie's hand. "Seems our wedding will have to wait," he said softly. "But nothing else will delay it. I promise you, darling."

"I will pass my days caring for . . . Clarence," she murmured.

Then she smiled softly. "Yes, I'll see to my . . . father's welfare."

FOURTEEN

The ship rocked gently with the waves as if the sea were a giant cradle. Brenda tossed fitfully in her sleep; then she awakened in a cool sweat to find Adam peacefully asleep beside her.

Pulling a blanket up around her and shivering from the cabin's damp mustiness, she continued to study Adam. Asleep, he looked as though he were a child, innocent and sweet, soft, with his lips relaxed and his dark hair laying in light waves across his brow and around his ears.

His features weren't hard and defiant, but gentle and smooth. He didn't appear to have the cold, savage heart of a pirate. But she knew him too well. He was a pirate. He had just shot her father and had left him to die. What would Adam do if he knew that she had seen Natalie inside a carriage in New Orleans and hadn't told him? Would he cast her aside, would she become like a leaf blowing unwanted in the wind . . . ?

She couldn't take that chance! No! She had lost her father, she couldn't take the chance of losing Adam!

With trembling fingers, she shook Adam's arm.

"Adam," she whispered. "Adam . . . wake up."

Throwing his arm across Brenda's chest, Adam growled darkly. "What is it?" he snarled. "It'd better be good, Brenda, to wake me up. I only got to sleep."

Brenda brushed his arm aside and leaned up over him. "Adam, I have something to tell you," she said. "But, I don't quite know how."

Rising to a sitting position, bare-chested, Adam tousled his hair with his hands, yawning. "Just say it," he said. "That should be simple enough for you."

He combed his hair back from his eyes and looked her way, frowning. "Well?" he persisted.

"Oh, Adam . . ." Brenda fretted aloud. She rose from the bed and slipped into her petticoat. She needed a drink of wine to give her courage to speak the words. They were only a few hours out to sea, yet she knew that she should have told him earlier—even at the very moment when she had seen Natalie!

Adam suddenly brushed past her and arrived at the liquor cabinet before her. He poured wine into two long-stemmed, crystal glasses and handed her one. He eyed her wonderingly as they each took a swallow of wine.

Brenda took another sip, then toyed with the glass, averting her eyes from his nudity. "Adam, I know that I must tell you this," she said softly. "I . . . uh . . . well . . . I saw. . . ."

The words seemed to freeze in her throat. She glanced quickly up at him, knowing his moods so well. She knew he would be angry. She only prayed that he wouldn't hit her.

"Damn it, Brenda," Adam growled, pouring himself some more wine. "You've never been at a loss for words before. Why are you now?"

"Because you're going to be so angry . . ." she murmured.

"And when has that stopped you?" he scoffed.

He went to her and with his free hand, drew her next to him. "You're my sea witch, my devilish kitten," he said thickly.

He kissed her roughly then shoved her away from him. "Now tell me," he growled darkly. "I don't like to be kept waiting. You should know that."

Brenda paced a bit, hearing the gentle splashing of the water against the ship and the creaking of the three magnificent masts as the wind moved the ship along its way. It was so peaceful now. But after she told Adam, she could expect havoc!

"Adam, I saw Natalie in New Orleans as we were leaving my father's warehouse," she forced herself to blurt in one quick breath. She watched color rise to his cheeks and his features once more became hard and intense.

"You . . . what?" he said in a shallow whisper.

"She was in a carriage, headed in the direction of my house," Brenda proceeded to say. "I know it was her, Adam. She looked directly at me. In the lamplight our faces were so clear each of us might have been a mirror at her own reflection."

A loud, snarling growl emerged from deep inside Adam as he threw his glass across the narrow space of the cabin. When it made contact with the dark paneling, splinters shattered in diamond twinkles all across the oak flooring, and the wine made red blotches wherever it landed.

"No!" he shouted, flailing his arms into the air. "It just can't be. She's surely wed to Albert Burns by now.

289

They were supposed to leave for New York immediately after the wedding."

He went to Brenda and clasped her shoulders, his fingers digging unmercifully into her flesh. "Who was in the carriage with her?" he growled, anger flashing in the dark pools of his eyes. "Tell me!"

Brenda flinched. "Adam, you're hurting me," she said flatly. "Let go this minute. Do you hear?"

"Brenda, if you don't answer me, by God, I'm going to knock your teeth down your throat," he shouted. "You're playing with fire when you choose to hold out on me."

"But, Adam, I didn't see who was with Natalie," Brenda replied, softening her tone of voice. "I didn't. It was too dark. I only saw Natalie because the carriage window framed her face. She was sitting next to it, looking in my direction."

Adam reached for his dark, coarse breeches and stepped into them. "Damn him," he growled.

Brenda crept toward Adam. "What are you going to do?" she murmured.

"It was Bryce Fowler," he snapped. "I know it was. I should've killed him a long time ago."

He jerked his black shirt on and fastened it at the front; then, even more angry, he placed his pistols at each hip. "I will kill him this time," he said. "He's interferred in my life for the last time."

As he took quick steps toward the door, Brenda rushed to him. "Where are you going, Adam?" she asked breathlessly.

He spun around. "To set the course back New Orleans's way," he grumbled. "I do believe I have some unfinished business there."

He glowered toward her. "And once we dock, you will stay aboard the ship," he added. "When I return, I will bring Natalie to join us on our voyage to Orchid Island."

Brenda's insides went cold; her face drained of color. "You will take her to . . . Orchid Island?" she asked softly. "But, Adam, why? Why not return her to Key West, to your father?"

"She can stay in seclusion on Orchid Island. My father will want that for her. At least until we feel it's safe for her to return to Key West."

"But if you shoot Bryce Fowler, surely no one else will be a threat."

"We will not take any chances."

Brenda grabbed one of his arms and clung desperately to it. "Adam, I wanted to share Orchid Island with you— alone," she pleaded.

Adam jerked himself free of her grasp. He laughed scornfully. "I didn't ever guarantee we'd be alone," he said. "Even now another occupies my house."

He swung around and left the cabin, leaving Brenda to stare blankly after him.

"What does he mean?" she whispered. "Who else . . . ?"

Worn out from the ever-building traumatic experiences of her life, Natalie climbed into bed, snuggling beneath the covers. With a sigh she lifted her hair from beneath her head to let it lay in midnight blacks around her face. She cozied down deeper into her pillow and let her eyes close, already feeling the peaceful, lethargy of sleep invading her senses. She felt proud of how she had been able to tend to Clarence's—No! She must remember to call him Father!

She knew that she had made her father comfortable after having seen to his wound. It had given her a deep feeling of satisfaction to help him, especially since she had caused him so much heartache because of her ill-fated voyage back to Key West.

Tears formed in her eyes when she remembered her father in Key West. That relationship had become a horrible nightmare since she'd discovered that he, in truth, was not her father, but was an aging ex-pirate who had most surely left a trail of blood sparkling red in the sea wherever he had ventured on his black, devil ship.

"And Adam . . ." she whispered.

A noise right outside her bedroom door startled Natalie. Eyes open now, she tensed, listening closely as she peered through the darkness. When a board in the flooring squeaked even closer to her bed, Natalie inched backward toward the carved, mahogany headboard, knowing that this surely wasn't her father. He wouldn't be sneaking around in the dark. He would have the aid of a lamp's light. And he most surely was fast asleep, after having become so weakened from the loss of blood.

Groping hands found Natalie. Coarse fingers quickly covered her mouth while another hand twisted an arm behind her. With a thundering heartbeat, Natalie squirmed and fought against the stranger in the night, only succeeding in hurting herself as both hands tightened on her.

"Don't fight, Natalie," Adam whispered harshly. "No matter what you try, you'll still end up in the same place. On my ship, headed for Orchid Island."

Natalie's eyes widened. Adam! It was Adam! Oh, why? She fought against his fingers sealing her lips. She grumbled, she kicked, but stopped suddenly when Adam removed his hands and hit her roughly across the face.

The snapping of her neck and the stinging of her face where his fingers had left their scalding imprints made Natalie quite aware of Adam's determination to get his way.

"Now get up," he spat. "Get some decent clothes on."

One of his hands lowered, to touch the swell of a breast. Harshly cupping it, the heat rose in his loins. He wanted her! Damn it he wanted her! But this wasn't the time. He let his fingers travel to the other breast, almost breathless from his need of her.

"Do you hear what I say?" he said thickly, stepping away from her. "And don't you let out a peep, or I'll be forced to hurt you further."

Natalie rose slowly from the bed, feeling a slow twisting in her gut. For so long, he had been a brother to her. Now he was only a man, yet more than that. He was a pirate, one who took what he wanted. Would he even take her body and use it as he pleased? A bitterness rose in her throat; she did not want to envision him with her in . . . that way.

Fumbling through the darkness, not having been a part of this room long enough to know her way around, she stubbed her toe on a chair. "Ouch," she cried, reaching to soothe the pain away.

Rubbing her throbbing toe, she tried to focus her eyes on his shadow in the dark, but saw nothing! It was as though she were standing in the dark pits of hell—with the devil standing near her.

"I can't see," she whispered. "Adam, how can I get dressed if I can't see what I am doing?"

She listened, hearing Adam moving around the room. Then she tensed when a kerosene lamp's slow glow climbed higher behind its protective chimney and reflected the evil glint in Adam's eyes. Now she could see the sneer on his slightly curved lips.

"I've lighted a lamp for you so make speed, my darling sister," he mocked.

His gaze traveled slowly over her thin nightgown trimmed in delicate lace. Through it, he could see the magnificence of her breasts, the gentle curve of her satiny hips, and the dark vee that seemed to crown her thighs. He took a step toward her. He had time. Yes, no one was . . .

His heart skipped a beat. In his haste, he had forgotten Bryce Fowler!

"Where is Bryce Fowler?" he growled. "Is he the one who brought you safely back to New Orleans?"

Blanching, Natalie cast him a sideways glance. "I've not seen Bryce Fowler for some time now," she lied.

"Who then?"

"A detective my father hired," she said smoothly, despite the anger she felt when his eyes raked over her again. Surely he wouldn't! Not Adam! She still held a remembrance of her sisterly feelings for him! He must also have such remembrances!

"You're lying," Adam growled. "And quit calling that man who paid to have you brought here your father. You only have one father."

He placed the lamp on a table and in two quick strides was standing over her. He grabbed her wrists, holding her immobile as his gaze went to her heaving bosom.

"But for now, none of those things matter," he said thickly. "What does is my ache for you. I've wanted you for so long."

He released her wrists, to place his fingers through her

hair. Groaning, he forced her lips to his and ground his mouth into hers while his tongue sought entrance between her teeth. One of his hands lowered, and reaching inside her gown, he made contact with her soft flesh. Intoxicated by her now, he would not be held back.

Natalie pushed at him . . . she struggled to free her mouth . . . then saw no other choice but to clamp her teeth down onto the invading spear of his tongue. With force, she lowered her teeth and suddenly tasted salt as his blood spat from the wound she had just inflicted.

A loud yowl tore him away from her. Adam began to dance around the room in pain, holding his mouth closed.

Natalie slunk away from him, numb with fright. When he recovered, what would he do to her? She glanced toward the door, considering escape. But how far could she get?

Then her hopes rose for an instant when she heard footsteps approaching from the hallway. Had Bryce once more stood watch as he had the other time? Had he seen Adam slip into the house?

With a racing pulse, she inched toward the door, hoping to see Bryce there, ready to defend her. But she stopped short when Clarence came ambling into view, pale, and holding his hand to his bandaged wound.

"Natalie . . . ?" Clarence said; then he took a step backward when he saw Adam at the far end of the room, glowering, with blood running from a corner of his mouth. He reached to protect himself when he saw Adam remove a pistol from his right hip.

Clarence began to shake his head back and forth as the barrel of the pistol was aimed toward him. He could hear Natalie's frantic screams as the gun exploded. Too quickly he felt a piercing pain in his abdomen.

In a brief instant, he was seeing Kathryn, loving her, kissing her, and in the next reaching for Natalie, seeing Kathryn in her. His mind then sank into a dull, blank void as his body crashed downward onto the floor.

Natalie covered her mouth with her hands, but her ears rang from her continuous screams. Adam rushed to her and slapped her, growling.

"Shut up," he snarled.

Natalie began crying, harsh, body-wracking sobs. She looked unbelievingly into Adam's eyes, seeing an intense, cold hatred. "Adam . . . why?" she sobbed. "You didn't have to—"

"I should have done that way before he found out about you," he fumed. "Damn, I even thought I had killed him. I just left him for dead a few hours back."

He replaced his smoking pistol at his waist. "Yes. I should've killed Clarence Seymour way before now," he grumbled. "But I hadn't counted on Bryce Fowler discovering you. I should've, though. The first time I saw him in Key West, I should've known what to expect."

Natalie ran to Clarence and knelt down beside him, fearing to touch him. He looked . . . so . . . dead. He was lying in a pool of blood and this time not from only a flesh wound. He had been wounded directly in the stomach. Surely many of his vital organs had been damaged.

With trembling fingers, Natalie felt for a pulse beat in his throat. Tears ran from her eyes when she could find none. She brushed some gray hair back from his face and then leaned down to kiss his cheek. "Father, I'm sorry," she whispered between sobs. "And, father, I know I would have grown to love you very much. You were so kind. You were so . . . gentle."

Her words halted when she felt the coarseness of

296

Adam's fingers around a wrist, urging her upward with a painful jerk. "Get dressed," he ordered. "We've got to get out of here. Someone may have heard the gunshot."

"I only hope," Natalie hissed, wiping her eyes free of tears as he shoved her away from him, toward the wardrobe. "Adam, one day you'll burn in hell. You and all like you."

Adam laughed hoarsely. "Until then I plan to live life as I want," he said, with a nod of his head. "Now get dressed or I'll be forced to put the clothes on you myself."

Natalie cast Clarence a sad look, feeling such remorse she found it hard to conceive of leaving him there alone and unattended. But if she hesitated much longer, she might even join him in death.

Yet, surely Adam wouldn't harm her. He would have to answer to Saul Palmer.

She drew courage from such a thought and looked angrily toward Adam. "Don't you touch me again," she hissed. "Especially don't try to touch my body again, or, Adam, I'll tell your father. He'll surely horsewhip you for taking such privileges."

Adam threw his head back in a fit of laughter. "You scare me, Natalie," he said, then once more grew quite somber. "Now get dressed."

Natalie swung around, feeling the full heat of his eyes on her as she chose a dress made of a heavy material so it might protect her from the dampness of the ship's voyage, and possibly even the invasion of Adam's eyes and hands!

Keeping her back to him, she cringed as she had to let her nightgown fall to the floor. Flushing, she hurriedly pulled a petticoat over her head and then her dress. She chose shoes with a rather low heel and a shawl to drape around her arms. Tossing her hair back across her shoulder, she once more glared toward Adam, letting him see that she was ready, though in her heart she truly wasn't.

"That's more like it," Adam snarled.

"Are we going to leave . . . him . . . just lying there?" Natalie murmured, nodding toward Clarence's lifeless body.

"I'm certainly not taking him with us," Adam said flatly. He went to Natalie and, taking her elbow, guided her toward the door.

Once more tears were escaping from her eyes. "Adam, it's so horrible," she whispered. She cringed when she was forced to step over Clarence's body. "He was so kind. How could you have. . . ?"

Her body ached as Adam jerked her away from Clarence. The stairs led them down into the parlor, and Adam propelled her under the orange-cast predawn sky in which only a faint edge of the fading moon peeked from behind a darker cloud cover.

The aroma of magnolia blossoms scented the air. Their perfume and the beautifully serene morning made it hard for Natalie to believe what she had been forced to leave behind. She had only found her father—her true father—but he had been taken away from her in such a cruel, cold-hearted way. It wasn't fair! But . . . what in life was?

Stumbling, she followed alongside Adam, hating the harshness of his fingers as they dug into the flesh of her arm. The cobblestones of the street were wet and slippery. Her shoes slipped, her shawl began inching from her shoulders, yet Adam forced her to move onward.

When they reached the riverfront, Natalie glanced anxiously around her, seeing only a minimum of activity, as though the world was awakening much too slowly on this morning when she so badly needed someone. But, as though Adam had read her thoughts, he leaned down into her ear.

"Don't try anything," he ordered. "We're going to walk slowly now, go casually toward my ship, and board it without drawing any attention. Do you hear?"

Natalie's eyes searched the moored ships. She prayed that Bryce hadn't left for Key West. But her hopes dwindled when she saw no golden hull. She was at Adam's mercy. She had no choice but to do as he bid. . . . "Yes," she murmured. "I understand."

She straightened her shoulders and held her chin proudly high. She would at least do this with dignity!

Ignoring the close observation of Adam's crew, Natalie crossed the quarterdeck beside him and then descended a short flight of stairs. He forced her to move onward through the dark shadows of a narrow hallway until he opened the door to a cabin and shoved her roughly inside.

Rubbing her aching arm, Natalie stood in silence, seeing only a faint light showing through the stained glass of the skylight overhead. Natalie tensed when Adam lit a whale-oil lamp and, smiling crookedly at her, held it in her direction.

"Someone else is sharing my master cabin," he chuckled. He gestured with his free hand. "This will have to do."

Natalie let her gaze move slowly around her. The room was small with only a bunk and a lone table beside it. The walls were of unpainted plywood and the aroma was that of sour grapes. She shivered and hugged herself with her arms.

"I wish to be left alone," she said blandly.

"And that you will be," Adam laughed. "But I will return. We have some unfinished business between us, you and I."

"Yes, we do," she hissed. "But not what you are thinking of. I hope to have a chance to pay you back for what you just did to . . . my father."

Adam grabbed one of her wrists and drew her roughly to him. "You've only one father, Natalie," he growled. "Saul Palmer. How many times do I have to tell you that. And, Natalie, how could you forget him so easily?"

"He is not my father," she said angrily. "As you are not my brother."

Adam chuckled. "If I'm not your brother then I have the right to do this," he said.

He forced her backward, down onto the bunk, and began fumbling frantically with the skirt of her dress. He placed his hot lips at the hollow of her throat and nibbled at her flesh while one hand traveled up an inner thigh.

Natalie pushed and shoved. "Adam, get off," she cried. "Surely you wouldn't!"

"I don't dare kiss your lips," he said. "Not with my tongue still throbbing from your angry bite. But I can kiss you everywhere else."

Remembering the soft, firm swell of her breast, his free hand reached to fumble at the front of her dress. But a sudden movement in the room made him look away from Natalie long enough to give her the opportunity to grab his hair and pull it.

Seeing only a blur of what he knew to be Brenda, Adam found himself being assaulted by two women at once, Natalie yanking at his hair and Brenda plummeting his back with her doubled fists.

"Adam, how could you?" Brenda screamed as her fists began to ache from hitting the steel muscles of his back.

With a growl, Adam swung one arm back, knocking Brenda away from him, and with the other he slapped Natalie's hands from his hair. Rising, he stood with his feet widespread, his hands on hips, glaring from woman to woman.

"So I have me two wildcats on my ship, do I?" he snarled, his eyes dark and his brows arched menacingly. "This is the first I've noticed a resemblance in your personalities."

Natalie inched up from the bunk, eying Brenda who, still stunned from Adam's blow, was slowly rising from the floor. "So you did board Adam's ship with him," Natalie hissed. "You are the other occupant in his cabin. I'm not surprised. Seems you both were made from the same mold. You are both evil!"

Attired only in her petticoat, Brenda shook her head, trying to orient her thoughts. She rubbed the back of her head where it throbbed from her fall. Then, gathering together her senses, she shook her hair back from her shoulders and glowered from Adam to Natalie.

"This will not happen again," she said flatly. "I won't let you two have the opportunity to be alone."

She let her gaze settle fully on Adam. "I'll kill you first, Adam," she hissed.

"Those are strong words," Adam said, straightening his hair by combing his fingers through it. "If you're not careful, it will be you who will be taking a last breath of life."

Natalie, remembering Clarence Seymour, realized just how easily Adam did snuff out another life. Then her heart slowed as she realized something else. Brenda didn't even know that Adam had killed her father!

Yet, maybe Brenda thought the first gunshot had killed him before Brenda and Adam had left Clarence wounded on the floor of his office!

However, it was Brenda's right to know how her father had died.

"And Adam wouldn't blink an eye while shooting you, Brenda," Natalie said with a toss of the head. She laughed a bit bitterly. "Not that I'd care," she added. Then she frowned. "But I did care about the man Adam shot only a little while ago at your house, Brenda." A deep inner sadness ate away at her insides when she thought of that wasted life.

"At my house?" Brenda said, arching an eyebrow. "What are you talking about?"

"Your father. Adam shot your father a second time tonight," Natalie said softly. "The second time he killed him, Brenda. Your father—our father—was killed by the man you chose for a companion. Adam. He cold-heartedly killed our father, and our father was unarmed, no threat whatsoever at the time. . . ."

Natalie expected to see Brenda show at least a bit of concern, but unless Brenda was a great actress, she showed no sign of remorse as she drew her lips into a narrow line and strolled, quite silently, from the cabin.

"Are we truly of the same kin?" Natalie whispered, not understanding how her sister could be so cold and unfeeling.

Brenda went to the side rail of the ship and clutched onto it until her knuckles were white from the strength she put behind her grip. She lowered her eyes to the splashy foam of the water below her and let her grief tear at her heart, suddenly feeling empty . . . yet, somehow victorious.

Yes, now even Natalie didn't have her father. . . .

ORCHID ISLAND

Go where you will, on land or on sea,
I'll share all your sorrows and cares. . . .

—Anonymous

FIFTEEN

As the ship approached Orchid Island, Natalie stood at the railing, peering intensely toward the somber green jungle that intermingled with valleys of lilac shadow. Heat was drawing moisture from the land causing a mist of sorts to wreath the tangled mangroves along the shore. Natalie was reminded of Bryce and his interest in this island, and she wondered when he might arrive to claim his fortune . . . and now her.

The anchor had now been heaved over the side and a small boat was being launched. Shielding her eyes from the intense rays of the sun, Natalie turned to watch Brenda being helped down into the boat. Then she jerked away as Adam reached for her. "I can leave the ship on my own," she said icily. She wanted to brag to him that Bryce would rescue her as soon as he discovered Clarence Seymour's fate. Bryce would know who was responsible and would also know who had abducted her.

She only hoped he would sail for Orchid Island when he found that she hadn't been delivered to Key West.

Lifting her skirt, she descended laboriously and seated

herself in the bobbing boat. She refused to look at Brenda. Instead she watched the shoreline as it drew closer with each hefty lift and fall of the oars manned by Adam's crew.

The air was moist and sticky with humidity. Natalie's dress clung damply to the sensuous curves of her body, and her hair hung in wet ringlets that framed her face and hung limply over her shoulders. A wild spray of water splashed her arms as the bow of the boat suddenly beached on the snowy white sand that edged the island.

Not wanting to be ordered around by Adam, Natalie climbed from the boat onto the sea-drenched sand. Feeling her heels sinking into it, she lifted the skirt of her dress and trudged onward until she was standing in dry, thigh-high grass. There she stopped to take in the full setting. There were many varieties of trees and beneath these stood a few *ajoupos,* palm thatch huts, apparently used by the ship's crew while not traveling the seas.

Orchids grew in the moist thickets alongside the streams that ran into the ocean, and wild cotton blossoms sparkled along the shore. The wind blew steadily from the sea, riffling the palm fronds and stirring the bamboo brakes and the guinea grass.

Natalie shook her hair back from her face, letting the breeze lift and dry it, so that, again, it might fall in lustrous waves down her back.

''Why did you have to enter my life?'' Brenda said sourly as, next to Natalie, she began walking away from the beach. Her own midnight black hair was also lifting in the breeze and if not for their attire, one would think they were twins.

Natalie still wore her heavy cotton dress, with puffed sleeves, full skirt and high neck. Brenda wore a delicate,

308

silk, lace-trimmed dress with a low-cut bodice that emphasized her bosom.

Each young woman lifted the skirt and straightened her back, hate a strong force between them as they moved toward a tall, white-pillared house that was now visible at the crest of a hill.

"It was not by choice, believe me," Natalie finally answered. "I was happy not knowing the truths of my past. Everyone was happy. But now? An innocent man is dead because of the truths revealed to all."

Brenda swallowed hard and averted her gaze from the direction of Natalie. "It's all because of Bryce Fowler," she hissed. Then she shot Natalie a defiant glance. "But he will pay." She laughed a deep, ugly laugh. "Ah, yes, he will pay. Adam will sink Bryce Fowler's *Golden Isis* into the depths of the Atlantic."

"I believe you forget who is truly responsible for our father's death," Natalie said flatly. "Adam shot our father. Not Bryce. It is Adam who should be the recipient of your venomous words. Not Bryce."

"I love Adam," Brenda said coolly. "I could never hate him, no matter the reason."

"Ha!" Natalie scoffed with a toss of her head. "I heard you threaten to kill Adam if he touched me again. Now does that sound like true love? Would you kill the man you profess to love?"

"Love and hate are one and the same," Brenda said.

Natalie grew quiet, remembering her own tumultuous feelings about Bryce. Yes, love and hate did blend. Many times . . .

They reached the house, a three-storied mansion with three great pillars reaching to its roof. Creeping, clinging vines decorated the walls, leaving only the close-shuttered windows and huge oak door visible to the eye. Mahogany, rosewood, and pine trees clustered closely around its structure, shielding it from the view of passing ships at sea.

After glancing at the house, Natalie's attention was drawn to a squared-off plot of land that displayed tall grave stones. Decorating the graves were beds of orchids, their purple and white colors a contrast to the green stand of grass edging the humps of earth.

Natalie's breath became shallow as she looked even farther, to where orchids clung to trees as far as the eye could see. Now she could understand how the island received its name.

But even more heart-stopping was the tall mausoleum that stood half-hidden beneath creepers and vines of orchids. Bryce had said that the treasure had been hidden inside a vault. Was the vault that he had spoken of so close? Is so, was it as undisturbed as this mausoleum, its stone door still closed, and its marble walls shining wherever they were revealed behind their cover of vines?

Having been so absorbed in her thoughts, Natalie hadn't heard Adam step beside her. When his coarse fingers circled a wrist, she flinched and tried to jerk herself free.

"On up the steps," he ordered, nodding toward the steps leading to a wide veranda that stretched across the full front of the house.

"Adam, unhand me," Natalie fumed. "I'm not about to take off in another direction. Where would I run to? You've done what you've set out to do. You've completely isolated me from everything and everyone I've ever loved."

"And this is where you'll stay," he growled. "At least

until father says it's safe to return you home to him."

"Adam, that place will never again be home to me," she sighed. She wondered where was her rightful place on this earth was? Suddenly she had no father . . . no family. But at the thought of Bryce her thoughts warmed. Yes, he was her life . . . her world. Oh, if he would only hurry!

"We shall see about that," Adam said. He gave her a shove up the steps and another through the door as he held it open for her and Brenda.

Natalie stepped into a room that appeared to be filled with white, ghostly images. Upon closer observation, however, as Adam began throwing shutters open at the windows, she saw that the ghosts were actually dust sheets carefully draped across all the furnishings in the parlor.

She looked slowly around her, absorbing the magnificence of the paintings in gilt-edged frames that decorated the walls, the intricacy of the cut-glass chandelier that graced a large portion of the tall ceiling, and the yellowed wallpaper that curled at the edges of the walls.

The oak flooring was dulled from age and lack of polishing, and the wide stone fireplace sat cold and devoid of fire.

Remembering Bryce's promise to make this their home one day, Natalie already felt a nearness to him and somehow knew the days ahead would not be so burdensome and lonely.

"Brenda, remove the dust covers from the furniture and go to the wine cellar and choose us an aged bottle of port," Adam said casually. "I'll see to it that Natalie is secured in her room upstairs."

Brenda swung around and studied him, danger in her

eyes. "Adam, remember that I am down here waiting for you," she warned icily. "Make sure you do not *join* Natalie in her bedroom."

Adam chuckled. "I have plans for another bedroom with the right sister," he said. "But later. Much later."

Brenda laughed throatily. She placed her hands on her hips and thrust her bosom out as she gave Natalie a look of triumph.

Natalie tilted her chin; then with a haughty air she climbed the stairs beside Adam. "And so I am to rot in a room until you decide otherwise. Is that the way it's to be, Adam?" she said flatly.

"It shouldn't be long."

"One night under the same roof with you and Brenda is one night too many."

"I've just decided I'd best travel on to Key West and tell father that I have you safely on the island," Adam said, taking Natalie by the elbow as the second-floor landing was reached.

He directed her down a dark hallway, opened a door, and shoved her inside. Then he stood glowering at her from the doorway, only seeing her outline against the darkened room. "And, then, little sister, I shall board my *Sea Snake* and go in search of Bryce Fowler," he snarled. "This time I won't be playing 'chase games' with him. I plan to pursue, catch, and destroy."

Somehow Adam's words didn't frighten Natalie. She had to believe that good conquered evil, and in this instance, Adam represented the evil force.

Yes, she would hold this thought. If she did not, she might become insane with worry for Bryce!

She felt the damp chill of the room wrap its icy shroud around her, causing her to tremble. She glanced around,

312

yet saw nothing but darkness. Once Adam was gone she would throw the shutters open and try to absorb some of the island's low-hanging tropical heat; for when night fell, she expected even colder temperatures.

Yet, if Adam did travel from the island, wouldn't she feel free to try to find a longboat in which to make her escape? She would not just sit idly by and let him do as he pleased with her! Certainly she would try to escape. It could be days before Bryce reached her. She didn't trust Adam. She trusted Brenda even less. . . .

She turned her full attention back to Adam as he began closing the door. "Before Brenda and I leave for Key West, I'll send her up here to you with wine and fruit," he said. "Enough to last until our return."

Natalie took a step forward. "Adam," she said, causing him to open the door again.

"Yes?" he said, raising his eyebrows.

"When approaching the island, I didn't see your *Sea Snake*," she murmured. "Where is it kept?"

Adam threw his head back in a fit of laughter. "Do you think I'd tell you?" he jeered. "The *Sea Snake* will leave the island when I do, and once I leave Key West the *Sea Snake*'s sister ship will deliver me to my black ship. So you are quite stranded on this island, Natalie. You might as well forget escaping. It's quite impossible."

Natalie's heart plunged and her hopes were shattered by the loud bang of the door slamming shut. When she heard the snap of a bolt lock being secured, she jerked her head back in frustrated agony.

"But I refuse to give in to melancholia," she argued aloud. Flipping her hair back from her shoulders, she began feeling around in the dark, gradually becoming aware of the slight rays of light trickling in around the closed

313

shutters of a window. With a racing pulse she let this light draw her toward it until she was finally touching the outline of the window. Her fingers slowly searched for the latch and once she found it she slipped it quietly back.

Breathless now, she inched one of the shutters open, relieved to find a tree's foliage hiding what she was doing. Then feeling even bolder, she pushed the other shutter open and inhaled the sweet perfume of the air. Although she let her gaze search through the thickness of the oak tree's weaving, swaying greenery, she couldn't see much from this vantage point. Only a faint sparkle of ocean could be seen in the far distance; then she caught sight of masts, not those of one ship but two. They were moored side by side in a cove. Separating the leaves, Natalie peered even more closely toward the masts and could now make out the ships more clearly. Her heart raced. She was seeing Adam's *Sea Snake* and a ship that had not delivered her to the island!

"So he has three ships," she whispered. "The *Sea Snake* must have two sister ships. . . ."

Natalie's eyes danced as she swung around, smiling. "Surely he'll leave one ship unattended," she murmured. "Maybe I can somehow maneuver a smaller ship from the larger one."

Then her smile faded. "But I am being foolish," she sighed. "I am only one person. How could I? And even if I did, I wouldn't know how to navigate it. I've never been alone on a boat. Never! I've never even handled oars!"

Creaking floorboards overhead filled Natalie with wonder. She looked toward the ceiling, her eyes following the sound of footsteps as someone in the room above paced about nervously. She listened more intensely. The footsteps weren't heavy like a man's . . . but light . . .

most surely a woman's!

"But . . . who . . . ?" Natalie whispered. Brenda was downstairs, probably entertaining Adam with a cheerful victory glass of wine, so it couldn't be her. "And only men make up Adam's crew. . . ." she reasoned aloud.

When the pacing stopped, Natalie went to the window and, leaning out of it, emitted a low gasp when she saw that the window just above her also had its shutters opened a mite. Hope sprang forth. It appeared that she wasn't that alone after all! Adam had brought another visitor to this gorgeous island and more than likely this was another unwilling victim.

With a thundering heartbeat, Natalie cupped a hand around her mouth. "Hello up there," she said in a loud whisper.

She tensed, hoping Adam or Brenda hadn't heard her through the downstairs windows. A flirting laugh, Brenda's, floated upward. Natalie could just envision Brenda clinging to Adam, teasing him with the evil slight slant of her eyes. . . .

Sighing heavily, Natalie watched a moment longer for a sign of life at the upstairs window; then she shrugged.

"I must be losing my senses," she said, wringing her hands. "I must have imagined hearing those footsteps. Maybe it was just the wind playing tricks on the old boards of this house.

"Or are my troubles causing me to become insane?" she desperately thought to herself.

Having the need to avert her thoughts, she let her gaze move slowly around the room, acquainting herself more intimately with her surroundings. It was evident that this room had been quite grand at one time, and maybe even

315

special.

The bedstead and matching furniture were of a heavy, carved mahogany, and the braided, oval rug on the floor appeared to have been made of neutral shades of velvet. A wardrobe with a yellowed, cracked mirror set into its door drew Natalie toward it. She opened it gingerly.

"My word . . ." she sighed. "At one time they had to be so lovely. . . ."

She let her fingers explore the limp, faded long gowns. They were so delicately old, she was afraid they might shred into a million pieces at the slightest touch. But she couldn't resist drawing one from a hanger and draping it over an arm to admire it more openly.

The lace trim on the cuffs at the end of the long puffed sleeves was yellowed with age, but the smooth, orchid-colored satin of the dress still held its shine and elegance and a faint aroma of perfume even lingered in the gathered folds at its waist.

A diamond brooch pinned into the braided satin on the lowswept bodice had been overlooked by the Palmer pirates. That oversight drew a low giggle from somewhere deep inside Natalie.

"I wonder who wore this," she said, holding the skirt out and then letting it flutter downward when she heard the bolt lock at the bedroom door being slipped aside again. She took a step backward as Brenda stepped into the room carrying a tray which displayed a bottle of wine and an assortment of fruit.

"I'd much prefer to let you starve," Brenda said stiffly. "But Adam insisted I bring you these before we leave for Key West. Seems his fondness for you hasn't lessened."

Natalie placed the dress back inside the wardrobe. "I

316

could not care less about what Adam thinks of me," she murmured.

She swung around and solemnly faced Brenda. "You see, I've never cared for him, not even when I thought he was my brother. I always suspected he had a heart of stone. I could see it in the depth of his cold, unfeeling eyes."

Brenda walked across the room to place the tray on a night stand, next to an unlighted kerosene lamp. "He isn't cold in all respects . . . especially when it comes to making love." She turned and looked arrogantly at Natalie. "But you will never have the opportunity to finding that out. You see, he will not share his love-making skills with you. I have proven to him which sister is the most deserving. I am the strongest. He knows that. He admires strength in his women."

Natalie closed her fingers into tight fists. "By strength, I take that to mean that you believe that aiding Adam to rob, even to kill, your—our—father is your show of strength. Well, I feel sorry for you, Brenda," she hissed. "I believe you don't know the true meaning of the word 'strength.' In truth, you are a weak person, in both character and deeds."

Natalie's words only increased Brenda's rage and her hatred for Natalie. She wanted to go to her and pull her hair from her head. But Adam was waiting. She rushed from the room, locking the door behind her. Nevertheless, she felt lightheaded and a strange emptiness suddenly seized her when, despite her resistance, she thought of her father and realized that he was truly dead. Brushing tears from her lashes, she went on downstairs, to Adam; yet she so missed her father. . . .

Going to the door, Natalie pushed and kicked it, frus-

317

tration building inside her. How could Brenda side with Adam? Couldn't she see that he was using her?

"But I musn't let myself start feeling sorry for her," Natalie scolded herself aloud. "I'm the one being held prisoner. Not Brenda!"

Again, she was drawn to the window. Barely breathing, she slowly inched her head outside, parting the leaves of the trees with her hands. She watched as Adam and Brenda moved in the direction of the *Sea Snake*. Then something else caught Natalie's eyes. Right beside the window was a large limb that had sturdy branches reaching from it in all directions.

She eyed the tree with enthusiasm, knowing how she would make her escape once the *Sea Snake* had set sail.

Then a coldness rippled through her insides. "But surely they've left someone to guard the house," she sighed heavily.

But she knew even that would not stop her from trying to fend for herself. In her disastrous situation, she had no choice but to keep a stiff upper lip to all that challenged her.

The creaking of the floorboards above her head caused her to tense once more and to stare questioningly toward the ceiling. She moved on tiptoe beneath the spot where the sound was most prominent. There was no doubt that she wasn't alone in the house. Someone was in the room above her. But . . . who? Would this person place her in even more danger?

"Surely not," she whispered. "This person must be locked in a room as I am. And I wonder for how long? Did Brenda also take this prisoner some food before she sailed for Key West?"

Natalie went to the door and pushed and pulled,

grunting from the exertion. "The house is old; the lock should be too," she grumbled. But no matter how hard she struggled, the lock would not give way.

She would have to climb from the window. Heaven forbid that she might fall from the tree limb! There would be no one to rescue her if she injured herself.

"Well, now I shall eat and drink my fill, in case I do manage to escape from this house." She sighed heavily.

She threw back the faded cover on the bed and arranged her skirt beneath her as she sat down on the sunken feather mattress. Reaching for the bottle of wine, she looked around for a glass into which to pour herself a small portion.

But seeing none, she took a tiny swallow from the bottle then reached for a ripe banana and consumed it almost greedily. After she had also devoured a small portion of pineapple, nourishing and sweet, she licked her lips and went back to the window. She felt energetic and sure of herself now. If the ship had sailed, she would soon be gone, too!

Once more riffling through the thick cluster of leaves, Natalie peered in the direction of the cove. Seeing no masts she knew it was indeed safe for her to try tree climbing! She reached out, shook the limb, and smiled when she found it to be quite sturdy. With trembling fingers, she pulled herself free of the window and tested her footing on the branch before moving one inch away from the house. And when she found that the limb could support her full weight, she began working her way down, cursing under her breath when she caught the tail of her dress on an upper branch. Yanking it free, she tensed when she heard a slight voice speaking from somewhere above her head.

319

Slowly turning her eyes upward, Natalie heard her own name being spoken. Who would know her? It was a woman's voice! But speaking her name? Then she felt a churning at the pit of her stomach when the voice spoke more loudly and a face leaned farther out of the third-story window.

"My God," Natalie said in a shallow whisper. "Myra . . . ?"

Natalie's heart hammered inside her at seeing her dear friend so pale . . . so bedraggled. And why . . . oh, why . . . would Myra be there?

Then she remembered her doubts about Adam. She remembered how he had reacted to knowing that Myra had been on her way to New York . . . and to. . . .

"Myra, how . . . ?" she said in a loud whisper.

"Just come and . . . get me out of here, Natalie," Myra said, reaching a hand toward her friend. "Hurry. But be careful, Adam keeps a . . . man watching."

A stirring beneath Natalie caused her to start and almost lose her footing. With a racing heart, she grasped more securely onto the tree limb, then died a million deaths when she looked downward into the face of a burly man who had thick, curling whiskers covering most of his face. His steel gray eyes were quite visible, though, and the iciness in their depths sent shivers racing up and down Natalie's spine.

"Come on down here, Missie," the man said, motioning with one hand, while the other rested on a pistol at his left hip. "Ye ain't goin' nowheres 'cept back in the house."

Natalie tried to scramble back up the tree but the fullness of her skirt and the rawness of her fingers slowed her ascent. When she heard the loud explosion of the man's pistol, she flinched and grew pale, but was relieved when she realized that this man was only discharging the gun into the air, past her, in an attempt to urge her to follow his bidding without any further delay.

"All right," she murmured. "I'm coming. I'm coming. . . ."

When she reached the ground, she stubbornly narrowed her lips into a straight line as the man roughly grabbed her arm. Though his grip hurt, she wouldn't let him know it. She just followed along beside him as she was forced back inside the house and up the stairs. She eyed him speculatively when the second-floor landing was reached and left behind.

"Where are you taking me?" she hissed. "Do you plan to place me in shackles in the garret?"

His wide-sleeved black shirt was open at his throat, revealing almost as much hair on his chest as was on his face. He looked threatening and even more evil than Adam. Muscles bulged at his shoulders and thighs. His lips lifted into a sneer as he glanced down at her.

"Adam thought ye might try escapin'," he said. "So he said if ye did, ye would probably know 'bout our other female visitor by then and to go ahead and lock ye up together. That way I will only have one room to watch 'cause that's what I'll be doin', Missie. Watchin' and listenin' for any more funny stuff. Don' have to worry 'bout ye climbin' from this third-story window. No tree limbs decorate it. You'd have a mighty big jump to reach one if'n ye'd take a notion to try."

Natalie felt a small ray of hope. At least she would be wth Myra. Together, surely they could come up with some means of escape. But Myra had sounded . . . so

. . . weak. Was she fit to escape? Did she have the strength to move from the room in which she'd been held captive?

Oh, Lord. Natalie calculated just how long Myra had been locked away like a criminal—since she had sailed for New York and that had been some time ago.

Now standing before the bolt-locked door, Natalie gave the man a sideways glance, focusing on his pistol. If she could just . . .

While the man concentrated fully on releasing the bolt lock at the door he left Natalie unattended. She grabbed the pistol from his waist and, stepping quickly away from him, pointed it toward him.

"Sir . . ." she said firmly, hating the trembling in her fingers and the ensuing weakness in her knees. When he turned toward her, she swallowed her fear and continued to stand, poised and ready to shoot the pistol if he so much as took a step toward her.

"Why, you little . . ." he snarled, eying the pistol with squinted eyes; then, daring her, he placed his hands on his hips. "Ye little snip," he snarled. "Didn't think ye'd have the nerve to try anythin' like this. Adam said ye were a genteel lady, to treat ye accordingly. I think Adam has ye figured wrong, Missie."

"Walk to the garret stairs," Natalie said in a near whisper, motioning with the pistol toward the narrow staircase at the far end of the hallway. "I'm sure I can secure you inside a room there. The windows are too small to climb from."

"Ye ain't goin' nowhere," the man said, lunging suddenly toward her, all hands.

"No!" Natalie screamed, pulling the trigger. Her body jerked when the gun exploded and she fell clumsily to the floor from which she watched unbelievingly as the pirate grabbed at his chest and began crumpling downward.

The sight of blood and the realization that she had just shot a man caused a bitter taste to rise in her throat. Oh, no! She was going to retch!

She turned her head away and covered her mouth with her hands, swallowing . . . swallowing. . . .

Then, when she'd fully recovered from her moment of sickness, she inched up from the floor and moved around the body, barely breathing. Despite a throbbing in her temple, she tucked the pistol beneath her left arm and worked the bolt lock to finish what her guard had started. Soon she had the door open, and peering inside through the semidarkness, she saw Myra curled up on the floor, silent.

"Myra . . ." Natalie gasped. She went to Myra, placed the pistol on the floor, and then slowly lifted Myra's head from the floor to study her face. "God, Myra, what's wrong?"

Myra slowly opened her eyes. She licked her parched lips before speaking in a low wheeze. "Natalie . . . thank God, Natalie," she said, letting tears run freely from her eyes as she reached a hand to Natalie's face.

Natalie settled down onto the floor beside Myra and eased her friend's head onto her lap. Smoothing the hair back from Myra's face, Natalie began to weep. "Tell me all about it, Myra," she murmured. "Do you even have the strength to do so?"

She looked around the room and saw the fresh tray of fruit and the unopened bottle of wine. Brenda had obviously brought Myra nourishment, too, before leaving for Key West. Then why hadn't Myra eaten . . . or drank?

It was obvious that she needed to do so. Her eyes appeared to have sunk deeply into her face and beneath them were black circles. She was pale, as though she had not been exposed to sunshine in a long time.

Natalie lowered her lips to Myra's brow and placed an affectionate kiss on it. "Oh, Myra . . . Myra," she murmured, cradling Myra's face and rocking a bit.

"I think I'm trying to miscarry my baby," Myra finally said. "I've tried not to make it apparent when Adam is around. I want to miscarry. I want to—"

"Myra, why did Adam bring you here?" Natalie murmured. "I don't understand, yet, . . . maybe I do . . . and don't want to accept the full truth of it."

"I'm sure you know, Natalie," Myra said, running her tongue across her lips once more.

"This child . . . is . . . Adam's?"

"Yes," Myra whispered, closing her eyes as tears ran from their corners in a silver, gray pattern. "He is the one who raped me. One night . . . as . . . I was . . . leaving Parrot Inn. He grabbed me in the darkness. He forced me to go to his ship. I don't know why he . . . chose me," she bellowed, pulling her knees up into a fetal position as a pain grabbed at the very pit of her stomach.

"Myra," Natalie gasped, seeing the pain etched across her best friend's face. "I've got to get you help."

Myra reached a hand desperately to Natalie's face. "No," she screamed. "Let it happen. I don't want this child. I'm sorry, Natalie, if I'm talking so horribly of your . . . brother . . . but I hate him."

Then Myra's eyes opened almost wildly. "Natalie, what are you doing here? Why are you being held captive? She looked toward the door. "And I heard a gunshot," she murmured. "Who discharged . . . a . . .

gun?''

Natalie lowered her lashes, not wanting to remember the moment she had pulled the trigger, the sick feeling that had encompassed her when she had heard the thunder of the discharge, or the sound of the bullet making contact with the man's flesh.

She didn't want to remember the blood oozing from the wound. Oh, God, she didn't want to remember any of it . . . but knew it would remain with her for the rest of her life . . . to haunt her. . . .

"I shot a man, Myra," she gulped. "I . . . shot . . . a man. The one who was left to guard us from escape."

Myra grabbed one of Natalie's hands and squeezed. "You did?" she whispered. "Natalie, why is any of this happening? Why did you have to shoot him? Why are you here? Why?"

"It's a long story, Myra," Natalie sighed, flipping her hair back from her shoulders. "One I don't even believe, yet it is all true."

"Tell me—"

"First, you tell me about Adam and how he's been treating you," Natalie said firmly. She once more glanced toward the uneaten food and untouched wine. "I see he's given you nourishment. Why haven't you accepted it? You look too weak to attempt to escape with me."

"I haven't eaten . . . because I am trying everything in my power to lose this baby," Myra fumed. "I didn't make it to New York to do it in the proper way, so I have tried in my own way. But all I have succeeded in doing is to make myself so weak I can hardly keep a clear head . . . and— These pains send me into such a dither, I don't even care if I live or die."

325

"Myra, you must tell me why you are here," Natalie said firmly. "It doesn't make any sense. Why would Adam abduct you from the very ship that is carrying you to a destination that would rid you of a child that neither of you want?"

"Adam wants the child," Myra whispered, swallowing hard.

"What?" Natalie gasped, eyes wide, face flushed.

"If it is a boy . . ." Myra said. "Only . . . if . . . it is a boy."

"Why?" Natalie asked, lifting an eyebrow. "Myra, he is cold-hearted, why should it matter to him what you have? I would think he wouldn't even want you to have a child of his."

"He wants any son that might be born of his union with any woman," Myra sighed heavily. "He told me this. He wishes to have many sons, to carry on the Palmer name and to carry on the piracy he and his . . . father . . . have been so vigorously involved in."

Myra's eyes widened as one of her hands covered her mouth. "Oh, Natalie, you don't even know about your father having been a pirate," she said weakly. "There's so much you . . . don't know . . . that I must tell you—"

Natalie deposited another soft kiss on Myra's brow. "I know," she whispered. "I already know everything. Probably even more than you. It's all like a nightmare, Myra. Like a nightmare."

"You know that this . . . Brenda is your . . . sister?"

"Yes. And how do you know that?" Natalie murmured.

"Adam told me," she said solemnly. "You see, he plans to hold me here until I have the baby. He plans to

326

have Brenda aid in the delivery of my child.''

"The delivery of your child?" Natalie said in a near whisper. "So he intends to keep you here during all the months of your pregnancy, for his own selfish reasons?"

Then she suddenly remembered what Myra had said. "Only if it is a boy . . ." Her insides turned cool at this thought. "Myra, if you gave birth to a girl . . . what then?" she dared to ask.

"I believe he would do away with both of us," Myra moaned, once more turning into a mass of quivering sobs. "What am I to do, Natalie? What am I to do? What are we to do?"

"We've got to get out of here," Natalie said, trying to urge Myra to a sitting position. "We must try to find a boat. Together, surely we can reach Key West. Orchid Island can't be that far away from our homeland."

Myra groaned wearily, feeling light-headedness sweep over her as she straightened her back and stretched her legs out before her. "Natalie, I just can't," she whined. "I would only slow you. You must go on without me." She doubled over in another fit of piercing pains. She clutched at her abdomen and bit her lower lip. "I'm too ill," she cried. "I can't move from this room."

Seeing her pallor, Natalie knew that Myra was right. No way could she be moved. Yes, Myra wanted to lose the child and would do anything to realize that end, but it was Myra's life that was in possible jeopardy now. If she aborted, the dangers were many.

Natalie rose to her feet and moved briskly around the room, inspecting it for cleanliness and handiness, just in case the worst happened and she had to help Myra deliver the child . . . or had to help with the birthing of a dead fetus.

It was quite evident now Myra was not leaving the island, nor was Natalie. She couldn't leave her best friend. To do so might cause Myra's demise.

Feeling the need of healthy sunshine to bathe the room of germs, Natalie went to the window and threw the shutters open all the way. She then turned on a heel and began to ready the bed and to pull dresses from the wardrobe to use as rags if needed.

These preparations completed, she helped Myra up on the bed, removed her limp silk dress, and left her to lie in her thin petticoat. Then Natalie poured Myra a glass of wine and lifted it to her mouth, tipping it gingerly to her lips until several swallows were taken.

While peeling a banana, Natalie glanced around the room at the expensive furnishings, the carpeting, and the satin draperies. The furniture was made of rosewood, and overhanging the bed was a graceful canopy with yellowed ruffles lining its edges.

It appeared that more pains had been taken with this room than the one in which Natalie had been confined. Maybe it had been used by her father. No! She must remember! She could not—would not—ever call him father again.

Maybe this room had been Saul Palmer's when he had made visits to Orchid Island. Possibly many times, when he said he was traveling to Cuba, he had actually been traveling to this island to check out his pirate son and the prizes he had taken at sea.

"Natalie, you haven't told me the reasons why you are here." Myra said weakly. "What has happened? How did you find out. . . ?"

Natalie handed the peeled banana to Myra, then sighed

328

resolutely. "It is so unbearably sad, Myra," she whispered. "My true father—he is now dead. Adam . . . shot him."

SIXTEEN

Helping to row the boat closer to shore, Bryce set his jaw in a look of keen determination. Now that Natalie was safe and sound with Clarence Seymour and Hugh had settled into a daily life in which he had no father to guide his every move, Bryce felt free to search for the treasure that had been constantly in his thoughts. Having found this hidden cove, he felt safer. But he knew that Adam Palmer surely had placed guards to watch every part of Orchid Island. Caution was the major factor now. One bullet and all would be lost. He hadn't waited so long to seek this island in order to receive a bullet in his chest as a welcome.

"Don' see a soul," Dominic growled from behind Bryce. "Can't imagine this island bein' deserted. Makes no sense."

"I know," Bryce mumbled. As his muscles flexed with each fresh rise of the oars from the water, he kept raking the feathered sea grass with his keen eyes. He had dreamed for years of arriving on this island. Then it had been only a lavender patch rising from the ocean, only a mirage. But now, it lay before him, beautiful in its tropical greens and mauves. If he had known earlier that this island would one day mean much to him he would have explored it long ago! But he had thought it to be only a pirate's haven . . . nothing else.

Grunts and groans from the men in the longboat filled the air as they moved steadily toward shore. The heat from the crimson afternoon sun bore down upon them harshly, causing sweat to glisten on their brows and upper lips.

Bryce welcomed a splash of water on his arms as a wave crashed against the side of the boat. Soon . . . soon . . . he would be stepping on the land that his father had talked of in such a dreamy way.

"But I must keep remembering that *he* was not my father." He sulked quietly to himself. "Nevertheless, I will take the island and Hugh will never know. It is rightfully mine because the key was given to me in confidence. . . ."

A shot rang out above Bryce's head, abruptly focusing his thoughts on the present. He ducked and yelled an order to his men, bidding them to resume rowing, while he withdrew his pistol from his belt. Tensing when he saw a movement in the waist-high grasses of the island, he aimed and sent a bullet through the air. He smiled when he heard a yelp of pain; then he watched a man slump out into the open. As several other shots rang out, Bryce ducked again and was glad when the boat finally made contact with the shore.

"Careful, men," he shouted, jumping from the boat. "We musn't let one damned man get away from us."

Bending his back, Bryce raced for cover as another shot whizzed by him. Then aiming, he watched for more

331

movement in the grass and once more hit his target when he released another bullet into the air.

Suddenly everything was quiet. All that could be heard was the sound of the surf, the squawking of the tropical birds, and the riffling of the wind though the palm fronds on all sides of him.

"I think we can move on now," Bryce said to Dominic who stood close by, pistol poised.

"Seems safe enough," Dominic growled, squaring his massive shoulders.

"You've got instructions on what to do when I near the house, don't you?" Bryce said. He didn't want to have to share the treasure with anyone. Dominic didn't even know what lay awaiting discovery on this island.

"Sure you'll be safe alone once you've made it to the house?" Dominic queried, scratching his thick brow with the barrel of his pistol.

"All you're supposed to do is follow orders, Dominic," Bryce stated flatly. "Like I said. You and the men stand back. What you must watch for is the arrival of the *Sea Snake*. We can't finalize the claim on this island until that ship is in the deepest pit of the ocean. So you all keep watch. Be sure to come and fetch me if you do see the approach of the ship."

"Aye, aye, sir," Dominic said, half-saluting Bryce. "Good as done, sir. But I still don't understand why you don' want me accompanying you to the house to check for the opium shipment. You know the dangers of working alone."

Bryce spoke into his face. "And you know the dangers of continuing to question my commands," he growled.

"Cap'n, get along with ye," Dominic urged, ignoring Bryce's building anger. "And good luck."

"I need it," Bryce grumbled. "But maybe we will find the opium to return to Clarence Seymour. If so, we should be paid quite well! First we deliver his daughter safely to him . . . then we also return his opium cargo! Yes, surely we'll be paid damned well."

"Thought sure the only reward you'd want is that prissy lady named Natalie," Dominc growled. "She sure did take charge of your life after you met 'er."

"I'll forget you said that," Bryce said from across his shoulder as he began moving away from Dominic through the thigh-high grass. "I've more important things on my mind than arguing with you about who should or shouldn't take charge of my life." He cast Dominic a sour glance. "One thing is sure," he said angrily. "You do not have a say in what I should or should not do!"

Bryce laughed to himself as he heard Dominic's low grumblings of anger. They sparred with words more than not. But they did have a mutual respect for one another and each knew he could depend on the other to fight to the death to protect him if that became necessary. That was why they had been together for so long. Ever since I bought my ship at age twenty, Bryce thought proudly. Ten years . . . ten long years . . .

Damn. He did feel guilty for not sharing his most tightly kept secret with Dominic. But the treasure would not be shared with anyone but Natalie! She was his world now.

The sleeves of Bryce's gold silk shirt responded to the gentle breeze as he moved steadily onward. When he spied the back of the mansion, ripples of excited pleasure splashed through him. He couldn't believe it had been so easy! He was actually only a stone's throw from the

333

house and he hadn't been stopped. He would have thought Adam would have left many strong men around the island. As it was, there were only a few!

Bryce's heart thundered inside him when his gaze caught the sun's rays bouncing off marble. That had to be the mausoleum.

The closer he drew to it, the more anxious he became. Soon! The only barriers between him and the silent, oblong tomb were colorful creepers and orchids hanging from the protective covering of various types of trees.

Almost in a trance, he hurried his steps, reaching inside his front breeches pocket for his ring of keys. He had placed the brass key on the ring so it could not so easily be lost again. He smiled to himself, remembering when Natalie had revealed that she had had it in her possession all along.

But his face suddenly indicated his confusion and dismay when he heard a voice yelling out his name. His pulse raced. That voice! It wasn't just any voice! It was Natalie's!

Swinging around, Bryce focused his full attention on the house. He laughed a bit nervously, wondering if he was slowly losing his mind! All he could see was the silent three-storied house behind its protective shield of trees and vines. There was no possible way that Natalie could be there. He had left her with Clarence Seymour.

Natalie's throat ached from calling for help, yet she was too frightened to leave the room. She had heard many gunshots. Was Bryce's life in danger even though she could see none of Adam's men near the house? Her heart beat wildly when she thought Bryce might rescue his treasure and go on his way unaware that she and Myra were so close in which case they would be left to Adam's

334

mercy.

She yelled again. Why didn't he hear her? She knew that she had called loudly enough. But the whining of the wind blowing around the corner of the house and through the thick branches of the trees made her understand. Her voice had either been drowned out by the rustling of the tree's leaves or had been carried away from Bryce's direction, maybe even out to sea.

"Natalie, I'm bleeding," Myra suddenly cried. "I'm miscarrying. I know it. Oh, God. It's . . . finally happening. Surely I'm not mistaken." She closed her eyes because of the pain and bit her lower lip. Then when the pain eased a bit, tears came. "Oh, how I want to be home," she murmured. She prayed softly to herself. "Oh, please, God. Let it be over soon."

Natalie went to Myra and cringed when she saw the blood spreading on Myra's silk petticoat. "Myra, oh, Myra," she cried.

Desperation seized her. She had to get Bryce's attention and if her voice wouldn't do it, something else must. She now felt compelled to stay in this room, not for her own safety, but for Myra's—in case the baby was suddenly expelled from her body!

Rushing around the room, Natalie gathered items to toss from the window. She chose the half emptied wine bottle, a kerosene lamp, and a hand mirror. And after placing each of these on the floor beneath the sill, she tried to penetrate the thickness of the leaves, grumbling when she was no longer able to see Bryce.

"Oh, where is he?" she whispered. When she had seen his ship's golden hull appear in the cove, she had hardly been able to quell her excitement. Then when she had seen him walking, unharmed, toward the house, she

335

had become unbearably excited at the hope of being rescued.

"But the damned gunfire," she complained to herself. She was ashamed that it had frightened her enough to make her stay in the room. Well, she had suspected Adam had more men on the island and now she knew that her suspicions had been confirmed! They had been there all the time. She was thankful none had bothered to come to the house and discover the death of one of their mates.

At the window, Natalie strained forward again, looking through the leaves of the trees. "Oh, Bryce, why don't you hear me?" she whispered. But she knew that he had other things on his mind than her, thought she was in New Orleans . . . safe.

"Bryce," she screamed again. "Please, Bryce, hear me. . . ."

She knew that if he didn't respond soon, she would have to take up the dead man's pistol and rush outside. Yet she knew that move was foolish! If she were killed, would Myra be found? What would become of Myra if anything happened to her? Yes, she did have a responsibility to her best friend. . . .

Bryce took a step toward the house, his heart hammering wildly against his ribs. Damn! It was Natalie! But how on earth?

He jumped as though shot when a wine bottle crashed to the ground a few feet away from him. His eyes widened when a mirror shattered into a million pieces next to the bottle, and then a lamp landed, breaking and spreading kerosene on green spread of grass next to Bryce's feet.

Bryce placed his right hand on his pistol and moved cautiously closer to the house, looking upward toward the third-story window. He paled when he saw Natalie leaning dangerously far out of it. "My God, Natalie . . ." he cried. "How did you get up there?"

"Bryce, please help me," she called. "And, hurry. Myra is here also and she's very ill."

"Myra . . . ?" he murmured. His thoughts raced, not able to put all the pieces together. None of it made any sense.

"Bryce," Natalie pleaded. "Why are you just standing there doing nothing?"

"I'm coming, darling," he said. He turned and glanced toward the mausoleum. His insides quivered strangely. Damn it, he was so close! Could he walk away from it so easily? Only a few footsteps and one turn of a key away from the family's hidden fortune. . . .

"Bryce . . ." Natalie shrieked.

Bryce kneaded his brow and shook his head to clear his thoughts. He had a choice . . . but he knew what it had to be. Natalie! She would always come first now that he had found her and had realized how important she was to him. The treasure would have to wait a bit longer.

Grumbling and with his right hand resting securely on his pistol, Bryce crept cautiously to the corner of the house. He checked to see if anyone was guarding the front door. When he found it safe to venture onward, he dashed into the house. He was curious about this mansion that was now his, but now could afford only to take a quick glimpse at it. Even so, it was clear that at one time the house had been magnificent. The pieces of furniture were faded and showed wear but they were grand and in good taste.

Footsteps rushing down the staircase drew Bryce quickly around. Once more, seeing Natalie's loveliness made all else leave his mind. Two wide strides of his long, lean legs took him to her as she left the last step to ease into his arms.

"Bryce . . ." she murmured, hugging him tightly to her. "I just knew you'd come."

She lifted her eyes to his and felt their penetrating blue dazzle her, making her knees weak from desire.

But this wasn't the time to let him cast his passionate spell over her. Myra needed to be taken from the island, to be delivered to the skilled hands of a physician.

Bryce framed her face between his hands as his eyes absorbed every inch of her beauty. His insides warmed at the nearness of her, but there were other matters to settle now. Why was she here? Many questions needed answers.

"Natalie, how in the hell did you get here?" he asked thickly. "I left you in New Orleans with Clarence. What happened?"

Tears sparkled at the tips of Natalie's feathery lashes. "Clarence Seymour is dead, Bryce," she said in a soft whisper. "Adam . . . killed him, then abducted me and brought me here."

Bryce tore himself away from her and stiffened his back. "Adam," he growled. "Damn. I thought you would be safe. I even had Abe stand watch. Why didn't he see what was happening? What was he doing? He was supposed to spend the night in the carriage across the street from Clarence Seymour's house. He was supposed to keep watch. All night."

"It was late, Bryce," Natalie murmured. "Surely he fell asleep."

"While a man gets killed and the woman I love gets kidnapped?" he roared, placing his right hand back on his pistol.

"But you said that he was only your partner in the banking venture," she said. "If he is not used to these capers, he probably wasn't able to stay alert."

"You can defend him after this?" Bryce said, gesturing with his hands. His eyes darkened into an ocean of fury. He clasped Natalie's shoulders with the tight grip of his fingers. "Where is Adam?" he said hoarsely. "His ship is not moored here. Where has he gone?"

"To Key West to tell . . . Saul Palmer that I am here on the island," Natalie said. "Then they will decide later when I shall return to Key West."

She lowered her eyes and wrung her hands. "You see, Bryce, Adam is going to seek you out in his *Sea Snake*. He plans to kill you." Her eyes moved upward, meeting his gaze of steel. "He thinks that after you're dead, it will be safe to return me to Key West, to resume my life where it left off before your arrival."

She swallowed hard. "Adam seems to think that I can return and be the same person I was before. He even thinks I can forget all that has happened . . . and become Natalie Palmer, the daughter of Saul Palmer, all over again."

Tears splashed from her eyes as she threw her arms about his neck. "But, Bryce," she cried. "That can never happen. Please don't let it happen."

He caressed the midnight black of her hair. "It won't happen," he growled. "It won't."

Natalie then jerked free of him and looked quickly toward the staircase, again remembering Myra. "Bryce, my friend Myra," she blurted. "She's upstairs, very ill. We must get her to Key West. To a doctor. . . ."

Bryce's face was etched with puzzlement. "How did

she get here?'' he asked sharply. "Natalie, don't tell me that Adam kidnapped her from her ship while she was on her way to New York. I remember you telling me of your worries about her.''

"Yes, Adam is also responsible for that,'' Natalie hissed, lifting the tail of her dress into her arms to move toward the staircase next to Bryce. "It is Adam's child she is carrying.''

She cast Bryce a troubled glance. "A child she is now aborting,'' she whispered. She shook her head in confused anger. "Oh, it is all so confusing, Bryce,'' she shouted. "Everything that has happened is one big nightmare.''

Then she touched his arm. "Until you,'' she murmured, smiling softly. "Now that you are here, the nightmare is slowly leaving me.''

"Seems we've much to do,'' he said thickly, draping an arm about her waist, helping her on up the staircase. "If Myra is that ill, we will have to travel to Key West. New Orleans is much too far.'' He seemed worried. "But it could be tricky, Natalie,'' he said. "If Adam is there, we just might run into him. I don't want to meet him on the streets of Key West. I want to meet him at sea. That is a chore I've been neglecting for way too long now. I've chased him for fun too long. It is time to get down to the serious business at hand, to rid the sea of that black reptile.''

"I believe that is what he wants, too,'' Natalie sighed heavily. "To meet you at sea. He thinks he has the most powerful ship, Bryce.''

She gave him a lingering look of concern. "In fact, it seems he has three ships at his disposal. You have only one. You will be outnumbered at sea, Bryce.''

"The scoundrel only travels on one ship at a time," he spat. "The *Sea Snake*. That is the ship on which he will pursue me. The others never travel with the *Sea Snake* when it is out for blood. Saul Palmer wouldn't want his business ships to be openly involved at sea in support of a pirate whom everyone hates. That would destroy his cover as the true leader of the pirates. He has been the silent one, but their commander. Adam only follows his instructions. You can be sure of that. . . ."

"I still find it hard to believe," Natalie sighed. "How did he keep it so hidden from me? All those years—"

"Natalie . . ." Bryce gasped as they reached the third-floor landing where the guard's body sprawled lifeless on the floor. He drew Natalie even closer to him. "Who . . . ?"

"I shot him," Natalie said dryly. "Bryce, I had to. It was the only way."

"Well, I'll be damned," Bryce chuckled. "You actually shot him? I knew you had spunk, but didn't know you had that much."

He knelt down beside the man and put his fingers on the man's throat. When he felt no pulse, he gave Natalie a long, approving look. "Seems this is one obstacle out of our way," he said. "You did yourself proud, Natalie."

Natalie felt her face heat up as a blush rose upward from her neck. "I'm not proud of having shot a man," she murmured. "In fact, it sickens me to even think about it and to see him there and know that I am capable of such violence."

Bryce looked toward the open bedroom door. "Seems you had no choice," he said. "Your friend. Is she in there?"

"Yes," Natalie sighed. She rushed into the room with

341

him beside her. She went to Myra and touched her brow. "I think she has a temperature," she stated. She swung around and faced Bryce. "We must take her to Key West. Immediately. Any further delay could cost her her life."

Bryce studied Myra, noting the perspiration lacing her brow and the feverish, glassy look to her eyes as she studied him back. Her sandy-colored hair clung to her face in wet ringlets and her cheeks were flaming red.

Then Bryce glanced toward the window, feeling torn. He was so close to having the treasure! Yet he did have to see to this woman's safety. Knowing he would have to leave the island empty-handed tore his heart. But he would return. Yes, he *would* return.

Bryce turned his attention back to Myra. "Natalie, you'd best get her fully clothed," he said. "Then I'll carry her to the boat. Everything else can wait until later."

Natalie's eyes widened with sudden awareness. "Oh, Bryce," she murmured. "The key. The treasure. You've come to claim the treasure. I'm so sorry. . . ."

"Now don't you worry your pretty head about that," he encouraged. He grabbed Myra's dress and threw it toward Natalie. "Here. Get this on her. Fast. The sooner we get her to Key West, the sooner I can see to your safety, then the treasure."

Myra leaned upon an elbow and breathed heavily as she slipped her dress over her head. "I think the bleeding has stopped momentarily," she whispered. "The cramping has even slowed a bit. Maybe I can walk under my own power . . . to the . . . ship."

Bryce paced the floor. "No. We'll have none of that kind of talk," he said firmly. "I'll carry you. There's no need to cause the bleeding to start again."

Natalie helped ease Myra to the edge of the bed where Bryce lifted her up into his arms. "Natalie, be careful now," he ordered. "Though my men are keeping watch, they might miss someone."

He nodded as he moved toward the door. "In fact, take my gun. And don't delay in using it if you have to."

"But I won't know your men from Adam's," Natalie said softly. "What if I should shoot a wrong man?"

"You won't shoot unless I tell you to," Bryce said, moving out into the hall. "Now come on. Let's make haste. Dominic's sure to be getting restless by now."

With trembling fingers, Natalie accepted the heaviness of the gun in her right hand. "You're sure you want to leave the treasure behind?" she asked, now moving beside him down the staircase. "Since Myra is no longer as desperately ill, maybe—"

Bryce stopped her words short. "No. I won't hear of it," he said, though he already felt the loss. "But I do appreciate your concern for my feelings."

"I know how much the treasure means to you," Natalie murmured. Once the lower landing was reached, she brushed on past Bryce, toward the front entrance. She slowly pushed the door open and stuck her head out, looking from side to side. When she saw no one about, she motioned with the barrel of the pistol for him to follow her on out onto the veranda.

The humidity of the afternoon assaulted Natalie's flesh with a damp stickiness as she ran down the steps ahead of Bryce. As she turned to give him an encouraging glance, she saw his gaze linger on the glistening mausoleum in the family cemetery. Not wanting to see the hungry need in his eyes, she turned back to where she was running and gasped in sudden fright when Dominic stepped out from behind a thick cover of marsh grass to stand looming before her, his hands on hips. His eyes became angry as he looked past her at Bryce and Myra.

"Damn," Dominic snarled. "What now? Where the hell did you come from? And who is that with Bryce?"

Natalie swallowed back her uneasiness and stepped to his side. "Sir, I do not have to answer to you," she said stubbornly. "If Bryce sees a need to tell you, then, an only then, will you know what has happened here."

With a pounding heart, she glanced over her shoulder at Bryce, before moving on through the thick grass toward the waiting longboat. Reaching it first, she shifted from one foot to the other, waiting.

The sun's rays, bouncing from the white sands onto the dark, heavy material of her dress, caused her to be miserably hot as she stood watching Bryce carrying Myra to the boat. Only after Natalie was secured in the boat, next to Myra, who she held safely next to her, did she feel the relief that went along with escape.

She lifted her face to the sea breeze, enjoying the freshness of the air as it eased her hair upward from her shoulders. She licked the salt water from her lips and fluttered her lashes when a splash of water tipped them with drops like sparkling diamonds. Then she remembered the gun. She laughed softly to herself as she lifted it into her hands and used its barrel to nudge Bryce in the back. She giggled almost drunkenly as he turned his blue eyes to her and smiled in return.

"I don't think I have the need of this any longer," she said, motioning with the gun. "Thanks to you, darling, I may never have to touch such a thing again the rest of my life."

Bryce's smile turned to a shadowy scowl. "I wouldn't

be so sure of that," he said flatly. "Just because we made it safely from the island doesn't mean that we are in the clear. Remember Adam. We might even come face to face with him before reaching Key West."

He took the gun and placed it in his belt, then resumed rowing.

"I owe you my life," Myra whispered to Natalie. "If you hadn't come—"

"Shhh," Natalie crooned, caressing Myra's cheek. It seemed that Myra was worse again. She seemed to be a bit out of her head as she mumbled soft rambling thoughts. And had Myra forgotten just why Natalie had happened to be on the island? It surely hadn't been from choice!

She dipped a hand into the ocean and brought its wetness to Myra's cheeks. Yes, she was burning up with fever! Would they reach Key West soon enough to save her. . . ?

They drew near the *Golden Isis*. As it rocked gently with the waves, it appeared to be a large, beautiful chariot, both powerful and graceful. She was proud to board it, and she hurried alongside Bryce as he carried Myra to the cabin next to his own, where he placed her gently on a bunk.

Natalie smoothed Myra's hair from her face and accepted the cool, wet cloth Bryce handed her. "Bryce, I'm so worried," she whispered, bathing the perspiration away from Myra's brow and upper lip.

She felt pained as she saw Myra's eyes close in a strange sort of sleep. "I hope the winds are with us today," she said further. "The *Golden Isis* must make a quick journey. If not, we may be too late once we reach Key West."

"I must give my orders to the crew," Bryce said, leaning to kiss Natalie's brow. "Once you have Myra as comfortable as you can make her come out on deck and be with me for a while. You know there isn't much else we can do for her but keep her as comfortable and cool as possible."

Natalie placed the damp cloth aside and rose to drape her arms about Bryce's neck. She kissed him lightly on his lips then sighed heavily as he gazed back at her with a quiet hunger. "I've missed you so, darling," she whispered, "I was so afraid. . . ."

Bryce kissed the tip of her nose. "You need never be afraid again," he reassured her. "I will see to it that you will never have Adam to worry about again. And then I will see to it that Saul Palmer is no longer a threat to you."

Natalie swallowed hard. She still held deep, warm feelings for Saul, though he was no more to her than a pirate who had set the course of her life much differently than her parents would have. Yet, despite everything, she felt deeply for him, and knew that she would always wonder about him . . . and yes . . . even miss him.

"No," she said quietly. "Don't even think that. That will not become necessary. I'm sure Saul Palmer will be no problem once Adam has been taken care of."

"You still care . . . ?"

"About Saul Palmer, the man who was my father for so long?"

"Yes."

"I cannot help but feel something for him," she said, casting her eyes downward. Then her gaze met his, boldly and coldly. "But as for Adam, I care not what happens to him. Truly I do not."

Bryce burrowed his nose into the depth of her hair and

held her even more closely. "Then, my darling, I see no problem," he sighed.

He drew away from her and held her at arm's length. "But for now, please see to your friend," he added. "I will see to my crew. Then please come to me. I need you."

Natalie glanced cautiously toward Myra. "But should I leave her for even one minute?" she questioned softly.

"Like I said, darling, once you have her bathed and cooled, and resting as comfortably as possible, there will not be another thing you can do until we reach Key West. Do not feel guilty for wanting to be with me. There is no need. You have already been a guardian angel to your friend."

He drew her into his arms and kissed her a hard, long kiss. "Come to me," he whispered huskily into her ear. "Soon. Soon. . . ."

"I will," she said, already feeling the strength of the pulse in the hollow of her throat. "Soon, my love."

She watched him walk away from her and close the door behind him. Vigorously, she swung around to attend to Myra. After getting Myra unclothed down to her petticoat, Natalie diligently began bathing her with cool water until Myra glowed like a rose petal and smelled as clean and fresh as after-rain. The bleeding hadn't resumed and if there was pain, Myra wasn't aware of it, for she was sleeping soundly.

Natalie stepped from the cabin long enough to toss the water in the basin over the side. And, wanting to be as fresh as possible for Bryce, she went back to the cabin and poured some clean water for herself. She enjoyed her skimpy bath, her thoughts already on what she and Bryce would soon be enjoying . . . sharing . . . .

In his arms, all else would be forgotten. Then feeling shame splash through her for thinking only of herself and the pleasures of the flesh, she placed a hand on Myra's brow, thinking maybe she shouldn't be left unattended after all.

Natalie's heart raced and her eyes widened. "She's cooler," she whispered. Hurriedly she ran her fingers along Myra's cheeks and down to the swell of her bosom. She laughed awkwardly. "She is cooler," she said. "The coolness of the water must have lessened her temperature!"

Placing a cheek to Myra's, Natalie hugged her friend affectionately, and although Myra slept, she whispered, "I was so afraid for you. Now maybe you're going to be well."

She drew away and studied Myra through a lazy haze of tears. "You may not even lose the baby," she murmured. "Will that grieve you too much? Don't you think you could love the child because you gave birth to it?"

Shaking her head and feeling foolish for talking to someone who obviously did not hear, Natalie started to rise from the bunk. But she did not get far. A cool hand reached out and touched her arm. Natalie turned with a start to see warm eyes smiling at her. Natalie's heart leaped with joy as she plopped back down onto the bunk and held both of Myra's hands in hers.

"Myra, you've awakened," she said, laughing softly.

"Yes, I have awakened and I heard," she said. "And you're right, you know."

"I am . . . ?" Natalie wondered. "About what?"

"The child. While in my drugged sleep, I dreamed of the child," Myra said, stopping to lick her lips, moistening their dryness. "It was a beautiful, golden-haired

348

child. My child. A boy. I couldn't not love him. No matter who the father is.''

"Then you do want the child?" Natalie asked, swallowing the lump in her throat.

"Yes," Myra murmured. "And to hell with Adam Palmer. If I do have a son, Adam would have to kill me first to get him away from me.''

Natalie lowered a kiss to Myra's cheek. "That won't be necessary," she laughed softly. "I believe Bryce has his own plans for Adam.''

Myra looked slowly around her. "Where is that handsome man?" she asked amusedly.

Natalie threw her head back, laughing softly; then she looked back toward Myra. "Now I know you're feeling better," she said. "When you begin talking like that I know you're going to be all right.''

"As long as I can relax and respond to what my body's trying to tell me, I think I can beat this thing, Natalie," Myra said, squeezing Natalie's hands affectionately. "Now that I've decided I want this child, surely God won't let me lose it.''

"I'm sure he won't," Natalie sighed. She glanced toward the door.

"Bryce is waiting for you, isn't he?" Myra said, following Natalie's eyes.

"Yes . . ."

"Go to him."

"You'll be all right?"

"Yes, all I need is rest now."

Natalie rose to her feet and then frowned. "But, Myra," she murmured. "This change in your attitude did happen so quickly. Are you sure . . . ?''

"I hadn't had such a dream before," Myra sighed.

"Then you are sure?"

"Yes."

"Well, then, I can relax," Natalie sighed. She combed her fingers through her hair. "Do I look all right?" she whispered, straightening her back. "I know my dress is ugly."

Myra again sighed, turning to her side and placing an arm beneath her head. "If I could only look as good," she laughed. "But it will be awhile. I know." She exhaled heavily. "Good Lord, Natalie," she added. "If you thought I was heavy before, just wait until you see me nine month's pregnant!"

Natalie's heart ached a bit. She still wasn't convinced that Myra wasn't going to abort. Maybe she already had! Myra surely wasn't aware of the blood that had passed from her body!

She patted Myra's hand. "You'll be beautiful," she said. "You are beautiful."

Myra licked her lips again and raised a hand to her hair. "I know how I look," she said. "My hair hasn't been brushed in days."

"When we reach Key West, things will be all right again."

"No," Myra murmured, her face shadowing with renewed tension. "It won't be all right. Mother wanted me to return to Key West with my womb quite empty. When she hears that I'm still with child, she won't even claim me as her own."

"Myra," Natalie scoffed. "She'll be so relieved to know that you're alive she'll forget that you're still with child."

Myra shook her head lethargically. "No," she said. "Her pride won't let her forget."

She wiped tears from her eyes. "In fact, I've decided that Bryce shouldn't deliver me to my parents' house once we return to Key West," she stated, looking guardedly toward Natalie.

"What?" Natalie gasped, hands on hips. "Where then?"

Myra fluttered her lashes nervously. "I want to go to Parrot Inn," she whispered. "I can stay there. That way, I can at least be near Hugh. Once he knows the truth of how I am with child, he won't hate me. He'll be sympathetic and let me stay there, at least until I'm back on my feet and can take up residence elsewhere."

"Myra, you're full of surprises," Natalie said, throwing her hands into the air. "First you manage to keep your pregnancy from me, your best friend, for such a long time, even after my own—the man I thought was my—brother raped you."

Natalie paced nervously. "And now? You refuse to go home?" She stopped and stood over Myra, puzzling. "I'm sure you're wrong about your mother. Do you not remember it was she who let you do as you pleased when it was I who was watched like a hawk. And what if Hugh doesn't understand? What if he turns his back on you? That could hurt terribly, Myra."

Myra sniffled. "He will understand," she said. "Though he has problems with women—sexually—he does love me in his own way. He'll be good to me, Natalie. He'll be so gentle. I just know it."

"For your peace of mind and physical health I hope you're right," Natalie sighed. Once more she glanced toward the door then back toward Myra. "I really must go now," she whispered. "My heart races so at just thinking of being with Bryce again. . . ."

Myra smiled a good-bye to Natalie and closed her eyes to drift into a peaceful half-sleep. Her fears were gone. How strange that one dream could steer her future in a much different direction. But it had and now she wanted to hold that baby of her dream in her arms and watch him grow into a strong, healthy man.

Natalie stepped out into the lengthening shadows of early dusk. The copper sunset had changed the *Golden Isis*'s colors into a pale, shimmering orange. Even the softly fluttering topsails had captured the color and held it; they blended beautifully into the backdrop of sheer blue ocean and the velvet ebbing darkness of night.

Breathing anxiously, Natalie spied Bryce at the ship's rail and was lost in the tranquil moment that had finally been afforded them. She absorbed his strong features, and admired his tall, magnificently proud height, the way his golden hair lifted and fell gently in the breeze, and the corded muscles in his shoulders when his fingers locked securely around the rail.

His gun belt had been removed and his shirt freed from his breeches so that its tail, as it blew softly away from his body, matched the fluttering of the ship's sails.

Sighing, Natalie went to him and, with a gentle tug at his left arm, urged him around to face her. Not caring that the crew was quite aware of her presence on the quarter-deck, she looked up into his eyes and smiled sweetly as her fingers moved over his bare chest.

"Darling, I love you so. . . ." she whispered, already feeling her drugged desire for him drawing her into a world that held only Bryce and herself.

Bryce lowered her hands and placed an arm about her waist, to guide her to his cabin. "Myra?" he said thickly, hardly able to keep from scooping her up into his arms and devouring her right there. But his men. He could sense all the eyes upon him and didn't wish to give a show! "Is your friend still asleep?" he quickly asked.

Natalie beamed. "Bryce, she is so much better," She sighed. "She's even awake . . . her temperature has lowered . . . and she speaks of wanting to keep the child."

She swung around and faced him. "And she wants you to take her to Parrot Inn instead of to her mother."

"My God, why?" Bryce gasped.

"She's afraid her mother won't even claim her back into the household now that she's still with child and unwed, and she has decided—yes, suddenly decided—she does want this child! She had a dream about the baby. The dream has made her change her mind."

"A dream?" Bryce said quietly. "That's a bit unreal, Natalie."

"But it is true," she declared.

"And it's a bit ridiculous to think her mother will treat her so badly, isn't it?" Bryce scoffed.

Natalie walked next to him, down the steps, into the narrow hallway and finally into the privacy of his cabin. "Not really," Natalie murmured. "Her child will be considered a bastard when born . . . unless . . ." Once more she swung around and beseeched Bryce, pleading with her dark eyes. "Unless we can get Hugh to marry her!" she said excitedly.

Bryce blanched. He took a step backward, the flickering of a whale-oil lamp revealing the shock etched across his face. "Hugh. . . ?" he said in a shallow whisper. As he usually did when concerned, he combed his fingers through his hair. "Does she actually want to marry that weasel of a man?" he said thickly.

Natalie's surprise showed on her face. "Bryce . . ." she gasped. "How could you say that about your own brother?" She giggled a bit and lowered her lashes. "Yet I guess it is true," she added. "Myra has told me of his problems with . . . women."

Bryce swung around. He went to his liquor cabinet and poured himself a quick glass of wine. In one swallow the glass was empty and he was pouring another. "It's a long story about why I think so poorly of my brother," he said flatly.

She went to him and touched a cheek with a forefinger. "What's a long story, Bryce?" she murmured.

His eyes were cloudy blue as he looked her way. "About Hugh . . . and . . . our mother," he said thickly. "One day I've some truths about my own family to reveal to you. You and I were destined to meet because of our pasts. I just know that to be so."

Natalie stood on tiptoe to place a gentle kiss on his lips, then he smiled as she licked the sweet taste of wine from her lips. "Must we continue talking of the past?" she whispered. She lifted a finger to his face and began teasingly tracing his features. "We have now. We're alone. Together. Can't you think of better things to do than just talk?"

A growl rose from somewhere deep inside Bryce as he placed his arms about her waist and drew her roughly to him. His lips crushed hers into his and he fit his body into the soft, sensuous curves of hers. His hands began their magical dance across her back, making their way to the buttons that held her dress together.

Natalie quickly drew in her breath when she felt the release of the buttons and the touch of his fingers making contact with her flesh. She moaned a bit as she stepped away from him and began to lower her dress before his feasting eyes.

"You too," she whispered. "Undress as I do. Please?"

Bryce's eyes gleamed. He lifted his shirt from his shoulders, pulled his boots off, and stepped out of his breeches just as Natalie dropped the last of her garments to the floor.

He stood there for a moment, letting the heat of passion burn brighter inside him as his eyes slowly raked over her loveliness. Her breasts were so magnificently large, her waist so tiny, and her skin so velvet. But his heart beat speeded up even more when he looked at the dark vee between her legs and the treasures awaiting him there.

His lips nibbled and teased her mouth and his breath, hot and anxious, almost seared her flesh. When he inched her toward the bed, she welcomed his body against hers as he lowered her downward.

Both of his hands traveled over the contours of her body, lingering longer at her most intimate pleasure points. Then when his tongue replaced his hands and began a slow, dangerous trail downward, she moaned with intense delight.

"Yes . . ." she sighed. "Oh, yes . . ."

Then he drew himself over her, entering her, and she lifted her legs around him and moved with him as he gently thrust in and out of her. His lips moved to the hollow of her throat . . . then to her breasts . . . then back to her mouth where he plunged his tongue deeply inside as both their bodies shuddered violently in those glorious moments of overwhelming, intense pleasure which left them both spent and breathless, yet clinging.

Natalie giggled as she laced her fingers through his hair. "You're a bit out of breath," she teased. "My, my,

Bryce. Am I worth all that labor?''

Bryce grumbled beneath his breath as he flicked his tongue over the pink tip of her breast. ''No,'' he teased. ''But I will pay you well for your trouble.''

Natalie's eyes flashed angrily at him and she rose quickly to a sitting position. ''What did you say?'' she hissed.

Bryce ran his fingers over the flat smoothness of her abdomen, smiling to himself when he saw her skin rippling pleasurably. Then he focused his eyes on her face and saw the humiliation his words had caused.

''Darling, you know I was teasing,'' he laughed. ''I remember how angry you were earlier when you thought I was going to pay you for our time together.''

He drew her into his arms. ''Darling, I do want to pay you,'' he added. ''But in the most appropriate way. I want to offer you my life. My name. All I possess and will possess. We must wed. Soon. Then no one else dare come near you again.''

''You really do mean it, don't you?'' she sighed, clinging. ''You do want me as your wife? Even after all that's happened . . . after all the trouble I have caused you.''

Bryce drew away from her and framed her face between his hands. ''For so long, I didn't think I could love a woman enough to wed,'' he said hoarsely. ''So much in my past made me hate women. But you changed that for me, Natalie. You changed my life and only for the better. . . .''

''Bryce . . .''

Bryce kissed her softly. She clung to him, wanting this future with him. But she wondered if he had so quickly forgotten the *Sea Snake* and Adam.

KEY WEST

*You kissed me! My heart, my
   breath and my will
In delirious joy for a moment
   stood still. . . .*

—Hunt

SEVENTEEN

Quite a stir was created when the carriage pulled up to Parrot Inn and Bryce stepped from it, carrying a weak and pale Myra. She clung to his neck and placed her cheek on his chest, relishing her brief moment of closeness with this delicious man. She loved the smell of him and the tautness of his muscles as he held her so comfortingly.

Oh, if only the child she was carrying would be a man of Bryce's stature and not a rogue—an evil Adam Palmer! What if her child inherited Adam's love of wickedness . . . of piracy?

She closed her thoughts to such preoccupations and let her gaze move to the door of Parrot Inn. When Hugh stepped into view, a soft pleasure filled Myra's being. To her he was a welcome substitute for Bryce Fowler. Though on the shy, weak side, Hugh was a kind and gentle soul whose voice could soothe even the devil!

"Myra!" Hugh said, rushing to meet Bryce's approach. "What has happened?" He glared hawklike toward Bryce. "Why are you in his company?" he said with deep scorn. "Is he the one responsible for your paleness? Has he offended you in some way?''

Myra reached a hand toward Hugh, laughing softly. "My Hugh," she purred. "No. Bryce did not harm me. He has rescued me. Aren't you glad to see me . . . to know that I am no longer being held by that damnable pirate?''

Natalie moved to Hugh and also spoke softly, reassuringly to him when Bryce brushed on past Hugh, ignoring him and his angry words.

"Hugh, we must talk," Natalie said softly. She watched Bryce as he disappeared inside the inn, obviously ready to deposit Myra where he damned well pleased, no matter what Hugh had to say about it.

Hugh turned, his face devoid of expression. "Where is he taking Myra?" he asked hoarsely. His eyes turned back to Natalie. "What's going on here, Natalie?''

Natalie glanced around at the staring group of people who were slowly gathering around, no doubt ready to participate later in some juicy gossip. "Please, Hugh," she encouraged. "Let's go into the inn. Let me explain.''

"Somebody had better explain . . ." he spat out angrily, moving his lean, lithe figure on through the door. The flowing sleeves of his orange, silk shirt swayed as he moved into the dim lighting of the tearoom. He stopped abruptly and turned to stare toward the staircase. Since his father had left him the inn, he had thought Bryce had decided to stay out of his life. In the end, Bryce had lost. Hugh had been the victorious one, having won ownership of Parrot Inn and all that his father had possessed in life.

But, somehow, Bryce still seemed to be the victor; he knew the ways of women and how to please them so well. Now, Hugh ached to run to Myra and confess his utter happiness at seeing her safely away from the pirate. He

360

had been plagued for many sleepless nights by worrying about her and wishing he knew a way to seek her out . . . to rescue her.

"But he did it. Not me," he thought sourly.

Though he was ecstatic that she was safe, the person who had delivered her safely to him had taken away the pleasure of their reunion!

"Hugh?" Natalie said softly, leaning into his face.

Hugh jumped as though shot. He cleared his throat nervously as he faced Natalie again. "I'm sorry," he said. "My thoughts were elsewhere."

The strumming from the usual lone guitar reverberated softly around the room and the aroma of broiled fish hung heavily in the air. Hugh pulled a chair from beneath a table and gestured with his hand. "Please sit down," he urged.

Natalie clasped her hands on the back of the chair and pushed it back in place. "Hugh, this is no time for tea and simple talk," she whispered harshly. "Let's move back out into the hallway where I can speak more openly, yet privately."

Furrowing his brow, Hugh stepped briskly away from her into the dimmer shadows beneath the stairs. "All right," he said, with a drooping pout to his lips. "Let's talk. Tell me about Myra." He cast another worried look up the staircase.

"It's quite a lengthy story," Natalie said. "But I want you to listen carefully. Hugh, maybe I'm wrong but I sense that you are a very lonesome man. Myra could change this for you. Please keep this in mind as I tell you everything that has happened to her."

"Just tell me, Natalie," Hugh said impatiently. "I do want to go to her."

Natalie placed a hand on his arm to comfort him as she began to tell the long story . . .

Having finished, she noticed the drawn expression that creased his brow and caused a slight quivering of his chin.

"Why didn't she tell me?" he asked thickly.

"And would you have understood as you do now that you realize the torment she has gone through to keep this ugly secret just that—a secret—something she had to cope with, alone?"

"I would have understood it even more if she had been the one to reveal this to me," he said thickly. "She would have shown her true devotion to me if she had trusted me enough to tell me the unhappy truths of her dilemma."

He cleared his throat nervously. "As it is, above all else, I cannot understand how she could have been ready to kill the baby. She should not have resorted to . . . killing an innocent baby before it had a chance at life."

His heart plummeted when he suddenly recalled Bryce and the way he had been conceived. By a man his mother had not truly loved—a scoundrel, who most surely had left a trail of unwed, pregnant women wherever he traveled!

All these years Hugh had despised Bryce for existing. He suddenly felt a deep inner shame. The sins of his mother had not been Bryce's fault. The innocent, unborn child growing inside Myra's womb had had no say about its deliverance into this world . . .

"Why didn't I see it this way before?" he whispered, kneading his brow.

"See what, Hugh?"

Hugh felt a blush rise to his usually pale cheeks. "Nothing . . ." he stammered. "Nothing at all."

"What will your decision be about Myra?" Natalie questioned softly. "Will you look after her for a while?"

"Her parents?"

"Word has already been sent to them."

"Then they will probably come for her."

"Myra doubts this."

"I will do what I can," Hugh murmured. Another blush rose from his neck to his cheeks. His eyes wavered. "But I don't know much about women," he said. "You see, the only woman I was ever comfortable with was my mother and she is—she has—now been dead for ten long years. I'll be clumsy. Myra will probably grow tired of my fumblings."

Natalie took one of his hands and squeezed it reassuringly. "You don't seem to realize just how much Myra cares for you," she said, smiling softly.

He lowered his eyes and smiled awkwardly. "As with most everyone, I am sure my voice is the full attraction," he said thickly.

"No. That's not the reason she wants to be with you," Natalie said firmly. "She loves you—the man—Hugh."

Hugh's blue eyes brightened. "Are you sure?" he stammered.

"Quite." Natalie laughed. "I'm quite positive. Why don't you go upstairs and find out?"

Hugh glanced from the staircase to the door and back again to Natalie. "Have you contacted Dr. Jamieson?"

"He's been sent for."

"Then let's go see if Bryce has Myra in an appropriate room," Hugh said, energy now reflected in his voice and quick gait as he moved away from Natalie and toward the staircase. "She should have a room on the sunny side of the inn . . . she should be able to watch the ship's. . . ."

Hugh took only a few steps on the staircase and then paled as he turned to Natalie who began climbing the steps next to him. "Natalie . . . ?" he said with an evident strain. "You didn't say how you happened to be with Myra. All you said was that Bryce had traveled to the island to rescue a stolen opium shipment and found Myra being held captive there. How is it that you are also with Bryce?"

Natalie swallowed hard, glad she and Bryce had already thought about all the questions that Hugh would ask. In no way could they reveal that the key had been given to Bryce.

"Why, Hugh, I just happened along when Bryce's Golden Isis moored at the quay," she murmured matter-of-factly.

"Natalie, you must know that gossip has spread about you fleeing from Key West in order to escape marriage to Albert Burns," he argued. "When did you return?"

Natalie placed a hand to her brow, caught in her web of lies. She thought fast and said: "Hugh, I had only returned to gather up a few of my things," she said, with wide-eyed innocence. "I guess the gossip that I am to wed your brother in the near future hasn't reached your ears."

Hugh reached for the side bannister, to steady himself. "God, Natalie," he gasped.

Natalie's heart jumped. "What's wrong, Hugh?" she murmured, paling.

"You can't marry . . . Bryce," he stammered. "You just can't."

Natalie swallowed hard, not understanding his reaction at all. Why should it matter to Hugh? It was obvious that there was no love between these brothers. But this reaction was a bit too much! "I don't understand, Hugh," she murmured, lifting a silken brow.

Heavy footsteps stopped at the head of the stairs and Bryce's cool voice drew all attention his way. "Yes, Hugh," he said. "What were you saying?"

"Bryce, doesn't she . . . ?"

"No," Bryce interrupted. "And, Hugh, it truly makes no difference."

Seeing his brother squirm delighted Bryce no end. He knew exactly what Hugh was thinking. That Natalie's father was Saul Palmer and that brother and sister were in love.

The humor of the situation tickled Bryce's insides. Hell. He would not tell him about Clarence Seymour. Let him be shocked and later surprised when he heard the full truth.

"But, Bryce . . ." Hugh persisted.

Bryce motioned with a hand. "Hugh, you have a very ailing house guest who should be your main concern at the moment," he growled. "I would urge you to look in on her. She's asking for you."

Hugh gave Natalie a long, questioning look, then sauntered on up the stairs, silent and brooding.

"The room at the far end of the hall, across from your private quarters," Bryce said flatly. "It was the only room that looked halfway clean. You ought to do something about the filth of this place, Hugh."

Bryce brushed past his half brother, stopping on the step above Natalie. He took her hands in his and recognized the questioning in the wideness of her dark, luminous eyes.

"Bryce, what did he mean?"

"I guess it's time I tell you a bit about my own life,

that has only been recently uncovered.''

"But, Bryce, what I want to know is why Hugh said I shouldn't marry you,'' she murmured.

"Darling, what I have to say will answer that question for you,'' he said thickly. He nodded toward the tearoom. "Shall we have a cup of tea while I tell you something that will be a shock to you as it was to me?''

Natalie welcomed his arm about her waist as they moved together on down the staircase.

The dark hallway afforded Hugh privacy so he might stand a moment and draw strength from inside himself before entering the room where Myra lay waiting. Natalie's encouraging words kept racing through his mind. Maybe Myra could be the answer to his loneliness. It didn't matter that she was already with child. He very much doubted if he would ever be able to father a child of his own. That one time with Myra, he hadn't even been able to make love to her. Something had been lacking. He hadn't had the ability to maintain the erectness required to fully enter her the way a man should . . .

"Hugh, are you there?'' Myra asked softly from inside the room.

Hugh felt a strange weakness in his knees as he made his appearance at the doorway. "I'm sorry it took me so long,'' he said with a quiver in his voice. "But Natalie took me aside and explained a few things to me.''

His eyes, traveling over her, noted how vulnerable she was, lying in the soft sunshine that filtered its way through the sheer, yellowed curtains of the one window in the room.

He let his gaze take in the paleness of her face and the way her hair lay about her head, a halo crowning her. The fullness of her face appealed to him—slender women did not—and the adoring look in her eyes drew him even closer to the bed.

A blanket was pulled to her chin, but its cover didn't hide the shape of her body. He couldn't help but stare openly at where her stomach should be beneath the blanket. No swell was yet visible. She couldn't be too far along in her pregnancy. If she had succeeded at ridding herself of the child, he would never have even known. . . .

"Do you mind that I have chosen to come to you for help?" she murmured, easing a hand from beneath the blanket, reaching toward him.

Hugh's hands trembled as he pulled a chair to her bedside. His pulse raced as he accepted her hand in his. "I wish you had come to me earlier," he said thickly. "Why did you decide to go to New York to do that terrible thing?"

Myra's lashes fluttered nervously. She was tired from the sea voyage and from the loss of blood. But she was also thankful—for this room, even with its drab, beaten-up furniture and dust-laden floors. At least it was a hideaway, a safe hideaway for a while.

"I had planned something different," she finally said. She turned her face from him, remembering how she had planned to trick him into marrying her, but his inadequacies had made that impossible.

"And what was that?" Hugh asked, leaning toward her. He crossed his legs and rested an elbow on his knee.

Myra slowly moved her eyes to him again and studied the sky blue of his eyes. Honesty was required now. If he was to trust her and stand by her, she needed to clear her conscience of all the shame that plagued her. At least that way she could search out his deepest feelings for her.

"I had hoped to be married by now," she said in a near whisper.

Hugh's back straightened and his stomach felt suddenly tremulous. His heart ached a bit when he envisioned her married to another man. Then a thought came to him. He was feeling jealousy for a woman! That was a first for him. Maybe there was hope after all!

"What man had you planned to marry, Myra?" he asked thickly.

Myra licked her dry lips and forced a smile. She was afraid, but she still had to tell him. "Hugh," she murmured. "The man I'm speaking of is you."

His eyes lit up and a small smile lifted his lips. "You wanted me . . . ?"

"The one night we shared more than tea, I had hoped for more than what we accomplished together," she said dryly.

She squeezed his hand. "Hugh, I had hoped we would—Oh, you know. Then I could have said the child . . . was . . . yours . . ."

Hugh's hand went limp in hers and the color drained from his face. He rose so abruptly from the chair, it tipped over backward. As it crashed against the floor, the sound echoed over and over again inside Myra's head. Tears hazed her eyes when she realized that she had made a mistake by telling him. Oh, why had she been compelled to do so? Had the fever warped her senses?

"Hugh . . ." she pleaded, watching him inch backward to the door.

"Hello, there." A pleasant voice spoke from behind Hugh.

Hugh spun around and laughed nervously at seeing Doc Jamieson standing there, his dark hair and mustache

368

blending quite well with his dark suit and the black satchel he held in his right hand.

"Come on in, Doc," Hugh said, sending Myra a downcast look. "There's the patient. Take good care of her."

He walked from the room and paced the hallway, sorting everything out in his mind. What she had schemed to do was scandalous! If she had stooped so low as to do that, wouldn't she be capable of all sorts of deceits?

He hung his head in his hands, shaking it. Maybe he'd best forget her. He could let her stay until . . .

Hugh's heart skipped a beat, remembering another woman . . . another pregnancy . . . another schemed marriage.

"Mother!" he whispered harshly. "She did exactly that and she was the most wonderfully decent woman on the face of the earth. Is Myra the same?"

Had he really found the woman that matched his mother in many ways?

"Hugh . . ."

Hugh spun around and faced the doctor as he stepped out into the dark shadows of the hallway. "Well? How is she?" Hugh asked quietly, almost afraid to hear the answer. If she had lost the child, would she no longer have need of him? Was she intrigued by him or the legal name she sought for her unborn child?

"She's in quite a weakened condition," Doc Jamieson said. "But, of course, you know that."

"The baby?"

"If Myra remains in bed for the next several weeks, the child will be born in six months. But bed rest is of the utmost importance now."

Hugh sighed. He clasped Doc Jamieson's shoulders

firmly. "Thank you, Doc," he murmured. "And you can be assured that she will get the rest and care that is required. I'll see to it myself."

"Your child depends on it," Doc Jamieson said, moving on toward the staircase.

Hugh's heart began to hammer inside him. He smiled a bit crookedly, suddenly his shy self, blushing because of the doctor's reference to "his child."

Then he set his jaw firmly and followed the doctor to the head of the stairs. "My child will be the healthiest in all of Key West," he bragged, surprised at how easily the words had come out.

Yes, it had been easy enough. The doctor had actually taken it for granted that the child was his since he was the one caring for its mother. Though Myra had been kidnapped by the pirate, no one had known why she had been abducted.

Yes! He would claim the child as his since no one knew the difference! And wouldn't that make him look quite the virile man! How proudly he would brag of a son! Yes, his son! He would concentrate on her having a son and that would surely make it happen!

"Thank you for coming, Doc," he said.

"Anytime . . ."

Hugh rushed back to Myra's bedside. He felt pain because of the hurt in her eyes. He sat down beside her on the bed and drew her gently into his arms. "The next visitor into this room shall be a preacher," he said huskily. He could feel her tensing in his arms.

"A . . . preacher?" she whispered.

"You will marry me, won't you, Myra?" he asked, then held her even more tightly when her tears splashed onto his silk shirt, soaking it through and wetting his

370

chest.

"Yes." she whispered. "Oh, yes . . . yes. . . ."

Clumsily, he lifted her chin with a forefinger and lowered his lips to hers with utter softness. Their tears mingled. . . .

The guitar played softly as a fog of smoke circled the tearoom where Bryce and Natalie sat in a dark corner, contemplating their lives.

Natalie sipped tea from her cup, still in a state of semi shock because Bryce had revealed to her that Saul Palmer was his father. She felt a bit numb, although earlier she had been silently longing to return to her childhood home, possibly even to see Saul Palmer again.

But it seemed every week brought more sordid news about him. Oh, how had she reached the age of eighteen without finding out the truth! How?

"Are you all right, darling?" Bryce asked softly, reaching to take her free hand in his.

"I wonder if I ever will be again," she sighed. "Life is so hard to understand."

She placed her cup down and looked intensely into his eyes. "How have you been able to accept all the truths, Bryce? Your life and mine have been based on lies. Isn't it hard for you to accept all the deceptions?"

"I'm focusing on the present and the future, Natalie," Bryce said thickly. "Ours. Together. This makes the past quite bearable. If it were not for our past, there would be no present . . . no us. So you see, Natalie, you must forget as I'm managing to do."

"It's not that easy, Bryce," she murmured, casting her eyes downward. "My past includes Tami and I miss my beautiful horse Adora. I can't help but wonder how they are."

"Before this is all settled, somehow you will have Tami and Adora as a part of your life in New Orleans," Bryce encouraged. "I promise you that, Natalie."

"Bryce, how . . . ?"

"You are not to worry, darling," he said.

"Now I must get you to New Orleans, to the safety of my house. Then I must return to my duties. Though Clarence Seymour is dead, I can deliver his opium shipment to his company. I owe him that much. So when I return to Orchid Island for the treasure, I shall also get the opium."

Natalie felt a shimmer of excitement. "Bryce, I don't want to go to New Orleans," she said anxiously. "Let me travel back to Orchid Island with you."

Bryce's face shadowed. "No," he said flatly. "It would be too dangerous. I am certain that Adam will be waiting in his *Sea Snake* this time."

"I will be just as secure on your ship as I would be in New Orleans," she argued. "If you will remember, New Orleans was not the safest place. Even Clarence Seymour wasn't safe. You must let me stay with you, Bryce."

"The crew wouldn't like it," Bryce said, shaking his head. "No. I'd best not. The crew would think you bad luck if we were to have a sea battle with Adam and his *Sea Snake*."

"Have I brought you bad luck at any time?" she asked flatly. "Have I, Bryce?"

He chuckled amusedly. "Some would say yes," he said. "But I'd say no."

"Well then? Why can't I go with you?"

He tipped his empty cup sideways, studying the damp residue of tea leaves at the bottom. Many had read their fortunes by such as these but he didn't believe in fantasy.

He pushed the cup away from him and leaned toward Natalie. "All right," he said in a near whisper.

His eyes narrowed and became a shallow blue. "But if we do run into Adam, and a battle ensues, you will have to stay in the master cabin, away from the horrors of the fighting," he said. "You do understand that, don't you?"

"Yes, I understand," she said, rising quickly from the chair. "I promise."

She rushed around the table and urged him up into her arms. "Oh, darling, I'd promise you anything. You know that."

"Anything?" he teased.

"Anything . . ."

"Let's return to the ship and set our course for Orchid Island," he said huskily. "I can think of many things I'd like to have promised to me while on our way there."

Linking her arm through his, she walked proudly with him from the tearoom. Then when the staircase came into full view, Natalie hesitated. "Shouldn't we first see about Myra?" she whispered.

"No, darling," he said. "She's Hugh's responsibility now, whether he knows it yet or not. And the only way he'll learn to live up to that responsibility is to be left alone with it . . . and her."

"But what if he doesn't want this?"

"He would be daft to say no to such a woman as Myra."

"But there is the child. . . ."

Bryce laughed mockingly. "The child should be even more important than the woman," he said. "It will make Hugh look a man. Something that he has not achieved by himself."

"The child is not his," Natalie gasped.

Bryce lifted an eyebrow. "And who should know but us . . . ?"

"There is Adam."

"Adam is the same as dead," Bryce growled.

Footsteps rushing down the staircase drew Natalie and Bryce around in unison. A different Hugh presented himself. His eyes were bright and color was high in his face. As he spoke, his arrogance was seemingly a thing of the past.

"Before you leave, I thought you might like knowing there is to be a wedding," Hugh bragged, yet not with his usual stiffness. "She has agreed to marry me, Bryce." He circled Natalie's hands in his. "She has actually agreed to marry me, Natalie," he shouted.

Bryce raked his fingers through his hair. "Well, I'll be damned," he uttered softly. He had hoped for this, but he had doubted that Hugh would do what was right for him. Yes, for once, his brother had made a wise decision on his own! Maybe there was hope for him after all!

Natalie's eyes danced. "Hugh, oh, Hugh," she cried. She drew her hands free and slung them around Hugh's neck and hugged him tightly. "I'm so glad," she murmured. "And you won't be sorry, Hugh. Myra is quite a wonderful lady. I've known her for so long."

With a tear sparkling in the corner of an eye, she took a step backward. "And thank you, my friend," she whispered. "Thank you . . . thank you. . . ."

"You will stay for the wedding?" Hugh asked, his hopeful eyes traveling from Natalie to Bryce.

Bryce clasped his brother's shoulders. "Hugh, my good man, we cannot stay," he said. "I've things to do. Please understand."

"The *Golden Isis,* eh?" Hugh murmured.

"Yes. I have travels to make and deeds to do," Bryce said firmly. He stepped away from Hugh and circled an arm about Natalie's waist. "And a wedding of my own to attend."

Hugh smiled sheepishly. "Yes, I know," he said.

Bryce's eyes widened. "You . . . know?" he gasped.

"Yes, Myra told me all about it," Hugh laughed.

A slow smile lighted Bryce's face. "Ah, yes," he said. "Myra. She does know the whole story. So you do see, brother, Natalie and I are not blood kin. Sorry I led you to believe differently. But you were behaving like an ass, you know."

Hugh's face became shadowed. "You've always thought me an ass," he argued.

"Yes, I guess I have" Bryce laughed.

"Bryce," Natalie gasped. "Please—"

"Only jesting," Bryce said with a toss of his head. "But I am not jesting when I say we must leave now. My crew awaits my return."

"I would like to see Myra," Natalie said.

"Myra is asleep," Hugh declared. "She is quite worn out from her traumatic experiences."

"You take good care of her," Natalie said, leaning to place a soft kiss onto his cheek.

"Good as done," Hugh said, ushering Natalie and Bryce to the door. "As good as done. And you two ride the seas with care. The pirate spares no one, it seems."

"The pirate will soon be no more," Bryce growled. He took a more careful grip around Natalie's waist as he guided her out toward a waiting carriage and helped her inside, where they settled down for the trip to the quay.

"Do you think it will work, Bryce?" Natalie said in a

375

near whisper.

"Hugh and Myra?"

"Yes."

"Myra will make it work," Bryce stated flatly. "She does seem to be a woman of spirit. Yes, she will make it work."

"Hugh seems so happy."

Bryce studied his thoughts for a moment, then sighed. "Yes, he does," he said. "Maybe there is hope for my brother after all. And, damn it, maybe even for the Fowler name."

EIGHTEEN

Blue and orange shadows danced downward from the skylight, settling on Natalie and Bryce as they lay entangled on the bed in the master's cabin.

"Bryce, are you sure you can concentrate on making love?" Natalie purred, as the tips of her fingers roamed across the tautness of his shoulder muscles.

"Do not worry," he said thickly. "Being with you doubles the excitement of the chase, darling."

He placed a soft kiss at the hollow of her throat. "It doesn't get in the way of my concentration. When I am excited, my pleasure doubles. I'm sure it's the same with you. We're so much alike, you and I."

"I want that to be so," she sighed. "I want always to be as one while with you."

"We are one," Bryce said, molding his body even more snugly into hers. "Let's savor the moment."

Natalie moaned when she felt the hardness of his desire against her flesh. "But . . . the . . . *Sea Snake?*" she whispered. "What if . . . ?"

"If it is spotted, Dominic will alert me."

"You plan to sink it?"

"Does that matter to you because you thought Adam to be your brother for all those years?"

A sort of emptiness settled in Natalie when she let herself think about Adam's possible demise. Though she hated him, she could remember times as a small child, when he had seemed to care for her in a brotherly way. But there had been so few of those times that it was a strain to recall even the slightest hint of feeling for him.

What she had to remember was the fact that he was a cold-hearted, murdering pirate with no feeling for anything or anybody.

"No, it is no concern of mine," she murmured.

She twined her arms about his neck and drew his lips to hers, welcoming the hand that separated their chests as his fingers circled a breast and gently squeezed it.

Their tongues met, sparking their passion into a raging flame. Bryce lifted his hips and entered her, causing a sensual sigh to escape from Natalie as her body shuddered with rapture. She responded to him, meeting his thrusts with sheer abandonment. It was as though her insides were molten lava—burning, scorching, flowing liquid from her head to her toes.

"I love you so . . ." Bryce said, sending his warm breath into the depths of her silken tresses.

Natalie linked her fingers through his hair, now breathless from the desire building inside her. "Bryce . . . oh, Bryce . . ." she whispered shakily.

She closed her eyes, already feeling a soft glow beginning inside her and knowing that their ultimate pleasure was near . . . and much too soon. She wanted to relish his touch, his embrace, the feel of him inside her for a more lengthy time . . . yet her body was the master of the moment and was already heeding the call of his unspent passion.

As his body shook and quivered, filling her with a delicious sweetness, she responded and fully enjoyed the pleasures of the flesh. . . .

Sighing, she clung to him. "I wish it could go on forever," she whispered.

"I . . ." Bryce began, but was stopped when Dominic's voice spoke from outside the cabin door.

"Cap'n, she's in sight," Dominic said anxiously. "Just off the horizon . . . makin' way for us."

Bryce rose quickly from the bed, his heart pumping wildly. He grabbed his breeches and stepped into them. "Are you sure it's the *Sea Snake?*" he yelled.

"Can't mistake that black devil," Dominic replied in a growling voice. "She's movin' at a fast clip as we are also."

"Get the cannons loaded," Bryce ordered. "We mean business this time. We must rid the sea of that vermon. Today!"

Inching from the bed, Natalie couldn't help but be a bit afraid. A sea battle could mean death to many. What if Bryce were defeated? It would be his ship that would find its grave this day, not the *Sea Snake*.

"Bryce, maybe you shouldn't . . . ?" she murmured, slipping her petticoat over her head. Seeing him already completely attired in his gold, silk outfit, she hurriedly pulled her dress on. His face was a hard-set mask of determination as he fitted his crisscrossed leather belts across his chest, pistols held in the loops at each side.

"The decision has been made," Bryce said flatly, securing his pistols. "You know that it is best for all concerned. This is a deed I gladly do without a commission.''

He sat on the edge of the bed and pulled on his shining, wide-topped black boots. ''I should have done it long ago,'' he grumbled. ''I won't even blink an eye while tasting the thrill of victory.''

''He's a true blood relative of yours, Bryce.''

''And Brenda is yours,'' Bryce argued. ''Is that automatically cause for changing one's feelings toward an individual? Does that fact magically make one care for an individual who has done nothing but wreak havoc from shore to shore?''

''No . . .'' Natalie sighed. She went to Bryce as, sparks of danger in his eyes, he rose from the bed.

''But do be careful, my love,'' she said softly, standing on her bare tiptoes to kiss his tightly drawn lips.

Bryce wrapped his arms around her waist and drew her roughly next to him. He devoured her with his piercing blue eyes. ''And, Natalie, whatever you do, do not come out on top deck,'' he said thickly. ''There will be much gunfire. You will only be safe down here, away from it all.''

Tears blurred her vision as Natalie reached a hand to his face and touched him gently on a cheek. ''Bryce, please, oh, please be careful,'' she murmured.

He took her hand in his, his eyes softening. Kissing each of her fingertips, he watched her expression, noting that her passion for him made her even more beautiful. He placed one of her fingers between his lips and sucked on it teasingly, smiling when he saw the pulsebeat grow stronger in the veins at her neck. Yes, he had succeeded momentarily in supplanting her worries with sweet pleasure. He felt like a cad leaving her like this, her need in her eyes, but at least he had lessened her fears a bit.

"You remember what I told you," he said, drawing away from her. "I must go. I want to see the look on Adam's face when our first shot is fired."

Natalie followed him to the door, trembling. "I'd feel better if I could be with you, Bryce," she murmured, reaching out for him as he opened the door.

"No," he said firmly. "I know what's best."

He nodded toward the door as he stood out in the hallway. "Now shut it, Natalie and stay put. When it's all over I will return victorious to you. We will celebrate the victory, you and I, in the best way possible."

"God be with you," Natalie said, then closed the door and leaned heavily against it, sighing.

Bryce rushed up on deck. At the railing, his tightened shoulders braced against the powerful wind. He smiled confidently as he watched the black reptile ship flying fast in the eye of the wind, toward his *Golden Isis*.

The white waves of the sea were rolling high; the rustling sails above Bryce were bending the masts. But nothing was as powerful as Bryce's heartfelt ambition to succeed at what he had set out to do.

He clenched his teeth together as the black ship came closer and closer, its weaving black flag flying free and bold in the wind. He knew that he must return that flag to Saul Palmer, to demonstrate his victory over the last of the marauding Palmer pirates.

But he knew that Adam Palmer would fight to the last man to keep Bryce from boarding his ship. He wouldn't allow the ship to be taken, boarded.

"Yes, I will have to concentrate on sinking her," Bryce said, glaring toward the tall, lean figure of Adam as he stood, poised, pistols ready in each of his hands.

"Cap'n . . ." Dominic said, sidling up next to Bryce.

"You'd best give orders to fire. The ship's gettin' too close."

"Yes, I know," Bryce said, readying a pistol in his right hand and leaving his left free to motion his crew to begin the battle. Now, almost able to make out Adam's features, Bryce raised his left hand and shouted, "Fire, men."

Dropping his hand to his side, he tensed as the cannons boomed in unison. The ship's deck shuddered violently from the explosions. Bryce barked out order after order and aimed his pistol as the Sea Snake crept closer.

The *Golden Isis* creaked ominously as her cannon fire was returned, some of the shot dropping frighteningly close to the ship's bow.

Bryce fired one shot from his pistol and then another, reloading quickly and firing again. The crew on the Sea Snake swarmed its decks like ants, the reflections from their pistols streaks of golden light; the pirates were frantic because fire had broken out both stern and aft.

"Keep firing!" Bryce yelled. "Show no mercy. That damnable ship and crew has fought its last battle!"

Bryce couldn't believe that Adam hadn't tried to board him and take his ship as a prize! He had to believe that Adam knew the *Golden Isis* couldn't be taken, but instead would have to be blown from the water.

Yes, it seemed that the two brothers did have something in common after all! A keen stubbornness. Neither would surrender to the other what he most treasured in life—his ship.

"Or Natalie . . ." Bryce whispered. "Does Adam know, somehow, that she is aboard my ship . . . ?"

Bryce tensed when he saw Adam standing amid black smoke and orange, dancing flames, aiming directly at him.

"No . . . !" Natalie screamed as she rushed to Bryce's side and shoved him down onto the deck just as a shot whizzed through the air above their heads. And when the sails began creaking and flapping violently above them, it was evident that one of Adam's cannons had delivered a deadly blow to the main topsail.

"Bryce . . ." Natalie shouted, covering his body with hers as sail cloth came crashing down to land close by them; it was aflame and dangerously near bottles filled with powder and pistol shot.

As the fire raged, Natalie rose from the deck and accepted buckets of water from the ship's crew. Panting, she threw water on the flames bucket after bucket of it until only charred remains lay smoldering and black at her feet. She cringed when Bryce was suddenly there, grabbing one of her wrists.

"Natalie, damn it, you could've been killed," he stormed. "Why didn't you stay in the cabin as I told you to do?"

Natalie squared her shoulders and tossed her hair back from her face. "And if I had, you would be lying wounded, maybe even dead, useless to no one, Bryce," she hissed. "As it is, if you will focus your attention on the sea instead of me, you will see Adam's ship sinking."

Bryce released his hold on her and swung around, eyes wide. He ran to the ship's railing and watched with a racing pulse as the *Sea Snake* slowly eased down into its watery grave. He tried to see through the billowing, black smoke and raging flames, to detect any sign of life . . . of Adam . . .

Then his breath stole from him when he saw the faint glimmering of a skirt as a woman knelt down by Adam, who lay lifeless on the *Sea Snake*'s quarterdeck.

"Brenda . . ." Bryce whispered, paling. "Damn it! I forgot about Natalie's sister."

Natalie moved to Bryce's side, numb from witnessing the full fight, now wishing that, somehow, this hadn't been necessary. She caught the last of Bryce's words, hearing Brenda's name.

She clasped the ship's rail and felt a weakness in her knees when she caught a glimpse of Brenda just as burning sails fell and covered her . . .

Nausea overcame Natalie and she turned her eyes from the gory sight. She lowered her head into her hands, gulping back the bitter gall that persisted in rising to her throat.

"Darling . . ." Bryce said, drawing her next to him. "I'm sorry you had to see—"

"Me too . . ." she whispered. "Oh, God, Bryce, me too . . ."

"Let me take you back to the cabin," Bryce encouraged.

Natalie shook her head. "No," she murmured. "You have your duties. I've already interfered too much."

A loud cheer erupted from the crew.

"Thar she goes!" Dominic cried triumphantly.

Bryce turned just in time to see the last of the Sea Snake bubble down below the surface of the water. A slow smile lifted his lips, yet a sadness of sorts accompanied his victory. He had never enjoyed anyone's death and he now realized that he couldn't feel proud of being responsible for these many deaths.

Adam. His own brother. Brenda. Natalie's own sister! Would he and Natalie ever be able to live with a free conscience?

Yet, Bryce had to remember that by sinking the *Sea Snake* and its crew, lives had been saved! Passengers and crews aboard other seafaring vessels could have been Adam's victims had he lived . . .

Natalie turned slowly and saw only water where moments ago the *Sea Snake* had been. Looking closely, she saw some floating debris. Not even one man had been saved. Her sister Brenda . . . dead. It was almost as though Brenda had never existed at all, the relationship between the sisters had been so short. The irony was that of what had once been a family, the Seymours, only Natalie remained and she had just become a part of that family.

She was no better off now than before. She still had no family because hers no longer existed.

Linking her arm through Bryce's, Natalie cast him a sideways glance. Fate had brought them together. Surely fate wouldn't part them. He was her world now . . . her only world . . .

"Cap'n, I've got ye a prize," Dominic said as he raced toward Bryce.

Bryce patted Natalie's hand and slowly turned his focus on Dominic. His eyes danced when he saw in Dominic's hand the black flag with the winding snake design on it.

"You were able to capture it from the water, eh, Dominic?" he said, leaving Natalie momentarily to meet Dominic's approach. He gladly accepted the wet flag, proud to spread it between his hands. He noted the ugliness of the snake's shape. How often he had seen that reptile take shape in the wind! Little had he known that one day he would take it as his prize to show to those who had talked of seeking and sinking the *Sea Snake*.

385

But only I succeeded, he thought smugly to himself, forgetting his earlier regrets at having taken the lives of so many. He had come on this venture to seek victory, and, by damn, he had won!

His gaze moved back to the water. An involuntary shiver raced up and down his spine. He knew that luck had been with him this day. He knew of many ships that Adam had boarded, taken as his own, then sold at foreign ports. This day, that could very well have happened to his *Golden Isis!*

"Thanks, Dominic," Bryce finally said, placing a hand firmly on Dominic's thick shoulder.

"Should I set our course for New Orleans?" Dominic asked, giving Natalie a quick once over.

Bryce went back to Natalie and placed an arm about her waist. He looked imploringly into her eyes. "Darling, I want to return to Key West," he said. "I must see Saul Palmer. You can go with me or I can take you first to New Orleans, to my private quarters. Whatever you wish, I will do. I understand how traumatic this must have been for you."

"Bryce, are you sure you want to meet with Saul Palmer?"

"It is a chore I must do," he said flatly. "I must deliver the *Sea Snake*'s flag to him. Personally."

Natalie blanched. "But while doing that, you will be delivering the news of Adam's death. It will be cruel . . . even more than that. It could be dangerous. For you, Bryce."

"This is why I hesitate to take you with me."

Natalie swung around, away from him. She went to the ship's rail and stared down at the restless abyss of the ocean. It seemed to match her insides. A part of her still wanted to be the girl who had been pampered as Saul Palmer's daughter, and a part of her wanted only to be Bryce's lover . . . wife.

She swallowed hard when she saw a broken mast suddenly bob to the surface of the water—the *Sea Snake*'s mast had broken loose. Adam's mast! Suddenly she felt the loss of Adam and Brenda and felt shame for having wished them harm. Death was too final. Somehow, she wished to have been given another chance, at least with her only sister. . . .

"Natalie . . ." Bryce said, stepping to her side. "You've grown so quiet. Has this afternoon been too hard on you?"

Natalie's eyes lifted to his. She knew that she had to appear stronger. Her strength was one of the traits Bryce admired most in her. "No. I am fine," she said firmly.

"Then, darling, you must tell me. Do you wish to travel to Key West or to New Orleans?"

Natalie knew she wasn't ready to face Saul Palmer just yet, not with Adam's death weighing heavily on her conscience. But she did have other interests in Key West. There was Tami. There was her horse Adora. . . .

"Key West," she said flatly.

"You are sure?"

"Yes," she murmured. "But, Bryce, I want to ask a special favor of you?"

"And what is that, my fair maiden?" he asked, lifting her chin with a forefinger.

"I want to get my horse Adora. I want to take her back to New Orleans with me. She's been mine for so long, I've missed her as one would a person."

Bryce moved closer to the ship's rail and gripped it with his hands. Fore and aft the hull groaned and labored since the sea battle, and the remaining masts nodded and swayed and bent. Some of his crew were stuffing caulking by the handfuls into opened seams; others were resetting the shrouds. Thank God for Dominic's experience and his mastery of the crew. They left Bryce free to deal with the other problems at hand.

"Adora?" he questioned her softly, bracing his weight against a splashy wave that leaped from the sea at him. He wiped the fine spray from his face and ran his fingers through his hair. "I guess it could be arranged. I did promise you this. Yes, I am sure it can be done."

Natalie smiled warmly. "Thank you, Bryce," she said, throwing her arms about him, drawing him away from the rail to her. "That will help lighten my burden a bit. I do so love Adora."

Bryce caressed her back and smelled the sweetness of her hair. "But how can we manage to get your horse?" he said thickly. "Saul Palmer will be a hard one to steal from."

"While you are inside talking with him, *I* shall be at the stables stealing Adora," she said excitedly. "Also, while there, I can question Matthew and see if he and Tami are all right."

She drew away from Bryce, eyes wide. "Maybe this time we can encourage Tami to return with us to New Orleans. Matthew, too!"

"You tried that once, Natalie," Bryce said, fondly touching the tip of her nose.

Her eyes turned downward. "I know . . ." she murmured.

"But we can try again, can't we?" Bryce chuckled. "Can't we, Natalie?"

"You mean it?" She sighed.

"Yes," he said. "I also promised you that, or don't you remember? Somehow, we will return to New Orleans with Tami and Adora, and if Matthew wants to be a passenger, he, too shall arrive in New Orleans with us."

Solemnly Natalie turned her gaze back to the sea. "But this must all be done without Saul Palmer's knowledge," she murmured.

An empty sort of ache settled at the pit of her stomach when she thought of him. Would she always feel this way when her thoughts suddenly dwelled on him? Oh, she hoped not!

She beseeched Bryce with her eyes. "It must be so, Bryce. I don't think I could bear to see him again so soon. Or ever. Do you understand?"

He drew her gently into his arms. "Yes, darling," he sighed. "Even *I* dread seeing the man. But I must. I truly must."

He knew that the deliverance of the *Sea Snake*'s flag was only one of the reasons he must come face to face with Saul Palmer. But could he reveal the truth to him . . . that he had lost one son this day to gain another? Did he even want Saul Palmer to know that he was his son . . . ?

What good would come of it? He would walk away from the man, having caused him pain by telling him he had a second son, but hadn't had the opportunity to watch him grow into a man—a man who, though he was his son, would still deny him parental rights!

"Yes," he thought angrily to himself. "I will tell him."

"But how?"

KEY WEST

I love your lips when they're wet with wine
And red with a wild desire;
I love your eyes when the lovelight lies
Lit with a passionate fire.

—Wilcox

NINETEEN

The art of disguise had worked again. Bryce smiled to himself as he was directed into Saul Palmer's library. Attired in a black suit and sporting a maroon cravat at his throat, he reached his fingers to the rust-colored mustache that had been placed above his lips and scratched at the glue that held it in place. Even the shaggy, rust-colored strips placed to cover his golden eyebrows itched unmercifully! But his matching wig lay perfectly in place, giving him the perfect cover! Saul Palmer would never guess his identity until Bryce was ready to reveal it.

Leaning on a cane and feigning a limp, Bryce stopped just inside the library. That powerful man, Saul Palmer sat, smoking, in front of a roaring fire in the fireplace. Though the retired pirate was aging, he still sported broad shoulders and a sizable chest. His hair, however, was gray as fog and quite thin, revealing a shining bald spot at his crown.

Bryce glanced quickly around the room, impressed by the many books lining the shelves and the expensive taste in furnishings. The aroma was not so impressive. Bryce loved a good cigar, but stale cigar smoke he could do without!

"Sir, please step this way," a white-gloved, negro servant encouraged him with a slight gesture of a hand. "Massa Palmer isn't feelin' too well. Please join him by the fire."

"Thank you," Bryce said, bowing gratuitously and wondering if Natalie was safe. She had gone around to the back of the house while he had approached the main entrance in grand style in a carriage appropriate for a visitor of means.

Forcing a trembling in his gait, Bryce made his way to Saul Palmer's chair, now quite aware of the dark eyes on him, following his each and every move. He couldn't control the rapid beating of his heart, and he felt as though he had stepped into a lion's lair, possibly to be devoured!

But he set his jaw firmly, determined to carry this charade through to the end. He would enjoy seeing the shock in this man's eyes when he handed him the *Sea Snake*'s flag!

Yes, it was cruel, but neither Adam nor Saul Palmer had ever stopped to worry about the hurt and pain they had inflicted on others! Yes, Saul Palmer was due his . . . and it would be his son delivering the mortal blow!

"I wonder what the servant meant by saying that Saul Palmer was ailing . . . ?" he wondered. He also wondered where his private guards were? Natalie had said that he usually was surrounded by men! But Bryce cast these thoughts aside when Saul extended a hand to him in friendship without rising from his chair.

Bryce pretended to steady himself with the cane and offered his other hand to Saul. "I want to thank you for letting me see you on this late afternoon, sir," he said throatily, feeling the firmness of the handshake, relieved that Saul hadn't offered the hand that was minus three fingers. "I just arrived in town and was anxious to discuss business with you," Bryce quickly added.

Saul raised his heavy eyebrows. "And what might that business be, sir?" he asked, feeling that the blue eyes of this stranger didn't match his hair coloring. He would have expected dark eyes like his own, or maybe even green. But not blue.

But it was foolish to wonder about such things with so much on his mind. Damn it! Where the hell was Adam? He should have arrived back home with the news that he had sunk the *Golden Isis*. He should be making ready to return to New Orleans and bring Natalie back to him! Where was Adam?

A coldness penetrated him when he wondered if Adam . . . possibly . . .

No! He wouldn't let himself think of those possibilities. Adam's *Sea Snake* had never failed him. Nor would it this day!

"Your business is cigars, is it not?" Bryce asked, releasing his hand and wiping it on his breeches' leg. He felt as though he had just shaken hands with the devil. It disturbed Bryce to remember just who this man was—his true father. . . .

His eyes slowly traveled over Saul, trying to see a resemblance, yet seeing none. "Thank God," Bryce thought. "At least that is in my favor." Only his mother's traits were represented in his features.

Saul gestured toward a chair. "Yes," he said quietly. "Cigars are my business. My factories make the finest. I use the best tobacco leaves from Cuba. Why? Are you interested in a shipment?''

Saul paused as he watched Bryce settle into a leather, wing chair; then he spoke again. "And where do you make your residence? Where might we do business with you?"

Bryce's eyes wavered. He looked toward the ceiling, then back toward Saul. "In New York," he stated flatly. "Could we do business in, let's say, one month? I would like to receive a shipment of your finest cigars. I plan to begin a thriving business on Madison Avenue. That is why I have come to you. I only want to deal in the best tobacco. I've heard that you are the 'king' of cigars."

Bryce glanced around the room. "Might I have a taste of one now?"

The Negro servant who had been standing silently by rushed across the room and brought Saul a gold, engraved case then moved back to his vigil beside the closed library door.

Saul slowly opened the case and extended it toward Bryce. "Yes, I do offer the finest to my guests," he said. "Especially prospective clients."

Then Saul frowned. "And you must excuse my rudeness," he grumbled. "I forgot to ask your name. You see, I've much on my mind this evening."

"Eh . . . ?" Bryce said, lifting an eyebrow. "Troubles? Maybe I should leave . . . ?"

"No. I'd rather have company to occupy my thoughts with concerns other than those of my family," Saul said, laughing absently. He now realized he should not have sent his men out to watch for Adam's ship. Being alone had set his nerves more on edge!

Bryce leaned a bit forward, anxious. "Family . . . ?" he asked cautiously. "A man such as you had . . . family problems?''

He laughed to himself as the distant look on Saul's face changed to a dark brooding expression and Saul cast him an ugly stare.

''Sir, that is none of your concern,'' Saul growled. ''I spoke out of turn. I must guard my words more carefully.''

Once more he offered the cigars to Bryce. ''Here. Please pleasure yourself with one of my finest,'' he added. ''And, please, sir. Your name? Since you will be my business acquaintance, names are quite appropriate, wouldn't you say?''

Bryce smiled darkly as he took a cigar and began circling it around in his fingers. ''Names . . . ?'' he said, once more lifting an eyebrow. ''Names can be quite interesting, wouldn't you say?''

Saul Palmer straightened his back at this remark and at the cocky manner in which this stranger was suddenly conducting himself. He watched, barely breathing, as the stranger rose from his chair, leaving his cane, unused, on the floor. He watched with even more awe as the stranger began to stroll around the room, no longer limping and quite straight-backed and broad-shouldered.

''Who . . . are you?'' Saul asked, slowly rising and placing the cigar case on the table next to his chair.

Bryce swung around, exhibiting quiet amusement in the depth of his blue eyes. He went to the fireplace and tossing the unlighted cigar into the flames, laughing throatily as the fire ate away at it.

''Who am I?'' Bryce spat, turning to face Saul quite openly. ''Do you really want to know . . . ?''

Saul ran a finger around the collar of his shirt, suddenly quite uncomfortable with this situation. Damn! Why had he sent all his men away? Maybe, just maybe, some had returned. He cast his servant a covert glance and nodded, hoping the Negro would go in search of help.

Bryce caught the nod and grew cold inside when the servant rushed from the room. Was the servant on his way to warn some of Saul Palmer's men that he was in a bit of trouble? Damn! Things had to get moving faster. Bryce wasn't sure how far away these bodyguards might be. And he had to remember Natalie who was also in danger of being discovered!

Only one chore could be done this time while in Saul Palmer's presence. He would wait and tell him at a later date that he was his son—his illegitimate son—who was ready to wreak more havoc in his life than Saul had ever bargained for!

Slowly lifting his lips into a smile, Bryce reached inside his vest pocket and let his fingers pull from it the *Sea Snake* flag. He stretched it out between his hands, letting Saul Palmer see the full size, color, and shape of it and chuckling when Saul's face drained of all its color.

"How did . . . you . . . get that?" Saul gasped, steadying himself against the back of a wing chair. "How?" he growled throatily.

"Then you do recognize it?" Bryce asked, emotionlessly.

Saul felt the need to compose himself. No one knew of his connection with the *Sea Snake*. Perhaps this was some sort of trick arranged by the authorities? Was this a duplicate flag? Had they begun to realize just who the *Sea Snake*'s captain was? It could be the end of Adam if they knew. It could be the end of himself. . . .

"No," he said, squaring his shoulders as he moved to the fireplace to place his back to Bryce. "I do not know of what you speak.''

"The *Sea Snake* flag?'' Bryce said, moving abruptly to Saul's side. "You are afraid to claim it as Adam's . . . as yours?''

Saul turned jerkily and glared murderously toward Bryce. He doubled his fists at his sides. "Who are you?'' he growled. "Why are you doing this? Why are you even here?''

Bryce beamed with delight. "So you still refuse to accept this as Adam's?'' he asked. He held it closer to Saul for further, closer examination. "Do not be afraid to take a much better look. I don't plan to turn you in to the authorities. Just examine the flag. You will see that it is the original . . . the *Sea Snake*'s flag. You will then have to accept that it was *I* who took it from your son's ship. As it is *I* who sank that ship to the bottom of the ocean.''

Saul teetered; his vision blurred. He grabbed at his heart and swallowed hard, unwillingly taking the flag in his other hand as Bryce shoved it at him. He clasped the flag and crumpled into a chair, now knowing the meaning of this man's arrival. This man who still remained nameless had come to brag of having killed his son Adam!

He wiped at his brow and then looked studiously up at the stranger, mortified as the man peeled off the mustache from his upper lip, then the false eyebrows, and then the . . . wig.

"My God,'' Saul gasped. "Bryce Fowler! It is you!''

Bryce pitched his disguises into the fire, no longer having need of them. Then he bowed mockingly toward Saul, keeping eye contact with him at all times. "The one and only, sir,'' he said amusedly. "I do hope you will enjoy the flag that I have presented you with. You see, it is all that remains of your devil ship and your pirate son!''

Feeling it was time to escape and still worrying about Natalie, Bryce lifted a hand into a mock salute. "And now to Orchid Island, sir," he said mockingly. "It is now mine, you know. . . ."

Bryce then fled from the room, his heart thundering wildly with each wide stride he took. He couldn't believe he had actually said that! It was a bold, open invitation for more trouble with Saul Palmer. But he knew that was necessary to rid his island forever of the pirate scum!

Once outside, he ran around to the back of the house, where the stables stood in the fast-falling dusk. Seeing Natalie's shadow standing next to her horse, he hurried to her, glancing occasionally over his shoulder and wondering just when he would be accosted by Saul Palmer's guards. Strange that none were already chasing him. Had Saul Palmer grown reckless in his older years? Or did he feel so secure in his way of life that he no longer felt the need to keep guards around?

But no matter. Bryce had at least half accomplished what he had come for. He knew that he would have at least one more confrontation with Saul Palmer, and he hoped then to have the chance to tell him the full truth.

Natalie stood trembling, clinging to Adora's black mane and watching Bryce hurry toward her. She glanced toward the house, noticing the dim lighting in the library. She wondered just how Saul had taken the news. A part of her still ached for him. Oh, how she hated the aching . . . and the knowing. . . .

"Natalie, we must get the hell out of here," Bryce said, lifting her hurriedly into the saddle. Then he glanced around, but saw no one besides themselves. "And did you manage to speak to Tami? Is she going to join us on our journey? Is Matthew?"

"Neither Tami nor Matthew are anywhere to be found," Natalie said solemnly. "I sneaked into the house. It seems they are no longer in the household. In fact, the estate seems quite dead. Did you see anyone in the house besides Saul Palmer?"

"One servant," Bryce said, mounting the horse behind Natalie. He reached for the reins and clucked, relieved to get away from the house and into a stand of trees.

"I don't understand . . ." Natalie said. Shivering in the briskness of the evening air, she took one last look at the house and saw a shadow of a man running across the yard, toward the stable.

"God, Bryce," she gasped. "We must hurry. I see someone."

She paused and peered more intensely through the fog that had drifted up from the ocean to dampen them with its misty droplets.

"The ship is near," Bryce said. "Don't fret, darling. But it is a good thing you managed to get Adora. On foot, we might have run into difficulties."

"You sent the carriage away?"

"No," Bryce said flatly. "Seems it was sent away for me. I guess the servant took care of that when he saw that I was there for more than discussing cigars. I guess that was a way to make sure I didn't get anywhere fast. They hadn't counted on me knowing of Adora."

He laughed and drew Natalie back more toward him. "They didn't count on you waiting with Adora to help me escape."

He threw his head back in a hardy laugh. "When he finds that I've taken the horse he will surely know that you were only a stone's throw away also, for he would have to know that I couldn't know of Adora.

The flapping of sails and the creaking of the ship were welcomed sounds as Adora drew to an abrupt halt where a gangplank waited. "Natalie, rush on board the ship," Bryce encouraged, lifting her from the horse. "I'll help board Adora."

He looked across his shoulder, having heard the faint sound of hoofbeats in the distance. "Hurry. We must make haste."

Breathless, Natalie lifted the skirt of her dress into her arms and ran up the gangplank; then she swirled around and watched as Bryce urged Adora on board. When her horse was aboard she stood clinging to Adora. She watched as Bryce shouted orders to the crew. Finally the ship was safely drifting out to sea, while on the shore Saul Palmer and the two men accompanying him fired pistols from where they stood.

Bryce moved to Natalie's side and draped an arm about her waist. "Well, at least that is done," he said flatly. "And they might as well quit wasting their time. We're too far out to sea for their shots to hit their targets."

Trembling, Natalie snuggled into the curve of Bryce's arm. "Now what, Bryce?" she murmured.

"Are you ready for some more adventure, darling?" he said thickly, lifting her chin with a forefinger, so that their eyes could meet and hold.

She sighed heavily. "I don't know. . . ."

"I would like to move on to Orchid Island," he said. "I don't want to wait any longer to claim what is mine there."

"Will Saul Palmer's . . . will Adam's men be waiting for you there?"

"Now that Adam is dead, the crew of the two remaining ships will return to Key West, to Saul Palmer, to see what his next move will be," Bryce said. "I'm sure they will then be ordered back to Orchid Island. We must be there to surprise them when they arrive. You see, we do have a head start. It might be best to get this settled once and for all. You can remain safe in the house during our battle—if there is one."

"Bryce, it sounds dangerous," she said.

"I have won so far, have I not?"

"Yes . . ."

"Then I will win to the end," he growled. "Orchid Island does not belong to pirates. It belongs to me."

He looked away from her, eyes sad. "And I must admit something else," he added. "I must share this with Hugh. I cannot continue to pretend that it is my island alone. Hugh is the true Fowler. I must tell him that the island belongs to the Fowler's."

Bryce directed his eyes back to Natalie. "And, Natalie, since Hugh has decided to be so noble, by marrying Myra, I've seen a side of my brother that has never been shown to me before," he continued. "I like what I saw. And I think father would have."

"But if you do that—" Natalie said, but was interrupted.

"No. I will not lose anything by doing that," Bryce said. "Hugh loves Parrot Inn. He will not want to leave Key West to live on a desolated island. He loves to sing. He only sings to an audience. There would be no such audience on Orchid Island."

He shook his head. "No. There is nothing to worry about. And my half brother is weak, much too weak to take charge of a complete island."

"I hope you won't be sorry," Natalie murmured. "But

surely you know what you are doing."

Bryce drew her into his arms and stared lovingly down at her. "Yes, I do," he said softly. "I always do. . . ."

ORCHID ISLAND

You gave me wings of gladness
And lent me spirit song. . . .

—Russell

TWENTY

Having left the ship safely hidden in the cove, Bryce and Natalie moved through the thick, waist-high marsh grass, keeping the house in view. Bryce, in his gold, silk outfit, kept one hand poised on a pistol; and Natalie, in a fresh, low-swept dress, clung to Bryce's free arm, her eyes wide with silent fear.

The island was deserted. But how long could it remain to be so? When would the pirates return? Could they arrive at any moment?

These thoughts kept racing through Natalie's mind, leaving her no free moments to appreciate the good side of the moment—that she was once more with Bryce . . . the most important person in her life now.

"Bryce, are you sure the instructions you left with Dominic are wise?" she suddenly blurted. "What if Saul Palmer comes firing on the island?"

"I don't think he will do that," Bryce said contemplatingly. "But I do believe he will set out in a longboat by himself. He still has it in him to want to get revenge on his own . . . by himself. He knows that I have come to the island. I told you that I so much as told him I would."

Bryce sighed heavily. "Yes, he will come by ship with a deadly crew of seamen, but he will come ashore alone—I know it—to kill the man who killed his son."

"But to let him come onto the island," Natalie argued. "You are just asking him to shoot you, Bryce. Why do you insist on meeting him face to face again? Wasn't once enough?"

"No," he said flatly. "It was not. You see, I have just one more bit of news to relay to him before we show each other the barrels of our pistols. And you need not worry about the outcome, Natalie. I will be the victor. You can be assured of that. No aging pirate is going to take the remaining years of my life from me. These years were meant to be spent with you. No, nothing will stand in the way of our happiness. Nothing."

A strange sort of ache crept through Natalie's heart. She stepped over a thick, high clump of grass, then clung more intensely to Bryce's arm. "Bryce, it is so sad," she whispered. "I don't even want to think about his dying. You see, I feel sorry for him. He did give me a home and treat me quite well for so long. In my heart, will he ever be anything but my father? I can't be so heartless as to forget all that so easily."

"Hah!" Bryce laughed, tossing his head back with a jerk. "You? Heartless?"

He stopped and, turning her face to him, glowered down at her. "Natalie, keep remembering everything," he growled. "Don't just sort through and remember the good things about that man. He is evil. He only played a game with you, pretending to be what he was not. You must remember that. Do you hear?"

Natalie hung her head a bit, biting her lower lip. When

she felt Bryce's eyes still on her, she raised hers to meet their challenging blue. "Yes, I know," she murmured.

"Then shall we go on to the treasure chest without further thoughts of Saul Palmer?" he asked softly. "In time, we will have no choice but to think of him . . . when he arrives on the island. But until then, let's concentrate on what we've come to this island for."

"Yes, let's," Natalie said, keeping pace with him as he turned and began to walk briskly toward the house. The sun was hot and hazy that afternoon, yet the steady breeze blowing in from the ocean was a reprieve. Natalie glanced toward the house, seeing its magnificence and knowing if the vines were shed from it, it would, indeed, make a grand house in which to take up residence and to raise children. . . .

"Ah, there it is," Bryce said, disturbing her thoughts. "The private cemetery plot where riches await the turn of a key."

Natalie looked cautiously from side to side. "But I still don't understand why there is no one on this island." She was worried, feeling this all was much too easy.

"The men who were not aboard the *Sea Snake* most surely make their residences in Key West," Bryce reassured her. "They work from there, following orders as they are given. And I am sure Saul Palmer has given them orders by now; he has told them of the death of Adam and the *Sea Snake* crew."

"Yes, that is what I'm afraid of," Natalie muttered under her breath, not wanting Bryce to hear.

She stepped high, then low over the roots of vines as she followed Bryce to the fenced-in cemetery plot. She sighed when she caught sight of the thick clusters of orchids draped from the trees next to the mausoleum. Bryce boldly stepped up to the tomb, but she stood quite still as he struggled with the heavy marble door.

"Damn! No wonder my grandfather didn't worry about anyone disturbing this place of death," he grumbled. "I may not even be able to get inside the mausoleum to find the chest. This damned door hasn't been opened for too many years now. It's sealed tightly shut."

Bryce worked and worked with his fingers until he succeeded in finding some small cracks in which to stick them. The rawness of his fingertips hurt as he continued to pull and tug; then when he heard a small creaking sound, he knew that he had finally made progress.

He stood back and looked at the door. It had budged a fraction. He spit on his hands and rubbed them briskly together, casting Natalie a shadowy smile. Then he went back to the door and began struggling with it anew. Sweat popped out on his brow and the muscles in his shoulders and lower back ached as the door creaked open even more, enough to fit a body through. He stepped back.

"You've done it, Bryce," Natalie sighed heavily. "You've opened it."

"Yes," Bryce mumbled, poking his head inside the door and seeing nothing but pitch black. He took one small step inside and flinched when a thick mass of spider webs covered his face and clung to his hair. He wiped this away and realized that his eyes were adjusting to the darkness, enough that he could see few vaults lining the walls on each side.

A deep shudder raced through him as he felt death all around him. The air within the mausoleum smelled of mold and dampness. It burned the insides of his nostrils; yet he knew that none of this mattered. He was so close! Now to find the vault that was not inhabited by a casket

. . . but by a chest.

Natalie crept inside the mausoleum, squinting her eyes, trying to see all that Bryce was seeing. She tensed when she saw him pull a vault out from its space in the wall and then put it back upon finding it occupied by a wooden casket. A strong aroma of decayed flesh rippled through the air. Natalie gagged. She rushed from the mausoleum, covering her mouth with her hands. She leaned her full weight against a tree, welcoming the cluster of orchids so close to her nose. Then when she heard weeds crunching behind her, she turned with a start and felt her knees weaken when she saw Saul Palmer standing there, pistol pointed toward her, legs widespread as he stopped to stare openly back at her.

"Natalie," Saul said gruffly, dropping his pistol to his side. "What are you . . . ?"

Natalie kept her hands to her mouth, not knowing what to say. She hadn't expected to see him this soon . . . so abruptly. She didn't have to say anything, though, for Bryce was quickly by her side, having heard Saul Palmer's voice.

"So you've come," Bryce said, placing his hands on his pistols. "I thought you would. But I didn't expect you so soon. You move quite fast for an old man."

"And what do you think to gain by letting me enter the island without even a fight?" Saul asked, glancing from Natalie back to Bryce. "I was ready to fire upon your ship when your first mate shouted out that you had said to let me come on the island, alone, to meet with you."

He tightened his grip on the pistol. "Is it a duel that you wish? Or what? I am prepared for anything of your choosing. Anything to get you off my island . . ."

Once more he looked toward Natalie. "And to have

her back with me.''

He lifted his lips in a twisted smile, glancing back toward Bryce. "For you see, young man, I shall win. Everything. You were wrong to come on the island alone—without the protection of your men. I will see to it that you are sealed inside that mausoleum, quite dead, along with the rest of the Fowlers.''

"But, you see, old pirate, you are wrong," Bryce smirked. "About many things. First, you won't kill me. . . . Second, even if you did, you would be placing me in the wrong mausoleum.''

"Oh . . . ?" Saul said, lifting his dark eyebrows. "And why is that, young man?''

Bryce squared his shoulders and stepped away from Natalie. "Because, sir, I am not a true Fowler," he said thickly.

Saul laughed gruffly. "And what kind of game are you playing with me?''

"Your mausoleum, if your family has one, would be the true resting place for me," Bryce commented dryly. "I hate to have to admit to that, but it is quite true.''

Saul Palmer took a step backward, his jaw tightening. "What's that you say?" he mumbled. "Have you gone daft, lad? Why would you think that you would be laid to rest in our place of burial? Only a Palmer would be placed there.''

Bryce clasped both his hands tightly on his pistol handles. He glared toward Saul. "Because, old, old man, it seems you are . . . my . . . father," he growled.

Lifting his pistol, aiming it dangerously toward Bryce, Saul growled like a bear. "Young man, your words make no sense," he said. "Only guns can make a decision between us.''

412

He glanced toward Natalie. "You step aside, daughter. This fight must commence, for I cannot stand to hear mockery from this man you have chosen to travel with."

"I am not your daughter," Natalie said softly, closing her hands into tight fists. "You've known all along that I'm not your daughter. How could you have played with my life like that? Did you think you were God? I could have had time with my true father had you been honest with me those many years ago."

"Your place was with your mother," Saul responded.

"But mother has been dead for so many years now," Natalie argued. "At some time you should have told me the truth. As it is, I hate you, Saul Palmer. Hate you."

Saul's eyes grew heavy. "So you don't acknowledge me as your father any longer," he said quietly. He glanced toward Bryce, now glowering even more deeply. "I have you to thank for all of this," he shouted.

"Shoot me then," Bryce said, thrusting out his chest, ready to pull his own trigger, knowing that he most surely would be the quickest. Youth was in his favor. "But if you do, and you kill me, you will never know the truth about a son you have had all these years and have been denied. What happened to you is similar to what you have done to Natalie. You denied her . . . as you were denied me."

Saul lowered the barrel of his pistol a fraction, paling. "You must be making this up. You just want to catch me off guard . . . to make me look awkward in front of Natalie."

Bryce chuckled. "Old man, what I say is quite true. You have had an illegitimate son all these years, one who was denied you because the woman you took to your bed chose another man over you."

"I didn't know," Saul murmured.

Bryce cast Natalie a victorious glance. "It's as I told you, darling," he bragged. "He has bedded so many wenches during his lifetime, he has no way to separate one remembrance from another."

"Why would my mother have wanted to stay with a pirate, a rogue, if he moved so freely from bed to bed?" Natalie whispered, trying to see Saul as her mother had seen him.

"Because she truly loved me, Natalie," Saul said quietly. "And I kept her as my wife, though we never wed, because I truly loved her. I loved no other. She would still be with me even now had I not . . ."

A pink color rushed upward from Saul's neck to his face. He lowered his pistol and stepped farther away from Natalie, realizing what he had just said. God, this was a day for finding out the truths. He glanced toward Bryce, seeing nothing of himself in the lad, yet why would the young man have said what he had if it had not been the truth? It wouldn't gain him a thing. Not a thing! Except . . . except a happy heart to see this old man squirm under their close scrutiny and tales of woe. . . .

Natalie lifted the skirt of her dress into her arms and took a bold step toward Saul. "Had you not what?" she said in a near whisper. "What were you about to say? It was about my mother, I know. Did you . . . do something to her?"

"Yes'm, he sho' nuff did." A female voice suddenly spoke from behind them all.

Natalie swung around and saw a disheveled Tami and a quite thin Matthew. She gasped and rushed to Tami, touching her gently on the cheek. "Tami, where did you come from?" she asked softly.

414

Natalie's eyes scanned Tami, seeing her torn dress and the emptiness in her eyes, eyes that had sunk so deeply into her head they looked like two hollow sockets. "Are you all right?" Natalie continued.

"It's been a struggle, Miss Natalie," Tamie said, taking Natalie's hands in hers. Tami glanced sideways at Matthew who stood with head bowed, weaving. "Matthew here ain't holdin' out so good. Thank the Lord I fianlly worked the door open in the garret. We've been locked there fo' days now."

"Oh, Tami . . ." Natalie sighed. "Why would . . . ?"

Then she suddenly remembered what Tami had said about Saul.

Natalie felt an iciness sweep over her and was afraid to ask the full meaning of those words. But she had to know. She placed an arm about Tami's waist and looking directly into her face, asked. "What did you mean, saying that about Saul Palmer?" she whispered. "Did . . . he do something to . . . my mother?"

A sudden shot rang out, and then another. Natalie clutched at Tami as she crumpled to the ground, blood spotting the front of her cotton dress. Then Natalie turned her eyes to the other person who had fallen to the ground—Saul Palmer, also clutching his chest. Natalie beseeched Bryce with questioning eyes. She didn't have to ask what had happened. She knew. Apparently Saul had shot Tami to silence her and Bryce had shot Saul.

Natalie looked desperately from Tami to Saul, feeling their eyes on her both, needing her. But something compelled her to stay with Tami. She fell to her knees and cradled Tami's head in her arms. "Oh, Tami," she sobbed, placing her cheek against Tami's. "I'm so sorry. Why, oh, why did this have to happen?"

Tami's long, lean fingers reached for Natalie, taking one of her hands. "Miss Natalie, listen closely to me," she whispered, gasping for breath.

"Yes, Tami. What is it?" Natalie cried.

"Don't have regrets about Saul Palmer's dying," Tami said, glancing over and seeing Saul clawing at his wound as he lay, ashen-faced, on the ground. "He be the devil. Truly he be."

Tami took a deep, rattling breath and then continued. "He . . . he killed your . . . mother. . . ."

Natalie's heart thumped wildly. "He . . . what?" she whispered harshly.

"During one of his . . . rages . . . when he . . . was earlier retired from piracy," Tami stammered breathlessly. "He choked her . . . he . . . killed her. . . ."

Natalie felt dizziness overwhelming her. She steadied herself as Tami grabbed desperately at her with her other hand. "I'm afadin', Miss Natalie," she whispered. "The Lord be with you. You always be like my child. Ol' Tami loves you. . . ."

Natalie froze inside as she watched Tami's eyes slowly close. She flinched as though shot herself when she felt the last shuddering breath released by her faithful personal maid and long-time companion. Crying, she lowered Tami's head from her arms and placed her peacefully on the ground.

"Oh, I feel so responsible. . . ." Natalie sobbed, rising, not able to take her eyes off Tami. She took a step backward when Matthew bent down next to Tami and began to chant something soft and mournful, resting her head on his own lap now.

Natalie backed away from Tami and looked, aghast, at Saul who, his breathing labored, watched her through half-opened eyes. She then glanced toward Bryce, trembling. "Did you hear what Tami said?" she asked quietly. "She . . . said . . . that he . . . murdered my mother."

Bryce placed his pistols in their proper places and then drew her into his arms. "Yes, I heard," he murmured.

Natalie kept watching Saul, ignoring the pleading in his eyes. "How could I have thought I knew the man so well? How could I have . . . even . . . loved him?" she whispered, tears escaping from her eyes to form sparkling rivers onto her cheeks.

"It was only natural," Bryce comforted her. "You thought he was your father."

"And all along, he held deep inside him the secret that had changed my entire life," Natalie sobbed. She jerked free from Bryce and fell to her knees beside Saul. "How could you have?" she screamed, clenching her hands into tight fists on her lap. "How?"

Saul's body jerked and his eyes closed as he took a last trembling breath that caused Natalie to flinch and rise quickly to her feet. She turned her eyes away and closed them tightly shut; yet she knew she would never forget this day. The loud rush of many feet advancing toward her caused her to open her eyes. She quickly stepped to Bryce's side when several men circled around this scene of death.

"Bryce . . ." Natalie whispered, grabbing for his hand.

"It's all right," Bryce said flatly. "These men are from both ships, mine and Saul Palmer's, but don't worry, darling. Saul's men now know what they must do."

"And what is that?" Natalie whispered.

"They must take their leader and leave," Bryce said flatly, placing his hands on his pistols. "They now know who the victor is. They have lost not only their leader, but all the glory that went along with him. They will scatter to the winds, each one finding a new niche in life . . . a new ship to travel on for most."

Dominic stepped into the circle, his massive physique something for any man to fear. "Cap'n, what's the next move?" he growled.

Bryce nodded his head toward Saul's Palmer's body. "See to it that that pirate is taken back to his ship and that his ship puts out to sea immediately," Bryce ordered firmly.

He watched as some of Saul Palmer's crew scurried to lift his body and began to carry it away, toward the oceanfront. Bryce's gaze settled back on Dominic. He nodded once more. "See to it, Dominic," he snapped. "Then all of you wait on the ship for my return. I need to be alone with Natalie for a spell. I have my own chores to do before setting sail for New Orleans."

"Aye, aye, sir," Dominic growled, casting an ugly frown at Natalie. Obviously he had not yet accepted her into his circle of friends. He walked stoutly away, ordering his men to return to their ship.

Bryce drew Natalie to him and kissed her softly on the tip of the nose. "Are you all right?" he whispered, holding her at arm's length and noticing her pallor and her bloodshot eyes that seemed to never run dry of tears.

She wiped her eyes. "Yes," she whispered. "Please don't worry about me. I'm strong. Or don't you remember?"

"Much has happened . . ." Bryce said.

Natalie cast a sorrowful glance toward Tami. Then she

focused on Bryce's blue eyes, always feeling better when they gazed into her own. "I know," she said. "But I can adjust. Please let's go on and see what treasure awaits you. You've been patient long enough. There will be no further interruptions. Surely there won't be."

Bryce eyed the open door of the mausoleum. "No. I don't think there will, he murmured. He released his hold on Natalie and took quick, wide strides until once more, he was inside the mausoleum, releasing the seals on the other vaults until he finally found the one that held only a seaman's chest.

"Natalie," he said in a drawn-out whisper. "I've found it."

His voice grew into a loud shout. "I've found it!"

His thoughts were no longer of death . . . of sorrow . . . of worries. The contents of this chest would sparkle away even the deepest pain or anguish.

With Natalie at his side, he reached with trembling hands to lift the heavy wooden chest from the vault, groaning at the immense weight of it. Struggling, he finally got it placed on the floor, close to the door where it could be seen when finally opened. He studied the chest. An initial had been burned on the top of it with a hot iron and the corners were a bit smashed. A strong aroma of tar arose from it.

Bryce studied the initial again. It was a battered *M,* and he wished it had been an *F* to make his possession of it even more valid.

"The key . . ." Natalie whispered, anxiously.

With speed Bryce took the key ring from his front breeches pocket and sorted through it until the brass key was found. Then placing it in the tarnished lock, he barely breathed as he turned the key . . . slowly . . .

419

slowly. Then he popped the lid open with one fast movement.

Natalie's hands went to her throat and a loud gasp escaped from deep inside her. "Bryce . . . look!" she squealed.

Bryce's fingers reached inside the chest, sifting through the coins. The jingle of gold was music to his ears. And there wasn't only gold. His eyes caught the shine of silver, emeralds, rubies, pearls, and even some diamonds.

"It's more than I ever dreamed of," he sighed.

He cast Natalie a wide-eyed glance. "We're even richer than I ever imagined we might be," he said thickly. He nodded toward the chest. "Look, Natalie. Bend down here and run your fingers through it all. It's ours. All ours . . ."

Natalie's pulse raced as she bent and touched and felt. "Bryce, I can't believe it," she whispered. "Surely there has never been such a treasure as this before. Are you sure it is ours . . . to keep?"

Bryce leaned back and clasped his hands before him. "That key has been kept by a Fowler all these years," he said firmly. "Yes, it is ours. Am I not the possessor of that key? The one that unlocked the chest?"

Then his face shadowed a bit. "No, I am not truthful in saying that," he added. "I must keep remembering to share this with Hugh and Myra. It could make their future much brighter. We can't be stingy in our wealth. Though in the past I have always disliked my brother, I will share this wealth with him."

Natalie placed her cheek against the broad expanse of Bryce's chest. "This day, I am filled with a mixture of feelings," she whispered. "But above everything, even the treasure, it is you I feel most blessed with. I hope it is the same for you . . . that this wealth you have found won't dim your love for me.''

"How could you even think such a thing?" he asked, drawing her closer and holding her more tightly.

"Though your words are generous, I see something strange in your eyes, darling," she sighed. "That's why I am wondering."

"It is the look of victory," Bryce beamed. He pushed her gently away and held her at arm's length. "But there is one thing lacking."

"And? What is that?"

"I would have loved seeing Saul Palmer's expression when he found out that there were riches here right beneath his nose all those years and he had never been wise enough to seek them out."

Natalie once more eased her arms about Bryce's neck. "Though it will be hard, we must forget Saul Palmer," she said. "We must look to the future. Our future. We have much to live for . . . be thankful for. Please. Let's leave this island and go to your house in New Orleans. Only then can I breathe more easily . . . only then can *I* forget."

"The chest . . ." Bryce said, kneading his brow. "If my men see me carry it on board the ship, they will know. They will want a share."

"Then what will you do?" Natalie asked, stepping aside and staring down at the coins shining in the rays of afternoon sun that shone through gaps in the leaves of the trees into the mausoleum.

Bryce began to pace. "They saw the mausoleum door open. All of Saul Palmer's men saw the door open. I wonder if they suspected anything? Even my own men saw the door open."

"Surely not," Natalie reassured him. "Why would they?"

"If not, we could place the chest back inside the vault and return later, alone, to get it," Bryce said solemnly. "Yes. That's what we must do."

"Bryce, are you sure?"

"Yes. It will be safe," he said, hurrying to close the lid to the chest. Then he groaned as he placed it back inside the vault. After that, he closed the seal and, taking Natalie by the elbow, urged her on outside. The heavy door squealed as Bryce once more sealed away the prize he would later claim.

Then his eyes fell on Matthew, watching as he knelt over Tami's body. Glancing toward Natalie, Bryce questioned her silently with a look.

Understanding his full meaning, Natalie knew Bryce was afraid that Matthew had heard what they were saying. She went to Bryce and fit her body into his, saying, "Don't worry about him. I'm sure our secret is safe."

"Just to make sure, we will take him with us," Bryce said flatly.

"I never thought you would leave him behind," Natalie said, inching away from Bryce.

Bryce laughed amusedly. "No, darling. I wouldn't have," he said. "But to be sure our secret remains just that, we will keep watch on him once he is aboard our ship."

"Please don't worry," Natalie sighed. Then she glanced down at Tami. "And, Bryce, what can we do with her? She should have a decent, proper burial."

"We will do all that we can under the circumstances," Bryce murmured. "There must be a shovel somewhere in the basement of this house.''

He looked questioningly toward Matthew and spoke sternly to him. ''Matthew?''

Matthew's eyes slowly rose upward. ''Yes sa?'' he mumbled.

''Go to the basement of the mansion and try to find a shovel. We must bury Tami.''

Matthew's eyes widened and his mouth dropped open. He stood and began to back away, cowering.

Natalie went to him and touched him gently on a cheek. ''Matthew, it's all right,'' she said softly. ''This is the only way. We won't be returning to Key West. She must be buried here. Please understand.''

Matthew inched away from her and moved toward the house.

Bryce placed his keys inside his breeches pocket and drew Natalie into his arms. ''Darling, soon this will all be behind you,'' he said, kissing her gently on the lips.

''Soon it will all be behind *us*,'' she corrected him.

NEW ORLEANS

Fold thyself, my dearest, thou, and slip
Into my bosom and be lost in me.

—Tennyson

TWENTY-ONE

The voyage to New Orleans was behind Natalie and she had just bathed and changed into something more attractive than what she had been forced to wear the past several days. Beautifully gowned in silk and lace, she had tiny white rosebuds pinned in her midnight black, upswept hair.

The bodice of her pale green dress was trimmed with delicate lace, cut very low to display the magnificence of her breasts. This dress was tight at her tiny waist and then flared full and long to her feet. Yards and yards of petticoats fluttered as she paced the full length of the sitting room, awaiting Bryce, who also had taken the time for a refreshing bath to remove the sting of the seawater from his flesh.

Candles sparkled among the prisms of the great, crystal chandelier overhead, bathing the parlor with golden light. Double glass doors opened to the other rooms of the house and, opposite them, another pair led to a rear balcony that extended around three sides of the second floor of this Creole house. The balcony overlooked a courtyard surrounded by high walls for privacy.

Natalie stopped her pacing long enough to admire the room, already feeling at home in Bryce's chosen surroundings. Seventeenth-century French and ancient Chinese tables and thickly upholstered velveteen chairs and sofas provided its main furnishings. Numerous paintings bedecked the walls and first editions of books were placed prominently on the wide expanse of an oak desk. A showcase of crystal beakers sparkled like diamonds through the glass enclosure of a display case at the far end of the room.

A trembling sigh, which accompanied Natalie's restless mood, escaped from between her lips. She so wanted to forget all that she had just gone through. But there were more feelings involved than her own. She had to remember Bryce and his losses and gains.

The sequinlike stars and the cradle of a half moon drew Natalie out onto the balcony. She had to hug her arms to her chest to protect herself from the chill of evening; yet the perfumed fragrances in the air warmed her senses and evoked a heady reeling sensation in her.

She closed her eyes and lifted her chin, inhaling deeply. The lush, tropical vegetation in the courtyard was almost the same as that in Key West. So often she had stood on her widow's peak balcony, there enjoying the flower-scented air and dreaming of a lover returning from the sea . . .

"Natalie, darling," Bryce said suddenly from behind her, drawing her from her deep thoughts.

Natalie swung around and saw his silhouette framed in the darkness of the doorway—his tall, lean figure, the broad swell of his shoulders and the powerful muscles of his legs. Though he was in shadow, she could see that he had also taken pains with his appearance and was now dressed in dark, snug breeches and an impeccably tailored evening coat.

When he moved closer to her, the smell of him overpowered the fragrances from the flowers. As he drew her gently into his arms and placed a kiss on the hollow of her throat, Natalie inhaled the fragrance of this man's rich perfume, the maleness of him, and the slight aroma of a cigar that he had most surely been smoking while readying himself for her.

"My home is now yours," Bryce said, gazing rapturously into her eyes. "And do you approve?"

Natalie reached a forefinger to his face and teasingly traced his chiseled features. "Darling, I could be happy making my home in a cave, if it meant being with you," she purred.

Bryce chuckled amusedly. "My dear, that mode of living will never become necessary. Not with the riches awaiting our return to Orchid Island."

Natalie drew away from him, leaning her full weight on the balcony's railing and clasping her fingers to it. "Bryce, I hope it was wise to leave the chest unattended," she murmured. She turned her eyes suddenly toward him. "What if . . . ?"

Once more Bryce drew her around and into his arms. "Hey," he said. "Is this the woman who just said she'd be willing to share a cave with me? Is the treasure chest so important to you?"

Natalie sighed, placing a cheek against his broad expanse of chest. "Darling, it is you I am thinking of," she said. "I worry for you. I know how important the chest and its contents are to you."

Bryce chuckled again and lifted her chin with a forefinger. "Now don't tell me you didn't get a faster heartbeat when your eyes caught the glitter of all those diamonds and rubies," he said. "Natalie, it's only human. Confess. Tell me. Which do you want to display at your throat first? A diamond necklace . . . or one of rubies?"

Natalie's thick lashes fluttered as she smiled. "Well, since you put it that way, yes, I am excited about what the key has unlocked," she said.

Then her smile faded. "But I feel wicked being excited about this while others . . . others have fallen on misfortune. Maybe it's not fair that we find such immense happiness at this time."

She once more placed her cheek against Bryce's chest and hugged him tightly. "I'm frightened, Bryce," she whispered. "I'm so afraid more terrible things are going to happen. Maybe even to us this time."

Approaching footsteps drew Natalie around. She smiled when she saw Matthew step out into the shadows carrying a silver tray which held crystal glasses and a lone bottle of wine.

"Massa Bryce, would you want your wine served here or in the parlor?" Matthew asked in his deep Southern drawl.

Bryce placed his arm about Natalie's waist and nodded toward the sitting room. "Inside, Matthew. In the sitting room," he said. "It seems there's quite a chill in the air this evening."

Beside Bryce, Natalie strolled into the sitting room where she eased down onto a sofa while he settled into a chair opposite her. She smiled to herself, when she noticed that Matthew's eyes had brightened. Obviously he was already content in his new surroundings.

Yes, he would be happy here, in a household that

would always be filled with the love and respect its members felt for one another. Maybe in time, Matthew would again have respect for himself . . . he had lost that during his years as a stable hand and servant to Saul Palmer.

The wine bubbled as it gurgled from the cut-glass decanter into the two glasses, one held by Natalie and the other by Bryce. Then Matthew bowed and immediately left the room. Alone, Bryce and Natalie glanced at each other admiringly.

"Why are you looking at me like that, Bryce?" Natalie asked, seeing the twinkle in his blue eyes.

"You've never looked lovelier," he said huskily. "I want to eat you up. I don't even know why we bothered to dress. The bed will give us much more room to explore our love for one another. It is quite different from that tiny bed we shared on the ship, it seems, from the very beginning of our love affair."

"Affair . . . ?" Natalie said softly, arching an eyebrow. She sipped on her wine, never taking her eyes from his handsomeness.

Bryce leaned toward her, giving her a salute with his half-filled glass. "Sorry, darling," he chuckled. "I didn't mean to offend. Shall we make a toast to something more, would you say, more lasting?"

Natalie's pulse raced, knowing what he meant. Now they were free to proceed with their wedding plans. No courtship ritual was required since there was no father to request it.

"And of what are you speaking, kind sir?" she teased, lowering her lashes, pretending bashfulness.

Bryce rose from his chair, urging her up before him. "Shall we toast our wedding?" he said. "One that will take place quite soon."

"Oh, yes, Bryce," Natalie sighed, lifting her glass to his. When the clink of their glasses filled the room, it was as though a pact had been signed . . . a pact of undying love and devotion between these two who had lost so much . . . yet had gained even more.

As Natalie placed the glass to her lips, she smiled devotedly toward Bryce, but stopped before taking a sip when the banging of the front door knocker reverberated up the stairs and into the sitting room.

"Who . . . ?" Natalie said, casting a quick glance toward the door that led to the staircase.

"I'll see," Bryce said, placing his glass on a table.

Natalie took a step backward, not knowing why she was afraid. She was safe with Bryce. Nothing could happen now. Surely nothing could happen!

With trembling fingers, she placed her glass beside Bryce's and, touching his glass where his lips had been, she listened closely to the drone of voices below, on the lower floor parlor. . . .

Barely breathing, Natalie crept to the door and then out to the top of the staircase, listening even more closely. Then she tensed. She recognized one voice. God! Was it Clarence Seymour? But, no! It couldn't be! He was dead! She had seen him die . . . in his house . . . after Adam had shot him. Surely she was hearing things, only wanting them to be true. Such a burden of guilt would be lifted from her mind if Clarence were alive. Nothing would bring Tami . . . Saul . . . Adam . . . or Brenda back. So many deaths! It was too much to bear when she let herself think about it.

Natalie's eyes widened when Bryce came to the foot of the stairs and looked up at her. When he reached out a hand, inviting her down, she smiled sheepishly and hesi-

432

tated. "Who is it, Bryce?" she whispered. "Who's there?"

"Darling, just come on down and see for yourself," he said, smiling, lifting his hand up higher, encouraging her even more. "I have a pleasant surprise for you."

Natalie stepped lightly on to the top step, then descended rapidly when she heard Clarence's voice, crisp and clear now, in the parlor.

"Bryce, it can't be," she said, her tone of voice light, yet slowly filling with excitement.

"But, yes, darling, it is," Bryce said, welcoming her at the foot of the stairs with the sweep into his arms and urging her on into the parlor.

Natalie's heart pounded wildly when she caught sight of Clarence standing next to the large stone fireplace. He was well! He was alive! He smiled warmly toward her as he stood tall and thin, his gray hair framing a face that was accentuated by his long chin and thin neck. His faded brown eyes misted over with sparkling tears as he reached his arms out to her.

"Natalie," he said thickly. "God . . . Natalie . . ."

Not yet having grown used to him as her father, Natalie didn't know quite what to do. But she was so happy that he was all right, she rushed into his arms and hugged his chest, to stifle the tears that crept from her eyes.

"You're all right," she murmured. "Adam . . . didn't . . . kill you . . . after all."

The thinness of his arms was obvious as he held her, as though in a vise, in his embrace. "And he didn't harm you," he sighed. "I have worried so about you."

To the side of her, Natalie noticed another man. He was larger about the middle, quite bald, and had hunched shoulders. Gold-framed spectacles rested on his broad nose. She stepped away from Clarence, smiling a welcome to the stranger.

Bryce came to Natalie and took one of her hands in his. "Darling, Abe here is my partner in the banking business," he said proudly. "And, Abe, this beautiful lady is to be my future wife."

Abe took a step forward and offered Natalie a hand, shaking hers when she accepted his gesture of friendship. Then Natalie looked back toward Clarence, feeling, oh, so good. "How is it that you are alive," she murmured. "I thought . . . I did think you were dead. I have been so troubled by having to leave you lying there. But Adam forced me . . ."

Clarence reached a hand to her chin and cupped it. "Now see here, my dear, don't you fret about that," he said. "I know Adam Palmer forced you. Let's just be thankful that we both are alive and well and able to look to the future."

Sudden pain raced around Natalie's heart. She glanced quickly at Bryce, wondering if he had told Clarence about Brenda. Clarence had gained one daughter . . . only to lose the other.

Bryce saw the look in her eyes, but he wanted to reveal that bit of news later. "And you say Abe here discovered you?" he said, moving away from Natalie to pick up a gold case of cigars to pass to the men.

Abe responded. "I did as you asked, Bryce," he said, accepting a cigar. "I stayed in the carriage across the way from Clarence's house. But Adam gave me the slip. He moved in the shadows. Got into the house without my seeing him. It was later when I heard the gunfire that I was alerted to the real trouble at hand. I was climbing from the carriage when I saw Adam rush from the house

434

half dragging Natalie. Sorry about that, ol' man. Sorry I couldn't prevent the shooting."

"Let's all go to the sitting room upstairs, have a drink, and discuss the rest of this," Bryce encouraged.

As he ushered Natalie out of the room and up the stairs, he glanced back over his shoulder at Abe. "And don't worry about how things happened," he said. "You see, you probably would have been shot, too, then there'd have been no one to rescue either of you. You and Clarence probably would've both died on the spot."

He guided Natalie to a chair in the sitting room. "No. Don't think about it anymore. It's a blessing that you were able to save Clarence by rushing him to a doctor."

Natalie cast Clarence a warm, tender smile as he sat down next to her. Suddenly the world was right again. At least her father had been spared. She would make it up to him for his many years of loss.

Then she felt her smile dwindle once more as she realized the time was drawing near when Brenda's fate must be revealed. How would he take her loss?

With cigar smoke spiraling lazily into the air, wine being leisurely sipped, and everyone relaxed comfortably in chairs, business concerns inevitably had to be discussed.

"And what are your plans now, Bryce?" Abe asked, drawing heavily on his cigar and crossing his stocky legs at his ankles.

"Before I tend to bank business, you mean?" Bryce chuckled.

"You could say that," Abe returned with a chuckle.

Bryce cast Clarence a long, lingering look. He had succeeded with his one commission, that of delivering Natalie to him. But he had one more thing to do before closing the book. He had to recover the opium shipment. Bryce had already decided when and how that would be done. The opium would be his cover while he rescued his treasure chest from Orchid Island. While his men were busy loading the opium onto his Golden Isis, he would, himself, be loading the chest and hiding it in his master cabin.

"I'm sure Clarence here wants me to get back to work for him, too," Bryce finally said. He raised his eyebrows, drawing on his cigar. "Isn't that right, Clarence?"

Clarence leaned a bit forward. "I must confess," he said, "I've had it on my mind." He reached and patted Natalie's hand fondly. "And now that I know Natalie is safe and sound, away from those scoundrels, yes, I would like to have my opium shipment back in my hands."

Abe flicked the ashes from his cigar and swallowed several sips from his wineglass. Then he eyed Bryce with a furrowed brow. "But we still have the *Sea Snake* to contend with," he growled. "Did you happen to see 'er while on your voyage from Key West? Is she still blackening the waters of the Atlantic?"

Bryce paled a bit and glanced momentarily toward Clarence, knowing the time had arrived for disclosures that would cut deep inside a man who had once loved his daughter Brenda more than life itself, since she at that time was the only one to love . . . to hold . . . to cherish.

Damn! It would be hard, telling him!

Feeling Bryce's hesitation, Natalie placed a hand on his knee. "Bryce, do you want me to tell . . . ?" she whispered.

Bryce shook his head. "No," he murmured. "That

would be too hard. It's hard enough for me, and I'm not related. No. I will tell—''

Abe leaned forward. ''Tell what? What's this you're hesitating about?'' he asked.

Natalie cast Clarence a sorrowful look, swallowing hard when Bryce rose and began pacing.

Bryce combed his fingers through his hair, then crushed his cigar out in an ashtray, focusing his eyes directly on Clarence. ''You see, it's this way . . .'' he said. ''Clarence, we've some bad news to tell you.''

Clarence hung his head, toying with his wineglass. ''I'm sure I know to whom you might be referring,'' he said thickly. ''I haven't heard from . . . her . . . since that damnable night Adam left me for dead.''

Natalie placed a hand on his arm. ''It is about Brenda,'' she murmured. ''Do you want us to wait until later? It's a shame to cast a shadow on your happiness now, just as it seems everything is going to be all right for you.''

Clarence's eyelids were heavy as he looked from Natalie to Bryce and then back to Natalie. ''No. Tell me now. Natalie, I will never be stronger than I am at this moment with you by my side,'' he said.

His eyes locked with Natalie's. ''You see, Natalie, I feel as though my Kathryn is back with me. You are much the same as she was. So lovely . . . so soft spoken . . . so sweet.''

Natalie swallowed the lump developing in her throat. She recalled that Kathryn had stayed with the Saul Palmer willingly, that her sweetness had not been reflected in her choice to remain with a man who was not her husband —to a pirate who killed and maimed without giving a thought to what he was doing. Then Kathryn had lost her life . . . at the hands of that man.

"Father," Natalie murmured and then realized what she had said. Father! It had come out so easily. She let her tears fall and they sparked on her cheeks as he squeezed her hand affectionately.

"I love you," he whispered. "Now, tell me. I'm ready to hear anything you have to tell me."

Natalie gave Bryce a quick look. "Bryce, please . . ." she whispered. "I don't think I can after all."

"Brenda is no longer alive," Bryce suddenly blurted out, feeling the torture was being dragged out much too long.

A slight gasp could be heard throughout the room as Clarence's body jerked slightly at the news. He took a quick swallow of wine then looked away from them all. "How . . . ?" he asked thickly.

Bryce shook his head, troubled. "God," he groaned.

"How?" Clarence repeated throatily, watching Bryce.

"She was on the ship with Adam Palmer when . . . when it sank to the bottom of the Atlantic," Bryce murmured.

Then he took quick strides to the wine bottle and poured himself a fresh glassful and swallowed it straight down.

Abe rose quickly from his chair, addressing Bryce. "You never told me," he said quietly. "When? How?"

"I didn't have a chance to tell you yet," Bryce said. "We've only been back in New Orleans a short while. But you know that. I sent a messenger to tell you of my arrival."

"But you didn't say anything else in the message," Abe said.

"I know better than to spread news by messenger,"

Bryce said flatly. "You are aware of that."

"Well? Then tell me now," Abe prodded him, pushing his glasses further up on his nose.

"Now isn't the time," Bryce said, glancing toward Clarence, feeling for him.

Clarence rose from his chair and poured himself a fresh glass of wine. "Yes. Tell him," he said stiffly. "I'd like to know the details. She was my daughter, you know."

Natalie rose and went to Clarence. "No," she whispered. "I would advise against it."

"I'm stronger than you think me to be," Clarence said, straightening his back. He went to Bryce and challenged him with a bold stare. "Tell me. How did Brenda die?"

Bryce began pacing and reciting the story from beginning to end. When he'd finished, he dreaded looking toward Clarence, but after he did, he breathed more easily when he found him standing quite alert and untouched. At least visibly! Inside, Bryce knew the man had to be dying a slow death to know that his daughter had died by the side of her pirate lover and had found the same watery grave as he.

"So when will you return to Orchid Island?" Clarence asked flatly. "I would like to accompany you on that voyage."

Natalie looked unbelievingly at Clarence, not having expected such a reaction. She glanced quickly toward Bryce, questioning him with her eyes.

Bryce nodded toward her, before speaking. "I plan to return as soon as possible," he said. "And you say you would like to travel with me, Clarence?"

Clarence cleared his throat. "Yes, I would," he said flatly. "The opium shipment is of much value to me. The

439

sooner I get it back, the sooner I can get into other things. It's been put to the side for too long a time as it is."

He smiled toward Natalie. "Yet, the wait was worth it since you have delivered my daughter Natalie to me."

Bryce lit another cigar and, drawing deeply from it, settled back onto a couch. "I'm not so sure if I can say yes to your request," he murmured. "I normally travel only with my crew."

Natalie went to Bryce and sat down beside him, clasping one of his hands. "Bryce, surely you can. This one time. Even let me go," she said anxiously. "Please? I want to return to Orchid Island with you."

"Natalie, I don't know. . . ."

"There is no further danger from pirates, Bryce," Natalie argued. "The voyage will be safe. I don't want to let you out of my sight again so soon. Please?"

Clarence sat on a chair opposite Bryce and Natalie. He leaned forward. "Yes, let her," he encouraged. "It would give us time together that we have never had before."

He winked at Natalie. "And since I see a wedding in the near future, I won't be seeing her much after that."

Bryce knew that Natalie wanted to be with him when he rescued the chest. But he hadn't planned on anyone else being there. Still Clarence's presence might provide an added distraction from what he, himself, had to do. Clarence could keep the men busy, instructing them to carefully load the opium shipment aboard the ship. Yes, that would be best. For all concerned.

He chewed on his cigar and then cast a warm smile toward Natalie. "Yes, darling," he said. "We can all make this voyage together."

"When?" she asked anxiously.

Bryce looked toward Clarence, glad to see the remorsefulness no longer in the depths of his eyes. The talk of a sea voyage and of recovering what was rightfully his had taken away the sadness—at least some of it—caused by Brenda's demise.

Yet, Clarence surely had known the news of her could not be good . . . whether she was dead or alive. She had chosen the seamier side of life instead of what her father had offered.

"We will sail on the morning tide," Bryce said, quickly rising from his chair. He crushed his cigar out in an ashtray; then he went to Clarence and extended his hand, asking, "How does that sound?"

Clarence rose from the chair and accepted the handshake. "I will be on the river front bright and early in the morning," he said.

He then went to Natalie and drew her gently into his arms. "I look forward to spending some time alone with you while aboard the ship," he said thickly. "It will be nice talking with you, hearing about your past, about you and what you enjoy doing with yourself. Yes, I look forward to that, Natalie."

He kissed her cheek and moved toward the door, nodding toward Abe. "It's best we leave these two lovebirds alone now, Abe," he said. "Seems we two old folk are only standing in the way."

He winked at Natalie and, turning, headed toward the staircase.

"Take care on the voyage, Bryce," Abe said, clasping his arms about Bryce and hugging him affectionately. "I'd like to see you enter our bank building in the next few days to say you have everything under control."

Bryce leaned toward Abe's ear. "When I return, do I

441

have a surprise for you,'' he whispered.

''What's that you say?'' asked Abe, stepping back from Bryce and pushing his gold-framed spectacles further back on his nose.

Bryce threw his head back in a soft laugh, then he directed his eyes toward Abe again. ''When I return, I will tell you all about it,'' he said. He shook his head. ''No. Better than that. I will show you.''

Abe laughed absently and went toward the door, nodding toward Natalie as he passed her by. ''You take care of that gentleman of yours,'' he said. ''He's quite a catch. But I'm sure you know that by now.''

Natalie linked an arm through Bryce's, smiling. ''Yes, I do know that, Abe,'' she said. ''There's none finer than Bryce Fowler.''

''You're going to spoil me, that's for sure,'' Bryce said, laughing.

''You love it,'' Natalie whispered, nudging him playfully in the side.

They walked casually down the stairs behind Clarence and Abe and bid them goodnight; then they strolled, leaning against one another, to the door that led them out into the moon-splashed courtyard. The sparkling fountain sprayed water into the sky, and wisteria swayed gently in the breeze. Banana and orange trees, palms and sycamores shadowed the flagstone walkway as Bryce and Natalie strolled, arm in arm, toward the staircase that led upstairs where the bed awaited them.

''Shall we . . . ?'' Bryce asked, bowing as he motioned toward the stairs.

''Yes, let's,'' Natalie murmured, so happy, so completely happy for the first time in weeks. Her sadness for Clarence had been lifted by his gentle acceptance of what had happened to Brenda. Somehow that made it easier for her to accept her sister's fate. Clarence Seymour was a special man. Clarence Seymour was her father! Clarence Seymour was alive!

When the head of the stairs was reached, Bryce swept Natalie up into his arms and carried her the short distance into the bedroom. A fancily painted kerosene lamp lit the room in soft, shimmering pools of gold light, revealing a rosewood headboard that graced a bed made with ivory-colored sleek satin sheets and pillows. The windows were curtain free and close-shuttered for the night.

But Natalie saw nothing else, for Bryce's lips on hers were stealing her senses, already deliciously dizzy with desire.

As he placed her gently on the bed, lowering his lips to one of her silky breasts, Natalie moaned and slipped her dress from her shoulders, freeing both breasts to his searching lips and tongue.

"Bryce, I never, never get enough of you," Natalie whispered, lacing her fingers through his hair and drawing his mouth even deeper into her flesh. His teeth teased her sharp peaks . . . his fingers kneaded and fondled.

Natalie tossed her head, loosening her hairpins. The small, white rosebuds tumbled free and lay amid the magnificent dark tresses of her hair. Her fingers went to Bryce's jacket. Having eagerly removed it from his shoulders and then his arms, she reached her fingers inside his shirt, stroking the blond tendrils of his chest hair.

When she ran a thumb around one of Bryce's nipples, his sigh of pleasure heightened Natalie's euphoria and she welcomed his hands urging the rest of her clothes away.

"I feel so free from worries now, Bryce," Natalie

443

purred, watching him remove the last of his own clothes.

"But you aren't fully free, darling," Bryce said, settling down on the bed beside her, molding her to the countours of his body. "You will never be free of me."

His fingers lifted her hair . . . his breath warmed her neck. She shivered at the exquisite, pleasurable sensation, and her fingertips traveled over the corded muscles of his shoulders.

"I never want to be free of you," Natalie whispered.

She trembled even more as his hands began igniting flames across her abdomen then lower, until she felt that her heart must be beating more strongly, but knew that this was only her need for him, growing to an almost intense burning passion.

Natalie strained her hips upward, welcoming the continuing caress of his fingers; then she sighed languidly as he eased atop her and entered her gently . . . smoothly. . . .

Twining her arms about his neck, Natalie moved her body with his. He kissed her throat, then imprisoned her against him as their desire increased.

When his lips bore passionately down upon hers, Natalie could feel her heart pounding in unison with his and she accepted the magical glow that rose inside her. She sighed as her pleasure exploded into an urgency, too soon leaving her light-headed and breathless. Soon he, too, achieved release, and she smiled, clinging tightly to him as he trembled violently and sent his love seeds deep inside her.

As he breathed hard against her neck, Natalie teasingly kissed his shoulder, tasting the manliness of him that spoke of spent passion. At this moment, she realized that she could never love him more. She smiled to herself, remembering her first doubts of him. The thought that he possibly was a pirate had intrigued, even excited her. Thinking he wanted her only for the diamonds he had seen her wear had angered her. But discovering that he wanted her, only for herself, had been cause for her to lose her heart, even her soul to him.

"I love you," she whispered, feeling goose pimples rising on her flesh when his lips became his words and sent fresh messages from breast to breast then lower, to the smooth curve of her hips.

Laughing softly, Bryce reached for the loosened rosebuds and lay them at each of her pleasure points.

"And now what do you plan to do?" Natalie chuckled.

"Once more enjoy my garden of love," Bryce said huskily, setting her on fire anew as his lips nudged each rose aside, supplanting them with fresh, warm kisses.

ORCHID ISLAND

The heart that has truly loved
  never forgets,
But as truly loves on to the close. . . .

—Moore

TWENTY-TWO

The *Golden Isis* was riding the crest of the waves, white clouds scudding above her on puffs of wind as the ship's sails shivered and flapped. Natalie braced herself against the wind, leaning into Bryce's body, both of them poised . . . silent . . . watching as Orchid Island became more than a speck on the horizon.

Natalie felt Bryce's body tense and his grip around her waist tighten. Damn. He had also seen it! There was a ship moored only a few feet from Orchid Island's white, sandy beach.

"Who the hell . . . !" Bryce suddenly growled.

Natalie glanced up at his face, noting the hard set of his jaw and the fight in his blue eyes.

"Do you recognize the ship?" she said in a near whisper, cuddling even closer to him when a splash of sea water sprayed her cotton dress. She reached a hand to the low-swept neck of the gown and wiped the water from her flesh.

"No," Bryce grunted. The silk of his gold shirt billowed in the wind and his hair lifted and fluttered from his shoulders.

Dominic raced to Bryce's side, then Clarence.

"Seems we're not the only ones with Orchid Island on our minds," Dominic growled, lifting a brass telescope to his eye and staring intently through it. "The ship's been left untended. Nary a soul on board 'er."

"Recognize the flag?" Bryce asked, now leaning his full weight on the ship's rail.

"Nay," Dominic said in a low snarl. "But 'pears peaceful enough. No cannon in sight."

"Just a peaceful ship out for a cruise, eh?" Bryce said, raising his eyebrows.

Not used to the sun's powerful rays, Clarence ran a finger around the stiff, white collar at his throat. Though in the import/export business, he rarely made it his business to travel. The disastrous voyage on which he had lost his wife, Kathryn, had kept him from the sea.

"Is Orchid Island known by many?" he asked thickly, fearing for his opium shipment. He had already lost so much he would hate to think of losing anything else so soon. Then Natalie turned her dark, luminous eyes toward him, melting his fears, and he suddenly remembered how he had been blessed by having been given her.

Bryce was remembering the many times he had chased the *Sea Snake* and how that the damnable ship had seemed to disappear on the horizon, lost somewhere among the purple valleys of island. Bryce had never pursued the craft further, thinking that unimportant. And all along the treasure had waited on that island! Just . . . for . . . him!

He reached inside his breeches pocket and jingled his keys. Finally he answered Clarence. "No," he said. "Because until I sank the *Sea Snake* the island had known only the footsteps of pirates on its soil.''

Then he thought, even when it belonged to Fowler family. They were pirates!

But he would never speak this aloud to anyone besides Natalie. At least not until the treasure chest was safely removed from the island.

"What's our next move, Cap'n?" Dominic asked, lowering his telescope.

"Take the ship in the back way," Bryce said sternly, straightening his back. He combed his fingers through his hair. "Drop anchor in the cove. We'll surprise whoever is on the island. And, Dominic, except for yourself, everyone will stay aboard until we can check out the island."

"Bryce, I want to go with you," Natalie said softly.

"No. You must remain on the ship until I know that it's safe," Bryce said flatly. He glanced toward Clarence. "And also, Clarence, it's best you stay on board. Stay with Natalie. When the coast is clear I will send Dominic for you both."

"Whatever you say," Clarence said, drawing Natalie to his side.

Then they all turned to the rail and stood in total silence as the ship drifted nearer and nearer to the island, and once the anchor was dropped, Bryce and Dominic landed by way of a longboat.

"Keep low," Bryce encouraged as he stepped from the sand into the thigh-high grass. "We'll circle around and take them by surprise."

"There was nary a man on the ship," Dominic said, crouching and keeping his hands on his pistols at his waist. "Best remember that. That means they're all on the island."

451

"A ship doesn't necessarily mean lots of men," Bryce reassured him. "It's not a warring ship. The crew could even number as few as eight."

"Eight is enough to put an end to us," Dominic grumbled.

"Dominic, something tells me that we've nothing to worry about," Bryce said. "If we did, we'd have seen men standing guard. So far we've seen no one."

The back of the mansion came into view. Bryce looked quickly toward the mausoleum. Through the haze of the afternoon heat, he studied the area around it most intently, relieved to see no one near the fenced-off family cemetery. He had just begun to worry that Matthew might have sent word, somehow, to someone about the treasure. But now he thought not. It seemed the treasure was not the reason for these people to be on the island.

Then . . . why? Who?

A flash of steel ahead of them caused Bryce to place an arm in front of Dominic to halt his approach.

"See that?" Bryce whispered, separating the grass and peering more intently toward the glare that had caught his eye.

"Aye, aye, cap'n," Dominic whispered back. "So there's one of the crew. Just wonder where the rest 'appen to be."

"Slow and easy, and above all else, quietly," Bryce said, removing a pistol from his belt.

Bent low, he and Dominic moved side by side until they found themselves close enough to the man with the gun to see to it that he wouldn't cause them any bother.

Bryce nodded to Dominic. In a flash Dominic brought the butt of his pistol down on the man's head. As the man fell slowly to the ground, Dominic cast Bryce a victorious grin and nodded for Bryce to follow him.

Looking up now, so close to the mansion he could touch it, Bryce had to wonder if anyone had seen their approach. The windows seemed to be all eyes, watching. . . .

Dominic grabbed Bryce's arm. "Cap'n," he snarled, nodding toward another stray sailor who was leaning against a sycamore tree, arms crossing his chest and head bent in a lazy slumber.

"I'll get this one," Bryce growled. He slipped up behind the tree, slipped around it, and covered the man's mouth with his hand. Struggling, they fell to the ground, but one blow of Bryce's right fist knocked out his opponent. Bryce heard a low chuckle as Dominic stepped into full view.

"Well, Cap'n, looks as though the coast is clear now," he said. "Seems as though most of the crew did stay on land close by the ship, protectin' it. Now what should we do? Go inside the house? Since there's no one out here, surely that's where the rest are."

"Don't know what anyone would be doing in the house," Bryce said, scratching his head.

"Takin' what don't belong to 'em, tha's what," Dominic said. "Such a beautiful house must have things of value to carry off."

Bryce's gut began to slowly twist. "Yeah," he said darkly. "Like the opium shipment, eh, Dominic?"

"Do you think . . . ?" Dominic said, his eyes growing dark with anger.

"We'd best find out without further delay," Bryce said, moving briskly toward the front steps of the house. Once on the veranda, he cautiously opened the heavy oak door and slipped inside.

"Damn . . ." he gasped, seeing the total disarray of the furniture. The dust covers had been tossed aside, and any furniture that hadn't been tipped upside down was split and torn; stuffing hung clumsily from the open torn upholstery.

"Cap'n, seems someone's lookin' for something all right," Dominic growled.

"Now what made you come to that conclusion?" Bryce stated sarcastically, casting Dominic a quick look.

The drone of voices and the muffled sound of footsteps overhead caused Bryce to tense. Then move quickly to the staircase to lean against the railing and peer upward. "Up there . . ." He motioned with the barrel of his pistol.

Loud crashes and bangs were evidence that whoever was searching hadn't stopped at the first floor.

"They're tearing up the place," Bryce said, anger crashing through him in hot flashes. No one had the right! He had fought for this island. It was his! And he would fight to the finish if necessary to claim it all over again!

"Let's go," he ordered angrily. He moved ahead of Dominic, taking the steps two at a time. Then when his feet made contact with the second-floor landing, he stopped short and took in a deep breath when Hugh stepped into view in the hallway.

"Hugh!" Bryce exclaimed, paling. "How on earth . . . why . . . are you here?"

"Bryce," Hugh gasped, teetering a bit with fright.

Bryce replaced his pistols in his gunbelt then went to Hugh and clasped his thin shoulders. "What the hell are you doing here, Hugh? How do you even know about this place?"

"Myra," Hugh said, his voice breaking as he glanced

toward the menacing figure of Dominic.

Bryce stiffened, now understanding. Myra! She had heard Natalie talk with him about the treasure while she had been waiting to be carried to the ship from Orchid Island. It hadn't even dawned on Bryce to worry about her. He had thought that all Myra had on her mind was to be rescued and taken to a doctor because she had lost so much blood.

But she had listened. She had even transmitted this bit of news to the man she loved. Bryce lifted his eyebrows, seeing Hugh in a different light. Never before had Hugh ventured from the land. But to find a treasure, yes, any man would venture out to sea in pursuit of it.

"Myra told me—" Hugh continued, but was silenced by Bryce stepping to him and covering his mouth with a hand.

"No need to get into it now," Bryce said, casting Dominic a troubled glance. He would not share this with his first mate. If he did so, he would have to worry about the crew mutinying to get their share. Such a treasure hadn't been found on any of the adventures they had shared at sea.

"Dominic, it's only my fool brother," Bryce laughed absently. "Seems there's been a mistake made here. His wife-to-be, Myra—you remember her, we rescued her and took her to Key West—well, she told Hugh some fool story that there was something of value hidden away in this house."

He nodded toward the staircase. "Go and get Clarence and Natalie. And get enough of the crew to empty the garret of the—well you know—the shipment."

Dominic glowered toward Hugh whose eyes were two wide pools of blue, and who stood, hawklike, staring frighteningly back at him. "Aye, aye, sir," Dominic growled.

A sailor, who appeared from one of the bedrooms, stopped short and reached for his pistol.

Dominic aimed his pistol toward him. "I wouldn't do that, lad," he snarled.

Bryce released his hand from Hugh's mouth so Hugh could encourage the sailor not to be alarmed. "It's my brother and his first mate," Hugh said, wiping his mouth with the back of a hand. "It's all right. Lower your gun. Go on outside and I will instruct you later as to what to do next."

"Smart move, lad," Dominic said, replacing his pistol in his belt. He turned and moved swiftly, yet heavily, down the staircase, leaving Bryce and Hugh alone once the sailor also had descended.

Bryce strolled around Hugh, hands clasped tightly behind his back. A slow smile lifted his lips. "So you've become a seafarin' man?" he inquired sarcastically.

Hugh's orange silk shirt, though flared at the arms, was partially, opened revealing his extreme thinness, as did his tight-fitting breeches. Again Bryce was reminded of his brother's shortcomings and failings.

"Why did you shut me up, Bryce?" Hugh grumbled, flinging back his long, golden mane of hair.

"Why did you come?" Bryce growled right back at him.

"To find the treasure," Hugh argued. "Myra heard you and Natalie speaking of it. Surely it's hidden somewhere in the house."

"You even thought you could find it in the furniture?" Bryce scoffed with a jerk of his head.

"Since I couldn't find a chest I thought you might have

hidden it piece by piece."

Bryce threw his head back in a fit of laughter and then sobered quickly as he placed a hand on Hugh's shoulder. "What else did Myra tell you, Hugh?" he stated icily.

"She knew nothing more," Hugh replied, shaking himself from Bryce and strolling to the staircase to peer downward.

"Hugh, damn it! Seems you've made an ass of yourself coming here like this, tearing up your own house and furniture."

Hugh swung around, his face pale, mouth agape. "What do you mean?" he said softly.

"Father left you Parrot Inn, didn't he?" Bryce teased.

"You know he did," Hugh spat out angrily.

"Well he owned much much more than that," Bryce said.

"What do you mean?" Hugh queried. "What else?"

Bryce gestured with his arms as his eyes followed. "This house. This island. It all belongs to the Fowlers," he bragged. He went to Hugh and leaned into his face. "Even a treasure," he drawled confidently. "Yes . . . a treasure."

Hugh took a step backward, clasping onto the staircase railing. "Bryce, none of this makes any sense," he mumbled. "Will you stop being vague and explain it all to me?"

Bryce laughed absently, combing his fingers through his hair. "I still can't believe you're here," he said. "Hugh. Pantywaist Hugh brave enough to leave Key West by ship in search of an island as well as treasure."

Hugh's hands clenched into two tight fists. "Don't call me names, Bryce," he stormed. "You must remember who the true Fowler is here. It is *I* who could refuse sharing any of this with you."

"I think not," Bryce said flatly.

"And why not?"

"*I* know where the treasure is hidden."

"Ha! And when you uncover its hiding place, then I will keep it from you if I choose."

Bryce once more leaned into Hugh's face. "Just you try it," he growled.

Hugh backed away, laughing awkwardly. "I didn't mean it," he mumbled. "But quit making fun of me. I do deserve better. And I wouldn't want Myra seeing you do that. I love her. We're already married. I want to give her the best of everything there is to give. That's why I came."

"How did you find the island?"

"I heard several men gossiping over tea about Saul Palmer's death," Hugh said. "Come to find out they were some of his crew. When they spoke further of Orchid Island, I decided to hire them to bring me here."

"And the ship?"

"It's only mine for this voyage. I paid well for its use."

"And what did you tell the men?" Bryce growled. "Did you tell them about the . . . uh . . . treasure?"

"No. I only told them that I was searching for a hidden diary that would spell out the exact words of a will of the Fowler family," Hugh bragged. "You see, I did use my head. Do you think I would want to share the treasure with those sailors?"

"And what if you had found the treasure while tearing up the house in search of it? What then, huh? Didn't you realize what the sailors would have done? When a treasure had been found instead of a diary, don't you know

458

your life would have meant nothing to those cold-hearted, gold-hungry pirates?''

''I have my pistol,'' Hugh said quietly, tapping a bulge at his waist, where a well-hidden pistol had been thrust.

Bryce exploded into a fit of laughter. ''Hugh,'' he said, forcing himself to sober down. ''One gun against that many? God, brother, have you ever shot a pistol before? Could you actually shoot a man?''

Hugh paled. ''Bryce, that's enough,'' he grumbled. ''You continue to make me out to be a fool.''

Placing his arm about Hugh's shoulders, Bryce guided Hugh into a bedroom, then to a window. He threw the shutters open and pointed to the mausoleum. ''I agree,'' he said. ''Enough of foolishness. And, Hugh, you couldn't find the treasure, could you?'' He chuckled a bit. ''Well, it's hidden away so well even the pirates never found it in all the years they inhabited this island.''

Hugh followed the direction of Bryce's hand. ''In the mausoleum . . . ?'' he gasped.

''Seems you've guessed right this time.'' Bryce laughed. He reached into his pocket and withdrew a ring of keys. Fingering through them he found the brass key and held it before Hugh's eyes. ''And this is the key that unlocks the chest of riches,'' he said thickly.

''How did you get it?'' Hugh asked, arching his thick eyebrows.

''Well, it's like this, brother . . .'' Bryce began; then he told the whole story, leaving Hugh even paler and more weak-shouldered.

''So father didn't trust me enough to give me the key,'' he murmured.

''Father didn't think you strong enough,'' Bryce stated flatly. ''Plus there were other feelings between you and he. You know that.''

Hugh's face flushed and his lips formed a narrow, straight line. ''I'm quite aware of those feelings,'' he said. ''But I was good to father. I took care of him at the last. You didn't. You left him to die without any further thought of him.''

''You knew there was much happening in my life,'' Bryce said angrily. ''You should know. You were the cause of some of that turmoil because you told me that damnable Saul Palmer actually was my father.''

''Bryce . . .''

From the hallway Natalie softly called him. Bryce spun around and rushed to her. He drew her into his arms.''The damnedest thing,'' he said. ''Seems Myra let the cat out of the bag before I was ready.''

''I'm sorry Bryce.''

He nuzzled her neck. ''It's all right,'' he said. ''It has gotten the dirty work out of the way. Now for the treasure.''

He drew away from her and glanced down the staircase. Seeing many of his crew heading up the stairs, he nodded to the men. ''On up to the garret with you and make haste. I'd like to set sail soon.''

He waited patiently until they were beyond hearing range and then hurried to where Hugh stood silently. ''All right, Hugh, if treasure is what you came for, treasure it will be,'' he said thickly. ''But we musn't let the crew know what we're up to. It could cost us. Plenty.''

Natalie lifted the skirt of her dress and hurried along beside Bryce, breathless. They had waited for this moment . . . and finally it had arrived!

She rushed across the lawn with Bryce and watched as he once more struggled to open the mausoleum door.

With a pounding heart she stood there, clasping and un-clasping her hands and finally sighing with relief when the door creaked open. She glanced toward Hugh; eager-ness shone in the bright glint of his eyes. And when Bryce once more opened the treasure chest, the world was theirs for the asking. . . .

The ship swayed gently in the water, the sun above only a pale image largely obscured by low clouds, which reflected an orange cast on everything.

Natalie clung to Bryce, watching the island diminish in the distance. Now it seemed to be only a mirage, some-thing that never truly existed. "I kind of hate to leave it," she whispered. "The island is so beautiful. But there are too many memories there. I know it's best."

"Seems everything worked out for the best," Bryce murmured. "The treasure was shared equally with Hugh . . . Clarence has his opium shipment back . . . and I have you."

He drew her into his arms and gave her a sweet, linger-ing kiss.

Then Natalie leaned away from Bryce, her eyes wa-vering a bit. "But, Bryce, something has been bothering me," she murmured.

"What's that, darling?" he asked, kissing the hollow of her throat.

"Since Myra is now married to Hugh, I can't help but wonder about the baby."

"What about the baby?"

"The child will, in truth, be Adam Palmer's," she said softly. "Don't you see? What if it's a boy? What if he in-herits his father's evil ways? When the child grows to adulthood, the island will possibly be his. Again a Palmer will have possession of Orchid Island. . . ."

Bryce paled and cast another glance across his shoulder; he was no longer able to see the purple reflection of the island on the horizon. Then he smiled triumphantly. "That doesn't matter," he said flatly. "We have possession of the treasure. There is no other brass key to keep hidden from generation to generation."

"Then you are truly happy? We have nothing to plague us, to keep us from just loving and enjoying one another?"

"No. Nothing," Bryce said, sweeping her up into his arms and carrying her boldly past his crew toward his master cabin. "But one thing is certain," he whispered into her ear. "I need to have my own son."

Natalie snuggled, contentedly against him, knowing they would enjoy making his wish come true. . . .

Taylor—made Romance From Zebra Books

WHISPERED KISSES (2912, $4.95/5.95)
Beautiful Texas heiress Laura Leigh Webster never imagined that her biggest worry on her African safari would be the handsome Jace Elliot, her tour guide. Laura's guardian, Lord Chadwick Hamilton, warns her of Jace's dangerous past; she simply cannot resist the lure of his strong arms and the passion of his *Whispered Kisses*.

KISS OF THE NIGHT WIND (2699, $4.50/$5.50)
Carrie Sue Strover thought she was leaving trouble behind her when she deserted her brother's outlaw gang to live her life as schoolmarm Carolyn Starns. On her journey, her stagecoach was attacked and she was rescued by handsome T.J. Rogue. T.J. plots to have Carrie lead him to her brother's cohorts who murdered his family. T.J., however, soon succumbs to the beautiful runaway's charms and loving caresses.

FORTUNE'S FLAMES (2944, $4.50/$5.50)
Impatient to begin her journey back home to New Orleans, beautiful Maren James was furious when Captain Hawk delayed the voyage by searching for stowaways. Impatience gave way to uncontrollable desire once the handsome captain searched *her* cabin. He was looking for illegal passengers; what he found was wild passion with a woman he knew was unlike all those he had known before!

PASSIONS WILD AND FREE (3017, $4.50/$5.50)
After seeing her family and home destroyed by the cruel and hateful Epson gang, Randee Hollis swore revenge. She knew she found the perfect man to help her—gunslinger Marsh Logan. Not only strong and brave, Marsh had the ebony hair and light blue eyes to make Randee forget her hate and seek the love and passion that only he could give her.

Available wherever paperbacks are sold, or order direct from the Publisher. Send cover price plus 50¢ per copy for mailing and handling to Zebra Books, Dept. 3293, 475 Park Avenue South, New York, N.Y. 10016. Residents of New York, New Jersey and Pennsylvania must include sales tax. DO NOT SEND CASH.

HISTORICAL ROMANCES BY EMMA MERRITT

RESTLESS FLAMES (2203, $3.95)

Having lost her husband six months before, determined Brenna Allen couldn't afford to lose her freight company, too. Outfitted as wagon captain with revolver, knife and whip, the single-minded beauty relentlessly drove her caravan, desperate to reach Santa Fe. Then she crossed paths with insolent Logan Mac-Dougald. The taciturn Texas Ranger was as primitive as the surrounding Comanche Territory, and he didn't hesitate to let the tantalizing trail boss know what he wanted from her. Yet despite her outrage with his brazen ways, jet-haired Brenna couldn't suppress the scorching passions surging through her . . . and suddenly she never wanted this trip to end!

COMANCHE BRIDE (2549, $3.95)

When stunning Dr. Zoe Randolph headed to Mexico to halt a cholera epidemic, she didn't think twice about traversing Comanche territory . . . until a band of bloodthirsty savages attacked her caravan. The gorgeous physician was furious that her mission had been interrupted, but nothing compared to the rage she felt on meeting the barbaric warrior who made her his slave. Determined to return to civilization, the ivory-skinned blonde decided to make a woman's ultimate sacrifice to gain her freedom — and never admit that deep down inside she burned to be loved by the handsome brute!

SWEET, WILD LOVE (2834, $4.50)

It was hard enough for Eleanor Hunt to get men to take her seriously in sophisticated Chicago — it was going to be impossible in Blissful, Kansas! These cowboys couldn't believe she was a real attorney, here to try a cattle rustling case. They just looked her up and down and grinned. Especially that Bradley Smith. The man worked for her father and he still had the audacity to stare at her with those lust-filled green eyes. Every time she turned around, he was trying to trap her in his strong embrace.

Available wherever paperbacks are sold, or order direct from the Publisher. Send cover price plus 50¢ per copy for mailing and handling to Zebra Books, Dept. 3293, 475 Park Avenue South, New York, N.Y. 10016. Residents of New York, New Jersey and Pennsylvania must include sales tax. DO NOT SEND CASH.